Object and Vist

Anka B. Troitsky

Copyright © 2022 Anka B. Troitsky
Published in UK by Greystone Consultancy LTD
ISBN: 978-1-7391959-0-8

Dedicated to the memory of my father,
Boris V. Troitsky, scientist and dreamer

Contents

I am grateful to my partner Richard and my daughter Dasha for their support and encouragement.
Also, to my editor Andy Hodges,
The Narrative Craft.

Chapter 1. 3416. Back on Earth – Vist

Had I died? I hadn't felt anything physical for a while. My body had gone. I panicked. If I had a mouth and lungs, I would have opened them all up with a long loud scream. A scream that would've made my own blood curdle and my ears pop. None of this happened. I did not hear that cry, as I had no ears.

I tried to concentrate on other feelings. I felt scared. Surely that meant I couldn't be dead. Only living things can feel ... or at least those with a fully developed nervous system. You can't feel by any other means, right? Yes, that's right! I also felt angry, but I'm not sure about what. Okay, calm down and think. I could think. Dead people can't think. Good news. I know my name for a start! Fine, I don't know ... I don't remember my name yet. But I love red wine and intense music. My hair is ... red? And I am left-handed. So far, so good. I felt better and a little calmer. My thoughts slowed down, becoming clearer and sharper.

I trucked through all the possible details: the names of my friends and the things I did last Tuesday, whenever that was, when I suddenly felt something else. My fingers on one of my hands. The skin on my fingertips was touching the surface of something. It was smooth, cold, and dry – a plastic kind of surface. It was flat and horizontal. Wow! I knew where the ups and downs were! It felt good, like meeting an old friend. A familiar something in the middle of nothing. I concentrated all my attention on that feeling. I was definitely conscious. But for how long? I was still not sure. What's next? My fingers slid in a circular motion. I discovered that the area by my side was curved, like in a canoe – or a coffin. But it was smooth and spongy, impact-absorbing. I could suddenly feel the rest of my body pressed against that surface with its own weight. Too much! I am not that heavy!

At the same time, the pain came. It started in the lower back and shot down the leg. I yelped like a puppy and heard a pathetic and scratchy noise this time. My leg was bent, and I felt my other arm for the first time, as it touched my knee. In that moment, the knee dipped into the soft lid of my "coffin." The pain receded, slowly and unwillingly like a guest who did not want to go home. I rolled on my side as far as I could. Looks like I was on my back before. I was dressed, but not sure in what clothing. Yet ...

My whole body convulsed and erupted. The hot liquid almost drowned me; it filled my nose and mouth in seconds, which forced me to twist my neck in a wild attempt to look downwards. I spat and coughed the acidic taste out until I could breathe again. Hey! I'd been breathing all this time and hadn't even noticed. I felt sweat on my eyelids. Where was I?

Suddenly, a transparent oval of soft grey light appeared in front of my eyes. A holo-screen! There was a face in it, but it was unfocused. I heard a voice, neither male nor female, with a metallic undertone and strong accent. It spoke, and the image became sharper.

"Hello, hello, if you can see and hear me, that means we made it. But first things first, can you move your arms? Are they free of straps? Quickly bring at least one hand to your throat. If your air did not have enough oxygen, you would probably have done this naturally anyway. The straps should unfasten automatically, and now you would have activated the necessary supply. You may not be good at anything else yet, but this is temporary, trust me. If you are still blind and can only hear me, press on your right hip; you should be able to hit the button. It will inject you with something reasonably helpful."

I had trouble remembering my left and right, but since I wasn't blind, I did not worry about it. The image was in full focus now. I could see a human face, a young person around forty-five years old, with dark shoulder-length hair on one side. Another half of the head was clean-shaven. A dressing had been applied to the top of their forehead, as if they had recently bumped their head on something hard. It was a well-chiselled face, but not pretty. The eyes were calm. There was no worry or fear in those eyes. I could tell that this person cared about what would happen to me. A friend, then. Good.

"Before we go further, we need to check the rest of you. I hope your eyes are working now, and if you can hear high-pitch beeping or see two white blinking lights from the corner of your eyes, then keep still, do not move just yet. Try to breathe deeply but slowly. You probably can't identify colours, and the sound of my voice may be distant or muffled. Can you hear a pulsating noise in your ears? I hope not, but if so, try to reach the ring on your chest and pull it. Now relax, and you should be ok in a few minutes. But we are good if you can see a steady blue light."

I rolled my eyes to one side and saw one colourful dot. It might have been blue – I wasn't sure. A faint smell of honey wax reached my senses.

"Now. Let me fill in the gaps. You are recovering from the effects of using the emergency escape pod. It is not a regular pod since I modified it to take an irregular course. Usually, you would be received by a recovery team, who would take care of you until you were well again, but they would have identified you before you regained consciousness. We can't allow that, can we? I changed your pod's landing coordinates, and you must recover by yourself, with a little help from your special suit and me."

This person was now relaxed and talking casually, as if talking to himself ... or herself? I still had difficulties there. He or she was looking down and sideways as if operating some equipment or moving objects next to the camera. It was rather therapeutic.

"Yes, it is dangerous and very risky. The chance of something going wrong is likely 34.7 per cent, but this is your third time. It was 86 per cent before father and I did some work on it. The very first trip made you the only survivor of the family ... Yes, you are probably remembering now. The second one took you towards the ship a few years ago, on its way to your mission called Object. Now you are back on Earth and have been apprehended by Cruisers. First, I had to reset the coordinates of the ship's hiding place, and then I had to take care of your landing. I had just a few seconds for that! Since the rest of our guys were already gone, no one could see me being clumsy in my haste and butting the control panel. No time to explain everything. All our pods are entering the atmosphere! It will be harder for them, as they are only humans. But you are not; you can integrate with technology. By the way, what you see and hear is a recorded message from you to you. I am you. Your name is Vist."

The face stopped talking, grinned, and then disappeared. I moved my hand to my face, and my fingers felt the dressing patch above my brow. I remembered how I did not want blood pouring into my eye, and I had applied this dressing myself right after the pod ejected. I remembered recording this very message just a few minutes ago. I remembered everything and every member of the crew. I became aware of the precious cargo attached to my back and chest.

The pod lid buzzed and hissed as it moved up and then to the right. The strong wind threw a handful of sand and dust into my face. I squinted at the black and yellow clouds of the dying Earth.

Chapter 2. 3411. Out in Space – Mars

MESH message
MJKavanaugh@@Parsecmail.mesh. The final record of Doctor Morris Kavanaugh (02.11.3411, 15.31 MN-time) Mars. Colony "Kansas-2."
Encrypted for personal viewing only, by his wife and colleague Futima Kavanaugh.

My darling, this letter is almost a message in a bottle, and I am afraid it might be the last one. I apologise if the sound is quiet; I can't get closer to the microphone. There is no way for me to know whether you will ever hear this, but even one chance in a million is better than none, and so I am taking it. I have locked myself in the Kansas-2 medical facility. In about twenty minutes, those cursed Cruisers will find me. Tom Darkwood, our captain, was against the landing, but his commanding base insisted on the order. Our passenger was too valuable to the Object mission to risk the pod transfer – no matter how well it had been modified. So Chang and Marta brought Wasp to the polygon. We were ambushed. Cruisers, armed with zappers this time, were waiting for us to identify to them the person we had come for. Wasp came under attack as soon as three of us – two troopers and myself – entered the lift.

Why did I go? I volunteered, of course. I was too damn curious about the new life support system. And yes, I can almost hear you calling me an idiot. I deserve it, my love. Anyway ... apparently, while we were going down to the cave town, the ship went back into orbit. Phil was shot on the first level when we were on our way to the pod launcher. I could not tell if he was dead or wounded, but Sandra killed two Cruisers, made me run through the quarantine ward, and pushed me into this room. Cough ... cough ... I could hear her swearing and shooting, but the sound became more distant, and I did not hear anything for a while. I panicked. Grrr! Cough!

Believe it or not, at first, all I wanted was to get out of here. I am not claustrophobic, but I was this close to banging on the door. Then I remembered that every med-suite in the old colonies had a terminal in the technician's room. Ugh! I found it, powered it up, and accessed MESH. Even if they destroy this terminal, the message will be waiting for you out there. I hope you'll find it, eventually. I closed the door to the tech room and just then noticed that I was bleeding. One of the rays had nipped my side, but I did not feel anything until I almost slipped on my own blood. My liver vessels have burned open, and I will bleed to death before they find me.

I tried to track Wasp only to see that they had taken off. I have no idea whether they picked up Vist or not. I hope they managed somehow. The Object mission must succeed. But for me ... what a meaningless death ... A punishment for my whims! So, whatever time I have left ... Cough! Ugh! I want to spend this time with you. I have found tetriconite, a syringe and bandages, and I hope I've bought myself a few extra minutes. I can't stand, I am on the floor, but I can see the tip of the microphone from here. It represents you for me now. Nothing else can. This microphone and your face in my memory. Cough ... phew ... sorry, my mouth is full of blood too. Your face, yes ... Remember when we went to Egypt on my birthday? Cough ... We had Prosecco with Belgian truffles and strawberries ... You were wearing a peachy bolero and matching sun hat. Gosh, you were beautiful ... cough ... Your eyes smiled ... I loved you always, but that day ... Grrr... Cough! Please remember that too. I can't tell you how ... tell Todd ... Evacuate ... both ... heh. You must try ...

miss you, *Futtie dear, I can't! Oh, damn ... Voice command: two zero nine ... Ugh! Send ...*

Chapter 3. 3416. Back on Earth – Tom

"Please confirm your name and title."

"Thomas Darkwood, former captain of Space Troopers Regiment EF-59."

"Date of birth?"

"17 May 3368."

"State of birth?"

"Greece."

"Cultural roots?"

"Dutch, Irish, Greek and South Africa. I can't believe you still have this section in your forms."

"Please just answer the questions. I won't tell you again."

The bald, still young, but weathered man touched his bleeding lip with his tongue and waited for the next question.

"Five years ago, the unauthorised vessel *WSP-41* performed a shift to Earth's only known colony in the constellation of Lyra. Was it you who was in command of that vessel?"

"Yes."

"On whose orders?"

"It was not an official trip. It was a decision agreed by many."

"What do you call your group? Do you work for the Resistance?"

"I never liked that name. We are the part of the human population who *don't* want to take blind chances."

"Careful, Captain. Blasphemy is not welcomed here."

"But sins are?"

The next punch was even more painful than the one before. The twisted bastard was aiming at the same spot, which was already raw and tender.

"My hand is guided by my Lord, you ... wretched man! To show you the right way, any means are good means!" A big, muscular Cruiser in a sky-blue hooded robe stood up straight and smiled, "But it is sinful for you to hit me back. That would be an act of malevolence. Now, tell me, why did you stop by Mars before you opened the wormhole for a shift?"

He took a few steps back and stared at Tom expectantly. Tom realised that he had been given a few seconds to compose himself. He squinted past the candles and tried to look around. We are not outside, he thought, but rather inside something big. The voices echo. It's not a cave. He dropped his head and briefly examined the tiled floor. A large hall ... or a cathedral? He tried to make out the walls, but the darkness swallowed them. A group of small candles failed to show anything useful. But Tom could not stop feeling that there was something important there, not far away.

"Time to answer," said the Cruiser and stepped closer, bringing his sweaty stench with him.

"We had to pick up a package."

"What was in the package?"

"Essential equipment."

"Do you want me to hit you again? We know you picked up a person."

"The equipment comes with an operator."

"Who was that operator?"

Thomas Darkwood sighed. They already knew. "Look, you can smash my face into mince if you like. I can't tell you much, even if I wanted to. This "operator" was a weird one – they kept away from everyone and did not speak much. I thought at first that it was synthetic. I mean ... really. Just imagine, it didn't need a medic to rise from the pod, it could access the entire database, it consumed minimum rations, and I don't think it slept at all."

"But it was not a synth," the Cruiser confirmed, before continuing. "Nobody builds synths anymore. For centuries they failed to produce synthetic life that would last a year. They're expensive and unreliable junk."

"No. This one was definitely a human. One of those who doesn't want to be known by other people."

"But who was it? Was it a man or a woman?"

"I don't know!" This was said with such strong emotion that the Cruiser surprised himself by believing this sinner.

"Hmm. We suspect they were a loader. We really could do with one. And the name? Surely they introduced themself."

The pause was too long to be polite.

"Vist."

Chapter 4. 3411. Out in Space – *Wasp*

"Friends, meet and greet our new and very important member of the crew – Vist. I am sorry, but until this moment, I could not reveal to you the true reason for making a stop at the Mars colony."

The captain, Tom Darkwood, made a broad welcoming gesture – almost a bow – with his arm and stood back, leaving me in the spotlight. I stood there and slowly looked around. Was I expected to say something? Why was this so formal? I should have visited Earth more often. The faces in the room did not look happy to see me. I scanned them quickly. There were eight, mostly from the British Isles. Two may have been Americans and the rest? I was not sure. One was old, two were female, five were white, one had a beard, one was seriously pissed off, one had CHD, and one was very shy ... those last two were a couple ... Those three looked incredibly strong. And yes – none of them liked my robe. They didn't like it at all.

"Vist? Is that all?" asked a short stocky man with a stylish grey haircut and something like a raincoat over his uniform.

"It's the only name we need," Captain Darkwood said.

"No. What I mean is ... where are the rest of the passengers? I was made to believe we were risking our lives and our mission was to pick up a good half-dozen specialists. We need a scientist, a doctor, and all those engineers, arty-farty people and linguists to make contact. This is just one—" the short man stopped and looked at me with some doubt. "One guy? Hmm."

"Well, Général. This is it. Vist is all those things and more. You know why we can't go in large numbers. This is your first shift flight, isn't it? The ship class WSP is not big enough, but it opens fewer wormholes, can shift faster, and we need to be fast."

"Oh my! You are one of those loaders, aren't you?" the Black woman with a French accent exclaimed, as she got up and walked towards me. She stopped, looking puzzled, and then smiled, "I never met one before. Nice to make your acquaintance. Is it Miss or Mrs? Vist."

"Just Vist," I replied, and the sound of my voice created a short moment of silence as usual.

"Oh, I am sorry. I thought you were a lady. Well? Are you?" Her smile turned into a puzzled frown once more.

"Blimey, Zina! Don't be so rude! Just because someone can multitask, you assume they are a woman. Welcome aboard, Vist!" A young man dressed in the yellow-and-black uniform typical for a maintenance officer stepped closer and stretched out his hand, "My name is Rod. Rodion Baker. I am looking after this baby ship. Tiny, isn't she? This is Zina Vurie, our single medical officer since we just lost our doctor on Mars. You already met Commander Lillypond. He is a general by rank, but we affectionately call him Général, after a light-hearted comment Zina made, which stuck! These three dishy blokes are all that is left of his squad after the last stop. Steven, Tolyan and Mik," he said, pointing his finger towards three stone-faced men, dressed in the same dark-grey armoured suits as their commander, but without the shiny pins.

Rod carried on. "These are our brave pilots – Marta and Chang Broadsky. They were assigned straight after their wedding day, but their honeymoon will have to wait until all this is over. Oh, that's a strong handshake, Mr Vist! Is that honey I can smell?"

"Just Vist, please."

Silence again. The look on Rod's face was priceless. The trooper named Mik scoffed quietly.

"This is just wrong, Tom," said Général. "Just one, whatever … loader. Too risky if you ask me. What if something happened to her … or him?"

"That is why we need you, Alan. Your job is to protect Vist. In fact, make sure that you and your boys don't allow Vist to be even stung by a fly – literally." The captain looked at each person in turn as he spoke, "This is it, my friends. We all have our roles in Object. We are here to deliver Vist to the colony and provide the best assistance we can. The Object mission is our last shot. If we fail, the Earth will not be able to afford another expedition, and desperate people will turn to the Moon Cruise project instead. You have all been assigned because you believed that the Colony of Noverca is our best option." The captain's eyes wandered from person to person in the circle and finally stopped on me. "Vist is important. And this is all we need to know about Vist."

I must admit that his pompous speech did not make it easier for me to fit in. I had to do something about it. "The captain informed me that three crew members followed the High Council order and went to the cave town. They did not have to."

The man they introduced as Général stood up. "Yes. Two of my troopers followed the order – Philip Altis and Sandra Paulson. Doctor Kavanaugh went too, but he volunteered. We didn't get any of them back, as we had to leave as soon as we landed."

"Even if I am not directly responsible for your loss, I still—"

"We have no confirmation of their fate. They may still be alive," said the trooper, a behemoth with a short light-brown beard. "Cruisers could not take over the whole cave town!"

"Easy, Tolyan," said Captain Darkwood, "Rod already informed the Resistance via MESH. They will follow it up appropriately!"

"Nevertheless, I would like to thank you all for risking your lives for Object and me," I said and smiled. "Rioja Gran Reserva, anyone? I hope you have crystal glasses."

I lifted the thermo-valise up to my ear and opened it. Six dark bottles glistened in the light of the small common room. No one moved. Nobody expected that because it was highly inappropriate. But shocks always worked for me before. I tried again, "You don't have to – all the more for me."

The awkward silence did not last for long this time. As soon as their leader nodded, everyone relaxed.

"I am afraid we don't have glasses," said Zina, smiling again, "but we do have poly-cups. They are transparent and make a bit of a ding noise."

Something changed in the atmosphere, just as I hoped it would – but not completely. Someone was still tense. Someone was still worried about me being here, perhaps angry ... or disappointed.

"With your permission, Captain?" I said to my host and opened the first bottle. "Thank you for letting me do this."

"We have spent the whole month in orbit before coming to Mars. And now we are going even further from home. I could not deny my crew a little taste of Earth. But I don't know how you managed to smuggle these bottles on board. Even in your sarcophagus."

"I cannot stay, I need to go," said a quiet, fair-headed woman called Marta, "I am on duty. We will manoeuvre in two hours."

An hour later, the conversation was flowing. It's amazing how easily you can stop people from probing you if you lead them to talk about themselves. All you have to do is to keep asking questions until you hit the right button. No one can resist their favourite subject. Initially, I thought Général would be the most difficult one, but the wine and chat about 4D games did the trick. He was of that age when a man slowly realises that he is not in his prime anymore, but he is still too strong and witty to live in the past.

Tolyan and Rod didn't need even that kind of attention. They had something more important to discuss among themselves. Rod, whose ancestors were most likely from India or Pakistan, occasionally slipped in a word or two in pure cockney. Tolyan was the biggest of the troopers. He looked like a huge Viking with his light beard and grey eyes. Rod seemed so small next to him, but he was spry and much smarter. It was clear they had known each other for a long time and very well. The blond guy, Steven, was more interested in the French girl. His blue eyes were betraying him despite all the banter and pretend indifference. No wonder. Zina was beautiful with her massive black braid, Jamaican profile, long neck and French accent.

Chang and the captain had many questions for me. The handsome young pilot kept very little of his Asian heritage – just his straight black hair, high cheekbones, eye shape and first name. He was keen to leave, though, to join his wife, but Captain Darkwood was like a party host who is not quite done yet, and who kept him involved in the conversation. The captain's head was shaved, and his adjustable glasses suggested his eyesight was deteriorating faster than opticians could treat it. These people were normal Earth people, and they socialised like all people of all times.

It was Mik who wasn't talking much. He watched me from his corner. His coarse black mass of hair was divided in the middle and twisted into two hard plaits, resembling a pair of short horns. I stood up and took the last bottle from my valise.

"You have to kill this one without me, guys," I said, "I need a real sleep and some time to recover fully from my awakening."

"Was it as painful as they say it is?" asked Chang, his narrow eyes twinkling.

"Depends on your perception, I guess."

"Marta had an urgent pod ejection too once," said Chang, "from the ship to the station. She said it feels like dying."

"I can agree with that description."

"But from the surface to the ship! I didn't think it was possible. Your system practically shuts down and restarts again to survive the speed and pressure. I hope I never have to do that. Not even a landing one!" said Zina. Her French accent was enhanced with alcohol.

"Good night, guys. I thank you for making me feel at home."

Everyone nodded or said goodnight, apart from Mik, I noticed. When I looked at him, he deliberately and slowly blinked and finished his drink. I left the room.

They will get used to it. I have been through this before, on Mars. First, they will wonder, then they will end up calling me "it" behind my back. Then they will stop hesitating before calling me by my name only and splitting into "he" and "she" groups. My sleeping cubicle was ready. Soon the first wormhole would be opened, and we will shift towards the Vitricus System in Lyra, towards Noverca. I needed to recharge.

Chapter 5. 3416. Back on Earth – Chang

The bright light made Chang close his eyes tight again. His head was ringing like a bell, but there was no pain.

"Can you hear me?" somebody was shouting from somewhere far away. "If you can, nod," said the same voice much closer, "If you open your eyes – that would be even better," whispered this female voice into his ear.

The light was gone. Or maybe it had not been there at all. He had probably just hit his head and saw stars. Chang opened his eyes and saw a female face in the blur, close but upside down. What a beautiful woman was bending over him! She looked familiar. After a few moments, Chang knew that she was his wife, and a couple of minutes later, he remembered her name.

"Marta."

"Thank you. You scared me, you ... no good for singing and dancing chunk of cabbage. If you had not woken up in the next five seconds, I would have left you here to rot, you old bony pig. I hate you. What are you laughing at?"

Chang used his right hand to grab Marta by the neck, pulled her face down to his lips, and kissed her.

"I love you too, ugly," he said.

Yes! They had made it. Both were alive, and nothing else mattered. Chang lay on his back, and Marta kneeled by his head. Next to her, Zina was flashing the med-torch into Steven's eyes, and Steven held his right wrist with his left hand. Chang carefully sat up and felt his body protest immediately.

"Slowly, Chang. Slowly. Remember, Vist told us not to rush it. Rest and try one thing at a time."

"Are you ok, my love? How many of us are here? Where is Tom?"

"The captain went north, and Mik went north-west. They are looking for Général and Rod, whose courses were disrupted. Tolyan is still unconscious, but he is going to be ok. He is strong. I was worried about you because of your heart."

"I have yours for a backup. Is there any water?"

"Here, but don't be surprised if you throw it up first."

Marta pushed the flask into his hand and got up.

"How is the blond doing, Zin?" Chang asked.

"Steven? He's a little pissed off. None of our troopers like being helpless. Even for a few moments. You should not have tried to open the pod by yourself, Steven. Did you panic or something?"

"Hell no! I just thought it was broken."

"Vist said to wait for at least five minutes for the air pressure adjustment. You could have damaged your lungs, bled internally, and popped the blood vessels in your eyes."

Steven frowned at Zina's words. "I am fine."

"You are lucky. Still, you have too many injuries already to add a broken hand."

"It is not broken, just bruised. How come Mikky and the captain are up and about already? Where is Vist?"

"Vist went on a different course, and don't ask me why and how. Marta was the first to come out, as she had done this before. Chang's pod sat too deep in the soft dirt to open, so she went to you next to help her. Your pod was resetting itself due to your efforts. So she went to the front line and got the captain and Mik up first. I don't know how they kept their guts in," said Zina, "they were covered in vomit, but Mik snapped out of it and woke me up. Together we pulled out Chang, Tolyan and you."

"You missed the sunrise, darling," said Marta to Chang, "I wish I could stand on that hill and watch it with you. Oh my! I can't tell you how much I missed a good, real dawn! You know, when you can actually see the sun going down!"

"Sunset will happen soon enough, Marta," said Chang. "Sure, we will watch it together. I am looking forward to the real night ... and real day, if I am honest."

Zina got up, looked at the sky and said, "I missed the dark sky and the stars ... and the sight of our bright Moon shining through the thin clouds. I hope it is still here. Also, is it just me, or is this not a real wind compared with the winds on Gera?"

Chang looked around to find himself in the Dead Forest. The ground was covered in ashes and rotten branches. Giant trees don't grow on Earth anymore. They were grey dead monuments with huge weathered trunks, left standing in the thin bed of rare but still living shrubs, grasses and ferns. This was such a contrast to the dark-green and purple-black woods of Gera! The open pods sat in small craters like darts, their points piercing the clay at a forty-five-degree angle, at an equal distance of twenty metres from each other. They were in the same order as if launched like bullets from a gun.

Nevertheless, Chang could see just seven of them. The gap between Zina and his pod was twice as large as the other gaps – Rod was missing, and the first one should have been second. There was no general among them. Chang's pod sat deep in the dirt a couple of steps away. He got up and walked on unsteady feet to examine the computer and load up the landing records. The holo-screen showed a map with the pods' locations and trajectories.

"I already looked at it," said Marta. "We were shot at! Shot from the satellite ZPE-cannon by Cruisers. They managed to hit two of us, but that was *after* Vist's pod went off course. Vist told us that they might attack."

"But look, it happened pretty low down. Général and Rod could not have fallen far. They should both be north-west of here, and just a few metres apart from each other. Do they have a signal?"

"Général was transmitting until a few minutes ago but not Rod."

"Crap!" Chang said, "Why is that?"

"The panel terminal only registered a ceased transmission and had no reason for it. Alan's pod told the story of being hit by two missiles. I assume Rod was hit too, just because they went down together," Marta mused.

"And Vist?"

"He was gone from the very start. There must be another reason. I suspect ..."

"What?"

"She ... he disengaged the course deliberately. Look at these readings: a 4.4 second delay to the scheduled launch and then ... this!"

"Is that why she wanted to be the last to leave? No, I don't buy that!" Chang brushed back his thick, overgrown black hair with both hands, "Why would she? There is no apparent reason."

Marta gently pulled his hands back down and looked into his eyes.

"Come on. This is Vist. You never know with him. I still think he is a dark horse and has his own purpose – a good one."

"Yes. Something must have happened in those 4.4 seconds."

Tolyan groaned, and Zina immediately left Steven to help Tolyan. She talked softly into his ear and checked his responses. Steven got up, swaying like a drunken man.

"I need to take a leak."

"Do not go far, and don't rush anything," said Zina without turning to him, "your wrist *is* broken, and I don't want you to take that bandage off. And don't punch anything else."

"Yes, ma'am. *Oui m'dame. Natürlich gnädige Frau.* This time, no sticky ucha-trees."

He made a few unsteady steps and disappeared between green shrubs. When

Tolyan could talk again, he also asked for water and about Rod but did not hear the answer. He said he was tired, then he curled up like a cat by the tree stump, and started to snore. Zina got up.

"I wonder how far the road is from here. I suspect that the satellite was controlled from around here somewhere. So where are those shooters? They will try and pick us up too."

"We are not too far from the Oak," said Chang, still examining the pods' logs. "According to this, we landed almost an hour and twenty minutes ago. If someone is after us, we really should not stay here much longer."

"Where will we go? If Cruisers are nearby, we have to disable our tech, but without access to MESH, we will not find our people."

"We just have to try. As long as we complete the mission somehow. Marta, help me to smash the pod's computers. The Cruisers must not have any of it. Captain's orders."

With these words, he pulled out the memory core, swung it like a club and smashed the panel of his pod with a few strokes.

"How will we find Vist without it?" asked Zina.

"Vist's pod is silent anyway."

"But if Vist is alive, he can fix his radio at least."

"We cannot carry the pods with us, and we cannot stay by them," said Marta, picking up a large rock from the ground and walking towards the next pod, "I will take my Field Portable Station just in case."

"I would destroy it too if it was down to me," said Chang, starting on the next pod.

"It will self-destruct if tampered with. Will that make you feel better?" replied Marta, moving from Tom's pod to Zina's.

Soon all the pods were ruined. Their panels were gutted, and the dirt around them was covered with shards, torn-out wires, and smashed memory cores.

"This is so sad," Zina said, sighing. "People like us should create, not destroy."

"Hopefully, one day we will create again," said Marta. "Look, Mik is back first. Have you found them, Mik? Where is the captain?"

A tall Black man approached them and looked around.

He made a face at the sleeping Tolyan as if muttering "of course" and then said wearily, "He is probably still looking because I found both of our pods over there, already taken care of."

Mik pointed somewhere behind his back, frowning at the destroyed equipment on the ground.

"Looted?" asked Marta.

"No, just smashed," answered Mik. "Not such a neat job as you have done here, more rushed, but the captain was not there to do that, so this may mean Rod and Général are alive ... or at least one of them. I saw a lot of blood."

"How much?" asked Zina.

"Not enough to assume anything, but enough to know that if they are both hurt, at least one of them was strong enough to smash the terminals. I looked around and found the used med-kit and evidence that the food had been consumed. One of them was sick. One of them had tried to build a stretcher and drag the other one for some time. Then the truck disappeared as if they just ... flew away."

"I am sure both of them were taken," Zina said quietly.

"Both? That would mean that they are both alive. Cruisers will not take a body. Right?" said Chang.

"They might. I can think of plenty of reasons: study, ritual, cannibalism. Yes, some sects are known to go that far."

"Maybe it was not Cruisers who took them. We have received signals from an R6-beacon in these woods after all," said Chang.

"Shouldn't they have left a sign for us then?" asked Marta.

"And for the Cruisers?" Chang sniffed. "No. Our men are too smart to do that."

"Yes. It was bad enough that the beacon attracted Cruisers too. I suspect it was Rod who was on his feet. He is not the strongest man I know, but Général is older, and this kind of landing could have left him very feeble, if not injured." Mik looked genuinely worried about his commander. Then he looked around with even more concern. "Where are my guys?"

Everybody turned and looked back at Tolyan's tree stump. The stump was there, but the trooper was no more.

"Steven did not come back," said Zina, gasping as she rushed into the shrubs after him but was stopped by Chang's hand on her upper arm.

"Don't!" Chang said to her and looked at Mik.

"Hide the girls," Mik replied to the silent question. He activated his zappers and disappeared into the thick shrubs like a cat.

Chang turned to both women. "Let's go, now!"

He grabbed Marta's hand, but a voice by one of the smashed pods said, "Too late! Come with us peacefully in the name of the Lord."

Three Cruisers came out from behind the pod. They were armed with maces and dressed in short green-and-brown hooded robes with a camouflage design. Their trousers were tucked into soundless leather boots. Somewhere on the left, everybody heard a struggle. Somebody screamed in pain, then Mik roared in frustration, and the woods went silent again. It seemed Mik did not go down peacefully.

"Hmm, I believe it just took four people to overpower your friend," said one of the Cruisers, who looked older than his comrades. He was tall and muscular; his hood was thrown back, revealing scars on his cheek and a deformed right ear. "We were just about to take your lovely, colourful trio when he arrived. Your captain has been taken already. The other two were not quite themselves and made easy targets. Looks like we have all seven now. We know who you are, so don't try anything."

Chang lifted his fist with a zapper towards the figures in front of him and received a strong blow on the head from behind. Before he passed out, he heard Marta's scream and thought, all seven? They don't have Général and Rod then.

Chapter 6. 3411. Out in Space – Rod

MESH message

RodionBaker101@@Parsecmail.mesh.

Rod Baker, maintenance officer. (05.11.3411, 09.10 WSP-time) Video correspondence, encrypted for the personal viewing of Master Ruslan Baker alone.

Hi dad. I thought I would send you this last message before shifting because it might be a long time before you hear from me again. What will be weeks for us, will be years for you. If all goes well, that is.

I am good and well, and I kept my promise about you know what. I also think I will need a new set of teeth when I get home since there is not one single sandy-beetle on board but only crackers and pellets. If we still have a home then, or if I even get back. Well, we are on our way. So far, it was almost botched: we lost people to the Cruisers fan club on Mars when leaving the solar system. The captain was right, and we should not have landed, but he had clear orders from the Resistance

Counsel. We ended up in a spot of bother; we legged it and had a narrow escape, as it goes. I was sure we would fail to collect our special passenger, but the station managed to deliver an emergency package. It has arrived on board Wasp inside the escape pod, the construction of which I wish I could tell you a lot about. Oh yes, sir! You would have been gobsmacked for sure! But I can't just yet. You know why. All because of that passenger – a very weird and dodgy character indeed! At first, I thought it was one of the defected Cruisers, as they chose to dress like an old-fashioned monk or something, together with other religious attributes. This one wears a baggy robe over the bio-suit, has a hairstyle like the famous Cassidy Nevada, and is very strong. Nevertheless, we can't decide if it is a bloke or a lass. Pretty olive eyes, a nice smile like a spiffing and muscular young man, but when she or he is serious, then this person looks like a very handsome woman, a Rubenesque Delilah under those robes, no doubt. Steven said it was a man because Vist (our new friend's name) did not flirt with him during the first hours after his arrival. This daft flutter suggested a bet – Zina should accidentally spill water over her front and watch if Vist would stare. Seriously? He thinks this would mean something?

Zina wasn't chuffed. She blushed and called him a wanker in French, but we are all intrigued now. And before you ask – the voice does not help. The rascal has an artificial larynx, and the voice is metallically distorted. We could have picked up a hair or an eyelash, but Zina's DNA tester crashed last night, and I had no time to look at it. It was Tolyan who asked bluntly, but Vist said, "I don't want you to know," and when Tolyan persisted in knowing why, the answer was, "Because I have a reason of my own." And that was it. Pretty naff, right? No one dared ask again, but we could not stop wondering. We are stuck together for a while, after all. Now we have something to occupy our minds, and curiosity is a natural quality of humans, isn't it?

But for me, it is not so much a him or her ... as you know. I am more interested in something else here. Dad, can you do me a favour? Contact Wesley for me and ask him to do a little search on this Vist character. If anyone can hack into a personal database in the Council logs – it will be him. And don't tell anyone else. I want to know for my own reasons. He ... or she is a loader! Believe it or not! Information about her will be well protected but not impossible to dig out. Not for Wes, anyway. Why is this person so important for the Object mission, and why did he have to hide in the Mars tunnels when he or she could be a great help to the Resistance? Surely the story of the colony could have been recorded instead, and there are more secure and less risky vaults than those for some loader's head. And, yes! Tell Wes to start with the best builders of the escape pods. I suspect his ... personalised sarcophagus also has something to do with her being a loader.

What else can I tell you? We had a good read of the colony chronicles. It is funny how people created a whole new culture. So many generations managed to keep English grammar very close to what they left with, but the spelling changed and became more phonetic; most articles and punctuation are now completely gone. Vist explained that although it is still English, it merged with all the other languages the first travellers spoke. As a result, they expanded their vocabulary and made the whole language richer, losing most of the punctuation. I am not sure it's a good thing, though. What if we will not understand them? What if they will think we are simpletons? I don't know. They might be smart arses, but they did not grow as we did. They may not use a stone axe there, but they did not even explore the other areas of that planet properly.

They are still on the same spot of Gera, on a continent one-third the size of Australia. When I mentioned this to Vist, he or she said (Listen to this quote from the record):

"Interesting that you mentioned Australia. It is remote enough to keep marsupials from spreading to the rest of the Earth for centuries. The colonists brought some Earth species with them to give them a chance to adapt and farm them. That is why Gera looks like the countryside on Earth, unlike the rest of the planet. Adaptation takes an unpredictable amount of time. The climate in that spot is more or less suitable, although only just. But there is another reason why they can't spread much. The colonists don't have a choice. Noverca is too close to its M-class dwarf and is locked with it tidally. You know what that means. Our Moon used to be like that. It spins on its axis, but unfortunately, one side always faces the sun. The dayside is too hot, and only the convection in the ocean cools it down. The words south and north have nothing to do with the poles of the planet. On Noverca they strictly refer to the unchanging dayside and nightside.

Gera is closer to the eternal twilight regions if you like. It is always mid-morning or early evening ... depending on what you prefer. Colonists call the place under the direct sun 'South' and the opposite spot 'North.' They called the colonised continent 'Gera' after their first year there, and the north parts 'Terrenia,' which started as the Mediterranean. They were obviously too busy to come up with new names."

Imagine, dad! (See what I mean about the voice? Bollocks, isn't it?) I wonder what their compass looks like.

I have to stop now. I will send it directly and hope you remember my encryption code to listen to it. We will be shifting in two hours. Wish me good weather. I love you, dad. I hope we all meet again. Toodle-oo! Yours, Rod.

Voice command six-eight-two, send.

Chapter 7. 3416. Back on Earth – Cruiser

He lifted his fist then stopped. There was almost complete silence. Tom Darkwood stopped breathing for a moment, expecting a blow that did not come. He realised that the brute had also frozen and was listening. What had stopped him? Tom tried to listen too. Did the flame of the candles just flicker slightly, or was it his imagination? He tried to remember Vist's lesson, "Close your eyes; it helps. Hold your breath and concentrate everything on your hearing. Listen with your skin, too, if you catch my meaning. You are an owl or a bat. You are flying from corner to corner – no sound or movement of air can escape you." There was a movement in the darkness. A rustle of fabric. Not a rough out-robe like that of the Cruiser in front of him, but much softer, like velvet or wool? Expensive. And yes, someone else was breathing there. Very quietly ... how far away?

The Cruiser slowly lowered his arm and locked both hands behind his back. He rocked on his heels and whistled a short tune. Then he slowly walked around Tom and casually strode a few steps away from him, behind the chair. Tom counted fourteen quick steps. With that height and this kind of walking, that had to be about nine metres. Tom concentrated everything on that spot. His heart and noisy pulse in his left temple really interfered, but there was nothing he could do about that. Unlike Vist, he could not stop his heart for a few seconds. But there was a definite whisper, confirmed with a quiet "yeah" from the Cruiser in reply. It was so soft. If Tom had experienced another punch to his head earlier, he probably would not hear anything but his tinnitus now. The Cruiser asked something, Tom could not make it out, but he picked up the answer, "Not ... now!" The whisperer sounded hoarse and frustrated by the question, but Tom could still just about hear him. It was very tiresome. Tom thought about how long it had been since he had last slept, and his whole body started to ache immensely. "Don't!" he said to himself. He lifted his head and saw the Cruiser in front of him again.

"Well, Captain Darkwood," said the brute looking down at his feet, "forget about this creature for a minute. Tell me about the planet. Yes, we learned soon after you were gone that you went to Noverca. What have you found there?"

"What do you mean? The life conditions on the planet?"

The Cruiser didn't respond; he had a sweet smile on his broad face.

Tom continued, "It is hard but manageable, just about as much as is possible by a red dwarf. In Gera's habitable zone, nothing is too life-threatening, but to survive, you need to be constantly alert and considerate. Outside of the zone, that is a different story. But even on Gera, mistakes can be the death of you or lessons to learn. Your worst enemy is yourself, and your best friend is too. Pretty much like it is here if you think about it."

"I see. Thank you," said the Cruiser, with a mock politeness. "Tell me about the people there. You have found the colony, haven't you?"

"Yes."

"What sort of society have they formed there? Do they worship the Lord, or have they become children of Satan?"

"Oh, that? They are highly religious. Yes."

"Wonderful! I am glad to hear that so far, and after such a long time, humanity still recognises the power of our creator. Tell me more. Here is some water. Here. Let me untie one of your hands. See, the blessing of the Lord is already upon you. Let's talk like brothers under the Lord's watchful eyes. Easy, don't try anything. We are doing so well."

The Cruiser released Tom's left hand, but his right wrist was pulled down and fastened to the chair's back leg using an orange cable tie. Tom brushed his fingers against the chair surface and noted that it was made of heavy plastic, at least on the outside. He sniffed at the cup and didn't smell anything but recycled water. He sipped a little but did not taste anything apart from his blood. He swallowed some, and his burning throat welcomed the cool relief. This was just water, after all.

"Thanks for that," said Tom, before adding sarcastically, "Brother, what is it that you want to know?"

"Everything!" The Cruiser either ignored the tone of voice or did not notice it. "Do they still remember the holy name? How do they pray? Who is the High Word-Bearer? Do they praise the Lord with sacrifice and blessed fasting? Do they protect their young ones from sins and sacrilege? Do they purify lost souls like yourself?"

Tom remembered the effortless conversation between Vist and believers of Noverca. It felt like ages ago, but surely he had learned something from it. It wouldn't be easy to do it with the same dignity while tied to a chair.

"Wow, where do I start? Don't they seem to have failed at the latter?"

"They must have had faith in you since they allowed you to live and to leave. Or do you have a story to tell me about you overcoming their force?"

"You tell me, brother. Doesn't everything happen according to the Lord's will?"

"You are right, my brother. Now we are talking! The Lord has a task for all of us. Maybe yours is to tell me about them."

The brute was smiling like a baby now. He pulled another chair from the darkness on his right-hand side and mounted it in front of Tom, leaning closer and breathing worm-stew stink onto his face. Tom was glad his stomach was empty, although he was so hungry that he would probably even gobble up cooked worms right now. Those fried larvae in White City were not too bad after all. He eyed the Cruiser's chair, its size, material and estimated weight. Was his chair the same?

"Okay," he said, thinking that he would probably enjoy this one for a change, "we have found two very different congregations there."

"Really? How different? Are they at war?"

"Not exactly. Some worship your Lord, or at least they use the same holy name."

The Cruiser again did not react, but Tom was not talking to him. He was talking to another one, the one behind him.

"Go on."

"They are the ones who would not maintain the peace, actually."

"Understandable, I say. Those who deny the true Lord must be found and delivered to him. Who is the holy leader?"

"They call him the High Martyr."

"A sufferer? Thank you, Lord!" The Cruiser dramatically threw his arms and face towards the heavens. "Please continue, chief; your words are sweet music to my ears."

Tom wondered if this man was truly mad or if he was just acting. His eyes glistened, his nostrils fluttered, his face turned from red to crimson, and his whole posture expressed excitement and exaltation. It was as if he wasn't punching Tom's face with delight just a few minutes ago and calling him a wretch.

"They are not a great group. Not anymore. There were less than eighty of them when we left the planet. And those who died since have only themselves to blame."

"No, you must be wrong. No one is to blame, praise the Lord. Hold on, did you say eighty?" The stupid smile disappeared for a moment, but then he grinned again. "The greater part of the colony then?"

It was Tom's turn to be surprised, "What? I don't get you?"

"The *Lyra* missions carried ninety-eight people each, divided between two ships. You can read that in every school book."

"Yes, but it was eleven generations ago. In about three-hundred-and-thirty Earth years, the colony's population grew to over five thousand. The initial number grew almost fifty times over, despite the high death rate."

"Oh. Yes, I forgot. So they all have become Adams and Eves! How wonderful!"

Tom was sure the Cruiser would have blushed a bit if his face was not red already.

"The New Eden was good for new children. Isn't that right?"

"Not really. Apples did not grow on the trees, and lambs did not wander about. The weather was not too harsh but still not great for a picnic. It was windy all the time – worse than here on Earth – with high radiation levels, and it was far too hot; the twilight never ends on that side. They had to build a far more civilised establishment to bring up kids. It was almost twelve years before the first twenty children were born. Two of them did not make it through the first year. Another one died at three, and two more in their teens. Illnesses and accidents are hard to avoid, even more so on a strange planet. But soon after, all the families had at least four children, and they developed a good education system."

This is not what the person in the dark wanted to know. His impatience was expanding and filling the room like smoke. Even the fat Cruiser sensed it.

"Forget about children, brother. What about the other group? Who do they worship if not the Lord? Satan?"

"A goddess!"

The Cruiser pulled an indescribable face, and Tom was sure he heard a gasp in the dark behind him.

Chapter 8. 3411. Out in Space – History

I will enjoy a proper landing for a change. Besides the *Wasp*'s ability to shift faster in space, it can also enter the atmosphere slowly, lower itself, and land gently like a skylark. This landing takes many hours, but you can stay awake and conscious all the time and even enjoy a view of Noverca's ocean. Nausea is not completely ruled out, but it's nothing compared to the recovery from a pod.

It was midday according to the ship timer. We already knew the colony was alive as we had picked up a few faint communications signals. They use radio – this is a good sign. They probably have their own version of MESH by now, but we haven't accessed it yet. Rod was visibly disappointed that the colony did not help with the coordinates. He opened a frequency for the captain, and then there was a surprise. The captain said "Gera ... Gera, respond, please. This is WSP-41 of Earth, the voluntary team of Object. My name is Darkwood. Thomas Darkwood. I am the captain. Would you please stop jamming your signals and help us to find your city?"

After a few attempts, a deep female voice on Gera answered, "Sorry for the delay, Object. My name is Raja Dalviny, a communications worker. I am not authorised to reveal our coordinates to you just yet. Hopefully, the reasons will be explained later, but I am sending you an image of the map with the coordinates of your landing spot. It will take you to the west foreland, south of the Terenian mountain range. Find New Portland, a small semi-island. Land there stealthily, get to the mainland and walk south-west along the coastline for about twenty miles. We will instruct a guide to meet you at the bay we call Laguna. He will take you to the White City, if you are who you profess to be. Take my advice, hide your vessel well, or take it back into orbit. Equip yourself for a long ramble, and don't forget food and first aid kits with wound sterilisers. I hope you received the Stranger-4 formula in one of the reports. Vaccinate yourselves with it as a precaution. Do not try the local food just yet. Filter and boil the local water before drinking. A single bite of a goon-fly won't kill you, but you will be unable to work for roughly a cycle. Clove oil fumes repel local bugs.

I am looking forward to meeting you soon, I really am. Over."

All that was thrown at us in almost one breath. And not another word was forced out of the mysterious Raja of Gera. Captain Darkwood had no choice but to obey the strange instructions. The *Wasp* sat in a geosynchronous orbit above our target, and both pilots joined the rest of us for a glass of fruit water and a briefing in the common room. Through the observation lenses, between masses of clouds, we could just about make out this small continent, less than three million square kilometres and shaped like a willow leaf. It stretched from the south-west, broken into smaller deserted and grey islands on the far southern coasts, to the north-east, where not very high mountains were covered in snow. To everybody's delight, the middle looked partially occupied by some kind of flora, with the white hem of salty shores at the edges. Equatorial ocean waters, where it was free from ice, looked incredibly green, but the so-called South looked less so. On Earth, Gera would have been an island, but here it was one of the largest drylands on the planet. Chang said that after four orbital loops around the Noverca, his satellite probe had scanned and confirmed eight big islands surrounded by smaller islands. Gera was so distant from the others, as if it had tried to get as far away as possible. The long chains of tiny islands were scattered in groups and lines across one big ocean, which covered the entire planet and distributed the heat to its nightside. Chang registered a large group of small but close islands that would collectively cover Madagascar, and a few groups that stretched out into complicated webs. Armadas of icebergs were also spreading into the dayside along currents and melting away as they drifted further south. According to Chang, you could probably travel around the planet just by sailing from one warm island to another in a small fishing boat and walking on the ice in the colder regions.

Général was the only crew member still in uniform. Everybody else had agreed to wear their off-duty clothing, ready for the vaccination, which would be followed by hot flushes – one of its known side effects. Three troopers wore their training suits; Rod and Zina wore shorts and vests, and both Broadskys turned up in casual yoga kimonos. Captain Darkwood looked much younger in his slacks and shirt. Everybody disapproved of my robe once again but no one said a word.

"Well, that was a warm welcome," said Steven, "with no questions asked."

"No point in asking," I said, "if they don't trust us. Why ask questions if you are not prepared to believe the answer."

"Vist, you sound like you expected that," said Général.

"I can judge only by what I read in the last reports," I replied, "the new society of the colonists does not treat time the same way their ancestors did. What is the opposite of the phrase time-wasters?"

"Time-makers," Zina volunteered.

"Oh? I like them already," said Mik, mounting his usual stool in the dark corner.

"So, any concerns?" asked the captain, "No? Good. Zina?"

"I brought self-injectors with our vaccine here; you all know what to do," said Zina, handing each of us a small yellow capsule called a stinger by those who use it a lot. "I already knew to bring clove oil from Earth, and I can pack up the rest of the medical supply. I have uploaded the chemical formulas for Stranger 1, 2 and 3, and if you want, I can synthesise them all just in case. Not sure what you want me to do about food, though. How much and for how long?"

"I recommend individual backpacks for every team member," said Général, slapping the back of his hand in search of a suitable vein. "Do we all go?"

"No, the Broadskys will stay with the ship," said Captain Darkwood, "but Chang and Marta, I would like you to take the jab too. You will go outside to collect samples while waiting for the update."

"Good, let them have their honeymoon, finally," said Steven and winked at the couple who were busy administering the vaccine to each other. "On the beach too! Hey-ho! The reports did say something about the sea, right? Is it safe? I could do with a swim!"

I snapped the top of the stinger off, pushed the now-revealed needle into the blood vessel on the back of my hand, and squeezed the yellow pipette between my fingers.

"The ocean is mildly radioactive, but so is the local soil," I said, "The water is saturated with salt and is very green with local plankton, but it is normal seawater. The report did not mention harmful compounds, microorganisms or stinging marine life around Gera. The ocean further north may be dangerously deep. However, I cannot say much about land wildlife without accessing relevant information. I assume we are taking weapons with us, anyway?"

"Tolyan," said Général, injecting himself and then wincing, "prepare eight zappers and hand blades. Everyone here except Vist is trained to use those."

"I will manage," I said and dropped the empty stinger into the waste container that Zina was passing around. She stayed next to me a second too long. I don't think she noticed that herself.

"Shall I leave it there then?" Général looked sternly at the captain, who smiled and nodded without saying a word.

"All done?" Zina asked, "Report any unusual side effects to me immediately, but we should all feel a little sweaty and chatty for the first hour. So drink plenty of water, everybody."

"Thank you, Zina," said the captain, sipping from his cup. "You are right, Alan, it is better to be light on our feet. If we need anything larger, we can come back for guns. Marta, what is the temperature like on the surface?"

"A bit hot and windy to my liking, but we will be fine. Right now, the spectroprobe suggests thirty-five degrees centigrade, but I hope it will be cooler by the sea. The humidity is low, the wind is strong, and the precipitation is at twenty-one per cent."

"Thank you, that is manageable. Let us just take the rest mats for possible camping and one emergency tent. Food – just bars and pastes until we find something edible. A small amount of water supplies and a couple of water purifiers, just in case. Zina and Mik, prepare backpacks for two days. We don't need much if the city is just a few miles away. If it is closer, I want to look around anyway. Chang, can we use that map they sent?"

"The continent was never mapped properly, so the map is not very good. It is not much different from the one we got from the reports," answered Chang, wiping his forehead with the back of his hand and activating the holo-screen in the room. "The picture was taken from space on arrival hundreds of years ago, then it improved just a little. It wasn't a priority, I guess."

"And I guess they had no way of taking a new picture. The ships could never fly again," volunteered Tolyan.

Chang shrugged.

"New Portland is here," he said, pointing at the corner of his screen. "Here are those mountains where Terrenia starts. They are not very high but they stretch deeper into the twilight regions, where the climate is much colder. The western coast curves south-west, and twenty kilometres should take us here, to the bay. This spot is not too far from the *Ark* landing place and the original colony coordinates given to us at some point, but they have not been updated since C-year 241. That is when the reports informed us about the city's relocation. The name White City was mentioned in the last parcel, but before, it was just *Ark*."

"Why was the city moved?" Zina asked, pouring more fruit water into the cups, and ensuring that everyone had plenty.

"They did not say," I answered, "but it could be for better conditions or to move away from the waste. None of the reports mentioned this change ever again."

The captain looked at me.

"Now, Vist, tell us more about those reports. What do they say that might help?"

"How about the whole story, Tom? My lads were never too good at history," said Général, interrupting him. He started to sweat but would still rather listen than talk.

"Hey!" protested Tolyan and Mik together, but Steven tightened his lips and nodded sarcastically, "That's right ... we are just knobheads, aren't we?"

"Well ..." said the captain, wiping his face with the sleeve of his shirt, "we have to wait for this vaccine to integrate into our systems. We have an hour to pack and four hours for a nap. That gives us enough time to have a little bedtime story. Let's first remind ourselves of what we are doing here. Come on, Vist. Ask us anything, and then fill in the gaps. I want to be confident that everyone here knows what Vist knows about the planet and Kepler's Object of Special Interest (KOSI). That's an order."

I picked up my personal screen projector from the table and held it in my right hand like a clipboard. It was almost as heavy as a large book, but I needed it to have as much contact with my hand as possible.

"Okay. What do we know so far? We have called our mission Object after KOSI. We have started our current journey from KOSI, the wormhole charger in Jupiter's orbit, which is protected from Cruisers. Its much older version allowed *Lyra* ships to open a series of slow wormholes to shift to Vitricus hundreds of years ago and then to echo the stream for feedback by *Jumping Postmen*. Since then, it was completely remodelled for vessels of the class Wormhole Shift Perambulation. They are long gone too. Only one of those still exists now – our *Wasp*. You all know very little about where you are going, just common knowledge."

"You have been on Mars for yonks," Rod said, "Common knowledge over the last few years is not great. People lost hope for Noverca and started to forget her story. But when I was a boy, my father told me about the expedition to another system that managed to colonise a planet humans could live on. What used to be just a number was then named Noverca, and its Class M sun was named Vitricus."

"Excellent names. I always loved them," Chang said, "Vitricus reminds me of my stepfather, a very short man with a very red face, harsh but kind."

"You are lucky you didn't have a stepmother, Chang!" Steven said, "Rod, you *are* good! Captain, make him tell us more."

Rod grinned with pride and carried on, "So the choice was made! After all, Kepler-452b in Cygnus was too far for bio-sleep, and Kepler-186f was still too cold, despite its Goldilocks zone. Perhaps we could have tried them now, with our new WH-shift ships, but thanks to the Cruisers, there is no study programme, no resources, and no interest in doing that."

"And no time!" Général added grimly.

"That's right. No time!" Rod said, looking rather absent-minded. He got up and strode around the room, gesturing and almost singing. "A few thousand years ago, Noverca wasn't a faff either. The average temperature was three degrees Celsius, with solar storms every hundred years that would blow the atmosphere away, and with weather too hostile for even a roach to survive. But it became Kepler's Object of Special Interest for a reason. For a few decades, scrutiny evidenced changes in the sun and, therefore, on the planet. Vitricus must have been a very old dwarf, but it started to change, becoming less active, and in a few hundreds of millions of years, it will whiten. It will be no good for Noverca, as the habitable zone will move, but for now, the energy flares have reduced enough for the planet's magnetic field to handle them. Noverca is bigger than Earth, and it has a massive working iron core. As you know, what we see and what is far away are not the same things. Vitricus is six hundred and forty light years away, and we only see its past, not its present. But everything suggests that in just a few hundred years, this planet could become good enough for us. Not easy-peasy – it may need a little bit of terraforming. It even has one moon, although it is a bit too large. The climate has been improving. The sea level has risen, and now the water moves faster, providing the planet with a circulatory system that assists atmospheric convection. Signs of organic activities have been very promising ever since."

"Good thing they are," said Marta suddenly. She had been almost invisible all this time. "Earth is doomed."

"Take over, Marta, please," I said. Marta volunteered to speak so rarely, that I could not miss an opportunity to get to know her better, even if this was due to vaccine side effects.

"You want me to? Okay then." Marta coughed and started talking quietly, but her voice strengthened with every word. "Things were changing on Earth as well. The scientists were an important and very respectful elite in those days. People worked hard to save the human race when the scientists confirmed the news about irreversible processes in the sun that would make the Earth, the Moon and Mars too hostile for life. Long before shift jumping through wormholes, the calculations had shown that Earth had just a few hundred years of habitability left. Mars would not last much longer. And Venus's resources would become unobtainable to us even sooner." Marta looked at Gera through the lens. She sighed, then continued, "And here is a young planet, identified as a possible new home and, unfortunately, too far away for existing ships.

Thanks to the Platinum Age, the best brains and craftspeople have built a long-haul fleet in just sixty-three years. They were huge, bulky, and clumsy and they had very powerful and effective technology for travelling to Kepler's systems, but building a ship was not enough. We wouldn't have had enough time, even if we had travelled at the speed of light. The best minds in the artificial wormhole study found the answer. They came up with the wormhole shift. This was a slow shift that opened a series of broad but short wormholes, allowing you to travel no more than twenty light years in one Earth year. This means that twenty-five or thirty years is all you need to get to those locations where potential planets were detected. In those days, the maximum safe period of uninterrupted bio-sleep for a human was thirty-two Earth years. The ships had to be controlled by programs alone, otherwise pilots' lives would have been sacrificed. Besides, what would be thirty-five years for the colonists, would mean humanity waiting almost twice as long – by the time the colonists had arrived and sent the first report by shift-postman." Marta stopped and used a poly-plate as a fan to cool herself.

"I did not know these numbers," Steven mused, "Is that why not all of them made it?"

"Hang on ... twice as long? That is not bad," said Tolyan. His face was pale, but his cheeks were like two tomatoes, "How come it is more than thirty times as long for us?"

"Because we are faster, silly," Rod said, panting like a steam train, "The *Wasp* has done half a dozen manoeuvres, and we are here in a month instead of in thirty-two years. The new vessel will be the most beautiful of all. If you were to evacuate from Earth just one day before I did, you would be here in a couple of days. I will leave a day after but arrive decades later to meet your grandchildren on Gera."

Tolyan pretended to cry in a high voice, "I will never leave without you, darling! Only together!"

When his laughter died out, Chang put his hand on Marta's back and said, "Just imagine what those people felt! That was great news and a reason for real hope. The whole of humanity was excited. Especially when the first two ships were sent to Noverca on the Millennium New Year celebration in the year 3000!" Chang sighed and dropped his head theatrically, "But then something went wrong, and Noverca has almost become a lost world for us."

"Yes, I will tell you what went wrong!" said Mik from his corner, his arms crossed, knees apart and eyebrows together. "The Platinum Age was over, and new religion grew like fungi. The cult formed in under forty years. Defence forces were split apart. Those traitors who joined the Cruisers made that cult stronger. What had been a noble army became an army of thugs and sadists."

"Come on, Mik," Tolyan said, interrupting as he took his sweaty vest off. "That noble army still exists. Hundreds of thousands of troopers still live and fight by the code."

"And another million do not," said Steven, breathing a little faster than usual, "Mik is right. This is what broke, killed, robbed, tricked and tortured more people than any alien invaders they were trained for would have done."

"Would you prefer an alien invasion?" Mik turned his wet face to Steven. "How many generations of soldiers retired like our general's grandfather without one real target shot?

Simulation after simulation! No wonder some felt wasted and became bloodthirsty. I am not one of them, but part of me understands."

"Stop it, lads," said Général quietly, and they obeyed at once, "I told you. Although his services had not been required when he was young, in his old age his training was priceless for my generation and yours. His resistance to the Cruisers' authority was a battle harder than anything else we had to face. But we became too distanced from KOSI history. Please, let's go on. Vist? Who will talk next?"

"So, who knows what happened then?" I asked, "Tolyan?"

"Gosh! It's like being back in history at school. Yes, sir ... ma'am ... hmm ... *Edrit' tvoyu!*" Tolyan cleared his throat and tried to impersonate a college teacher. "The Moon Cruisers started massive propaganda that resulted in all resources being withdrawn from the KOSI relocation project. More and more people were brainwashed into believing the dying Earth had a presupposed destiny. There is no need to look for another system, they say. Forget about KOSI, they say. Even thinking about it is a great sin. This disaster is the Rapture as foreseen in the old books. The Lord has good reasons to punish people who started to forget him, and he would want to make them pay for the Platinum Age. He would destroy the Earth to test the faith of real and loyal believers. Those willing to put their lives in his hands would build the largest ship and set off in a random direction, picked purely by faith! The Lord would deliver them all to their new home, which will be their heaven, their paradise, their reward for their faith, just as was promised thousands of years ago," said Tolyan before he gulped the whole glass of water in one go, then burped and bowed. Rod, Steven and Chang applauded.

"Blimey!" Rod said.

"You do know your history," said Mik, still frowning. His wet, divided hair looked like shiny black Velcro, "I have seen that ship. They did not build it. Their Lord provided it millions of years ago ... just for this purpose. They are building SRS reactors and stasis tanks and adding new life support equipment to the lunar stations. They hope to ride the Moon like in one of the oldest sci-fi flicks, but not by accident. Like hell yeah! These motherfuckers want all humans to drift on it to nowhere just to be caught by the gravitational force of a massive planet or a star."

"The Lord would not allow that to happen, don't you get it?" replied Steven, taking his t-shirt off and using it as a towel on his upper body, "Hey, Vist! How come you are not sweating?"

"I am. My bio-suit takes care of it."

Zina insisted on everyone having their cup refilled.

"That Moon idea makes some sense," said the captain, returning to the subject. "The Moon needs the energy to break out of orbit and set off in the safest direction, away from the most obvious large objects, and then survive on energy from the Space Radiation Station. It would work for a short while. Maybe even long enough to get somewhere ... in theory."

"Not even that," said Chang in his almost-soaking wet kimono, "They hope to use certain natural processes on Earth to break away from it. Nothing will be left alive there when they launch. Everybody will have to be on the Moon at that time. A massive establishment has been built under the surface besides SRS power stations, stasis chambers, storage, chapels, etc. Most of the people will be bio-sleeping in stasis tanks. A small group of technicians will use nuclear power to push it to wherever they choose to go. The problem is that, even if they break away from Earth, it will not be as easy to break away from the sun's gravity as they think. Even if they get much further away than Pluto's orbit. I think the Moon will become just another Pluto or Sedna at best – if the angle and speed of flight are right. They have no means to control it. Once the converters and solar panels fail, and the energy storage unit expires, the life support system will malfunction, and everyone will die in their sleep."

A moment of silence reigned among the still-alive Cruisers.

"Some deliverance, ha!" said Général, as he sighed and grimly lifted his brow.

"There is talk that they have already abandoned this unbelievable project," Tom said quietly.

"And if they have, then what are they counting on?" Chang asked.

"Guess! Why do you think they attacked us on Mars?" replied Tom.

"To stop Object from succeeding?" suggested Steven.

"To exterminate our loader?" said Rod.

"To stop us, they could have burned the entire Mars colony and killed Vist with it. They wanted Vist alive," said the captain, looking at me with reddened eyes.

"Why don't they just join Object?" Zina said. "They could have combined forces and have a better chance."

"Good question!"

"Forget about those mugs!" said Rod. His face was covered in sweat like a leaf in the morning dew, "Let's talk about the colony."

But the captain ordered everyone to finish their drink, return to their cubicles to get some rest, and prepare for the landing.

"We will talk more another time," he said, "Let this hour be a useful recap of why we are doing what we are doing. Here is our chance to restart the project and use the KOSI station charger to evacuate humanity through a new type of wormhole. If we manage to overpower the cult in the next few decades, upgrade the

KOSI station, and build a decent fleet, we can shift them all here. I still hope to live to see it happen for my grandchildren, even if I just pack their bags and see them go. They might have a real chance."

Chapter 9. 3416 Back on Earth – Father Ontha

Tom used the moment of confusion and moved like lightning. In a single burst of energy, he pushed his feet down and grabbed the leg of the chair with his tied-up hand. He smashed it down on the Cruiser's head, with all his weight behind it. The brute hit the floor with a thud. The chair was now a mass of sharp plastic splinters.

All that was left was a leg tied to Tom's wrist, like an assassin's blade. Tom did not check the state of the big Cruiser. He turned back and saw a streak of light through the closing door and a dark figure disappearing behind it. Tom was a poor runner with his numb legs, but he charged towards the light. He leaped like a clumsy cat and fell by the threshold as the door closed.

But a second earlier, his hand touched and grabbed the soft folds of fabric, trapping it in the door just in time. He twisted it around his fist, then got on his feet, and pushed the door open. For a moment, he was blinded by the bright light of a fire.

Outside there was a narrow corridor of ancient brick walls with torches every few paces.

The fabric in his hands was a soft, perfumed mass of a mazarine-blue robe with nothing in it. A few steps away, another Cruiser in a long undershirt disappeared around a corner, his movements that of a clumsy older man. Tom dropped the robe and started after him. When he reached the corner, he saw a tall Black man, with two hard swirls of coarse hair, standing over the old man's body on the floor.

"Mik? How—"

But Mik stepped over the body and grabbed Tom by both shoulders. He tossed him aside like a child, and Tom hit the wall. When he looked up, he saw his fat torturer from the interrogation room coming around the same corner. The Cruiser did not have time to consider Mik. The young trooper crushed his windpipe with one chop of his hand.

The brute made a strange noise and fell to his knees. His eyes bulged even more, filled with horror and disbelief. His hands clutched his throat. He looked at Mik but did not see him.

Mik grabbed the man's dirty big head and twisted it, as if he wanted to unscrew it. He let the corpse drop to the stone floor. Tom looked at

Mik standing still between two bodies and did not know what to do or think.

"How?" he tried, but Mik had already lifted him up, before throwing Toms's arm over his shoulder for support and leading him back towards the interrogation room.

"No time," he said. "Let's move."

They passed the interrogation room and continued until they came to another door. Mik released Tom and carefully put an ear to the crack between the door and its frame. He held his breath and listened.

Tom stood still, wondering, when Mik said quietly, "It's dark in there. Captain, if I'm wrong, we will both probably die here. But if I'm not, then some of our crew is in this room. Why don't you stand behind the column while I try the door?"

Tom showed Mik the plastic shard attached to his hand.

"No, let me try. Just look at me. You are in better shape to do something right if you are wrong."

"But I might be better for the job inside since I am still in good shape."

"That's an order, Mik!"

"We are not in the *Wasp*, Captain. That part of our mission is over. Here I take orders from my commander."

"Let's do it together then. At least you can use me as a shield."

"With all respect, Captain, you are not tall enough to be my shield."

"I will be your half shield."

Mik hissed but argued no longer. He pushed Tom against the wall next to the door, took a torch from the wall, and pulled the handle. No result. He pushed the door. It was locked. He kicked the door and waited. Nothing. He walked back and charged at it like a bull. A second later, he was lying on the floor, groaning and clutching his upper arm.

"Wait here," said Tom, wincing.

He picked up the torch and walked back to the discarded robe. He felt much better; his legs and arms were working now. He found nothing in the robe, but on the old man's body, he found what he had hoped for. There were four keys, fastened together with a wire. The keys looked old and rusty, but the cables, although old, were ordinary, electrical, with traces of yellow and green insulation. One of the keys opened the door. Mik stepped in first.

The torches lit up three figures on the floor. One was on their side, tied to a tipped-over chair just like Tom had been. It was Zina. She looked unconscious. Another was Marta, kneeling with her hands tied behind her back, head down and swaying from side to side with a quiet and constant moan. The other was lying face down in a pool of blood. Chang was dead, and Marta, half-mad with grief, could not even put her arms around his body. When Mik and Tom stepped closer, Marta lifted her face. It was covered in blood and tears, swollen with fresh bruises. It was hard to say if she recognised them or not. But she immediately, with her eyes, found her husband's body and released a cry like a wounded elk. She jerked her whole body in an effort to cover the few steps between them, crawling on her knees towards Chang, falling forwards and pushing her forehead into his side. Then she went quiet. Her back started to convulse in silent sobs.

The two men looked at each other and, without a word, went to free both prisoners from their bonds. Tom looked around and saw a small table in the middle of the room. The surface was a sight from a nightmare: bloody clothes, surgical knives, scissors, saws and bone cleavers of different shapes and sizes. He noticed a plastic bowl with a mixture of red and white gore. He tried to avoid looking closer and picked up a small knife – one that appeared not to have been used this time – and squeezed the handle. Chang! Nausea and grief overwhelmed him. Damn you all, you bastards! He used the knife to rid himself of the remains of the chair leg on his wrist, but before cutting Marta free, he tried to lift her off Chang's body. She struggled and wailed, but he took her face into his hands and forced her to look into his eyes.

"Marta ... Marta ... Listen to me. It's me, Tom. No, don't. Look at me ... I need to get you out of this room, and then I will free you. Yeah? Yeah? Can you hear me?"

She stopped struggling for a moment and allowed Tom to pick her up. She was much heavier than she would have been if Tom had not been beaten and if she had not half fainted. He carried her to the room where he had been questioned earlier, laid her on the dark-blue woollen robe, and wrapped the folds around her. She seemed to be quiet now. Mik brought Zina and laid her next to Marta. Then he took the old man's body to the second room while Tom stripped the big Cruiser of his blue robe. Both men returned and then dragged the fat dead brute to the same room. They gently wrapped the dead Chang in the sky-blue robe, carried him out, and locked both Cruisers inside. Tom noticed that Mik had also armed himself with a cleaver from the torture collection. They closed the door on the inside and looked around their room carefully. Not too far from the door was a stone bench covered with several large cushions stuffed with dry hay or straw. Tom found his backpack among them, and his vest, his unused med-kit, pocket watch and map, but his weapon was gone. This is probably where the old man sat before Tom broke free. Also, in the room, he found chair splinters on the floor, four or five whole plastic chairs, an ancient coffee table with a bucket of water, a few plastic cups, wires, ropes and a large wooden club, which had probably been used to knock Tom out when they caught him. No sharp tools, though. They did not intend to cut him – yet. Or was there a shortage of torture tools in the castle? Nothing in the room offered him a clue about their captors. Both women were now free of their bonds. Marta cradled Chang's upper body in her arms. Tom would not let her unwrap him, but she no longer cried. Zina drank water from the cup greedily and told them what had happened.

"They threatened to rape us first. Then they brought Chang into the room and beat him hard in front of us. Every time Marta fainted, they punched her in the face. Then they brought those ... things and—"

"Don't," said Tom, "You don't have to."

But Zina shook her head. Her eyes were wet, but she did not sob; she just shivered.

"They were cutting pieces off him. They asked him if he wanted to kiss his wife goodbye, sliced his lips off and tried to press them against her face."

Tom remembered what was left of Chang's face and felt sick again. Zina closed her eyes and rolled on her side, hugging herself and shaking even more violently in her grief. Mik stood with his back to them. A few minutes passed in silence.

"Any orders, Captain?" he asked without turning.

"How did you happen to be in the corridor? How many of us are here?"

"They don't have all of us, as far as I know, but then we were captured yesterday, soon after they got you, I guess, in the landing location. Thanks to Chang and Marta, the pods were destroyed as intended. We were brought here in the electro-truck that travelled for about forty minutes. Given its speed, I reckon we are almost twice as far from where we should be. They separated us this morning. I was in this room before they brought you here. I heard the screams from the other side of the wall, and these bastards were preaching at me! Preaching! Talking about how people like me are valuable to the good cause because of the will of the Lord. I played along and said I wanted to know what they would have for me in return. They made a few promises: my life for a start and some privileges in command. I said I would help turn the others if they took me to them. They seemed to like that idea, but they are not stupid. The fat one almost took me to Steven, but your old friend must have given him a signal. The guy with the missing ear took me to the guy they called a doctor. He examined my wounds, gave me food, and told me to rest in the tent. I pretended to sleep, and he came to me with a needle. The doctor is now in that hammock instead of me, enjoying the afterlife in heaven and treating angels with haemorrhoids." Mik turned around. "You see, I let them think it was me there if someone were to walk in. The one without the ear was just outside. I took him down and stuffed him under the desk. I made my way back to this room, hoping that they would take Steven here next, but it was you already dealing with them."

"Why Steven? What about Tolyan?"

"They were both hit on the head, but Steven still hadn't fully recovered from his injuries and lost consciousness. They took Tolyan away first, but they did not bring him back. He was not in the doctors' tent, so – I don't know."

"And the others?"

"I did not see Général or Rod here. I still hope they got away."

"And Vist?"

"I am afraid Vist has crashed the pod." Mik looked Tom in the eyes. "The reading shows that it went off course right after launch. According to the trajectory, it would have crashed at least a hundred kilometres away from the rest of us. Captain, it is better this way. These mystics will be more dangerous if they get hold of Vist. Why are you smiling?"

"She is fine. Better than the rest of us."

"She?"

"Or he. Mik, let's try and get the girls to safety of some sort. Then we will try and find the rest. We will try, of course, to get on with the Object mission, but even if we never see Vist again, the mission will be completed. All she ... he ... will need is a computer to upload everything up to MESH. Zina, can you walk?"

"Yes," said Zina, "I think one of my ribs is cracked, and my head hurts, but I will manage."

"What about Marta?"

"She received a few face punches, but nothing else that I know of ... but I think it's best not to move her just yet. She needs a minute or two."

"Marta," said Tom. He touched her skinny shoulder, but she recoiled. "We need to go soon. Prepare to leave this place."

But Marta moaned and started to swing back and forth again, clutching Chang harder.

"I will kill every single one of them for Chang," Mik said, hissing through his teeth.

"Okay. Let's make a plan first," said Tom before turning to Zina, "What do you know about this group?"

"They seemed to be in a hurry but had not questioned me yet. They hurt me only when I tried to defend Marta. They tied me up and told me to wait for my turn. Also, they were well pissed off when her Field Radio Station's self-destruct was activated before we arrived here."

"What did they want from Marta?"

"Cooperation, the *Wasp*'s coordinates, the colony's coordinates, Vist's location and everything she knows about Vist. Sounds like they wanted our ship and a pilot to do something against the Rebels or even against the colony."

"In this case, they could have made use of both the Broadskys. All they had to do was simply threaten one to hurt the other. Chang is a man of valuable skill. Why kill him?" asked Mik.

"They did not intend to kill Chang," Tom replied quietly, "did they?"

"No, they avoided damaging any vitals," said Zina before sobbing again, "I tried to tell them about Chang's condition and that he might not survive the torture, but they knocked me out."

"Any hints of why they are interested in Vist so much? And in the colony?" asked Tom.

"I don't know," replied Zina.

"Why don't we ask them?" said Mik.

"How and who exactly?" Tom replied.

"Your old friend."

"But I thought?"

Mik continued, "No, I did not finish him off. I played with his spine, he will never run away again, but he will be out for a while."

"He felt dead. Are you sure you did not overdo it? He is quite old."

"Let's check him out."

Tom sighed. "Mik, I sometimes forget how dangerous you guys are. Zina, are you okay coming with us? You might have to revive him."

Zina managed to get up, and all three carefully came out to the corridor and locked the silently crying Marta up in the room. The place was strangely quiet and deserted.

"Where is everyone?" asked Tom, "I expected the whole cult to be upon us by now."

"No one has alerted them yet. Looks like I hid the evidence well enough."

They unlocked the door, then entered the room with the two Cruisers inside. The big brute was already cold, but the old man was still alive, although in a bad state. His skin felt like ice, but a closer examination found a weak pulse and shallow breathing. Mik was well-trained, indeed. He knew how to harm an organism to any degree he wished. He would have probably made an excellent torturer – or a surgeon. His knowledge of anatomy and physiology was just as vast. But he was not trained to fix the damage he caused. "What for?" he would ask.

"Is it a coma?" asked Tom.

"I don't think so. Let's try to wake him up the conventional way first," said Zina, slapping the old man's face with a menace quite extrinsic to her profession.

The old man was not that old – maybe eighty. He did not look feeble, just bony and dry, with a face full of lines and liver spots usual for his age. Zina was still in pain, and her slap only made his jaw wobble. Tom took her place.

He shook the man and slapped him on both cheeks until his eyelids twitched and a hoarse groan escaped his lips.

"Bring some water, Mik," said Tom, "to liven him up again."

The old man opened his eyes and briefly cried out. He was in pain. Tom lifted him a little and sat him up, leaning his broken back against the body of the dead brute. The pale blue eyes circled around and fixed on Tom's face.

"Hello. We meet again. Please confirm your name and title," Tom said, using the words that probably started all interrogations here.

The man hissed quietly, replying "Sssinner."

Tom ignored that.

"Who are you, and what did you try to do to us? Where are the rest of my men?"

The cackle or cough shook the old man's body.

"What is your name, Cruiser?" Zina asked.

The man closed his eyes. Mik returned with a cup of water from the room next door. He was about to splash it into the man's face, but Zina stopped him.

"Wait."

She walked to the horrible torture tools, paused for a moment, and then picked up a pair of scissors and the bowl full of Chang's blood and skin. She stood over the old man.

"Look at me, son of dullard."

The old man slowly opened his eyes and granted Zina a mocking look. His lips parted as if he wanted to say something, but in the same moment, she sent the whole content of the bowl into his face and pointed scissors towards his nose. The old man's expression changed dramatically. Fear and disgust filled his eyes, and he started spitting and shaking his head. Maybe now, he finally realised that he could not move a finger.

"Listen, you piece of dead worm. You have killed my friend, and I won't hesitate to cut your nose off too if you don't tell us ..."

Tom pulled Zina off and wiped the man's face with a fold of the Cruiser's long white undergown.

"Let's talk like brothers, again."

"Why," the old man said, struggling, "why can't I move?"

"This is what the Lord has decided to test you with. Your spinal cord now has a tear. It can be fixed, and you will be able to dance again if you tell us what we need to know. Or have you guys destroyed all the stem hospitals while we have been away? What did you call them? Samael's temples?"

"You will burn. You are children of Satan. The Lord will reveal to you the holy true—"

"Okay, you refuse to help us. Why don't you think about it, while we look around your castle? Maybe we will find someone more cooperative among these Mooners."

Tom got up and walked away, signalling to the others to follow him.

They were by the door when the old man called after them. "Wait!"

Tom stopped and turned around but remained where he was.

"I will tell you if you take me with you. I need ... the therapy."

"Okay." Tom stopped and waited without taking a single step back to him.

"We are not Mooners. My name is Ontha. Father Ontha. I am one of the leaders of the Moses Movement."

"Really? I thought your brothers exterminated your party in the Lord's name long ago."

"Not everyone was executed. Over the last few years, we have grown in numbers. We are in strong opposition to them now. We do not want to escape the system on the Moon. I want to lead my people to the land chosen by the Lord!" Father Ontha paused to rest. It was clearly hard for him to speak. "The Moon Cruisers are blind, and they don't see that the colony is the only way for us to unite with our creator. That planet is our Promised Land."

"The Moses Movement? Aren't they Cruisers too?" Zina asked.

"Well, they are," said Tom quietly, "it looks like the cult has broken down again. Some of them are not stupid enough or fanatical enough to plunge themselves into certain death." He addressed Father Ontha again. "So you want the colony?"

"Yes-s-s," said Father Ontha with much effort.

His pain appeared to have become excruciating. It was obvious this man never imagined that one day *he* would be in such agony in this room.

"But why not just leave the cult and join the Rebels? Oh, I see you will lose power over your followers. You want to go there by yourselves."

"The *Wasp!*" Mik said suddenly, "Is that why you want the *Wasp*?"

The old man closed his eyes again and did not answer.

"How many of you are there? The WSP ship is tiny."

"It does not matter how many," Zina said bitterly, "They are going to leave most of their own people behind. Only the worthy ones will go to paradise, right? The few leaders perhaps, or just him, with a few loyal servants and a pilot." She paused and clasped her arms together, as if from a draught, "This is why they need Vist. They will not need anyone else. They hope to enslave him and then try to take over the colony, like newly arrived messiahs or something. You scum! Vist will never help you!"

"How godly of you," said Tom to Father Ontha, "Is that how the Lord treats his children?"

"Lord? They don't give a damn about their gods," said Mik with contempt. "They are a bunch of hypocrites who trick useful idiots into serving their needs."

"Nothing ever changes, I guess," said Zina, shrugging and then wincing with pain, "Let his Lord take care of him now!"

Father Ontha opened his eyes and looked at them with concern. Tom walked towards the door.

"Don't. Please ... Have mercy! No ... Aaaah!"

His screams filled the corridor as Tom, Mik and Zina left the room and locked the door once again. But these walls were now used to this kind of sound. Sobs and curses followed them to the next room, where they found Marta kneeling by the body. But this time, she was not holding Chang, but instead had the sharp plastic chair splinter in her hand. Her sleeve was rolled back. She was still.

"Marta, don't!" said Zina, gasping as she held up her hand and slowly started towards Marta, "Give that thing to me. No need to be ..."

"Don't worry," said Marta calmly and dropped the splinter. Her voice was lifeless and dull, "I was going to, but it won't change anything. The pain will stop, but I am not an animal to be put out of my misery. You still need a pilot. I will see the Object mission complete, and maybe then."

Chapter 10. 3411. Out in Space – Landing

"Only Marta can land the ship like she is putting a baby in the cradle," said Captain Darkwood after the ship had powered down and the background noise of the engines had died out. Forced to hear this noise day and night, everyone was almost shocked by the sudden silence. "No offence, Chang, but she is the best of the best."

"I would never argue with that," answered Chang as he locked up the control board. Marta took her hands off the control panel, rubbed her palms against her trouser legs, and resumed breathing again.

The captain was strapped to his chair between the two pilots. The rest were strapped to their seats in the ejecting sector. All were dressed and equipped for an emergency landing according to protocol. Fortunately, this time things went much better than on Mars. After the long and gradual entry into the atmosphere, the *Wasp* had emerged above the ocean, practically gliding over the water, then over the beach and the broad grassy meadow. Chang suggested they land in a small valley between two rocky hills of the semi-island. He scanned the small wood for a nice flat spot; something they could later use for a vertical take-off. Marta brought the *Wasp* between the trees like curtains and made it disappear under the treetops. The ship filled the woods with clouds of lifted dust, extended its landing platform, folded its wings, and perched itself on the dry grassy clearing. Captain Darkwood watched the strong winds blow away the mixture of smoke and steam in a second and then got himself out of the chair.

"Well done, crew!" he said, turning the microphone on. "Is everyone ok there? Welcome to New Portland, I guess."

"Yes, Captain, we are all good. It was a jolly good landing, considering the unknown geography! No one needs to change their pants or replace any teeth." Rod's voice came from the speaker and was almost inaudible through the excited noises in the background. "Kiss those Broadskys for me. They know how to treat my favourite ship!"

"Everyone, stand down from emergency mode. Rest and re-equip yourself if necessary, then meet me in the common room for breakfast at 10.00 a.m."

The captain turned the communicator off, put both hands appreciatively on the shoulders of his pilots for a moment, and then made for the door.

"Captain," said Marta.

"Yes?" Captain Darkwood stopped and looked at her.

"I understand why you want us to stay with the ship, but we have seen no signs of human activity for miles around here. Are you sure the *Wasp* would not be safe enough to just leave locked up? Maybe we should all go. You may need everyone's help."

"If I was sure that we are not walking into trouble, then yes – I would leave the ship even if my heart bled," Tom answered, "but so far, things with these colonists have not been as simple as expected. Let me repeat myself – if the Object mission were to fail at such an early stage as this, then I would need someone to inform the Resistance on Earth. You will have a chance to go home if something happens to us. If, for some reason, you lose that chance, then send a message to Rezeda or anyone else on the Oak. Our shift-postman will take less than a month to reach home. You have to keep the Resistance updated as long as you are alive. For now, we will be on the frequency TR-1–210 every 6 hours. You will be getting mine or Vist's logs and will know what to do."

"Captain, what if everything does turn out well?" asked Chang.

"Then you will relocate to the new coordinates in aircraft mode and join us wherever we are," Tom said, "We will go over all of it once again at the final briefing. In the meantime, I need to talk to Vist."

"Yes ... Vist," Chang said, "Do you trust this person? I am still not sure I am comfortable around him. It's almost as if I feel a threat deep in my guts."

"Feelings are not a good tool of cognition," said Marta to Chang, "Vist is simply unusual and probably learned to behave differently in Mars's sub-town. I have been there twice and can confirm that in such a large place with such a small society, you just get in the habit of communicating differently to how we do in our overcrowded settlements. The fact is, he has not done one simple thing that would have made me doubt him. Admit it, my dear: he has been pretty consistent all this time. I trust Vist."

"This argument is good enough for me," said the captain with a smile and left the cabin.

Marta and Chang looked at each other.

"You still think so?" Chang asked as they both got up to start the routine register of external conditions.

"Absolutely," answered Marta, "Did you watch his eyes? They are different every time we mention Vist."

"I am not convinced," said Chang, turning the cameras on and activating the projector. The south-facing camera sent an image of a black mass of tree leaves and the dim red sun above it to the holo-screens. The north-facing view was dark with a few ripples of light. Chang carried on, "Forget about that. Check out those auroras above the northern horizon. Must be a glorious light display there in the nightside sky. The sun is very active indeed. We need to get active too. I look forward to being alone with you here in this strange place. Look, if it was not for that red dot, it could easily be a lovely but windy 5.00 p.m. teatime somewhere in Dzharylhach Park."

"It is too red, but it is hardly a dot. Vitricus looks almost as big as our sun," said Marta, looking at the screen and putting her arms around Chang's waist.

"It is almost half the size of our sun," said Chang, kissing her neck, "but we are much closer to it."

"I know. I wonder what the local time is. What hour it is right now on the colony timer?"

Chang kissed Marta once again and carried on downloading measurements into the *Wasp*'s journal.

Marta went to check the sampling equipment and said, "You were on duty when Vist explained the time here. Darling, I can't imagine how they can even have a calendar here if they have no day and night. How can you maintain your sense of a twenty-four-hour rhythm on this planet?"

"Perhaps it's for the best because Noverca rotates slowly anyway, for almost a year, and the moon rushes around it in a nine-day orbit. The sun hardly moves. Words like evening, morning and noon shouldn't even exist in their vocabulary."

"They don't," Marta replied, running the *Wasp*'s routine diagnostics. "Without a circadian cycle, they have to rely on technology for such a simple thing and measure minutes and hours the same way we do – using watches and clocks. Oh, Chang! Remind me to check the upper filters later. Right, so people still need to sleep every few hours in a pretty consistent sleeping cycle, despite the sun's position in the sky. The colonists decided at the very start that the length of the day would remain the same, but now they call it "a cycle." The concept of day and night is now purely geographical. Seven cycles still make a week, and the month follows the length of the female period cycle. Yes, Chang! That is hard to ignore. Unfortunately, the local moon is not so synchronised with it, but hey! A name is just a word."

"Fair enough. Shame you can't see the stars much. Those clouds are thin, but they don't allow you to see the sky's true colour. At least we can see the sun through them. Have you initiated the shift self-test?"

"Yes. Hey, Chang?"

"Mmm?"

"I have a malfunctioning auger here, but the marine sampler is fine."

"I will fix the auger. If not, it's no big deal. Rod is a very forgiving guy. We can always take soil samples the old-fashioned way."

Chapter 11. 3416. Back on Earth – Miller

The miller slammed his palm down on the control panel, and the millstones stopped rotating. The windmill blades still turned with a creak but were not that noisy. The miller listened intently, then looked at the door, and shouted, "Casp! Hey Casp, is that you?"

The doorway was a dark hole in the brightly lit yellow wall; it looked like the mouth of a cave leading to a staircase and into the barns. The pale face of the miller's assistant Casp appeared in the black hole. He stopped and looked at his boss through his round goggles with a pitiful tremble.

"Okay, let's hear it. What have you done this time?"

The young man in an apron and long gloves generously dusted with flour did not answer but just stumbled into the operator's cabin. Behind him, a hand clasped down on his shoulder and pushed him in unceremoniously. Casp looked terrified. He swung sideways, clinging to the wall and allowing the figure in the long hooded robe to make their way into the cabin.

"Oh, not again!" exclaimed the miller, "You have no mercy and no shame! Guys, you were here just last week and took sixteen sacks. Don't tell me you ran out already. This week Thieves took four sacks. If you take any more, I will lose my profit and the mill itself. The fields in the whole region are dry and—"

"Quiet!" The stranger interrupted him with a deep and calm voice. "I am not interested in your flour."

"Sir? Then why are you here? And ... I don't think we have met. Is Brother Patrick with you?" said the miller, squinting at the doorway.

"Is this the Daisy Mill?"

"Yes, it is."

"Then I am in the right place. If you know Brother Patrick, then it is in your best interest to assist me. Do we understand each other?"

The miller didn't nod but asked, "So what does the brotherhood want now? You know we have no corn this year. There are no more goods rafting along the river, and I have only one worker left."

The visitor pushed the hood back and produced a rubbery-looking backpack from the endless folds of his robe.

"I need to use your MESH terminal. Don't worry. I will not compromise it or take it away. What do you have here?"

The miller wiped his hands on the front of his shirt and stepped away from the control panel. He pulled the pair of antique glasses from his pocket and tried to clean the white dust off the lenses, only making them worse.

"Is this your first time or something? I can see you bumped your head recently. What's wrong, sir? You should know what we have here. All my machines are practically prehistoric."

The miller put his glasses on and examined his night visitor, who asked, "Are you connected to MESH?"

"Maybe."

"I think you are."

"Who are you, and how would you know that? None of your brothers ever cared about that junk. Are you looking for an excuse to accuse me of blasphemy? I need what I need to operate my mills. Without them, you will have no use for me."

The two men stood face to face now. The young Casp pushed his goggles to the top of his head. He used this moment to slip behind the guest into the doorway, and he disappeared into the darkness.

"Sir, I won't ask again. I have very little time. I am not here to intimidate you. In fact, I am asking you to help me. I will trade my supplies with you for a few minutes on your computer. I just need to send a message to my friends, and I don't want the brothers to know about it. Do we have a deal?"

The miller hesitated. "Do you have any medicine?"

"What for?"

"I need antibiotics, and something for the pain?"

"How many? Age? Estimated body mass?"

"One, six, about fifteen kilos now. She has lost some weight."

"Do you want me to take a look at her first?"

"Are you a doctor?"

"Yes. I am as well."

The miller's face suddenly twisted in horror, "Casp, no!"

The visitor turned, and the next second, Casp pulled the trigger. The discharged shotgun threw the hooded figure back, and he lay still on the floor. The bag flew off towards the wall. The miller rushed towards the body, then stopped, turned around, and looked at his assistant in horror. Casp's smug smile melted away under that stare, "Master Herman, he is a Cruiser."

"He is not. Casper, what have you done?"

"But ... the robe. He is with the Moses sect or worse – the Mooners."

The miller bent over his visitor. "He came alone, without the Word-Bearer, and he has medical supplies. He was going to trade. Cruisers don't trade."

After these words, Casp rushed to the visitor's bag and grabbed it. The miller thought out loud, "There is just one doctor in the castle.

This one does not look like Doctor Munny ... he is much younger. And this robe is the wrong colour. Neither navy nor sky blue. It is almost a reflector! And why is half of his head shaved?"

"You believed him? Master, he was trying to trick you. Damn! How do you open this thing? I have a knife!"

"Trick me to what end? A Cruiser who wants to use a computer? That's not exactly the best trick to get whatever they want. They have known about Tsuyoi Hachi for days now." The miller took the limp hand with two fingers, feeling for a pulse.

"They knew you needed medicine. Maybe they were trying to find out if you are hiding Rebels. You work nights, after all. Master Herman, I can neither open nor cut through this bag of his. What is it made of? I have never seen leather like this before. Is it made of dragon skin or something?"

The miller ignored him, then said, "He also doesn't wear their insignia." He touched the man's chest, lying on the floor, "but he is wearing the breastplate."

A strong hand grasped the miller's wrist, and a hoarse voice said with a strange metallic undertone it didn't have before, "An armoured vest actually. The bag is made of ucha-silk, and so is my clothing. It's a bit heavier than my old robe but much softer. Dragons don't exist." The visitor opened his green eyes, the colour of which reminded the miller of the pickled gherkins he loved so much. The travelling visitor released the miller's hand and said, "You are right. I am not a Cruiser, and I would have told you that myself, but I had to be sure about you first. They have made even their loyal servants very angry recently."

The miller has regained the ability to speak, "I never served them! I have been robbed by them on a regular basis!" This time the miller grabbed the visitor's arm to help him to rise, and continued, "Are you a Rebel then, sir?"

"I am one of the Resistance supporters. I work towards the same goals but by different means. My name is Vist. Take me to your little girl first."

The miller turned to his assistant and said, "Casp, return this gentleman his property and get rid of that gun at once. I will deal with you later and ensure you never find it again. If anyone shoots mystics in this house – a Welshman shall," he added, stubbing himself with his thumb.

Casp handed the bag to the visitor and said, "I am sorry, sir. I was a bit desperate. My sister injured herself in the kitchen. She is feverish now, and I couldn't … I thought you were one of them. We asked the Cruisers for help, but they only promised to pray for her. I hate them enough to kill them."

"Well, now that we have all introduced ourselves, let us all get on with our business," said Vist, following the miller up the stairs to the third floor of the mill tower.

The miller was either a slow climber or just felt like talking. As they ascended, he said, "Eight years ago, I advertised for more help on the MESH work market and found myself a whole family there. Kawa Peterson, a widow with an eleven-year-old son named Casper, came from Gogo to work the mills with me. A year later, she became my wife. I had two dozen employees back then and four mills like this one, but after the Cruisers took over the government, I lost my staff and most of my mills. One mill was destroyed by a jet crash, another was bought off me by a local electrical company, and one just malfunctioned because of a lack of maintenance. This mill became useless, even for them. The climate is changing too fast, and the windmills needed an upgrade each year, which I was unable to afford. I keep Daisy in good condition because my family depends on it. The flow of grain is also not great. Most workers went back to the market; some followed the Cruisers after being brainwashed. Now I have only Casper the Great here. He is a hardworking boy, although he can be clumsy sometimes and a terrible judge of character. I hope, sir, that you forgive us both for this misunderstanding."

The night was unusually quiet. All thirty of the six mills' broad blades creaked in the wind and spun slowly. There were two sets of windmill vanes on each floor, but on the third, they were almost motionless and almost silent. Casp reappeared unarmed and followed them in silence, without taking his eyes off Vist. A room that served as one of the bedrooms was quiet. A beautiful woman with black hair and slanting eyes rose from the edge of a bed on which a small child was resting. She stared at Vist in horror but visibly calmed down when Master Herman started to talk, "Kawa, relax. This is a friend."

He kneeled by the bed and unwrapped the bandage on a tiny hand.

"Sir, this is my Hachi and her mother, Kibono Kawa. As you can see, Hachi has inflammation around her wound. She tried to be a big girl, helping her mother, but she burned her hand badly. My lovely better half here knows what to do if you give her what is needed to stop the infection." He turned to the woman. "Kawa, we have the medicine. Now I need to show this gentleman the way to the office."

Vist had already built a short row of small bottles and boxes on the table and pushed a bunch of stingers into the woman's hand.

"Inject one of these now, one in twelve hours, and then just one per day for a week. It's a mild anti-inflammatory drug but very effective. Apply this ointment around the wound but not on the burn itself. Leave it covered with this bandage. No matter how bad it may look under the transparent membrane, do not change it for four days. I will give you three of these. Let her take lots of warm fluids and high-protein food. These pills are painkillers, but I have a single dose with me. I am sorry. A word of warning, lady: in a couple of days, the hand will start itching like hell. Don't let her scratch it. This is all I can do."

"Sir," the woman said with a voice like a little girl, "I don't know what to say. Thank you! Nobody sells remedies of this quality anymore. Where did you get these from?"

"Out of my own med-kit," said Vist, smiling. "Fortunately, I have had no great need for it on my journey so far. I have reduced the dose for your daughter's age, so she has enough to not need to go to the hospital. I wish you both farewell."

When Vist and Master Herman returned to the tower staircase, the miller said quietly, "Sir, for what you have just done, not only can you use my computer but you can also move into my best room for free lodging and stay for as long as you like."

"Thank you, but I have big plans for the next fifty years."

"I would not plan that far. The world is ending, in case you didn't know. It may not last fifty years, and my little girl will never be an old woman. In fact, sir, you look like someone who hasn't been around for a while, or who has come from an entirely different world or time."

"In a way, you are right on all three counts. I have been away for a few weeks, but it has been a few years on Earth."

"Sir!" Casp said, "You are an astronaut!"

"A passenger."

They walked into another furnished room, like a small library with a writing desk.

"I must admit, Master Herman, that when you said the word 'office,' I didn't expect to see a study. I thought you ground flour day and night."

"Just at night. My mill generates electricity and flour for us, but the wind is too strong during the day. It breaks the blades, and I have to fold them up. I use solar generators from dawn to dusk, but you know how little sun we get these days. All I manage is to charge the main battery. What else can I do? You can't get hold of ZPE-converters or Zappers nowadays, not even on the MESH black market. Ooh! Coming here is good exercise, but I get out of breath every time. Here you will find what you need. The right screen flickers a bit, but my connection is steady.

We are quite high up, and that is an advantage. The Cruisers hardly ever bother to climb this far up. They are usually more interested in my barns and the storage rooms in the cellar. The real treasure is in this room. I write my poetry here in the daylight after a good sleep."

Master Herman powered up his desk, and four holographic screens appeared above it.

"It is not as old as you made me believe. I would love to hear some of your poems when my task is done, Master."

"I would love to read you some, but I am afraid it must wait until morning. I need to go back to work. Casper, you stay here and don't bother Mister Vist with questions, but answer anything he may ask. Casper is much better than me with all this technology. He has all the access codes. Thank you again. Knowing Brother Patrick, I can see now what you meant about my interest in assisting you."

Chapter 12. 3411. Out in Space – First Camp Lecture

This was very impressive. During breakfast in our first camp, we were surrounded by a group of real, alive and very earthly plants. These plants had adapted to the windy wilderness and could photosynthesise with great effort under little light. Few looked completely alien, but some were almost the same as on Earth. Although the foliage was not so thick, the leaves were broader and nearly black in the red light. Some trees looked old and were probably the first to have been established here on the flat land and on the sunny sides of the hills. Most were evergreens, but a few resembled deciduous plants that had been seriously tampered with. I could see tall thujas and a group of holly trees on my left. There was something like a purple plum tree on my right, with leaves only on the very top branches. Beside it, I could see various ferns, conifers and one unknown dead tree covered in the lianas of a chestnut-coloured climber. Right in front of me, on the other side of the camp, there were a few tubas of sarracenia – the size of a human leg, probably feeding on local insects, beside a not-very-healthy-looking-but-real aeonium and a barely green and rather disfigured ginkgo. You could almost imagine yourself in a botanical garden on Earth if only these trees were not much smaller than normal, incredibly dark and with the appearance of wet nylon. A few native luminescent plants had survived this alien invasion, and they made these woods look like theatre decorations. They grew between those trees in some kind of symbiotic relationship, adding their ghostly white glow to the ungenerous sunlight in the darkest parts of the wood.

On my copy of the colony reports, I took a quick peek at the diary of the first botanical scientist on this planet. Robert Bianchi was a hero in my eyes.

We waited for Steven and Zina, who brought tea and served it in cups made of the latest type of polymers that, despite being so thin and light, never burned your hands, never got stained, and were practically unbreakable. We did not have those on Mars. They were too expensive.

Rod soaked the torch in a mixture of clove oil and the pink wax of lucerna rosea – a highly flammable local fungus that looks like a bowl of luminescent pink liquid. Rod lit the wick, pushed the handle into the soft soil in the middle of the circle, and sat down on his mat next to Tolyan. The fumes from the pink wax would propagate mushroom spores many kilometres from here.

"I am ready for another lecture now. I would ignore most of it if I had to worry again about those bastards. Ah, don't you wish it was a little more parky?"

"You stink of oils, Rod. All the insects of this planet will now avoid these woods for a decade," Tolyan said, and Steven laughed with him. Mik did not laugh.

"Let's start," said the captain.

And I started. "As you already know, the expedition to *Lyra* was composed of two vessels launched every few years. Each pair of ships carried ninety-eight people, and everyone on board was a skilful and resourceful expert in at least four fields of work. They were born into this mission, carefully selected for their abilities, and free from all known inherited disorders and predispositions. The very fit, healthy and fertile colonists aged between twenty-five and thirty-five entered those ships with full knowledge of their purpose."

"Poor people," Zina said with a sigh, "everything was decided for them. What sort of life was that?"

For a moment, I thought that the glance she gave me was flirtatious; I did not pause to find out. "It was a good life by most standards. They grew up with their parents in Canada's famous Resort of Hope. They had a busy childhood full of fun with many reasons to love life and value it. They all found love and formed couples among themselves. At the age of twenty-five, they were given a choice to withdraw. From the thousands of potential colonists, hundreds of individuals were found unfit for various reasons, and only eight couples decided to leave of their own volition and start their families on Earth. The succeeding colonists had to be seriously overeducated, even by today's views, trained in many skills and crafts. They were committed to going. It took a few decades to select and bring up the fortunate four hundred and ninety couples, and to build the KOSI launching station and WH-shift ships. Also, those ships carried vast collections of essential equipment – from a simple hammer to the most sophisticated devices of that time. Also, they brought vast stores of food and of pharmaceutical and medical equipment, including a field surgical van. They had spare parts, materials, clothing, an e-library, plenty of entertainment, a portable school, a portable kitchen, workshops, a chemical synthesiser and a few robots for heavy lifting and digging. They brought many other useful and lasting items and substances. It was a one-way ticket; they knew this and devoted their lives to it. One of the vessels in each pair could permanently transfer into a huge military or fishing submarine, while the other could become a fortress and a first dwelling station for the colonists. But that is not all. They brought dormant embryos, zygotes and the seeds of thousands of species of animals and plants. As far as I know, they used only about fourteen per cent of those species for the first few generations, as it became clear that this planet was not yet ready for most of them. The rest had to wait. They even brought microorganisms and, of course, a human gamete bank for possible future use. The KOSI wormhole charger station and Lyra missions were the greatest events of many centuries.

Everybody knows the famous names of those Lyra vessel pairs."

"Oh no, Vist Sensei. We don't!" Tolyan said, giggling and imitating a schoolboy. The captain ignored him, and so did I.

"Only one of Lyra's pair of ships made it here. *Noah-8* and *Ark-8*," Mik said. He did not smile. He hardly ever smiled and laughed even less. But his big brown eyes brightened for a moment, and his voice rang out. "*Noah* was deadly! Even by today's standards. It had an arsenal better than ours here on *Wasp*. As a boat, it could fight on the surface and be submerged. It was capable of manufacturing Harpoon-L29 torpedoes on board during action or battle, and it was able to extract chemicals from seawater as raw material to make fuel."

"Yes!" I was impressed. "It also had a large cargo space. Fortunately, in this case, most of the weapons were stored away on land, as there was almost no threat and no predator encountered. It could be worse, but the planet was much more welcoming than expected. *Noah* was mainly used for studying and obtaining some marine life for the scientists to deal with, for food and for resources. I wonder where *Noah* is now."

"Chang scanned for it," said Rod, lying down and stretching on his mat, "but the signal jam they used prevents us from detecting even its metal. I never heard of this ever being possible until now. Maybe they broke it apart?"

"I hope not," said Général, turning his poly-cup over to let it clean itself, "I want to see it. It is rare antiquity even for me."

We drank more tea, then spoke about the value of old items and sentimental attachments to things before quickly returning to the story.

"The objective was to occupy one small and remote continent in the planet's optimal meridian, away from the hot dayside and frosty nightside. Making changes to the ecosystem was unavoidable. It was not enough to claim the status of carrying out terraforming projects, but the colony could not survive and preserve the local natural environment simultaneously. And, of course, humanity needed to ensure that this planet could become a new home. Even if it was just a small habitable fragment of it that they named the Belt of Noverca, which we used to call the Comfort Zone. Due to the colony's initially modest size, the decision was to take one step at a time and settle in a nice and quiet land before crashing in. This is how a computer program chose Gera when the colonists arrived, still in stasis. It happened to be the best spot in the Belt of Noverca – far enough from the nightside not to freeze, close enough to the dayside to see where you are going. It was still a bit hot, gloomy and windy there, but nothing could be done about that. The amount of ocean water that circulates on the surface of Noverca along a very fast current is the true reason for sustainable living in this zone – caught between an icy haze and a red furnace."

"They must have already changed the whole planet somehow. Sorry for the interruption, but," Captain Darkwood said before sniffing the air, "there is less methane here; the percentages of oxygen and carbon dioxide have increased and not only in one continent. I am sure of it."

"That's right," I said, "the atmosphere has changed, but hardly because of a small colony in just over three hundred years. The natural global changes are still at work. And yet it is a very smelly planet, although methane itself is odourless."

"Yes, Captain. We can smell hydrogen sulphide and that stupid cabbage-like plant with black leaves, clove oil and me," said Tolyan and laughed.

I continued. "The colonists settled reasonably close to the seaside because there was more oxygen. The plankton was a major source of oxygen here, and until they grew these trees, the ocean was the sole source of oxygen."

"That ocean is pea soup," Steven said, "Have you seen the colours of those waters?"

"So what about these weird, almost black plants?" Zina asked, "I have never seen anything like this on Earth. And I have done my homework on plants, even the extinct ones."

"I don't believe they are original Earth plants, nor are they aborigines," I said. "They might be a product of natural and artificial selections, mutations, genetic rebuilds or all those factors. They were obviously not a priority, since the reports say very little about them. Farmed plants grow with artificial light in colony climate-optimised greenhouses. Nevertheless, the colonists obviously have done some work in encouraging plants to adapt in the wild. It must have been a remarkable project – playing with genes. That cabbage plant that Tolyan pointed out – it absolutely has to relate to Earth's *Brassica* genus, although it smells remarkably like human sweat. The flowers look less like mustard blossoms, though, and the smell was probably changed to attract something to pollinate them. Maybe even those flies."

The unchanging sky was getting on everybody's nerves. It was hard to track time. This planet made you feel stuck in one moment for eternity. The lack of change and the same length of shadows would take a while to get used to. It was not bright enough to feel like it was day, but it was not getting any darker or lighter – a strange sensation. Only lots of fast clouds and the distant northern lights made a difference here. You could not see any stars in the almost purple gaps between them.

The first goon-fly buzzed through our camp. Rod added a few drops of oil to the torch. The flame was bright in the gassy air, but now we could smell some cloves. No one was dozing off; as everyone was listening, I went on. "According to the project description on Earth, they had to very slowly introduce this planet to the colony and the colony to the planet, with a thorough study of local resources and all possible effects and side effects. The rough landing was an unfortunate complication but without serious consequences. Since the air had less oxygen then, they had to gradually change the air on the ships, increasing their red blood cells before exposing themselves to Noverca's atmosphere. They had to send probes out, taking hundreds of samples of air, water, soil, small animals and chemosynthetic plants. At first, most colonists were busy studying biochemistry and non-biological factors before letting them into human systems. The lab was busy analysing and testing microscopic life and its possible effects on the human organism. Colonists donated their own tissue samples to help and synthesise a few antibiotics and vaccines to protect themselves and stimulate their immune systems. It took not days, not weeks, but years before the first colonist stepped out without a protective suit. The Earth received its first reports much later when just a few people still believed that the colonists had not perished in space. It took a while for the records to be delivered by shift-postman transmitter, and they were years out of date, but this was something to celebrate for sure."

"What about the other pairs? There were ten of them, if I remember correctly," Steven asked.

"Out of the ten Lyra expeditions, *Ark-2* and *Noah-7* sent very inaudible signals only once. *Noah-10* was clear, though. It was not an automatic signal. Someone was awake to send it. The message was short and informal: 'The mission was unsuccessful. Good luck, see you in hell!'"

"Would you bother to stay formal if you are dying and a hundred people in your care are dying too?" Mik said, then asked, "What happened to them?"

"We don't know. We also don't know what happened to the other six pairs; they had to jump through several different wormholes, broad but short. They were not very stable; anything could have happened. Maybe the others had malfunctioned or were destroyed before they reached their destination. Maybe they crashed on other planets. Maybe they got lost in space or died in a hostile local environment, in poorly chosen landing spots, with a miscalculated chemical capability or infection, or they simply failed to wake up. *Ark-8* and *Noah-8* were the lone successful pair, as we know. I can believe that the people on *Ark-10* and *Noah-10* – either frozen or burned – realised that they would never be able to step out and, unable to return or even relocate, simply exterminated themselves with Adieu."

"With what?" Tolyan asked.

"You know," Zina answered, "the euthanasia pill on Earth that could be prescribed to people over ninety-nine if they asked for it. It became illegal when the Platinum Age was over."

"Mass suicide? Really? Bollocks! That is just shite!" said Rod.

"Our colonists here were the most fortunate. They first took in filtered oxygen, followed by water in the second week, soon after the ships had completed their transformation. Then Sir Robert Bianchi and his two assistants focused on using local soil and seawater. But for more than a year, they were doing nothing but studying every cubic nanometre of this place, using just what they had brought with them."

Zina clicked her fingers, "Of course! Bianchi! He had made most remarkable discoveries here."

"I suspect you might enjoy listening to this, Zina," I said, then accessed the log, closed my eyes, and read out loud, "Alexandra is still not sure, but I am confident in my theory that life can travel in space inside a chunk of ice. On this planet, it was either partially seeded by Earth long ago or originated here and somehow travelled to our system. I danced with excitement when Luke returned with those seawater samples. The seawater is very green; I had never seen such a phytoplankton concentration. My hopes were high already, but finally, it was confirmed. Photosynthesis! This ocean is full of cyanobacteria, but this algae and tiny free-running cells of unknown taxonomy are full of chlorophyll. Oh! They were like old friends to me. Yes, I was pleased enough when local life happened to be carbon-based and at least partially energised by respiration. But the land flora was chemosynthetic, obtaining carbon from methane. I knew something else had to produce oxygen here! And voilá!"

"Surely it was not the same bacteria," noted the captain. He looked tired and preoccupied. He had changed somewhat since we first met.

"No. Not exactly, but this is what excited Professor Bianchi. He found DNA strands similar to our archaea and some prokaryotes. This was enough for him to come up with his theory. Maybe it has already been confirmed here since then. I hope to find out soon. I cannot help but wonder if some microorganisms they found here arrived with the earlier ships, and were planted unintentionally, unlike deliberately released cultures in a controlled environment."

"It's possible," Rod said, "after all, the *Lyra-8* pair was launched almost fifty years after *Lyra-1*."

"I must say I care very little about that," said Général, "I am more curious about their food, Vist. What did they eat here? A black salad?"

"At first, simply what they brought. Then the first attempts at farming produced plant food in the hydroponic chambers of *Ark*. The first animal zygotes activated were chickens, pigs and goats, but only after enough vegetables and grains had been grown to feed them. Everything happened indoors at first, all based on intensive recycling. *Ark* was a large ship, and it had to unfold into an even larger dwelling and self-sustaining station. The colony itself was small at first. Only two people died during the first year, in an accident. So, as you can see – so far, so good."

"Why do I suspect there is bad news ahead?" Steven asked, waving a fly away from his face.

"No, nothing special happened here for a while," I said, "there were good years and bad: sometimes more people died, sometimes more babies were born. They had famines and epidemics, natural disasters and depressions. But Gera, despite all the discomforts and inconveniences, was an extraordinarily welcoming land. When the first farm was established as a separate settlement away from *Ark*, exposed to the air and adapting to the new environment, it was a complete success. The colonists did not need to rush and try the local forbidden fruit. They were happy to grow new varieties of potatoes, carrots and other vegetables. Fish were killed at first for scales and fat only. The fat was a good fuel, but then the pink wax was found. The local plants were checked for useful properties, mainly to extract chemicals. Local animals were approached with extra care and studied but they were found to be less useful than the plants. Some species remarkably resembled Earth's arthropods. Some cold-blooded creatures here have some kind of womb and feeding features that served as mammary glands. Nothing large or very threatening lived here. Some deadly insects had to be made extinct on this continent. But as far as the early reports show, there were no man-eating plants, lions, tigers or bears."

"But why did they keep these cursed useless bugs alive?" Tolyan asked, "And I am sure you mentioned predators before?"

"There was and may still be a creature they called the svoloch. It was described not as a predator but as an omnivore with cannibalistic habits and as big as a leopard. But it attacked during its mating season. What else is here? Oh yes! There is a venomous vergiftigen – a small reptilian creature – and a big bad fish in the deep northern sea, but only its teeth marks were found on the boards of *Noah*. No one knows its real size or appearance, but the teeth were twelve centimetres apart. And as for the flies: Rod, flies, are not useless. According to the report of Alexandra Ken, their venom is a great anaesthetic. An extract from just four of them can shut down your nervous system for up to 6 hours without any harm. In the woods, of course, you would not wake up after a few bites because a swarm would strip your bones clean, but on the surgical table, you will never suffer and wake up to recover with no pain for another day or two."

"Couldn't they synthesise the venom?" asked Rod, still unsatisfied. He couldn't stop ruffling his hair. "They managed to synthesise antibiotics and other things. Surely these bastards are trying to nest in my mane. The first thing I will do in the city is shave my head like the captains. I am also sure I am allergic to that pink stuff."

Chapter 13. 3416. Back on Earth – Wesley Parera

"We have to go back for the others, mate! Even if no one else was shot down, I am worried about Tolyan's landing."

"Rod, listen to me. My orders were to find two knocked-off pods. Tolyan is as fit as a bull, but *this* man needs medical attention. Cruisers have already taken your friends – I am sure of it. You know me, wouldn't I try if I saw a single chance? Plus, I can take just one more on board, maybe two at most – if they are thinner than me. Let's reach the Oak and get some help."

The giant of a man, dressed in black with a yellow strip of engineer's insignia on his sleeve, fastened the second belt across Général's chest and returned to the control panel.

"Wes, are you sure he will make it?" Rod asked, bringing Général's seat into a horizontal position and adjusting his oxygen mask.

"I am a mech, not a med, just like you," Wes answered. "Let's get him to Selest and hear what she will have to say about this. Do you want to help? Go and see what you can do with this shaking in the back left leg."

"Shaking? I don't feel any."

"The other three legs are perfect, but you will see, once we start walking on the ground, that the rear left shakes. Like this."

Wes shook his head, making his brown cheeks and lips wobble like jelly. He clicked a few switches, started the engine, and pulled the locking handle as if he were lifting a heavy load. Wes pushed both of his hands into the driving gloves with attached cables and lifted his fingers like a pianist ready to play. The spider-like vehicle was hanging between two giant dead trees on four limbs like a hammock. Mechanical phalanges gradually let go of the thick branches they were grasping and, after carefully testing the lower parts of the trees for support, wrapped around them like an ape's hand. The four-legged spider climbed to the ground, raised its body above the ferns, and carefully took two steps forwards.

"Good girl, Itsy. Take it easy. We have a patient on board. Rod, we are far away enough to leave footprints. Let's walk. This way, we will be much faster."

The tetrahoder walked between the dead trees soundlessly and elegantly, like a living creature.

"You called this one Itsy?" Rod asked with disapproval. "You are one cheesy American son of a—"

"Ha! Look who's talking." Wes laughed in a high-pitched voice. "You called your harvester prototype Galosha and the last cloud-chaser you crushed – a Dandelion. A Dandelion ... For goodness sake! It was eighty tonnes and not even yellow!"

"I am the one who built it and I can call it anything I like, mate."

"Well, I have not built a tetrahoder, but I kept this one and Bitsy in working condition in your absence. It was five years, dude. You have to start telling me about the colony."

"I will tell you everything but not yet."

"When we get to the Oak, we will have no time for stories. For a start, we will take care of Commander Lillypond, and then you will have to start patrolling on one of the hoders right away. We are short of people, man."

"I can't drive them no more. I lost my middle finger on another planet."

"Serves you right! So there is justice, even in the world of disbelievers. Hopefully, now you are more polite to your friends and enemies. But about your driving skills: you can still operate our spiders, but half-blind. If you leave cameras and all the visions to the robot, you don't have to control it yourself. You can see the screen, can't you? Ever since your father built the rear limbs that copy every movement of the front ones, it has become much easier to drive in a stable environment. Work of a true genius. But your mission ... man. Did you find the loader and the colony and make working contact? Come on."

"Yes! Wes! Cor blimey Guv'nor! I don't know where to start, but I must eat first. We landed in the escape pods: you know we haven't eaten for twelve hours – captain's orders. We had to wake ourselves up on landing, and he did not want any of us to drown while honking."

"I have food here. Do you want any wheat paste with spinach and cheese?"

"Wesley, any chance you have – you know – my favourite?"

"Rod! Sandy-beetles? I missed you, dude! You old bug-eater! I have almost a kilogram on board! There, in the blue box."

"Oh, Wes! Really? I love you, mate!"

"I bet Tolyan still hates them?"

"Tolyan prefers molluscs, but I am working on it."

Rod's fingers shook when he tore the lid off the plastic thermo-box. He pulled out a greasy grey paper bag and scooped a handful of dry brown severed beetle abdomens, each the size of a walnut. He placed one between his teeth and gently cracked the insect's chitin shell. He sucked out the yellowish chewy ball, spat out the remains of the chitin into another hand, and moaned with delight when chewing. He closed his eyes and swallowed.

"Mum used to cook stew to die for with sandies, but I always loved dry smoked ones with spicy salt and khmeli-suneli. There was a farm near our town in Essex where they fed them with raps and gutted them manually. This is heaven! Thank you, old friend."

"I keep them merely because they last for months; I still find them too fatty for my diet."

"No way is your worm stew better than this."

"Hey! There is a potato worm stew and a peanut worm stew. You have to know the difference. Nick the Catalonian is the best cook and makes them almost odourless. He does wonders with his recipes ... minty chickens on a skewer, fishcakes, caterpillar chipolatas or pickled mushroom *aperitiu*."

"Nah ..." Rod threw the handful of empty shells into the waste hatch and scooped up more of the segmented treats. "Nothing beats the taste of a properly farmed insect. Not even a chicken."

"I don't know. If only those birds were a little bit bigger. In the Dark Ages, they were big enough to feed a family. Now you need two on the plate to make a decent meal. But I think the old legends just exaggerate."

"They don't. The colony has animals that don't exist on Earth anymore. They have cows, goats and pigs. Their chickens and ducks weigh up to four kilograms and can match the size of a wild cat. And so are their cats. They have claws and sharp teeth. Everything is like in the books, although the Earth trees they grow there are so damn small. No taller than twenty metres and one hug thick. You wouldn't be able to climb up them in this hoder. They would snap like a pencil."

"No way!"

"Yes. But I think that is due to environmental differences. Their dogs are smaller too. They don't saddle them."

"Tell me the whole story. Tell me about the loader."

"No, Wes. *You* tell *me* about the loader. Did father pass my message on?"

"Yes."

"And? What is she ... he?"

"That is the problem. Nobody knows. But I did what you asked and tracked down all the records on the best pod designers."

"Have you confirmed the connection?"

"Not quite, but there is enough to suspect their identity."

"Tell me. I want to know. I'm pretty cheesed off, actually! I think the captain is in love ... and Zina too, but even they are not sure what Vist is really up to. That bastard is impossible not to like and, at the same time, so easy to hate. We all want to know. Not just out of curiosity. It is hard to trust him ... her ... knowing nothing about his past. He is very strange and secretive. And the last thing she or he has done is not helping. We don't even know where he is now. By the way, the leg is shaking, you are right."

Wes took a deep breath and drove his quadruped vehicle in silence for a few moments. It was quiet in the cabin; Itsy walked between pillars of dead trees like a real insect – silent and fast. Rod waited for a minute, then took the el-tools and diagnostic gears from behind the wall straps, shifted his seat to the left rear joint panel, and started the limb test. He had known Wesley Parera for a long time and recognised his friend's long silences when thinking.

Finally, Wes said, "Okay. I will tell you what I learned, and you can make whatever you like of it. Your conclusion may differ from mine, but here is your peer assessment at work. When I got your message, I was going to start with the Council, but your father, Master Baker, pointed me towards his colleague Maiser."

"What did Maiser have to do with it? He was dead for at least a decade. By my time, anyway."

"Do you remember twenty-eight years ago – by my time, as you know – there was an incident on the orbital station Jupiter O-12? Everything accomplished there was gone, and what was left in MESH – articles and publications – was not enough to recreate its findings or understand what had happened. The research settlement was destroyed in the blast big enough to blow up a small moon. In fact, Europa was the closest body and experienced a detectable ice melt on the facing side. That is how bad it was, and of course – there were no survivors. At least as far as the officials concluded."

"Yes. How many died?"

"Six people. At the time, there was just one family in the dwelling."

"I remember. I have read about it. What was their name? The Unevs?"

"The Anevs. A couple – Gleb Anev with his wife, Karagoz."

"Terrible. They had young kids!" Rod turned the torch on and peered at the colourful wire rows behind the panel.

"Three. Twins in their teens and a male toddler. Plus, there was Gleb's sister Rebekah. They were all participants in the special-breeding programme. The whole family was already genetically enhanced, fit, multi-skilled and versatile in so many professions that even your dad, Baker, the senior, would be no more than an apprentice for their nineteen-year-old kids. They belonged to the first and only generation born and bred to make data-loaders. A few years later, that generation was the first to be exterminated as an abomination by Cruisers. The next one did not make it to adulthood."

"As far as I know, Cruisers tried to capture a few that managed to escape the slaughtering on Earth and the orbital stations a few years ago."

"No more than half a dozen, but they were also assassinated. Do you remember the loader bounty hunters? What did they call themselves? Unloaders? Your mysterious friend truly may be the last one alive. Anyway ... back then, the Council of Relocation Project had news of massive progress that this little bunch of geniuses had come up with. The rumours were that the Anevs family found a way to open a single wormhole and designed a vessel to travel through it much faster than the existing shift ships. They proposed to evacuate in small ships that could be mass produced or even be built in the private garage by skilled individuals, like you and me. Those vessels can be sent in large groups, in turns, along a narrow but very stable and long stream. It's easy to imagine what that would mean. But the Council kept it a secret, just in case Cruisers sabotaged it. They wanted to protect it. Looks like they failed. The accident was not an accident. The new technology was lost apart from a few publications that helped make the WSP ship class, made by Vatslav Maiser and his pupil – your father."

"Yes, our *Wasp!*" Rod took another laser tool and added, "Can you stop for a sec? Okay, thanks. Go on but don't run. If I remember correctly, KOSI WH2-openers were also Maiser's design."

"Apparently not. I have no information on whether he took the credit as plagiarism or to protect someone."

"Protect whom?"

"A survivor."

"You think someone survived the explosion?"

"There were plenty of discussions about one of the Jupiter anomaly probes. It had recorded a very vague signal of a small object leaving the site just a few seconds before the kaboom."

"A ship?" Rod turned off the diagnostic pad, placed his hands and ear on the wall, and listened.

"Nah. A ship would be easily registered even by the satellite probe. It was small enough to be an escape pod."

"That is impossible!" Rod thought for a moment, "Even if it was intact and successfully launched, No! Where would it go? There was no other life-supporting station anywhere close enough. It's certain death."

"That's right. We have no idea what happened to it. Then there was a claim made by one of the media reporters that one of the twins has survived, maybe by just not being on the station during the explosion or by leaving it earlier without a proper official arrangement."

"It's unlikely but not impossible, right?" Rod pushed the panel lid back on and clipped it in place. "That should do it."

"Thanks, it's much better – I can feel it. But this is when it becomes interesting. The twins were not identical. There was a boy and a girl. Which one survived? Is your loader one of them?"

"Which one?"

"No idea ..."

"But what exactly did that reporter say?" Rod put the tools away.

"Someone who knew the family recognised the face in the crowd during the big event when the last shift-postmen from the colony were being encrypted. He thought it was a boy because they had a shaved head, but he was unsure. He spoke about it with another friend, who confirmed that both twins used to shave their heads to look as similar as possible. The reporter could not prove his source of that information and was not allowed to publicise the news. Maiser suddenly moved his laboratory to Mars a few years later and almost halved his team. For ten years, no one outside of the Council heard of his work and then – Ta-da! He is back with complete blueprints for the WSP engine and is ready. The escape pods cannot just bring a person safely back from orbit; they can also take someone to the orbital station or to a ship from the surface. Sound familiar?"

"Yes, and he was very unwilling to publish the details. I remember now. I was sure he was protecting the technology from Cruisers!" Rod turned to check on Général and changed the oxygen cylinder that was beeping its "almost empty" tune.

"He did that too, for sure. But in my opinion, he had Anev's kid in protective custody. Where did your loader spend her last fifteen years?"

"On Mars … studying reports from the colony."

"What if this Vist is the surviving twin and a loader who concealed their origin and gender, then changed their name and face?"

"And voice."

"And laid low, making themself much harder to track down."

"Of course. Vist would have been in double danger all their life. On the one hand, threatened with extermination as a loader; on the other hand, possessing technology for which any cult is ready to kill."

"And they did. Okay, they did not want to kill Maiser, but he died during that kidnapping attempt nevertheless."

"Did he leave anything in MESH about the people he worked with?"

"Almost nothing. In the few articles, Maiser referred to his most 'valuable assistant,' but that was after he returned to Earth. He could have meant your dad. Master Baker told me that even he wasn't told everything about the origin of those designs."

"Okay ... wait," Rod scratched his head of newly grown hair with all nine fingers. "I know that Cruisers desperately searched the solar system for a loader ... for any remaining loaders. Are you telling me they might know about Vist being so much more than that?"

"They can't know for sure. Maybe Cruisers suspected something, or they tortured someone on Mars ... or they had a spy at the Institute or the archive."

"Or it was Vist's doing. We need to find Vist. That son of a bitch broke away from the landing trajectory and went off course at the last moment. I have no idea why. It couldn't be malfunctioning – I have made sure of it myself. Maybe he knew about the ambush. Maybe he was trying to get away from us for a reason."

"Do you suspect Vist is working for Cruisers? If Vist is a twin, she should hate them."

"That may be so, but I watched Vist for weeks and saw what they are capable of. He or she does not hold the same values as the rest of us. Always wanting more. Vist doesn't do anything without reason. None of us understood most of his reasons. Someone with Vist's ability could not just join Cruisers but could take over them, lead them, or pack them up into the Moon's tunnels, and send them all to hell."

"But then what about the rest of the people?"

Rod sighed. "Maybe Vist does not really care about other people or ordinary stuff. People can do incredible things when obsessed with revenge ideas."

"Does Vist appears to be obsessed or irrational at all?"

"That is the thing about Vist. You can never be sure. You can never fully understand Vist or predict his behaviour. I hate that."

"No wonder Cruisers are afraid of loaders."

"We all should be afraid."

They both went quiet. Wes's wired fingers moved fast through the air, driving the hoder. Finally, he shrugged his massive round shoulders.

"I don't know, man. But something tells me Vist isn't an evil person. If we don't understand something, it doesn't make it bad. To trust is not the same as to believe. That creature sounds anything but stupid. She might be a superhuman but surely she wouldn't lose her humanity for such things. She – sorry mate, I prefer a lady version – she wouldn't be simple enough to do things out of passion, as she wouldn't do it based on religion."

"I don't believe that any of the fathers are religious either. They never believed; they always sought power and control. Who knows what Vist really wants? What if he does want to be one of them? Or to even replace them all? A single leader of the sect, a Cruiser with the library in his head. Imagine ... practically omniscient."

"Scary. Tell me more. What else did she do?"

"On the day we met, this was the first time I witnessed the independent lift from the planet in the new pod type. Vist has done something to it. That sarcophagus worked together with a bio-suit. Do you get it? Together!"

"That is very impressive. And here I thought *you* were a genius."

"Stop it. I still am because I am not a loader but a man. My genius is natural and is therefore – truly mine!" Rod snapped his left fingers in the air and carried on, "So, I understand why Cruisers might want to get Vist, but what do they want with the rest of us?"

"Those Mooners would do anything to stop a KOSI evacuation. They are messing with us, and they don't want the Resistance to use your findings. You brought us hope; they might lose too many followers, their labour. Who will build and serve stasis chambers on the Moon?"

"Why are *you* sure we brought you some means to get to the colony?"

"If your loader is one of Anev's kids, you might. If we ever find her."

"If Vist is still alive. Listen, Wes, I was thinking ..."

The tetrahoder suddenly stopped before the giant oak tree, with almost bare branches that covered half of the sky. Itsy bent all four legs and lowered the cabin to the ground, almost disappearing in tall green shrubs and grasses.

"Tell me later. We arrived at the first outpost," Wes said, "I need you to wait here while I go and check if it is still safe to approach the tree."

He switched the engine off and, with a loud grunt, pulled himself up from the seat that was way too small for him.

"I will come with you," Rod said.

"No. You will wait by the hatch. I need to see if there is any evidence of unwanted visitors. Gerda was supposed to have greeted us by now."

"Okay. Signal to me if the coast is not clear. Make a sound like an owl."

"Dude, owls are extinct."

"Bats are still around. Make a sound like a bat."

"Flap-flap. Don't be an idiot. We are not loaders to communicate at such frequencies, remember? Just wait. Get your general out of here if I am not back in five."

"I can't drive Itsy." Rod waved his hands in the air.

"Hit auto-retrieve, and she will return the same way we came here. At least you will have distance and time to think."

Wes opened the side hatch, and the two friends stepped outside on the marshy ground of what used to be a forest bed. The soil was rich with rotten remains of leaves and barks, twigs and roots. Mosses and ferns had taken over thousands of years ago, growing large and dark in the heavy air.

Wes kept saying, "Do not wander off. Just wait. If I am not back soon – run. If you hear something out of order – run. If I manage to shout a warning—"

"I know, run."

Both suddenly stopped, frozen on the spot. They were still looking at each other, but all their other senses were turned outwards to absorb the new noises and scents in the air.

"No need for that, Wes!" a tall woman in leafy camouflage said, stepping out from the green shadows, "You are safe."

She was a mass of brown and green rugs. The stench of rotten straw and stewed worms hit them like a wave. Only her narrow face and blue eyes were just visible through the grey veil.

"Gerda! I started to wonder whether you would not be welcoming us this time. Cruisers are everywhere. I have counted four parties of Mooners on the way to these guys."

Gerda and Wes greeted each other in a Rebel manner – both gestured as if they were tearing off something hanging on their chests and discarding it. She nodded at Rod.

"Mooners have been snooping around the Oak like never before since the latest news. You got just one astronaut?"

"Two. The commander is inside and needs help. Is Selest around?"

"She is in the med-branch. I will message the guards so they don't stop you. Hello, are you ... oh! You are Rod Baker, aren't you?"

Rod did not know what to say, so he just nodded. The woman's appearance and manners had left him with a strange thought. He remembered patrolling scouts to be very different. More professional and better equipped. So much had changed in just five years.

The woman spoke again. "It's a big honour for me to meet my son's hero in person. He is an engineer too and worships every machine designed and built by the famous dynasty of Rodion and Ruslan Baker."

She would have likely uttered more things Rod would have wanted to hear, but Wes said that Général was almost out of oxygen cylinders, and so he pushed Rod back inside Itsy.

A minute later, the tetrahoder was almost galloping through the safe zone of the Resistance state before climbing up the oak trunk like a spider. A few hours later, a brave Commander Alan Lillypond opened his eyes in the medical unit, where people don't cure patients with prayers and trinkets.

Chapter 14. 3411. Out in Space – Blobsters

Vist turned video binoculars off and said, "That foam is no ordinary sea foam. I want to take a closer look."

"Careful, Vist," Zina said, "what chemical reaction creates something like that? You don't know whether it is dangerous?"

"The reports mentioned them, and the harm was described as ... I quote, 'paper cuts.'"

"Paper cuts?" Steven winced.

"I don't understand it either. Fancy having a look?" Tom said.

Now the whole party was curious. They started down the slope and towards the water. Then they approached the white dunes that looked like snow hills lit by the red sun. Everybody could see that this was not a pure white but a rather yellowish-grey mass of bubbles with green and brown stripes, like the ones you can see on marble. In fact, the bubbles themselves looked like a great collection of marbles clustered together. But it was their size that shocked them all. Most of them were as tiny as mustard grains. The rest were the size of all sorts of round things, with diameters up to the size of a beach ball and a few much bigger. The larger ones had been thrown higher into the cliffs, probably by a tide or storm.

Vist crouched by the foam with a scout shovel, picked up one spherical object the size of an apple, examined it, dropped it back, and smashed it up with a handle.

"Hollow inside! So it is a bubble, like an eggshell. These broken-off shards can give you a deep cut, no mistake about that."

"I wonder how they form," Rod said, "Surely ... what waves can beat up a foam like this? Why aren't they stuck together? How do they solidify without being popped by the sharp cliffs? Vist, did you read anything about them?"

"Yes. They are not formed near the shore. Professor Miteck wrote that the initial cause is organic because of the DNA fragments. He believed there has to be an organism that uses ocean salts and its own secretion to make those bubbles as its eggs or for waste disposal, nest or shelter, transport or storage. And he was right. It turned out to be a prop in a mating ritual. He studied small sea animals in the Laguna and observed their life cycle. He noticed that these small sea creatures attract a mate of the same sex every few months with which to exchange genetic materials like our tiger-slugs used to do. The bubble does not serve any other purpose but a demonstration of maturity and the actual size of its creator. The young creatures (he called them blobsters) make tiny bubbles, but they grow every year, and their bubbles get bigger each year. But they are small in number, as they are part of the food chain and various sea predators feed on blobsters of a certain size. Miteck observed how the water surface in the bay turns into the most spectacular display when millions of bubbles surface, float and get discarded once the happy couples unite. Miteck did not report their lifespan, but he noted that the biggest spheres were three to four metres in diameter. He said the bigger the blobsters, the further away in the sea they live, but they always return to the same bays to mate."

"Never mind how big the biggest bubble is. I want to know how big the biggest blobster is," Tolyan said.

"Not so big. The bubble is twenty or thirty times the volume of the creature itself. Miteck captured a blobster the size of a mouse with its bubble the size of a pumpkin. They are bad swimmers and usually crawl on the seabed. When the time comes, the blobsters produce a soapy, glue-like liquid, mix it with saturated sea salts, and take it to the surface by filling it with air or waste gases. When floating, they ride under it and look for similar structures using their antennae above the water. They must have eyes on the tip of their antennae. The sea is usually calm during the mating season, and the sun reflects well off the white surface. I wonder how they know when it is the right time ... without any seasonal change here."

"Fascinating," Tom said, "But we must be close. If this is the Laguna, our destination is not far."

"I wonder if the White City has that name because of the white bubbles," Rod said.

"You mean they use them as garden ornaments?" said Général.

"It's just some salt and spit ..." said Steven. "Vist, surely it is brittle."

"I don't know. It was as hard to break as a slate, but only on the outside. Maybe the bio-compound in its structure makes it particularly strong. Why else would the rain not dissolve it?"

"This is a very interesting biology lesson, but can we go, please?" said Mik impatiently.

"Are you afraid it will be dark soon?" said Tolyan, laughing. "It is not going to be, you know."

"Yes, I know, but I prefer to have more information about the unknown threat rather than the local fauna."

"Mik is right," Général said, "I, too, would prefer to study the colony as much as we can before we enter it. Let's go, Vist."

"Okay, but Captain, I suggest we leave our weapons behind before entering the place. Do not take anything that could be used against us if the colonists get hold of it."

"Why, Vist? Do you expect a threat?"

"We don't know their current number or their intentions. They have been very cautious with us. I think we should be too."

"How can we be careful if we are not armed," Steven asked.

Tom looked at him.

"We have other skills. Vist, do you also think if we look less threatening then ... hmm, I see. Alan? What do you think?"

Général looked pensive for a moment.

"I agree that we have to be careful. Storming right in could be ... regrettable. I suggest we separate off. Let me and my lads go in first. We will take a couple of locked-up zappers and a blade. We will signal that the rest of the locals are not hostile."

Tom hesitated for a minute then said, "I like the idea of separation. I will go first. Steven, Tolyan and Vist will come with me. Alan and Mik, your orders are to take Zina and Rod back if the colonists kill us on the spot. If things are not that bad, but something else goes wrong – take charge and act accordingly. We will try to maintain radio contact the whole time. The earpieces need to be on all the time, so charge them when you can."

The whole party resumed their journey towards Laguna. Their converters charged their equipment during the walk, the northern wind started to cool down the air, and the sun rays danced in the clouds in a very earthly way. A group of flying animals crossed the sky silently, heading towards the open sea.

They found the highest hill after three hours of walking and used it to look around. Steven said that the hill's size and shape reminded him of the famous hill in Edinburgh, where his father came from before moving to Australia. So the mountain was immediately named Steven's throne, and everyone was in a better mood despite the tiredness.

Chapter 15. 3416. Back on Earth – Arthur

Mik knew his way around the castle ruins better than anyone else. Partly because he had already had a chance to walk about. And partly because his training allowed him to process every piece of information that found its way into his mind. He was not as good as Vist, who appeared to see through walls and ten feet into the ground. But even without thinking, Mik absorbed the visual details of distances and sizes. His ears and nose could recognise the type of weapon fired nearby. His intuition could sense the enemy approaching, even in his sleep. This is why, during the short break in the food storage – their first stop, Mik sat up and said, "I was right. He is here. Don't move, guys. I won't be too long."

Moving silently and swiftly, he slipped out of the large crate where all four were hiding. Earlier, Tom suggested that if the Cruisers tried to recruit Mik, they would probably try the same with other skilled men. Mik was certain that both troopers were smart enough to do what he did – pretend to accept the offers first and go into action soon after. But he wasn't sure about Commander Lillypond if he was captured too.

Mik really hoped that the Général would get away. He was a stubborn old man. If they tried, he would most likely refuse to play along, and they would kill and eat him.

"Not right away, sunshine," Mik said to Zina when she gasped. "Didn't you hear about their protein processors? They treat people like livestock in special ways, control them with drugs, and then turn executed prisoners and their own dead into protein supplements called Angel Flesh."

This was their reason to make their way to the kitchens first. They were not hard to find. Worm stew has a very peculiar smell despite attempts to hide it with fresh mint, which grows like a weed everywhere. They were also very hungry and needed to eat since the Cruisers had not offered them anything but water for two days. They avoided dry discs of Angel Flesh, stacked like large coins in the smoking chambers, but filled their vest pockets with dry fish sticks, potato bars and tubed vegetable paste. It looked like the Cruisers were already stocking up for a long journey. Mik suggested resting and waiting. Tom agreed. Ready to go at any minute, they waited for someone to turn up.

They waited for a good hour. Tom seemed worried that every minute here might mean more suffering for his men. But Mik was confident that there was only one interrogation chamber in the castle ruins because torture is messy and noisy. Cruisers preached purity and tranquillity; therefore, the rest of this settlement should be clean and quiet. Tom doubted it but still could do very little. After all, they had no idea how many Cruisers were in the castle.

When Mik went out, everyone kept perfectly still. Finally, the sound of rapid steps on the spiral stairs indicated that two people were coming down. They were likely carrying something very heavy and had evidently encountered Mik on their way down. Tom, Zina and Marta heard some brief commotion, a thud and the sound of a man trying to scream as someone squeezed his throat. After a moment of silence, Mik reappeared, dragging a Cruiser by the leg across the stone floor. This one was wearing a sky-blue robe, much like the one on the large torturer earlier, but far shorter. He was dead. Mik concealed the body in the half-empty crate of grain and went back. He returned slowly, carrying Tolyan over his shoulder.

He groaned under the weight of his friend, "Not dead. Drugged for preservation. Let's hope he has not overdosed."

He laid Tolyan on the pile of flour sacks decorated with tiny daisies and returned for the second Cruiser. This one was alive but seriously disoriented, dressed in a short, hooded brown robe. Mik sat the man up against the wall and forced his head up. The frightened eyes blinked fast and swollen lips trembled.

"I will give you one chance," said Mik, "Are you ready to come back to reality?"

The man looked no older than twenty-five. He nodded frantically in fear.

"Do you know your priests have betrayed you? They are not taking you with them. You will die here after they leave or even before that."

"No." The voice was also young. "You are lying. It's impossible. Father ..."

"Ontha?"

"No, Father Deessa and Brother Patrick said that we are all expected in the Promised Land. The Lord has a place for us. Our destiny."

Mik got up and walked to the nearest shelf. A stack of Angel Flesh rained on the boy's head. Mik threw it with a gesture like a rich man throwing a handful of coins to the crowd of beggars at his feet.

"This is your destiny."

The boy's face was already distorted with horror. Now it looked almost petrified for a few seconds, and then he breathed heavily and fast.

Zina stepped out of the crate and approached the young man, pressing her hand over her hurt side.

"Hi," she said, "I am Zina. What is your name?"

The boy looked at her, and his breathing slowed down a little.

"Arthur."

"Listen, Arthur. We are not the bad guys here. We don't share your faith, but does that make us monsters?"

"Brother Patrick said that those who deny the Lord embrace Satan. You are sinners and he wants—"

The attempt to be brave did not last.

"Yes? What does Satan want?" Zina asked.

"To ... doom the human souls."

"Why?"

"I don't know."

"What happened to *their* souls?" asked Zina, pointing at the Angel Flesh discs on the floor.

"They are with our Lord now." The young face expressed pure panic and disgust too. "They have been redeemed for their contribution to the cause."

"Do you want to end up like this? Do you wish to contribute? You probably will, whether you die today or later," Mik said.

"No, I don't want to."

"But what do you want?" asked Zina.

"What?"

"If I could grant you one wish, what would that be? What is it you want more than anything?"

It looked like the boy was thinking not about what he wanted but whether he should talk about it.

"I want to be with Sophie and my dog, Droog."

Zina smiled. Her good eye narrowed, while the other almost disappeared under swollen bruises.

"And I bet it does not matter where?"

"That's right," the boy said with new defiance in his eyes, but this time it was not addressed to Zina.

"The Earth is dying, you know."

"I know."

"So what will you and Sophie do?"

"Brother Patrick—"

"Yes, they promised you the holy land. Do you know where that is?"

"I ... no. I don't. Another planet or something."

Tom was already standing behind Zina.

He joined in. "But will you believe me if I tell you?"

"I don't know."

"You don't know much, do you? But I suppose it's better than *no*. Listen closely, just in case you are smart enough. Suppose you learned at school about the colonisation programme and orbital wormhole charger KOSI built near Jupiter in the smart past. In that case, you should know that the holy land your fathers are talking about is an establishment on one of the planets where people already live and grow in numbers. Humanity has already survived this way, and from what we saw, whether we join them or not, they will be fine. Your sect is not capable of building a ship that can take you there. Let's see. Everything you have here, where did it come from?"

"The Lord providers ... our prayers are answered."

"Really? Do you truly think so?"

The boy nodded unconvincingly. Tom carried on.

"Where is your real father?"

Arthur looked at him and then looked sideways.

"He was a sinner. He is dead."

"Has he been dead for long? Is that why you don't like Angel Flesh? I can tell you how the Lord provides. I might not guess all the details, but I can tell you the main story. Maybe a member of the cult made the robe you are wearing. Some skilled woman, perhaps like your Sophie, is kept alive for that purpose. If she refuses to work, she will also become a sinner, and her only salvation is to be eaten. The people who produced fabrics for those robes are probably dead already. And so are those who used to make food, medication and everything the Lord provides for you. He must, mustn't he? Your fathers have to make sure he does. If they fail, more people will go another way. So people must die to keep the faith of those who live. But they live only as long as they believe. And who decides all that? Those who possess the power of persuasion ... by word, or by fist." Tom pointed at his own purple lips and Zina's black eye as he spoke. "Your father was probably a farmer or hunter, and he refused to feed your cult in the name of the Lord instead of trading his product on the MESH market. Cruisers were probably just taking what they wanted by force every year, but time was running out. He could not produce much anyway, and the sect was competing with Mooners, Thieves and other marauders. So, to take everything from your father, they killed him and everyone else in the family who protested. Right? Are you grateful that they spared you? How old were you when that happened? Or were you already brainwashed by that time?"

Arthur did not reply, still staring at the floor.

"My point is, without people who actually make things, your Lord will not provide anything. And when all sinners have been eaten, whom do you think the fathers and brothers will start on? The cult will eat itself unless they find a way to get to the colony and start the same self-destructive process there. So, the next thing the Lord has to provide is ... what? That's right. The ship? This time they want *my* ship. It has already been to the colony and back. This lady," he said, pointing at Marta, who stood grimly by the crate, "is my only surviving pilot. Your brothers tortured and killed her husband, trying to ensure the Lord provided your cult with transportation.

The problem is – my *Wasp* can sustain fifteen … maybe even eighteen people if they are in stasis tanks. So, if your fathers get hold of it, who do you think they will take with them? You? Sophie? Your dog, Droog? I doubt it."

The boy looked at Tom with worry.

Tom added, "You probably want to ask us what you should do. To save your life? To save your loved ones?"

"Are you ready to sin?" said Mik.

Zina elbowed him in the chest, "Don't confuse him even more, idiot! Leave that to his fathers."

Then Tom said, "If saving lives rather than souls is a sin, then the Lord himself should set an example and not bother with your Promised Land. But if you care enough, go to those people who can make useful things and do wonderful things – who can build enough ships to take even dogs. Be one of them and help them take you to the holy land, hell, paradise, the colony, anything you want to call it – the place where you can live your life like your real father tried to live his."

"How can I do that now?" said the boy, looking as if some wheels in his head had started to spin really fast, "It's too late for me."

"It is not. You are still alive, young and capable, aren't you? Do you want to help and come with us to the Resistance?"

"Yes. But my—" he hesitated and looked unconvinced once again.

"I know you want to take your loved ones with you. But I do not know yet if I can trust you. So we can't let you just go and get Sophie. If you tell us how we can get her and your dog, we will bring them to you. Deal?"

The young Cruiser bit his lip.

"You don't really have a choice, boy," Mik said, "you either help us or join your friend in the grain? My job is to kill those who are a threat to us. I would not risk my life to save yours unless it is worthy."

Arthur seemed about to start hyperventilating again, but he pulled himself together and sat up straight.

"What do you want to know?"

"First, about our friend here. What did you give him?" asked Tom.

Arthur glanced at the grain crate. "Len injected him with five milligrams of Bliss."

"Oh shit!" Zina marched towards Tolyan and gently lifted his eyelids with her thumbs.

"Zina?" Mik asked impatiently.

"Your friend is having a good time," Zina said, "but when he wakes up, probably by tomorrow evening – he will be very sick. Don't worry. He is healthy and strong, and he will live, but if you find my bag with everything still in it, I should be able to neutralise the drug. Why Bliss?" she asked and turned to Arthur.

"This way, we share the divine delight with sinners, to show them the forgiveness of the Lord and to open the door to heaven ... Before processing them."

"You were going to turn Tolyan into food, as I thought," said Mik quietly.

"I can see why some of you get persuaded so easily. When did you start taking it, and how much?"

"A year ago. I am a novice, so I am on a solution of less than one milligram daily."

"You are not far gone then. Just enough to control you," muttered Zina, lowering her head to Tolyan's chest and listening to his breathing.

"Arthur, back to business," Tom said, "How many Cruisers are in the castle and what is their rank?"

The young man pressed his hands to his face and took a deep breath.

"I really don't know much. We are not allowed to ask difficult questions. I am sure this castle is one of several settlements of the faction... and the smallest settlement. Two days ago, I started working in the kitchens and helped Len to prepare thirty-seven portions of worm stew daily. Father Ontha, Father Deessa, Doctor Munny, the Word-Bearer – Brother Patrick. There are guards, Brother Cog, Brother Mark, Brother Otto, Big Pete and the twins. Jade, the stitcher, is not a sister, so she lives in the camp with us. There is Sister Volna. She mainly manages twenty-three novices, including myself, Sophie and my friend Nat. They all live in tents behind the northern castle wall. We have two animals here: Droog the dog and Lisa the goose. And there was also Len, the chef."

"That makes thirty-six. Did you miss somebody, or did one of you take a double portion?" asked Mik.

"I don't think so, I don't know. Perhaps Len made a mistake."

"Was Len your friend?" asked Tom.

"He was a cook. I was ordered to help him."

"Who had the missing ear? And who are the twins?" asked Mik.

"Judaea is one of the twins. His brother Jod chewed his ear off to make him different when they were novices. So I was told, anyway."

"So apart from the novices and the stitcher, we have six people left to deal with. I assume the torturer was Big Pete? Where are the novices, and where do I find your leaders?" asked Mik.

"The novices will work in court sheds but only until evening service; then, they must return to the camp. They will try to stop you only if ordered. Father Deessa, Father Ontha, Sister

Volna and the Word-Bearer spend most of their time in the tower. I am not sure about the guards, but one of the brothers is always at the main gate."

"What do you know about the other prisoners?" asked Mik.

"I did not know we had prisoners. Len called me to his meat shack and told me to help take this guy to the kitchen storage. The other one looks a bit like you, but white. He is still there, also blissed."

"Steven?" Mik was glad and angry. "What are they doing taking drugs?"

"He is in a bad way. Looks pretty battered," Arthur said.

"He was like that before we got here. Let's hope they did not add anything to it," said Zina and turned to Mik. "You better find him fast. Marta, please help me with Tolyan. His feet and hands are getting cold."

Mik went for the door.

"Okay. I will return to the doctor's tent and look for the bag. Where is that meat shack?"

"Go left at the top of the stairs... about sixty paces by the broken wall," said Arthur. His voice was slowly filling with determination. Mik thought this boy would never turn so easily if he was a devoted believer. How many of them hid their true thoughts?

"What are the chances someone will come down here?" he asked.

"Len takes supper to the fathers and the Word-Bearer an hour before the service then feeds the rest. Some novices would have to help him, but not until they are called in."

Mik took the boy's wrist and fastened it to the table leg with a cable tie. The orange tie looked suspiciously identical to those used on Tom earlier that day.

"Sorry, kid, I promise I will cut you free when Steven is here."

Mik and Tom moved towards the stairs. Both women began to rub life back into Tolyan's numbed hands and feet.

"Fisherman—" Tom stopped and looked at Arthur.

"My father was a fisherman at Romeo Reservoir. They killed him last autumn when he refused to give up all his pikes and eels. My mother died when I was eight. They told me if he did not die, he would have sacrificed me to Satan. I never really believed that."

Chapter 16. 3411. Out in Space – the Village

They spotted it miles away, just as Tom hoped. It was white, as much as anything could be white under the red dwarf. The part of the Laguna that cut its deepest curve into the land had a small grey beach cleared of salt bubbles. It was obvious that the clearance had been made and maintained by human effort. Some posts and rough fences had been built around the small wharf, creating bubble-free areas and the gate for boats and rafts that rested on the grounds nearby. The salt bubbles covered the rest of the beach and surrounding cliffs. A few were floating on the waves like sculptured icebergs or buoys. Some of them were much bigger than those encountered before, but the biggest ones were not on the beach. It looked like they had rolled away from the beach and lay about five or six hundred metres away in the nearest meadow. From a distance and from above, they appeared like a bizarre collection of game balls of different sizes left by a giant child on the lawn. They were white and grey, as if someone had partially covered them in mud and ashes.

"Is that the White City? Where is *Arc*?" Tolyan said in disbelief.

"This place might not be the whole colony – too small. Obviously, the main base is elsewhere," Tom said.

"Then why did that woman on the radio … what was her name again?"

"Raja?" Zina said.

"Yes, her. Why did she tell us to come here?"

"I don't know," Tom said, taking his glasses off to clean them. "She mentioned the guide. Perhaps there is a reason why they wanted us to be introduced slowly to their world. This is a place where we can be checked out and checked in. Guys, your eyes are better than mine. How far away is it?"

"No more than three kilometres," answered Tolyan, and the rest nodded.

"Two kilometres and eight hundred metres."

"Vist, stop showing off," Tolyan said.

"I am going to test that," said Steven with a challenge in his voice, "If you are just a hundred metres off ..."

"In this case, two thousand, eight hundred and twenty-six metres."

Vist's smile was almost handsome and so disarming that Steven sniffed and dropped the subject.

At the bottom of the hill, Général, Rod and Zina settled on the small opening, surrounded by some shrubs and something that incredibly resembled bramble but with bright-yellow prickles and inky leaves. The whole arsenal was packed away and left under their care, except for the E-40 beam guns, which Steven and Tolyan wore on both hands. These secret weapons looked like fingerless gloves with a full thumb and a small bulge on the back of the hand. They should not attract any attention. The device – a ZPE-converter – could convert environmental zero-point energy into any desirable type of usable energy. It solved the power problem on Earth during the Platinum Age and created a new way of sending small objects through parsecs of space, such as shift-postmen. Ultimately, they also solved the weapons problem for the Resistance. Cruisers, unable to produce anything good, seized a few of these guns, but not for long, as they could not maintain them. What everybody called zappers would silently shoot a thin deadly beam of instantly converted environmental energy upon pointing your fist and pressing your thumb into the knuckle side of the index finger. Punching your enemy with that fist could also be more devastating than a knuckleduster, but the weapon couldn't be damaged or triggered by anything except your thumb. The glove was completely harmless until it was unlocked by a voice command.

Mik followed Tom's group for another few hundred metres until the white settlement became visible again, and he took a watch post in the tall brown grass. Tom, Vist and two troopers carried on towards the nearest white sphere. Soon they noticed a network of paths around the settlement. The paths all led towards the spheres and disappeared between them. The travellers followed one of the paths and soon had to cross a small creek. The bridge over it was nothing but two logs of scaly-looking trees.

"Vist," said Tom, "how old are your journals from this colony? This looks too primitive even for a satellite of the main dwelling."

"The latest entrance was made eighty-one years ago. The colonists only had half a dozen shift-postmen with them and sent reports every thirty years. The latest one stated that it was their last device, but they hoped to build their own soon. That was a promising sign, but nothing else came through. The very first shift-postman was a clumsy transmitter the size of an average parcel. Upon reaching the solar system, its signal could transmit information back to the KOSI station after following the echo from the stream of wormholes. The maximum distance was no more than ten light years at the time, with only sixty-four charges of the ZPE-converter, which means sixty-four jumps. The last one started transmitting sixty-five years after the update report was recorded, and we know nothing about what has happened since. The data was very scrambled in places but mostly readable."

"I assume all six parcels have been in the Mars library ever since," said Tolyan.

"No, Mooners destroyed them all after I read them. All records were distorted too. Except for this one." Vist's head tilted slightly forwards.

"Anything could have happened here in almost a hundred years," said Tom after a pause.

He was going to ask Vist another question but forgot about it because of a momentary distraction. Vist was walking and answering at the same time. On the bridge, it looked as if Vist had lost her footing and was about to fall. Before thinking, Tom jumped forwards and grabbed her hand for stability. Her hand – Tom was sure of it now – was the small hand of a distressed woman. He paused to make sure the balance was restored. It felt like he was helping a woman. She leaned on his arm for a second. It was nice. Tom scrutinised Vist's face for an answer. She was still looking under her feet, at her next step. Only for a second did she meet Tom's eyes with a nod. Was it confirmation or simple gratitude? Tom dismissed the question as inappropriate, let her hand go, and they all carried on towards the spheres. He had to focus all his attention on the ground under his feet. It should not matter. He would have helped Vist even if she were a man. He would have.

"So there were just six parcels in all this time?" asked Steven, "Not much. Why didn't they take more with them?"

Vist's voice was lower as they approached the settlement, "Well, if the mission is unsuccessful, you only need one parcel to convey that, if you can, and not many have even managed that. We received the first one so late – everyone thought none of the ships had made it. We expected them to land thirty-five years after the launch, but we did not consider a few variables. The luckiest pair, number eight, landed successfully with minor damage. The wake-up call did not activate straight away, and nobody knows why. They sent their first parcel in the forty-first year after leaving Earth, and it took sixty-five years to reach us. The report contained very basic information and excellent news. Only one person did not wake up. We received another shift-postman thirty five years later. This is why they count their time on the planet in generations – every thirty five Earth years. Counting time by Noverca orbit or axis spinning is not easy for obvious reasons."

Captain Tom looked at Vist again: straight back, square shoulders. The damn robe did not allow him to imagine the loader's figure. As far as he knew, all loaders wore robes over complicated bio-suits full of equipment and compartments on their chests, sides, hips and even on their backs. Technically the bullet- and ray-proof suit was robotic wear, which only loaders could put on and connect to. It was a wearable laboratory designed for field research and distant study. Loaders dressed in it could gain additional strength, agility and stamina. And at the same time, this structure – although not particularly bulky – hid the shape of the person inside annoyingly well. Tom interrupted his own thoughts in disbelief. The realisation that he really wanted Vist to be a woman was unsettling. How much time had passed since he had been with a woman? That must be it. A gnarly but welcomed explanation.

The conversation had to stop at that point, too, as they approached the first sphere. They saw a man between two small salt orbs almost the same size. The man was busy trying to fit a long stone slab on top of the balls as if he were building a bench, but the slab kept sliding off. Every time it happened, he would pick up a small rock and hit the salty tops, trying to chisel them flat. It was visibly hard work, and the man dropped the stone before he had made any reasonable progress. He tried to fit the slab again, balancing it on his hope more than on the salt spheres. He stood up and looked at the approaching party. He did not appear surprised by how they were dressed or equipped, but he looked at their faces intently as if he expected to recognise some of them. He was in his forties but looked older because of his long hair and beard, each braided into a long single twist, one on his back and one down his chest.

Unmistakably it was a human, undernourished and weathered, but definitely born from the Earthlings. Later, Rod said that in his childhood, he had imagined a book character who looked just like this person – a shipwreck survivor who lived on an island for a long time. His skin looked dark with a touch of purple – most likely an environmental trait. The skin shimmered on his forehead, nose and cheeks as it was smeared with sprat scales. His outfit was likely made of some locally produced fabric – pale, stringy and knitted into a simple long tunic. Grey leather belts were strapped around his waist and across his chest. A few grass-weaved pouches were attached to those belts. This man's face was probably handsome when he was younger but now he had a serious expression of concern and distrust. He did not walk towards the guests. He stood on the same spot waiting for them to approach.

A few steps away from the man, Tom put both hands up with open palms and spoke out. "Greetings, friend. I really hope you understand me. Do you?"

"Why wouldn't I? Do you people really think we are so wild here that we forget how to speak?" said the man abruptly and clearly, "What are you doing here? Are you lost, or are citizens starting to leave in packs now?"

The man spoke in English, but in this short speech, he used at least eight words from various languages. Further encounters with other colonists soon revealed that they spoke in the same linguistic mixture. Tom thought for a moment and decided to play it safe. "My name is Tom. These are my friends, Tolyan, Vist and Steven. What is your name?"

"Gareth."

Such a common name sounded strange here.

"And what is the name of this place?"

"We call it the village. Who are you, and what do you want? And what's wrong with your skin? Are you sick?"

"We are explorers heading to the White City. Would you help us with directions, please?"

Gareth's grunt changed into a frantic burble as he spoke.

"You have lost your way? An expedition? Or, you are not from there?" Gareth finally looked at their clothes more carefully. "You don't look like farmers; you cannot be from another village. Oh!" He looked at Tom's face. "And the way you talk, you are from another colony. Ah! Praise the Lord! The divinations are true, you finally came!"

He grabbed his head with both hands, stared at his guests, and appeared to be thinking fast, obviously trying to choose the best course of action.

He suddenly addressed Tom with a happy and welcoming gesture. "Please be guests in my house. Come, chief. You can rest and take shelter for the sleeping hours here. This is a real blessing and honour for me."

He led them around the sphere to the front door facing the rest of the village. Gareth's home, as suspected, was inside a salt sphere. In fact, it was two spheres – one about four metres in diameter and another a little smaller. They were buried next to each other in the ground by about half a metre and filled with grey soil – just enough to make a flat floor inside. The vegetation around them made the home look like giant eggs in a blackish-green nest. The larger sphere had a covered doorway leading into the second sphere. Small round windows, a few inches in diameter, were not cut out for light but for ventilation. The doors were made of something that looked like bamboo stems fastened together; a few curtains were made of nothing but stitched semi-transparent petals of a pale alien flower.

The salty sphere was adequately lit inside with stingy sunlight that shone through its shell. It had obviously been scraped and scooped inside to make the room larger and the walls thinner. The thinner the translucent walls, the more light they allowed through. The floor was compacted clay-like grey soil covered with primitive rags. The furniture was also very simple – a low shapeless stone table in the middle, leather cushions and several blankets and pillows scattered on the floor by the opposite wall. The doorway into another round room was hidden behind an animal hide, like an oiled brown goatskin. The house was reasonably clean and resembled a gathering place of some hot, eastern country of the pre-tech age.

"Here," said Gareth, bowing and gesturing to guests to use the cushions, "Mi casa es su casa. Please rest here. You can sleep in my bed, chief, if you like. Be comfortable. I can't offer you any dinner just yet. The food is not shared until the bell hour as the cycle ends, but you will find water in this jar and—" He looked up as if he had had a sudden idea. Then Gareth rushed towards the doorway of the second sphere and disappeared behind the goat hide. A moment later, he reappeared, dragging a young girl by her wrist. He pushed her towards Tom, who he recognised as a leader and said with pride in his voice, "Here is my most valuable offer to you, chief! My young daughter! You can please yourself for free. I expect no rent. I wish for nothing but your friendship."

He posed, waiting for an answer and trying to read the reaction on Tom's face. The girl was in her teens; she was dressed in a knitted tunic, similar to Gareth's, only shorter. Her skin also had a lilac hue and sparkling freckles. She had just one belt around her waist, a light coat of the same fabric and a necklace made of the same damned salt spheres, the size of large pearls. Her hair was unevenly cut short; she was better washed than Gareth and looked disinterested and subdued at first. The girl was very skinny, but her partially covered breasts were large. She looked around, noticed the intense examination of her own person by Vist, covered her chest with both hands, frowned, and appeared suddenly very worried and serious.

"We are grateful, but to accept this offer would be against our traditions," said Tom. "I hope this will not offend you."

"Not at all, chief. Is there anything else I can offer?"

"Only one thing. The way to White City."

The girl, who was about to leave, stopped and glanced at Tom with interest before disappearing into her room.

"Ahem, yes. Of course," Gareth frowned again, "but I don't think I should be doing this alone. Why don't you rest here and wait? I will run as fast as possible and deliver the wonderful news to the High Martyr. He will know what to do. He will show you the way."

"So you brought us here to distract us?"

"No, chief! I genuinely wanted to welcome you, but I am just a humble villager. If I just point my finger at where to go, the rest of the villagers won't have a clue. Oh, my Lord! Our deepest prayers have been answered."

"Prayers again? This is not a manner of speech, is it?" Vist said, sounding surprised for the first time.

"Just wait for me, please. I have to do it the right way."

It was obvious that Gareth could not make them stay, but he was desperate to tell someone about their arrival. At this point, he looked more worried than excited.

"We will come with you," said Tom, "If you can't show us the way to the city, show us the way to your leader."

Gareth had to give in. He stepped outside, and the whole party followed him between the salt spheres – some white and some darkened with mud – to the heart of the village. Most of these round houses were made of just one, two or three spheres. Tom spotted a few vegetable beds with something growing in them, a couple of huge chickens, and one goat that appeared to be painted bronze. Outside their homes, a few villagers, dressed like Gareth and his daughter, stopped and stared at the travellers with glazed eyes. Some stood in confusion, and some followed the group a few paces behind. Gareth made inaudibly squeaky noises under their stares and strange gestures with his hands, and sometimes he hopped like a child. But he did not say anything sensible to any of them.

The person Gareth called the High Martyr lived in a house made of at least six spheres. The biggest bubbles were not only joined together but also assembled into a pyramid. It formed a two-storey house with stone stairs and solid doors. He probably had a bedroom, kitchen and bathroom. Maybe even a storage room or study.

A guard by the front door heard Gareth's explanation, and his purple face changed remarkably from a serious expression of authority to one of astonishment and even adoration.

He opened the door and screeched in a high voice, "Hey, Kendra! Take Gareth in!"

Gareth disappeared, but the guard stayed without moving a centimetre as if his feet were rooted into the ground. He was breathing heavily and staring at the newcomers with an unchanging flabbergasted expression. The travellers were left waiting and wondering.

"Wow," said Tolyan quietly and sarcastically, "what sort of civilisation can't even build a proper palace for their leader?"

"The sort that is going backwards. The sort that offers their daughters to strangers and can offer their guests nothing but water," Steven said.

"Tom." Vist's voice was low, almost a whisper, so the guard would not overhear it. "The girl didn't care much about being offered to you but was very worried when I noticed that she was breastfeeding."

"What? Was there a baby in that room?"

"Definitely not."

"But then—"

The door opened again, and a tall skinny man appeared in the doorway. He smiled, and his hands rose theatrically to the skies. His pale face was patchy like a turnip. His tunic was made of a real-but-worn fabric of faded orange, decorated with seashells, salt pearls, crystals and small metallic parts of various devices. There was some hat or crown on his head, but apart from a strange symbol, it was hard to describe. The symbol resembled a cross or star with four rays and a circle in the middle. Another sect, another symbol, thought Tom, and a total lack of imagination. No matter what you draw as your mark – a cross, a sun, moon or star – its vagueness together with half a kilogram of jewellery compensates for the rest and makes it all the same.

"Welcome! I cannot express how excited I am about meeting you. We always believed that sooner or later our prayers would be answered," said the skinny man. His gaze passed over all four of them and stopped on Vist's robe. "I am delighted to see a fellow priest. I compliment you on your markings, brother. So beautiful and ...

dark. My name is Shafran. I am a High Martyr in this lovely community of true worshippers. I can't wait to hear about where you are from and how long your walk here was. You must be tired and hungry. Would you allow us to offer you hospitality in the name of our Lord?"

Vist and Tom exchanged looks. Tom hoped he understood Vist correctly. He saw an expressionless face, but the olive eyes opened a little wider for a split second, then squinted a little before becoming warm and attentive again. Whatever it meant, Tom interpreted it as he should not do what he normally would have.

He turned to the High Martyr. "Thank you. We came from the north-east and are trying to reach White City. Our journey here took a long time. We want to speak with Raja, or with anyone representing this society."

Tom briefly examined the small group of people behind Shafran with disappointment. None of them looked like communications officers. They looked like a bunch of old homeless beggars, or a group of actors in a low-budget theatre production about homeless beggars. Especially the old woman by the High Martyr's left shoulder – she was dressed like a wood witch in rags and strange clothing decorated with fragments and trinkets. Her necklace was made of bits of an electronic device of unknown nature.

This old woman said slowly, looking at Vist rather hatefully, "They could be telling the truth. The question is, which north-east and a long time of travelling how? They are different from us, a different race."

"Quiet, Kendra, not now." Shafran smiled again, then looked at Tom. "Please don't feel offended, but there are no rajas, sultans, kings or tsars among us. We are all equal in the Lord's eyes. You can count on our assistance, of course. After all, the Lord teaches us to help our brothers. But first, please allow us to thank him for such a wonderful occasion. We never have guests. People usually come alone and come to stay. And we always know exactly where they are from. But you ... you are not from White City, I can tell. Please, join our prayer, eat with us, and treat us to a good story."

"We—" Tom started, but Vist interrupted him. "We are in a hurry. We have rather urgent business in White City. We need medical supplies unless you have a decent supply of tetrapropalozine. All we can afford is a short rest, and so we will leave soon, Your Grace."

"Tetra...? Eh? Massimo?" Shafran turned his head to the right, and the young man stepped forwards from the group of followers.

He was short but athletic, healthy-looking and bright-eyed. He could have easily been from Kenya or Ethiopia if his skin hadn't been the colour of deep purple. He was dressed the same way as all the villagers, but he probably had a special court position, as only he and Kendra had been marked with metallic bits of dismantled equipment, although not as heavily as the High Martyr. Massimo's right ear was pierced and decorated with a single intricate earring.

"It's a medicine, my priest. Cursed stuff!" Massimo's voice was also young and somehow sounded unwilling.

"Oh, I see," said Shafran without a smile this time. "You do not rely on the Lord's mercy to treat illnesses?"

"Your servant is correct, my priest," said Vist. "But I need this chemical for a very different purpose. Not for treating my brothers. None of us is sick."

"This priest is telling the truth – but what is his purpose?" said the old woman and was ignored.

"I am glad to hear that, Your Grace," said Shafran, smiling again and welcoming the whole group into the opened door with both arms. "I want to know more about your pilgrimage. Please come in. It is not sleeping time yet, and waking time is not soon."

Tom looked at Vist again but saw only calmness and confidence. Clearly Vist had already tested Shafran, who had already failed that test.

"I will ask for your permission to leave my own guard here," he said to Shafran and nodded at Tolyan.

"Of course!" said the High Martyr with the same smile, but his eyes became cold. "We will send him some food too. It's time for a bell hour."

As the hosts and guests walked into the salty castle, the clouds in the sky looked like the folds of a giant velvet curtain, shining with red rays and golden reflections from the sun, which added even more to this remarkable feeling of a theatrical performance in which everyone played a part. This play is a story of an unknown script with an unknown ending. Like the music marking the intermission, the strange strikes of a bell pierced the air to mark the end of the cycle. The crowd of gaping villagers turned like one person and drifted in one direction to receive their share of daily rations. Soon, there were only two figures outside of the castle door. One was a savage guard with something like a spear in his hand, dressed like an ancient tribe warrior but far too skinny and confused. The other was a strong young trooper in military space uniform, with a light-brown beard, appearing completely unarmed but more dangerous than all the villagers put together.

Chapter 17. 3416. Back on Earth – Brothers

"Is he dead?" Tom asked.

"I am afraid so," Mik answered.

"He was not as tough as we thought then."

Captain Darkwood stepped over the body on the floor and picked up the mace dropped by the Cruiser in the short blue robe.

"We need to find another one," he said, throwing the mace into the thick mass of bramble.

"How about you let me defuse the next brother, somebody who will still be able to talk? We might finally get some information. Otherwise, you will kill them all before we get to those fathers."

"Okay, go ahead, but remember, they are fanatics on at least two and a half milligrams of *Bliss*. They will not be very cooperative, and if you use that cleaver ... This one must have been Brother Mark."

"No, he is the second twin, the one with both ears. Jod?"

"How did you know the one by the gate was Otto?"

"I did not. Who cares?"

"Who killed *him*?" Tom asked.

"Maybe Steven's on the loose? The meat shack was empty, after all. I have found all our weapons in the armoury apart from Steven's blade. Let's hope he has it."

"Zina said he has a broken wrist?"

"That's right. At least now she is reunited with her bag, but I couldn't tell if anything is missing from it."

Tom and Mik slowly walked to the end of the wall and peered around a corner. The shadows were long, and the sky was darkening. The evening sun was still yellow, and the wind was warm, but after many months on Noverca, under harsh and dark Vitricus, both men perceived this weather as rather cool and quiet. To their eyes, the green grass and leaves of the Earth flora were too green. In fact, all other colours appeared a little too bright to the point of being irritating, like the colours of toddlers' toys.

"So ..." Mik returned to the interrupted conversation. "The Cruisers' leaders are fathers, their subordinates are brothers, their slaves and servants are novices, right?"

"That's right," Captain Darkwood replied.

"So who is the Word-Bearer? There was no such title when we were leaving Earth."

"I am not sure, but it could be some kind of preacher or decipherer of the old texts."

Both men reached the end of the ancient wall and the only round tower that still stood tall in the hill castle. The highest narrow window on the darker side was lit with the glare from the fire, but the lighting was still faint in the twilight.

"I just can't get used to the absurd. Cruisers live in the old ruins and use candles and torches, sleep on straw, and cook on clay stoves," Tom whispered, "The only electronic technologies that I have seen here so far are a protein processor, a freezer and a chemist's centrifuge."

"They could have been worse," said Mik quietly, "they could have lived in the salt bubbles."

"You know, if they were on Noverca, I am sure this is exactly what they would have done."

"No, this gang is more aggressive, it has stronger forces. The villagers did not even have maces or swords. Steven and Tolyan saw just spears and wooden clubs there. Our Cruisers would never stop trying to take over the city and its ZPE-converters."

"And whatever happened to *Ark-8* would also have happened to *Noah-8*."

They walked slowly round the cylindrical tower, staying close to the wall and listening for nearby foes. Mik, who was going first, stopped and stood still for a few seconds. Tom waited in silence.

When Mik turned back to his captain, his voice was barely audible. "I can hear two people talking. Let's try Vist's technique to make sure."

Tom nodded. They closed their eyes and held their breath for a whole minute. This works better when no one is punching you in the face at the same time. Tom allowed himself to become aware of the background noise, the rustling winds in the bush and the creak of dead trees. He pressed his ear against the wall and heard dripping water behind it. Tom channelled his focus to the wall's stone and sent it forwards. Now he could hear those voices too – one male and one female.

He concentrated all his attention on those voices and heard the words.

"... for about an hour. Then I will go and look for him myself," the woman said.

"As you wish, but he should have replaced me ages ago. Forgive me, Lord! Sister Volna, I am hungry and am starting to think something is seriously wrong in the dungeons. I have not seen any of my brothers wandering by the court."

"Don't worry, Brother Mark. I will pass your concerns on to Father Deessa, who will deal with them. Right now, I need you to ensure that no one disturbs the Word-Bearer for an hour or two. I will order Len to find you a second beer and Father Deessa's second portion of worm stew."

The woman laughed, and the door slammed shut, almost like a clap of thunder. Tom jerked, sighed and opened his eyes. It looked like the Cruiser called Mark was now alone at his post. Mik had already disappeared behind the wall curve. Tom started after him and soon arrived at the door a few metres away. Mik sat on the chest of a short stocky man in his prime with a red face. The man couldn't move his arms, but his legs frantically kicked the air and the ground he lay on. He obviously could not call for help as he had trouble breathing, but Mik's hands let go of his throat only when he stopped struggling. Tom picked up an axe, which belonged to the man called Brother Mark, and let it fly over the concrete fence.

"Careful Mik," he said and crouched next to the man's head, "if the novice boy spoke the truth, this is the last guard in this settlement. This time *you* will overdo it."

"You know I won't," Mik answered and woke the Cruiser up with two rather mean slaps on both red cheeks. "Mark? Are you alright, sweetheart? Wakey-wakey. My captain wants to talk to you."

Mark gasped for air for a few seconds, coughed and opened his eyes. He looked terrified, but there had to be a reason for him to be appointed to such an important post. The man tensed all his muscles up and freed his right arm. He must have been trying to reach his lower back when Mik took him by surprise. A small dagger was clenched in Mark's white fingers. The Cruiser roared hoarsely then tried to bury the blade in Mik's thigh but only managed to cut it.

Mik was faster. He twisted Mark's wrist with his left hand, causing him to drop his weapon, and with his right fist, Mik broke the Cruiser's nose and split his brow.

Tom recoiled. "Oh, man! Control your prisoner. Pick him up before he drowns."

The round face was covered in blood.

"Not bad!" Mik said to the man, "A couple of centimetres to the left, and you would have severed the artery. Where did you learn to do that?" He turned the Cruiser face down like a sack and held him with his knee, "Let me guess. Your father taught you to be a guard. He was a deserter from the space trooper regiment, wasn't he?"

Tom picked up the dagger and leaned over the Cruiser again. "All I want from you is a little update. You see, Mark? Okay, I will call you Mark. You know who we are. We have been away for a while. Can you be so kind as to tell me the political situation in these parts? Also, I am curious about the evacuation stage for both sides, unless there are more than two plans."

"I won't talk to sinners," said the Cruiser.

"Really? That's a pity. Your brother Big Pete and I had a lengthy and very productive conversation about what I was up to. Now he is too busy contemplating what he heard, and I was left with no choice but to seek your help."

Mark groaned and puffed in response. But he did not try to get away anymore. His face swelled up and changed colour from red to ... something more common among the citizens of Gera.

"Okay, let's speak your language. If you don't talk to me, I will ask my friend to hurt you more. Then we will go upstairs and—"

"No!" the Cruiser shouted and tried to get up. "You must not disturb him! Father Patrick is the Great Word-Bearer. You will anger the Lord, and we all will die on the spot."

Mik pressed his knee harder into the Cruiser's back.

"So what is it going to be, brother? Shall I bind you or kill you?"

"I will tell you only what everyone knows. But don't expect me to tell you any secrets. I would rather die and join the Lord prematurely."

Mik pulled a cable tie from his pocket and fastened both of Mark's hands behind his back.

"Where did you get so many of those?" Tom asked.

"Borrowed from Judaea, the twin," Mik replied.

Mik got up, turned Mark on his back and dragged him away from the door by his legs. "Don't be noisy," he said to his prisoner when Mark tried to protest.

Tom followed them to the sunny side of the tower and found a spectacular view of a real sunset. The building stood on a high cliff. You could see the endless forest that used to be a sea bed from this spot. On the horizon, the thin line of the ocean was barely visible, and it glowed under the sun like molten gold. A few clouds added to all of this, a series of horizontal lines with different colours and brightness.

Mik pulled the brother up and leaned him against the wall. Tom found disinfectants and elastic bandages in his aid kit and passed them to Mik for his cut.

"How bad is it?" he asked.

"I will live," Mik answered, and after dealing with his wound, he searched the Cruiser, saying, "Here is a nice and quiet corner where you will answer all my friend's questions. I will be back in a few minutes, and if he is not happy, you will join your brothers since I can't guarantee your meeting with your Lord. Now I'll have these keys, thank you!"

Chapter 18. 3411. Out in Space – Shafran

This room was almost an architectural building. The four largest spheres we have seen so far were cut and joined into the shape of the quatrefoil. I wondered how long it had taken for Shafran's subjects to chisel them into shape, smoothen and join the edges, and make the one large and almost square hall with rounded corners. Blobster salt was as solid as a rock. Without modern tools, this would be a task our ancestors had to face when they built pyramids and castles. The labour had to be well encouraged by reward or fear.

The raised floor was made of grey clay tiles. The whole ceiling was covered with a network of glowing garlands. The room was brightly lit with thousands of luminous buds of this climbing plant that Professor Miteck called *dryadalis qui laternis*.

In the middle of the room, we saw a long, very low table, just a couple of feet above the ground. Some simply dressed people were busy loading it with food. The urgency in their movements indicated that they had received their orders at rather short notice. There were bowls and boards, clay jars and strange bottles that looked like they were made of a large dry fruit shaped like a leathery pear but longer and brown. The local food looked colourful, but there was little variety of dishes: a couple of types of fruit, some kind of bright-yellow crumbling bread, grains and herbs, deep seashells filled with greenish oil, fried white sea animals that could have been a bizarre-looking fish, prawn and serpent at the same time. Small pink chunks on skewers were probably meat and there was one huge bowl of something that looked like giant frogs' eggs. This bowl was placed in the middle of the table with extra care and ceremony.

After the table had been laid, a few villagers, including the over-excited but now very timid Gareth, stayed in the room behind the High Martyr's chair, nervously giggling and looking at the food with the mercury-coloured eyes of a hungry beggar. Only two people, besides the High Martyr himself, behaved differently. The young, friendly Massimo stood by the table ready to assist, and the old woman in the corner with the face of a deeply insulted cleaning lady in the embassy quarters of Mars.

"Please, make yourself at home," said Shafran, pointing at the scattered cylindrical cushions on both sides of the table. He took his seat at the head of the table, which looked like a broad legless throne.

"I expected to see salt orbs even here, serving as a dinner set," said the captain quietly.

But Massimo, who happened to be right behind him, answered, "We tried that, but they spoil the taste of food," he smiled. His teeth were too good for this village. He offered me his hand and helped me to sit down. His skin was also not as rough as I expected; it was darker than that of the other villagers, but his smooth cheeks were those of a man who eats well. He continued, "Nevertheless, they are excellent for storing fish and meat. Salt keeps them fresh for many cycles."

Tom looked at Massimo, took his place by my side on the cushion pile, and asked, "So what is the chef's recipe of the day here?"

Steven did not sit down but stood behind me with a straight back and his arms crossed across his chest. Shafran was watching us. Massimo was answering and, at the same time, helping us to get comfortable at the table, moving cushions around and covering our knees with long homespun towels. "The bread is chewy, but it is a good source of energy. The sea dweller was boiled in six fresh waters, so it is not as salty as the one you can get outside these walls. Try those bark flakes dipped in spicy oil if you like sweet food. They are hard to come by, Your Grace."

"And what is that?" asked Tom, picking a conical bluish fruit the size of a peach but as solid as a melon.

"Tock! My absolute favourite!" said Shafran, "Don't you have tocks in your parts? We dig them up from the shore sands further away from Laguna. No one knows how to grow them within the village grounds, but hopefully, in one lucky cycle, we will get a newcomer who will be a gardener or farm herbalist. I would love to grow enough for every villager," he said, then he picked up one of the tocks, rolled it between his palms, pierced it with the skewer, and lifted it above his open mouth. A thick whitish liquid slowly poured onto his tongue. Shafran swallowed and continued, "Your visit was unexpected, so we had no time to slaughter a goat in your honour, but if you stay longer, we will have a goat or at least an egg-laying bird. Oh yes! Our caviar will not let you forget this meal. It is an outstanding delicacy of all times, I have heard. A true sign from the Lord that this land is indeed our new paradise."

"A dish of all times?" Tom looked puzzled.

"Correct me if I am wrong," I said to Shafran, "but my priest is probably referring to a dainty of ancient Earth. Certain fish eggs used to be appreciated in the early times for their unusual taste and rarity. They were not to everyone's liking but prestigious when served on the elite table. How did you learn about them?"

"Every legend has some truth in it. My predecessor left us historical records about how the Lord marked the right place for us to reward loyalty with pleasures. Those records describe many pleasures true believers can be rewarded with – food that makes your stomach happy, a drink that does the same to the head. The knowledge has passed to your loyal servant also by the wish of the Lord." He bowed his head slightly and his smile widened. "I have answered your question. But I also want to know how *you* know about fish eggs. I don't believe you have had a chance to see the same records since you are a stranger to our land."

Safran looked at me with a friendly but intense expression.

I returned his look. "We both have the same origin and the same history. Why shouldn't we both learn it? Records are just one of the Lord's ways of passing on knowledge. Would you not agree, my priest?"

Shafran was clearly not stupid. He frowned for a second and smiled again. "Of course! The Lord is omniscient. He sends the same message to all his children. And I want to know how he speaks to you?" Shafran's eyes moved from my face to Steven's and stopped on Captain Darkwood. "Are you the leader of this expedition?"

Tom understood my game and played along. "I am a leader of the holy guardians assigned to protect honoured pilgrims. I am not the one to know the true cause of their mission. I am not to be tempted to judge their goals."

He looked at me, trying to ascertain how impressed I was. Well done, *mon capitaine*!

The High Martyr spoke again. "I see you have a holy test of your own, Your Honour. What about you, young man?" he said, looking at Steven. "Are you a guard too, no doubt? I see you are also here to protect your priest?" He looked at me again with increasing curiosity and muttered to himself, "Priest or Priestess? This strange voice, I can't explain it."

He looked at Steven again expectantly, but the young trooper had also chosen the part for himself to play. He pressed his lips firmly together. His eyes opened wide, expressing a total disengagement from reality.

It looked like Tom had also never saw Steven looking so stupid and determined at the same time, so he eyed him intently and said, "Permission to answer is granted, soldier."

Steven relaxed a little and said with the same dull expression, "My assignment is to follow orders and to protect my grace with my life. I am to starve for my grace, I am to burn for my grace, I am to die for my grace, I am to kill ..." with these last words, Steven stared at the High Martyr, "for my Grace!"

Shafran's face turned a little paler than it already was. The silent group of followers became even more silent. The old woman Kendra moved deeper into the shadow behind Shafran's throne.

The High Martyr pulled himself together and looked at me again. "Tell me, Your Grace. Are you a governor of your settlement, then? I have heard about the mechanical voice of your ancestors, which was described a lot like the one you speak with. It fascinates me!" Shafran said, carefully examining my robe and Steven's uniform from a distance, "Where is your settlement? Your clothing and ... things tell me that you have won."

"Won?" Tom looked at me.

"Oh, I am so rude. Eat first!" Shafran put his palms up. The tock juice was dripping off his fingers, "Eat, rest! We will talk in good time. Here, start with this sea-dweller meat." He picked one of the skewers with pink chunks and offered it to Tom, who was closer to him.

I was relieved to see that none of my comrades had moved.

I put my hand up, signalling my declining the invitation, and said, "Many thanks, but our fasting commitment does not allow us to be distracted by food. You tempt us with this wonderful nourishment, but the Lord sends us this test for a reason, which we gladly accept as a challenge to gain his favour."

Shafran froze for a moment, then took one chunk off the skewer with his teeth and said, chewing at the same time, "I have no choice but to respect such devotion to your cause. I know fasting was a popular way to honour the Lord in the old times. I am happy to say I can at least contribute to your test and prolong your temptation in the name of the Lord's glory. And if you don't eat, surely you have to drink. Does your test include dehydration? Let me pour you the nectar of this Eden. The pears of its garden bring you closer to the Lord."

Shafran lifted the ceramic cup as if to make a toast.

"I am sure they do, but we are humble pilgrims. We are under an oath that does not allow us to consume anything that can cloud our minds. The punishment will be severe. As you know, the Lord can see everything. Nevertheless,

I am grateful for your offer. We drank plenty of blessed holy water on our journey. Thank you once again."

Shafran's face changed expression with every word spoken, from understanding to cheeky flamboyance, then to sharp realisation and finally – acceptance. He nodded with regret and in total agreement, looking down at his cup.

"The will of the Lord is respected here. My heart is glad that you follow his directions so thoroughly. Tell me, my dear guest. Is your friend outside also under oath? I ordered some food and drink for him."

Tom's face became tense, but I spoke first once again, "Then you have to call it back unless you warned him that your flask contains fermented juice that is highly alcoholic and, perhaps, has strong hallucinogens. If you did not, the honest gesture could be misunderstood. You might upset him."

Shafran again looked at Steven and then at one of his followers, who immediately disappeared through the front door. Tolyan was not a fool, but I wanted to see what would happen if I threatened Shafran again. I think he started to get our message. He made another sign to his servants, and they began removing the food and drinks from the table as promptly as they had served it earlier.

"I must admit," he said, "that despite my full understanding, I am deeply hurt by your decline of our hospitality."

"I can apologise and thank you again."

"Oh, but you can do more than that. You can satisfy my innocent curiosity and tell me about your quest. This is also a matter of great importance for my people and their faith. What are you seeking in the White City? You have still said nothing about your home and about yourself. Give me something, for goodness' sake!"

"I will tell what my Lord allows me to reveal to a stranger. When I am done, you will honour the Lord by giving us directions to the White City and assisting us so we can continue our pilgrimage. On the way back, we might *possibly* share your food and drink with you, and I would be delighted to exchange more stories about our cultures. Believe me, my priest, I want to know about you as much as you want to know about me!" I leaned forwards and gave him a smile of my own; one he could misinterpret in dozens of ways. I added, "The Lord might grant us the pleasure of such an exchange beyond imagination. Our Lord rewards nothing more than patience."

Shafran emptied his cup in one mouthful but swallowed his drink with effort.

"Your words are making me drunker than these dream-pears. But, Your Grace, isn't it true that our Lord teaches us to fight temptation? How do we balance patience and endurance?"

I sat back and replied, "You are the High Martyr. The Lord has already marked you with the power to hear his wishes. He sent me to the White City and placed you on my way to it. This means that you are part of my quest. I will complete it with your help, and we will celebrate together. My people have a lot to offer."

The High Martyr eyed me with new interest. It looked like Shafran had made up his mind about me.

He talked again, and with every word, there was more and more lust in his voice, "As you can see for yourself, we are a small and humble settlement. We are nothing more than servants of the Lord. We trust his way of deliverance and completely rely on his guidance. We use his gifts to build our modest shelter, to fill our guts with the manna of this New Eden. We make clothing with what he provides, and he protects us better than our parents. And we would be fully sustainable as a society if it wasn't for the selfishness of certain neighbours who keep the best Lord's gifts for themselves. They have everything else, but we have the truest gift of all. Our love! Love is the answer. It will bring us to our Lord and to each other."

Shafran looked excited but I suspected he would not forget his own immediate desire so easily.

"Now tell me what you can!" he said, "I want to know what your needs in the White City are, and – most importantly – where you from are?"

"Your words are as tempting as everything else you have offered to me. Very well! Here it is, my priest. We are from another city. Call it Dark Rock. It is cold, and survival there is hard. We want to relocate, and with the Lord's help, we heard of the White City. Maybe we will all go there one cycle, but so far, it is my quest to travel there with great hope of finding the truth, of learning about their faith and of learning whether the prosperity of the city, technology and medications are truly granted by the true god or ... by his rival."

Shafran's voice sounded squeaky. "I can tell you all that! You don't need to go to the city. In fact, your very lives will be in grave danger there! You have to know this!" Shafran almost got up from his throne. His face went crimson, and he started to talk frantically. "The White City citizens – we call them Otekans – indeed worship a false deity. They are corrupted by selfishness and a lack of care for their own brothers. They enslave each other; the strong make the weak work beyond their strength. There is no peace, no rest but constant labour and the battle of those who can do more and take more: a battle between lucky people and those who haven't done anything to deserve such discrimination. There is no equality. Otekans do not care for anything holy or for anything truly spiritual. They don't care for the pure eternal soul or for unconditional love. They despise any deep feelings. To be emotional, to feel, is almost a sin. They are cold and cruel in their judgement. There is no shared opportunity; there is no fair chance for those born unfortunates. They worship a goddess of mockery. O'Teka hides in her temple and offers no guidance; she does not speak to all with the same word, and she doesn't treat people evenly. She has no priests to unite the community or to teach her true meaning to those who might be confused or not very smart. Everyone interprets her words as they please, even their young ones do this! Imagine all the wrong interpretations and heresy! There is no order but great chaos in the human mind! They create and grow abominations among themselves and ..." Shafran stopped and dropped his shoulders in apparent despair. Now he looked consumed by sadness. "Unfortunately, their numbers are great, and the ancestors' technology is under their control. There was a time when some of us managed to escape, but Otekans did not share technology that would allow us to build better houses or to get more food. If only we could overpower them as we did a few generations ago. Your Grace! Don't go there, I beg of you! Not yet! I will do my best, Your Grace, to save you time and tell you anything you need to know. I am bound to tell the truth in the name of the Lord!"

He looked at me with a true plea in his eyes.

I turned to face him. "And I would believe you. But if you were in my place, would that be enough for you, or would you want to see such an important tragedy with your own eyes? I understand your subjects need you to interpret the meanings of the Lord's word, but do you honestly think I need it too?"

I looked right into his eyes again. Tom sat next to me and coughed briefly. I was convinced he concealed a chuckle. From the corner of my eye, I noticed Massimo's white teeth as he flashed a brief grin. Shafran frowned a little. His pupils were so dilated that his bluish eyes looked almost black.

"So you still want to go? I pray, don't. Stay with us, join us," he said and looked at Steven, standing still like a beautiful stone statue. Shafran carried on, "You are obviously a race of great warriors. You have the technology to make good clothing and probably many more great things. Together with your people, we may prosper, become stronger and even take over the city. With their energy devices, we can do everything. All the people of Gera will have enough food and shelter. I believe our Lord wants to restore the balance and remove the injustice. You spoke the truth – it was his will and deed to bring you to me, to us!"

Here it is. He is about to say those words.

"You and I can rule this world together! Lead our people along the path of the true children of our only sovereign, together!"

Yes. He said that. How predictable.

I sighed. "It is as it is. We are strong, and we have everything. We have better quarters and food. We have fast transport and luxurious ways to celebrate," I said, and Shafran's face brightened for a short moment. "Although we are not so much warriors but traders. Let me ask you, what can you offer in return? What do you trade?"

He appeared to be thinking when the old woman Kendra bent over his ear and whispered something while looking at me malevolently. Shafran smiled again.

"I am sure we have something you want. My adviser reminds me that my followers are still waiting for their share of food and rest. I say, let us all rest! The sleeping hours are upon us, and we all need to close our eyes and dream of the Lord's blessing. Your Grace! You are welcome to stay in my home; you will be safe here. Your guards will be welcomed into the best houses in the village. There are women and soft beds. Everything for you to relax and cool your feet."

I had to interrupt him.

"My priest, I am grateful again, endlessly, but I also have to remind you that we are in a hurry. We have rested greatly· in your lovely home and in your company. The conversation was most enlightening. I feel warned and prepared now for the unknown. But we have to be on the move."

Tom got up and helped me to rise in my role of sovereignty. Shafran also jumped up. He looked lost and was obviously struggling to remain calm and hospitable. His face almost reflected the hatred in the eyes of old Kendra, who was no longer in the room.

"Fine!" He said and forced another smile, "Since Your Grace is almost as stubborn as me, I will keep my word and show you the way. When you leave the village go east, away from Laguna.

You need to make your way between the hills and follow the stream. You must have crossed it if you came from the north."

"We have seen the bridge, Your Grace. Thank you once again."

Captain Darkwood also said his thanks, and Steven nodded silently. Massimo accompanied us outside, and we found Tolyan surrounded by a small group of villages staring at him as if he were a museum exhibit. Tolyan's pose was exactly the same as Steven's in the palace. I wondered if Mik and Général would have naturally assumed the same pose if they had been here. We needed to regroup with them all, but our deception plan had to go on a little longer until we were left alone. Our friends, of course, heard everything and will make their own way towards the hills. The villagers did not follow us far. Whether they lost interest, got hungry or had to follow a sleep schedule, I don't know. But Massimo walked with us for another few hundred steps, pointed towards the hills, and wished us farewell. We walked forwards slowly until he vanished from sight.

Then we stopped and waited. Général, Mik, Rod and Zina did not make us wait for too long. They expressed their opinions about the villagers and the High Martyr, and then they congratulated us all, especially Steven, on our great acting skills and had many questions for us.

Soon Général looked at Captain Darkwood and at me, then asked, "What now? Where to? The east?"

"Of course not," I said.

Tom nodded, "Vist is right. No way did Shafran show us the right way. First, he tried to drug us, scare us, seduce us, and finally – separate us. So I assume he is about to send his men after us if they are not waiting between those hills already."

"I doubt he will send someone to ambush us or risk an open attack. He could see that his men are not a match for our 'great warriors,'" said Steven, grinning.

"What about an armed spy who will try and cut our throats in our sleep?" said Mik. "He doesn't know that our numbers have doubled, but it can just take one blade and a bit of stealth to—"

"I cannot imagine any villager coming close enough to you. Even if we have no one standing on guard, you will sense the spy in your sleep before he finds us. And so will all my lads," said Général with pride and almost indignation in his voice.

"So where shall we go from here?" Rod asked.

"And where is the guide we were promised?" Zina asked.

"My advice is to carry on south," I said, "I am sure we are still to meet our guide."

"I am hungry," said Steven, "those sea-dweller kebabs looked rather good."

"We will stop for a break in one hour," said the captain. "We need to be a good distance away from Shafran and his tricks. Also, we need our sleeping hours too."

We resumed our journey as soon as our backpacks had been divided between us once again. We walked in line, crossing the meadow. The tall grass was thick, and we left a long furrow. My hope was that the strong wind would cover our trail. The clouds above thickened and fell down as short-lasting rain. The soft grey soil absorbed the water almost as fast as the hot wind dried everything up. Soon we re-entered the woods and found a place to stop. We had a lot to talk about. After all, we had made our first contact and a rather disappointing one. Captain and Steven were busy describing the village and the feast to the rest of our group. Tolyan told us about his own experience of the village. He saw a small herd of goats brought back from the meadow for milking. They all shone with a hint of bronze, and their devilish eyes were like tiny mirrors. He saw four fishermen pushing a cart with some sea creatures they caught in the tidal trap. He counted about fifty people approximately the same age as Gareth, and half a dozen younger people in their thirties. If there were any small children, Tolyan had not cast eyes on them. The villagers were mostly men, and a few were older men. He said that someone from the palace came to him with a tray, but he made that little purple woman disappear by growling at her. The troopers laughed and made jokes about this little adventure. Tom appeared to be deep in thought. Zina and Rod argued about possible reasons for the colonies' degradation,

and I could not stop thinking about one word our
host dropped during the visit – won?

Chapter 19. 3416. Back on Earth – Mik

Using the key he took from Mark, Mik entered the tower and locked the door from the inside. He heard rhythmic beats as if someone had just started playing a heavy music record upstairs. The spiral staircase took him to the second level, which had one round dining room with a round table in the middle and a very round and very drunk man in a fine, dark mazarine robe that was identical to the one they took off Father Ontha. The man sat at the table with his face pressed against a platter of wild berries. He was snoring. He obviously had, at some point, let go of the glass of wine lying next to his hand. The wine dripped from the edge of the tablecloth. Each drop sparkled like a ruby bead as it passed through the narrow ray of the low sun.

There were several dirty bowls and spoons on the table, a pot of yesterday's worm stew judging by the smell, a few slices of bread on the plate, and some empty bottles.

Mik watched the man for some time until the light was gone, and a cold draught entered the room like a thief through the small castle window.

Mik approached the man and said into his ear, "Hey! Are you Deessa?"

The man did not react. His condition was not one of pretence.

"Do yourself a favour and sleep a little longer," Mik said and left the room. He ascended the stairs towards the music source and passed two more levels with empty bedrooms. He found few wooden beds with straw mattresses and pillows, simple furniture and no sign of any technology.

"Nothing here either, no computers, no radio transmission systems, not even a good old telegraph," Mik said after he finished searching the second bedroom. "Brothers and fathers, how do you communicate with other congregations from here?"

He approached the vanity table and picked up a small syringe with a few milligrams of the creamy liquid still in it. After dropping the syringe and crushing it under his foot, Mik looked at his reflection in the mirror. His skin glistened demonically in the darkened room. Two stiff swirls of wire-like hair stuck out like horns. Mik grinned, turned his chest-worn flashlight off, closed his eyes, and listened. Some sounds were coming from the loft room above his head. The musical beat was much louder now, but now Mik could hear something else. Someone screamed, but the sound was muffled. Mik moved swiftly and soundlessly, reaching the top of the tower in a few seconds. He stopped by the loft door, which was made for a much shorter person, and listened again.

Now he could hear the female voice clearly. "Lord's mercy upon you, my master! More pain, more suffering for the forgiveness of our sins. Pray for our souls, I beg of you!"

There was a sound of air whistling, followed by a high-pitched scream. Mik carefully pushed the door, allowing the music to fill his ears. The door opened slowly, revealing a scene Mik did not expect. Maybe a bed with two crazy lovers, or a woman being tortured by a sadistic mystic – a sacrificial ritual of some sort? He was not sure of what he expected.

At the far wall, a fire burned brightly in a large marble fireplace that looked completely mismatched in the loft. Against its background, Mik clearly saw the black silhouette of a huge cross built of two railway sleepers in the centre of the room. It stood in the middle of a circle of candles, but they were faint against the bright hearth. Loud and very old techno music flooded the room, coming from some ancient player with a single speaker. Mik saw a dancing woman in her thirties between the fireplace and the cross. She was naked; her body was painted below her breasts and above her knees with intricate stripes of red, gold and silver paint. Long black hair was loose over her shoulders. She stopped dancing and kneeled before the cross. Mik could not understand what she was doing at first. It looked like she was kissing the cross repeatedly. The cross was partially draped with red chiffon, obscuring the full view.

A minute later, the woman got up and picked up a small whip from the floor. With her left hand, she wiped her mouth, then she raised her right hand and said "Pay for our sins with your torment!" as she flogged the cross, making that airy whistling sound as she did so. In that moment, Mik realised that someone was crucified on the other side of the cross, facing the fireplace. This someone screamed with pain and then groaned with obvious pleasure. The woman roared indignantly when she spotted Mik squeezing through the door, bending slightly.

When he lifted his head and looked at her, she screamed again in horror, dropped the whip, and grabbed her blue robe from the floor. As soon as Mik went around the cross on one side, she sneaked to the door on the other side, wrapping the robe around herself as she went. She looked at Mik with her large eyes, like a person who was afraid and defiant at the same time. Mik did not stop her, and she soon disappeared behind the door mumbling some kind of prayer or threat.

Now Mik stood in front of the cross and looked disgusted at the crucified man, who was tied to sleepers with thick rope around his wrists and ankles. He did not hang on the cross but stood with both feet on the floor. He was stark naked, still aroused, incredibly slim, and he could not move at all. He looked the same age as the escaped woman. His sweaty skin was dark but much lighter than Mik's. He had long hair and a short beard; his spread arms were covered in countless black dots left by a needle. His thighs were striped and reddened by the whip, and his head hung down. As the man slowly lifted his head, his manhood drooped. Mik thought that two surprises in one day were more than he would normally have in a year. The eyes that looked out at him from under thick bushy eyebrows were the eyes of a mad man. The man's wet, bony face was distorted by a mocking grimace. He squinted short-sightedly and started to shake and jerk like a fly in a cobweb.

"Brother Patrick, I presume?" Mik started but was rudely interrupted.

"You have come ... You have come, you demon!" The man shook so violently that Mik expected him to fall together with his cross, but the structure was well fixed and didn't budge. The man howled, "Go-o-o-o ba-a-ack! You can't take me-e-e-e ... I belong to my Lord! Yes, demon ... I am his loyal son! I am here to pay for their sins! You ... Satan! Go away, son of a whore!"

"Hey, stop it!" Mik said and took a step back, dodging the well-aimed spit, "What's wrong with you?"

"A-a-a-a! Somebody help me-e-e-e!"

The man's eyes rolled back, and he now shouted as he threw his head to the right and left, almost to the beat of the music.

Mik looked around. The loft was full of bedroom attributes but without a bed. He found a basin bowl and a jar of water on the bedside table. He emptied it on the man's head. The Word-Bearer did not stop screaming and shouting unpleasantries. Mik even picked up the whip but thought better of it and dropped it, wiping his hands on his trousers. Finally, he sat on the short bench by the wall, far enough from the Cruiser and his saliva, and waited.

He did not have to wait long. One music track ended, and the next one started. Mik could not tell if it was different or the same record. Soon, the Word-Bearer's struggle slowed, his cursing turned into a faint mumble, and he dropped his head and went limp.

"Tired?" Mik asked, as he got up and turned the music player's volume down. "Ready to talk?"

The man on the cross jerked once but did not look up.

"I take that as a yes," Mik continued, wondering if there was any point. "Are you Patrick?"

The Cruiser jerked again but added, "Patrick ... Patrick is the name the woman gave me when I was cut free from her filthy bowels."

"Excellent. You're on the cross for the sake of … what?"

"The sins, the sins of many … My brother died on the cross. He wasn't the first. Before him, my older brother, chained to a rock, paid with his liver for the people he loved. I have to suffer on the cross, day and night … forever and ever and ever!"

Patrick lifted his eyes towards the ceiling and started to hit the cross with the back of his head.

"Suffer? I thought this is what you perverts do for fun!" said Mik with a certain discomfort in his throat, followed by the taste of stomach acid at the thought of what that woman did to this man. The trooper had not eaten much, had had no rest for two days, and was starting to feel a little lightheaded. The cut on his leg bled again. The fire died out, and the smell of smoke was pleasant, overpowering the stench of sweat, sex, drugs and urine in the small room. Now the only light in the room was produced by dozens of candles around the cross.

"Day and night, week after week, year after year, with only my Lord and Father to talk to," mumbled Patrick, swinging his head again.

Mik felt another wave of nausea. Is this what the Word-Bearer meant? They used this poor madman as their own personal Jesus Christ, interpreting his gibberish to fool others and maybe even themselves. How long had he been crucified for? He spoke of days, weeks and years. How can that be possible? Not without a daily dose of Bliss, surely.

"What about that woman?"

"No-o-o-o. No more of her. Temptress, sinner! Who-o-o-ore! She tempts me, she hurts me, pinches me, bites me, pulls my..." The man tensed again and started to cry. Real tears rolled down his concave cheeks.

This face was covered in sweat, perhaps mixed with tears. Had he cried before? Had Mik mistaken the cry of real pain for moans of pleasure?

What am I to do with you? Mik thought, but he did not say anything out loud. Should he put the poor creature out of his misery or set him free? Mik was unsure of whether he was ready to take on a burden like this. He could not even think clearly in his current state. In any case, he needed to deal with two more Cruisers downstairs. He would need help to get the mad and unpredictable man out of here. What if he doesn't just spit but also bites? Mike decided he should return with the captain or with Tolyan if the big trooper was up and about. He got up and limped towards the door.

Chapter 20. 3411. Out in Space – May

I was not listening to him anymore ... we were not alone here. All the noises and voices in my head were mixed into clouds that I pushed away and left outside of the imaginary clear tunnel. The tube of my tunnel appeared like a growing stem and rushed in one direction and picked up human breathing and a heartbeat ... two heartbeats ... three.

"Vist? Did you hear me?"

Without moving a muscle and still staring at the fire, Vist suddenly said, "We have visitors."

Everyone instantly became quiet and motionless. Three troopers looked at Vist, then at each other. Tolyan nodded at Général.

Mik said, "Not a threat."

"I can hear one," said Steven.

"There are two over there." Vist's head turned to the left and green eyes peered through the wood's shadows. "But we only need one more cup."

Everyone followed Vist's gaze.

"Come out," called Tom, "we are not hostile."

That someone was further away than Tom thought. They all waited for a long minute while Général grumbled about civilians having better scanning accuracy than his lads did. Unthinkable!

The girl appeared behind the tree and stopped, letting everyone see her in full light. Her side bulged with a broad sling; a child about eight months old was strapped to its mother's body. The girl was a child herself, no more than seventeen years old. Zina pulled a spare cup out of her bag and filled it up from the pot. Rod got up from the mat and offered the girl his place, settling himself down on Tolyan's bed-pack.

"It looks like we have two guests for sure," said Tom before adding, "You are here for a reason. We saw you at Gareth's house, didn't we?"

Indeed, it was the same girl Gareth had offered Tom a few hours ago. He saw her for just a few seconds, but it was the same unevenly chopped hair, short dress and thin coat of the same rough, unstained fabric, and the same uncertain look on her face. Although she had looked more worried the first time they had seen her.

"You are not afraid of us," said Vist's metallic voice, and the girl's eyes opened wider. "What are you afraid of?"

"I don't want to be found here," said the girl with lilac skin, "and I am afraid you will say no."

Her voice sounded deep, boyish and not frightened at all but concerned.

"No? What do you wish to ask of us?" Tom said.

"You are going to the White City. Please take my child with you."

"Just the child?" Tom asked.

The girl looked at her baby with tenderness.

"I won't be accepted there. I never heard of anyone who left and was then taken back."

"Weren't you born in the village?"

The girl sat down on Rob's mat and took the cup from Zina with both hands.

"I only knew one who was and lived to grow up. This place is not good for children. Nadezhda is my third daughter; the first two didn't survive. Agonya was born too early, but there are no incubators in the village. White City has them, though. Tristeza died two months after birth. I have learned enough to keep this one alive, but I am not sure how long I can do it for. I keep her in the cave, not at home. Father and his guests don't like the noises she makes. Grand, the leader of the colony, will be over the Moon and back when he sees you! You are from Earth, aren't you?"

"We are!" the captain answered, astonished.

Now everyone could see how different this girl was from everyone else they had met in the village. She did not have that glazed look in her eyes. She did not beg; she did not have that nervous laughter covering up her true feelings. She did not say a single word for no reason. She did not say more or less than was needed at the time. She waited for their questions.

Zina asked the first one, "What is your name?"

"May. This food is delicious, thank you. What is it?"

"This is potato soup," said Zina. "If you like it, you can have more. Let me hold your baby, and you go ahead and help yourself to those nutritious bars too. Oh! Is your baby sparkling?" Zina gently brushed the sleeping girl's cheek with her finger and looked at May, "When I saw you, I thought you were wearing make-up or some kind of purple ritualistic paint. Vist? What is it?"

"I don't know. I am sure we will find out soon enough."

Obviously, this girl was hungry and had probably never had a chance to fill up properly before now. She was beautiful in her youth and resembled a fairy-tale creature in a magic forest. Her skin looked so delicate and thin as if its lilac colour resulted not from some pigment but from the blood vessels under it. Tiny reflective scales sparked in the areas of her body that are usually exposed to the sun the most. Her dark hair had the same shine as those scales, and her irises looked as if they were made of mother-of-pearl. And yet this almost elfish creature was a human girl who sniffed and squinted with pleasure, as all teenagers do when they eat something delicious.

"Tell us your story, May. Tell us about White City," said Tom after May emptied the third cup and asked for no more.

And this human girl started her narrative by the campfire so far from Earth. She spoke easily, without waffle or repetition, as if she were reading a book. Everyone listened and tried not to interrupt when possible. Rod recorded her story in the log and transmitted it to the *Wasp*. This was the second contact and the second description of the White City they had heard that day.

May was born in the city just like everyone else there. She and the other kids spent most of their time at school, learning, playing, trying various skills, discovering personal talents, making friends, listening to music, dancing, exploring outside the city walls, researching, and growing into people with purpose.

Family time was priceless, although she could see that her parents were somehow different. They seem to prefer to spend time with

May separately. The older May grew, the more she became convinced that something was wrong. She was concerned, as she loved both of her parents. She asked her mother, "Are you happy?" Her mother seemed surprised but not by the question. May asked about such serious things at the very start of her adolescence.

"Not completely," replied her mother. "But I am happy that I have you and that you are doing so well. I am happy that I have another very productive cycle at work and that my garden is in blossom."

"But?" May asked.

"I am afraid your dad has changed too much. I am worried," her mother said.

"What is wrong?" asked May.

Mother looked sad, "I think he deceived me. I think he invested enough in our family and has now decided to be himself."

May did not understand much, but when her father wanted to spend time together, she asked him the same question. Her father was flicking through a list of shows in his amulet.

"Where is it? Where is it? Here! Classic stuff. I know you don't like it, but I do. Try for my sake to have a good time."

"Father, I just asked you..."

"I heard. The answer is – no. No, no and no. How could I be happy in this cage? I can't do anything. I hate my job. I have to break my back for every scrap of pleasure. Oh, just stop that. Why are you looking at me like this?"

"I thought you loved baking. Mum told me you used to be the best in the whole district."

"Damn right. I was in love with your mother, so I tried very hard. Do you think she would have coupled up with me if I had made no effort? So practical! So calculating. So romantic." He said the last word in a bitter and harsh tone. "But I hated it! Yes, yes, I know. I discovered a new recipe. I once accidentally fell asleep and left the dough on for half a cycle instead of for two hours. I thought it was ruined, but it turned out okay. I did not fancy starting all over, and so I tried to bake it. The bread doubled in size and melted in your mouth. Of course, our nerds became curious and took yeast samples from my supplier. One of them studied it and wrote an article in an issue of 'O'Teka's offerings' about the mutation of the cells. I bet he gained extra credit for my discovery."

"But why couldn't you do that yourself?" May asked.

"Why would I? My job is to make bread. Isn't it?"

"But nobody would have stopped you. The credit would have been yours if the scientists had reassessed and approved your offering."

"Do I look like a writer to you? Anyway, I had already married your mother, and you were on your way. She was not going anywhere."

"But she is not happy."

"She just doesn't love me anymore." Now father looked sad. "She is incapable of maintaining deep feelings for me. She always wants me to do more, learn more and try different things. Never enough. Never satisfied. She is ashamed of me now since she has become a Grand Gardener, but she is also the wife of a simple baker."

May paused and looked up.

"Did you talk to your mother afterwards?" Rod asked.

"Yes," May continued, "Mother said she loved my father and wanted to be with him, but they could not even talk about anything else but his business being ruined by others. By that time, there were about a dozen Grand Food Masters in White City and on the farms. They fed the whole colony and supplied stores and restaurants. All colonists work hard and train school kids on how to build their skills and find their purpose. They are always busy getting supplies, selling products, researching and working with engineers on new tools. Some kids would always love a particular trade for a purpose and build up their own business for it."

"What does purpose actually mean?" asked Général.

"Exactly that. It's something you love doing, a way of express yourself through your work. Most school kids dream of working outside the city on the Empire project. This was a big plan to move further east and west, spread the colony, and build more establishments, farms and towns so that the population could grow more rapidly. Everyone has to find their own purpose. That is why every master will always find one or two apprentices to take over or form a branch. Competition is welcomed in the city."

"So your father did not fit in?" asked Mik.

"No. Mother died in an accident a year later. I was thirteen at the time, and her sisters invited me to move into their house. But they were too late. I did not see my father for two cycles and hoped to see him at the Farewell Ritual, but he reappeared just before with two guards. He said he was leaving the city, because nothing was left for him after my mother's death, and no, he was not forced to leave but wanted to go. The guards allowed him to pack his clothes and food; he had to leave his amulet behind but could take some simple tools, although nothing could be used as a weapon. I cried. I had already lost one parent, and now the other was doing the most horrible thing to himself. If you leave the city, you are banished from returning there forever."

"Tell us more about this banishment," asked Tom.

"It is the worst of what can happen to you if you don't – as your friend put it – fit in. We were told at school from the very start that doing something wrong would harm us one way or another. It is bad manners to say what you don't mean, take what is not yours, cause any deliberate harm to another by action, or use any sort of force. If caught, you have to go to rehabilitation without your amulet, but only once. Rehabilitation consists of an isolated chamber where our coaches talk to you daily about ethics, consequences, values and O'Teka and human history on a different planet called Earth. The sentence can be just a few cycles, or it can be much longer. But you are welcome back, and people don't treat you differently. They might not like you or may avoid you, but they will not talk down to you with contempt. The more calmly you accept the punishment and take it with honour, work harder and improve your skills, the quicker you will re-establish yourself in the city. I know people who lived their lives after one rehabilitation, never got exiled and died with the dignity of old age, surrounded by their loving friends. But there are others. They do wrong again. Maybe more than once, but there are only so many times you can get away with things that are so uncommon. These people *have to* leave."

"How often does that happen?" Zina asked.

"This happens so rarely that even my mother could not remember the last time. But some people choose to leave. On the day they make that decision, they are just as lost as the banished ones. Usually, it will be someone who has already served rehabilitation. They pity themselves, can't stand that feeling of being marked, and see themselves as strangers to the colony. It is just a feeling, but it can overwhelm your reasoning. After a while, they choose to leave and seek themselves outside the city walls. They usually die, get killed by a svoloch, or end up in the Salty Village."

"But your father never served rehabilitation," said Tom.

"That is why no one in my family understood why he was leaving. Father tried and failed to sneak out. He was arrested and went through the usual resignation process. The main principles of city life are: look after yourself, have a purpose in life, don't gain at the cost of others, help the colony to grow and develop, and protect it from harm. So people learn quickly to enjoy life if their purpose is well chosen. Father did not choose well and yet decided not to sell his business and try to find the purpose again."

"Hang on, look after yourself? You are not allowed to look after other people, is that so?" asked Zina, gently cradling May's daughter in her arms.

"Of course you are. It is simply not expected of you or taken for granted. If you look after each other. That is what we call family and friends, don't we?"

"What if you don't have family," asked Général, "and lost your legs in an accident? Are you doomed because you cannot look after yourself?"

"You can," answered May, "and others will look after you if they are grateful, and they have a reason to love and respect you, but mainly because they are able and want to. They don't have to, though. Plus, you will still be able to do something. You just have to find a new purpose. Some people will help you with that too because it benefits everybody. Doctor Hawk will make mech-trousers for you, and you can walk wherever you like. It is a robotic leg that can be plugged directly into your spine. My aunt Shar designs and upgrades a new model every five years. There we have mech-gloves, mech-glasses ..." May's face suddenly lost its glow, and she dropped her head, "I mean ... *they* have."

"Directly into my spine?" Général looked worried.

"So the villagers are the banished ones?" asked Tom, "How did you get here? Did they banish you too?"

"Yes. Because I also left willingly. It does not happen often. If people are exiled for a repeated crime just once in one's lifetime – two or three leave voluntarily every year."

All this time Vist was sitting almost still, deep in thought, occasionally shifting the embers in the fire with a long stick. Then Vist said, "The High Martyr, he suffered the forced exile, didn't he? So, if you leave by force, you are canonised by the villagers, but not if you leave voluntarily. But why did you leave? Did Gareth convince you?"

"Yes. Father was hoping to find the village of the true believers but said he would rather die than never see me again. Father said he was sick of being a slave; the only way was to get out of the white cage. He wished to do what he wanted, and god would look after him this time. I asked father, 'but what about O'Teka?'

He laughed and said, 'She does not look after us, doesn't want anything from you, and doesn't tell you what to do. She is just ... there. And you can come to her if you want, but you are not forced to. What kind of god is that? No leadership whatsoever. Goddess of wisdom? Ha! She gives you wisdom, and that is it. Do what you like with it. She's useless!'"

"So you do have a goddess for a deity." Vist's voice displayed interest. "Do you have a church?"

"Oh yes, a temple. Full of bibles. Billions of files. You can pick a bible there, upload it into your amulet and pray as much as you like."

Chapter 21. 3416. Back on Earth – The Word-Bearer

"Hey, come on, man! It was a joke. I am not crazy, just a bit high. Ha ha! You have to admit, I've got you! Got you, big boy! You have to laugh it off. Don't go, mate! Don't leave me here. I am getting pretty uncomfortable. I need to move my arms and stretch my legs. Untie me, and we will have a good chat. I have wine!"

Mik stopped and looked back over his shoulder. Two perfectly sane, although glistening, eyes were looking directly at him, as far as he could judge in the candlelight. Mik narrowed his eyes at the happily nodding man and said, "You *are* good! You fooled me. I am probably too hungry to think clearly."

"Laugh it off, man. A good prank deserves some credit, right?"

Mik returned to the bench and sat leaning forwards, with his elbows on his knees. He was so tired. The pain in his leg turned into throbbing waves.

"So all this was a fetish, and you are not some ... son of god in captivity."

"Sister Volna is a real professional in her craft. You should try her sometime. But you guessed it – I am a Word-Bearer, Brother Patrick. I am so good at delivering the Lord's word that even the fathers do what I tell them. I am very talented in the art of persuasion, as you can tell from your own experience." Patrick laughed, but he did so with great effort. His position bothered him.

Mik picked up a candle and lifted it to the wrist of the Cruiser. It was too dim, so he dropped it and used his bright flashlight. The Word-Bearer thought Mik was about to cut him down and waited patiently. The wrist was marked with callouses from the rope. It looks like Brother Patrick visited this cross quite often, but after being tied up for an unusually long time, his hands turned violet from the lack of blood supply. All that shaking caused the rope to rub on the skin, blistering it and drawing a few drops of blood. Mik wondered how much pain the binds would have caused the man if he had less Bliss in his system. Mik turned the music volume up to the maximum and walked towards the door again.

"Hey! Come on, man! This is a bit heartless. You can't leave me here to suffer!" The Bearer had to shout over the noise.

Mik stopped.

"Suffering is what you preach," he said without turning back and without worrying about being heard. "Yesterday, I would have killed you without hesitation for what you have chosen to do to other people. This morning my captain showed me that the best way to deal with mystics is not to remove them from your world but remove yourself from theirs. I am leaving you to do exactly what you expect from me and from everyone, but not from yourself. You've made your bed, now lie in it, son of god."

The last words were said at the same moment as the music paused.

"I am the son of god," the Cruiser said, starting at the same time as the music, so it sounded almost like a song, "We all are ... because he is omnipotent and omniscient. If it wasn't for him, none of us would be here. He is the Lord! I am his son, and you must release me! Surely you don't want to repeat our ancestors' mistake and be cursed forever. He is god now! I am his son! I am a son of god! I am a god! I will return."

Mik was already too far downstairs to hear him. The music was still playing, but even that became nothing but a rumble in the walls now. In one of the bedrooms, Mik found the woman, Sister Volna. She had already tried the locked tower door and had no other option but to sit and wait. The woman was very attractive, with witty eyes and a well-proportioned figure, which was now fully wrapped in her robes. Her hair was braided, and her face was red as if she had cried. Mik looked at her, wondering whether he should question her or take her to the captain. She interpreted this silence in her own way.

"You are a man," she said.

"Last time I checked," Mik replied automatically, still thinking.

"When I saw you up there," she pointed at the ceiling with her eyes, "I thought you were ... him."

"Whom?"

"The messenger from the dark Lord." She got up and sheepishly approached Mik. "You are so big and dark … and your hair." She lifted her hand to touch his hair, but he politely led her hand aside with his index finger. She stood back and opened her robes.

"If you are a man, then you need a woman. I have a lot to offer to a big strong—"

"You don't know what I need, lady. And you are not my type."

She closed her robe, but Mik noticed that she had washed the paint off, and now there were red marks from a sponge on her stomach.

"Oh, I see. You are one of those who don't like women … or men in robes."

Now her voice was sulky and girlish.

"I recently developed a great respect for certain people in robes. Or at least for one person."

"So what are you going to do with me then? And what have you done to our Word-Bearer?"

"Didn't lay a finger on him. You are coming with me."

"What for? Can't you just leave me too?"

"I am afraid not. Will you come quietly, or shall I knock you unconscious?"

"Wait. I want to leave. You see, I am sick and tired of this place. I would have left ages ago, but if I do, one of the novice girls will have to replace me, and they are all way too young not to be freaked out by his preferences. What you saw is just the tip of the iceberg. You know what I mean, it is a figure of speech. There were icebergs on Earth hundreds of years ago – large chunks of—"

"I know. It is not me who you have to persuade. I don't believe a word you are saying, but I am not the one who makes decisions."

"So you just follow orders?"

"Yes, but that does not stop me from having an opinion of my own."

The woman picked up a large black scarf and covered her hair, letting the ends hang on her back.

"Until someone orders you not to," she muttered and followed Mik downstairs.

On the way down, Mik passed the closed door to the dining room without checking on

Father Deessa. The trooper was too tired to realise his mistake at the time. Outside, Mik did not find the captain in the same spot where he had left him with the red-faced Cruiser. Brother Mark was still sitting against the wall, looking at the last traces of the dying light to the west horizon. Looking but not seeing. A short arrow protruded from his chest. Only hunters used crossbows on Earth. Mik looked down from the cliff and saw nothing but darkness. Where could an archer shoot from if Mark hadn't been shot at point-blank range? He would have stood right here. Then where is the captain?

"Oh-oh-oh!" Sister Volna howled and sobbed. "Brother Mark! Who did this to you, my poor dear sweetheart?"

She rushed to the corpse, but Mik grabbed her by the elbow and pulled her back to face him.

"There shouldn't be anyone else left here. I saw no crossbows in the armoury. Who knows how to shoot here?"

The woman's face, distorted by grief, suddenly changed again, and looked at him with its usual cautious defiance.

"Who knows how to shoot? From such a distance, anyone could shoot." She pulled her arm back and straightened her stray scarf. "And there's only one crossbow. The hunter's son dragged it all the way from home; he stole it from his father when these brothers convinced him to join the Cruisers. He hid it under his bed. The girls and I knew of it and no one else."

"Why would he shoot one of his own?"

"Ha! He wouldn't. Mark was after him, understand? The poor kid had no place to hide and was too embarrassed to say anything. Mark simply wouldn't let him be. I figured the brave little novice came here and seized the opportunity to do what he had wanted to do for months."

Mik had no other choice but to bring Sister Volna to the kitchen. Here he found the captain in one piece, Tolyan awake but pale, Zina and Marta – once again nursing Steven back to health, and the young Arthur – freed from his fetters. There was also a new face – another young man in his twenties, sitting on the empty crate, hugging his crossbow.

"What took you so long, Mik?" Tom asked, "I hope you don't mind, but I cut Arthur free at the request of his friend. This is Nat. He was a Rebel before we even came here. He just did not know it."

Mik pushed Sister Volna towards Tolyan, who was sitting on the floor. He looked like a man with a deadly hangover.

"Are you strong enough to watch this woman?" Mik asked. "Be careful. She has learned a lot from the Word-Bearer."

Tolyan answered with a nod and a single but painful hiccup.

"What happened?" Mik asked the captain.

"This young man appeared when Brother Mark and I were disagreeing about the meaning of life. First, he pointed that thing at me, and Mark cried joyfully, 'Shoot him, shoot him!' It looked like brave Nat hesitated, so Mark shouted at him, 'Shoot him, you son of a whore ... shoot him.' He called him all the names under the sun until he said something like, 'You are my bitch, and you will do what I say!' Guess what happened next? Nat's hands stopped shaking. He turned and pinned the bastard to the spot like a beetle.

It took less than five minutes to explain our situation to him. When he heard that Arthur was helping us, he demanded to go to him immediately, and then he demanded the binds be untied. He is a very demanding young man. Take a break, trooper; that's an order. We are spending the night here, and I will update you in the morning."

Mik looked at Sister Volna, who sat on the crate next to Tolyan but far away enough not to smell him much. She had a pretty smug expression on her face.

"I would still be cautious with these Cruisers," Mik said and turned to Nat. "Why did they kill your father?"

"My father is still alive," answered Nat, sounding not like a kid but a mature man, "because I left. It was the only way to keep him and the rest of the family unharmed."

"And your weapon?"

"It's mine. I earned it on my sixteenth birthday trial. Tradition."

Mik took another look at Volna, but this time she pretended to talk to Tolyan with interest. Tolyan's face was wet, and his beard curled up more than usual. Mik studied Nat in detail. The young man strangely reminded him of someone called Massimo, who he had met before in a different world. He noticed uncertain but smart eyes, and in his motionless pose, something really was reminiscent of a hunter. This boy should not be a mystic. He should train in the military academy. He was wearing the brown robe of a novice, but it failed to hide his broad shoulders and his strong neck.

"So you can shoot well," Mik said.

"He can, believe me!" said Steven suddenly, whom Zina had finally left alone, as she was about to check Mik's injury. "He shot me too, and he aimed well to cause me no more than a flesh wound."

Mik turned and examined his squad. It did not look good. Steven, already hurt by a svoloch and with a broken hand from the landing, had been beaten by Cruisers and now shot in the leg with a crossbow. Tolyan had a bump on his head and a minor concussion. Apart from that, he was in one piece but still recovering from the Bliss overdose. Mik himself was hungry, exhausted, bleeding and close to fainting.

"So what has happened to you? Why didn't you end up like Tolyan?" He asked Steven, sat down and let Zina change his blood-soaked bandage. He grabbed the mug of soya milk and a piece of garlic bread offered by Arthur and ate greedily.

Steven said, "They knocked me over in the woods. I came round tied up in the darkroom last night. I heard two people talking about how to administrate what they called Bliss to me. One of them called Otto said that an injection is not good because I am bleeding from my cuts, and Bliss will bleed out too, and it is better to make me drink it with water. Seriously, they have no idea about human physiology. He held my head up and told someone he called Len to force it down my throat. I did not resist so as not to choke, and I was really thirsty. It was a glass of water with something bitter dissolved in it. I was lucky they left soon, and I puked the whole thing out. Some of it had still gotten in and made me sleepy. I don't know for how long, but it was a good nap. When I woke up, I was alone in the stinky shed, still tied to the butcher's bench. I broke free by breaking the bench. The door was unlocked, and I went to look around. I found the courtyard, removed the guard outside the gate, and took his axe. Then I found the dungeon, and someone was crying in one of the rooms. I axed the door to pieces but found ... you know what I found. Then on my way from there, I discovered the dead Cruisers in the armoury and dwelling area in the medical facility. I recognised your style, Mik. Then I checked out the tower and received an arrow in my leg on arrival. I swore and heard the captain shouting, 'no, no, this is one of my men!' The lad did not get to the bone, and I thought, one hole more, one less, what's the difference. And funnily enough, it did not hurt much. I think that the drug was still ..."

But Mik did not hear the end of the story. He was fast asleep.

Chapter 22. 3411. Out in Space – O'Teka

"And how does this praying help you?" Zina asked, cradling the child in her arms.

"It helps me very much. Through prayer, I learned that my purpose is to heal people using local resources. The White City has highly sophisticated medical facilities. They focus mainly on changing people so they don't get sick, and they have many more facilities to improve treatments for those who get sick anyway. Most of the medicine is synthesised. O'Teka gave me knowledge of people on Earth called herbalists. I was the best in my class at botany; I knew all the local herbs and their properties. Ask me anything." May's eyes shone once again.

"So, this is how you managed to stay alive here and protect your baby?" Zina said coldly, passing the child back to May. "What did you give her? Did you keep her drugged all the time?"

May frowned. "No. In the past, my father insisted on giving her a drop of dream-pear juice so she wouldn't cry and disturb the guests. But recently, I found another way – a place to hide her. We needed to sneak out quietly to bring her here, so I made her sniff a pinch of losheka's pollen. It is harmless and is used by dentists in the White City to treat children without hurting them much. This is the first time in six months; I practically live with her in Inessa's cave and go to my father's house to clean, cook and work."

"You are a village herbalist?"

"No, I know a lot, but I must keep it a secret. Only my father knows about it now and my friend Inessa knew. She was a village herbalist but was blessed by the High Martyr and died a few months ago."

"I have more questions about your goddess, but still ... Why did you follow your father, knowing that you will lose everything?" said Vist, glancing briefly at May.

"My father told me I must go with him. It is just him and me now. We are all that is left of the family. We will look after each other and be free together. I was younger and felt sorry for him. I also believed him when he said, 'Do you really want to wait for another two years for your work experience with healers? Come with me, and you can start your own scouting tomorrow. All the herbs out there are yours.'"

"But he did not look after you when you found the village, did he? Your friend did, am I right?" said Zina.

"Yes, Inessa cared for me, but my father doesn't let men hurt me. He rents me out for one hour every cycle, apart from the six cycles of blood. He always shares payment with me, lets me ask men for food, for cooking herbs that are hard to get, and he keeps all the dream-pears to himself. If he consumes too many pears, I have to hide in the cave by the shore in case someone tries to take advantage of me while he is unconscious. Inessa was a good woman; she let me use her cave. She left the city a generation ago because the man she loved married someone else. Being a healer, she survived here for a long time. She said she had been serving her own rehabilitation all these years and was happy to help me. I became her new purpose. She had been secretly helping some villages until one of them told the High Martyr. The High Martyr did not want to bless Inessa because he was also using her help ... secretly. But the villager said it loudly during the gathering, so he blessed them both: her for meddling with the Lord's will and him for accepting her blasphemy when he was sick. The villager lived after the blessing, but Inessa was too old and skinny. She died."

"What is a blessing?" Mik asked.

"The permission of the Lord to redeem yourself. You have to give everything you have to those who need it. So the rest of the village will go to your house and take what they want. You can keep what is left, but you must give the others all your daily rations for ten cycles. This way, the Lord purifies you, and you become blessed. Your sin is forgotten forever."

"So Inessa starved to death?"

"Not exactly. I tried to bring her food, but she refused, saying they would bless me too if someone found out. I was already feeding my daughter, so she would have been inadvertently blessed too. Inessa was under surveillance and could not go to the woods and feed on fungi or fruits. So she died. I went to her house afterwards. They took everything that could be used. But they did not take all the herbs because they didn't know how to use them. I found some remains of blue roots and realised she took them when the suffering became too much. She preferred to go rather than be blessed."

"Does your father regret leaving the city?" Général asked.

"Only when there are no dream-pears. If he had them all before falling asleep, my father would start saying how he did not know about all this when he persuaded me to come with him. I think he regrets leaving O'Teka."

"That is terrible!" Zina exclaimed, "Looks like nothing changes. Humanity repeats the same mistakes over and over again. I don't get it– how is it possible? I understand the villagers worship god to avoid responsibility and for the High Martyr to stay in power. But White City sounds like an advanced civilisation. A temple? Are you kidding me?"

"Maybe it is symbolic," said Rod, "or that temple is just an environment where you can think, focus, reflect or meditate? Some form of Buddhism?"

"None of that." Vist sat up straight and looked at everyone in turn with a eureka expression. "Don't you get it? The goddess of wisdom never tells you what to do, never wants anything in return? She is just there. A temple full of bibles. What was the one thing colonists brought with them, in the form of billions of data units? Billions? Books! The bibles of O'Teka. Biblioteka ... *bibliotheca* is an old word for library in Latin and a few European languages. They worship knowledge! *Praying* means reading ... or learning. The *bible* is just a word for a book there. Any book! Definitions ..."

"Any book!" said Tom. "Cycle means day, bible means book. Language evolution is faster than biological adaptation. If you can take control of biological evolution by altering genes, then you can also take control of the language and ideology of your society. Zina is right – nothing has changed. People will always want to worship something, to believe in something. Especially if you are stuck on a different planet and there are a handful of you against the hostile world. You don't need to resurrect a personality cult or make up a god. You just need to choose a good object of worship and name it. Use a holy word to name something rational, and this will help you get through harsh times believing in only things that can really help you. May, tell me, do you know the words logic, reason, rationality?"

"Of course. Those are the names of the saints. Logic teaches us to weigh all the available facts before deciding. Reason teaches us to absorb what we hear and see and use it together with what we already know. Rationality is not a saint, but a grade at school for solving test situations. It is a little harder to get than Respect or Pride, but if you get it, Cognita will become your saint. We have other saints. Ethica, she helps you to see the difference between right and wrong. There is also Judge, Modesto, Loyalta, Honesty and Esteem."

"Fantastic!" said Rod, "but surely you don't believe in the afterlife? Do you go to hell when you die as a bad guy?"

"Of course. If you are a failure in life, you will end up in Oblivion after death."

Rod looked disappointed for a moment but then smiled again. "Which means you will be forgotten. Your name will not be associated with anything worth recording. Am I right? How interesting!"

"What about heaven or paradise?" Général asked, "What is your afterlife alternative?"

"Those are different words. Heaven means sky in our language. Paradise is the name of the garden in the middle of the city. I know they used to have different meanings in the human past. But you seem to understand it all correctly." May turned to Vist. "If you write your own bible that can help someone or tell an interesting story, this will be your afterlife. You will live in the temple's data and in people's memories for as long as there are people to pray for something useful from your offering. Or at least pray for it once. That is what you would probably call Paradise ... Talking about gardens! Mother had a trophy from the special ceremony – the Achiever. It was the year when she became a Grand Gardener. Visit her garden for me when you reach the city, please. It probably belongs to her apprentice now, but her trees are still there. They are large and old, seeded by the founders and moved to the city from their landing place."

"Si hortum in bibliotheca habes deerit nihil ..." Vist whispered and slouched in front of the fire again, inhaling the smell of clove oil.

Everyone was quiet for a long time. May cradled her sleeping daughter, who was accustomed to sleeping outside. Vist looked at the fire, and Tom looked at Vist and May in turns. Steven cleaned up the plates and cups, and Zina packed them back in the case. Mik and Tolyan went out to check the perimeter. Lying down on his back, Rod stared at the fantastic shapes and layers of the thick and thin clouds. Général was muttering something to himself, shaking his head and frowning.

Soon Tom said, "What shall we do with the baby if we take her with us?"

"Find my aunties Rosemary and Shar Zhonjey. They will know what to do. Every child is precious in the city. Nadezhda survived for almost a year in the village, so she is very valuable. Doctor Hawk and Professor Nguyen will be interested in her immune system. I am sure she will have to go through quarantine, but then she will be looked after like all other kids. She will have pretty dresses, and she will go to school. She will find her purpose."

"Come with us," said Zina, "I am sure your family will accept you. Your daughter needs her mother."

"Most importantly," said Steven, "your reason for leaving was to be with your father. It is different from sneaking out and following some sect of real mystics. Surely that should count for something."

"They will never trust me. I have lived among the villagers for so long and have learned too much about their ways. And my father – the High Martyr will bless him if I go. He has a bad liver and will surely die."

Général sneered and shook his head once again.

"What if we kidnapped you?" Steven said, "There! Let them blame me personally because I have stolen the villager. I will tie your hands and blindfold you."

"I doubt it will work," said May. "The High Martyr saw you leaving. Also, the villagers always talk of taking over the city one day. They just don't know how to get past all the technology yet. The citizens will suspect me of being a spy, sent to sabotage something. This has happened before."

"We will tell them too that we have kidnapped you," said Steven.

"I would not lie in the city if I were you," said Vist with a smile, still not looking at Steven or May. "I don't believe your father is in any danger because your running away does not threaten the High Martyr's position. He won't miss you. He never visited your house and never sent for you."

"No," May said without regret, "how did you know?"

"I agree with Vist," Tom said, "but you should come with us, May. If it doesn't work, I will escort you back myself. Alan, what do you think?"

Général nodded. Rod put his hand up.

"With my vote, we are in the majority."

"I am sure the guys will agree too," said Steven.

"And what do you think?" said Vist a little louder before glancing up.

Everyone looked at each other in confusion. Apart from Mik and Tolyan, who were still on the cliffs, everyone else here had already agreed. They looked at Vist, who was staring at the fire again. Was this question addressed to May?

Vist spoke again, "Massimo. I know you heard every word. Come out."

The leaves rustled on the top of the black tree near the camp. A few flakes of bark flitted into the flames. The slender, athletic figure dropped down in front of Vist, next to the fire. Everybody else gasped and stood up. Steven and Général pointed their zappers at the squatting man. The man straightened himself. Indeed, it was Massimo.

Chapter 23. 3416. Back on Earth – Sophie

Just outside the castle wall, a twenty-one-year-old ginger girl woke up in a small tent and checked the place next to her. It was still empty. Arthur had not come back last night from his chores.

A dark and sticky feeling of panic had returned, and she called out quietly, "Droog? Droozhok?"

There was a movement outside of the tent and a high-pitch whine. The sheepdog descendant's huge black-and-white head pushed into the tent and forced its way through the gaps between the knots.

Sophie felt better after hugging the broad furry neck.

"Where is your master, big boy? Ah? I have worried myself sick. Why didn't you find him? Oh yes. He told you to guard me, didn't he? You will never leave my sight now, until he calls you off or until you die."

She put on her colourful gypsy skirt, trainers, t-shirt and brown robe, tied her orange curls with a green scarf and started to undo all the knots of the tent entrance one by one until she could get out. The other dozen tents were still sealed, meaning she was the first to get up. She was very hungry. Everyone was. Dinner hadn't arrived last night, and no one could enter the castle yard without an order.

It was late when the whole group felt something wasn't right. At first, no one thought to go in and check why there was a delay. Sophie and some other girls first asked Jade to go, but she said she is a stitcher, not a sister, so why should she be punished for everyone else's concern?

When it became dark, Sophie went into her friend Nat's tent. She was worried, not so much about the food, but about Arthur. He was supposed to work in the kitchens that night. Nat went to the gate and immediately came back. He called everyone out and said that Brother Otto was dead in the gateway.

"What happened to him?" Jade asked. She was a bony woman, about seventy years old, and the only person in the castle not dressed in a Cruiser's robe but in a cardigan and patchy duster instead.

"I am not sure. But Otto's weapon is gone, and his neck is broken," Nat answered. "I say this is not the work of Thieves, but professional killers. We might have been overrun by the Mooners or Rebels."

"Rebels have guns and use lasers when they want to be stealthy," said another young novice, a Black boy with long dreadlocks tied together with a blue bandana. "Must be the Moon people. They would take his axe."

"If that is right, why has no one come here?" asked the girl next to him. Her chest was decorated with a few rows of tin necklaces and colourful shells. She was the youngest in the group, no older than thirteen.

"They might still do that, Yazabella, later tonight or even in the morning," Nat answered. "I will go and check it out. Who is with me?"

"What for? You are better off on your own," said the short youth in the baseball cap, "If you learn something – great, but if they catch you – then they will catch whoever is with you, too. Even if we all go, they can just pluck us one by one. We are no match for them."

"You might be right, Russell," Nat said and went to his tent. He came back with his crossbow and a handful of arrows.

"Don't go, Nat. You will anger the Lord," said the girl in the robe that was too big for her. It could have almost passed as a sister's long robe if it were blue.

"Vira is correct," said Russell. "What happened has happened by His will, and we must not intervene."

"Or maybe it is the Lord's will for Nat to go. That is why the Lord gave him his bow!" said Sophie.

That stopped any other objections from being raised.

"Lord be with you!" said Jade, the stitcher, and she turned to the others. "We can all help you the best way we can. We will all be praying for your safe return, won't we? Let us hope that our other brothers are alive and our fathers are just taken as prisoners and not killed. And we will pray for those killed and beg our Lord to look after Brother Otto's immortal soul."

She walked slowly into the circle of young novices with her arms spread invitingly. Russell put one arm on her skinny shoulder and lifted another in the same manner. Vira ducked under his arm and beckoned Yazabella to take hers. The boy with dreadlocks already had his arm on Jade's other shoulder, and soon, the rest of the novices hummed some complex prayer and closed up this group hug, swaying to the right and left.

Sophie did not join the prayer.

"I want to come with you," she said to Nat, who covered his face with his hood and started towards the gate.

"No, Sophie. Please. It will be easier if I don't have to worry about you. Plus, if you come, then so will your Droog, which means goodbye, stealth. Go to bed. Everything will be fine. I will bring Arthur back to you. I promise!"

But he didn't. Neither did he come back himself. His tent was empty, and the others were asleep as if everything was all right. Sophie decided to go and look for Arthur all by herself, or rather, with Droog. She planned to go around the castle walls and through the gaps and cracks to see what was happening. She pulled a small saddle from the tent, spread the leather folds on the ground, covered them with a blanket, and made a kissing noise with her lips. Droog immediately lay down on the blanket and lowered his head. Sophie pulled the straps under his front legs and warped the dog's chest into the saddle folds. She fastened the buckles on his back, sat in the saddle and strapped herself to it. Now it looked as if the dog was wearing a leather waistcoat with a seat on his back. Sophie made another kissing sound, and the dog rose. Sophie scratched the right side of the dog's neck and said, "Let's start this way, Droog, like a good boy."

The dog turned right. They started along the northern wall of the castle, down the hill, where the deadwood started and where the wall was more broken. On the back of the dog, the girl was able to look over the ten-foot-high concrete fence that compensated for the crumbled masonry. She gently touched the dog's shoulders, making it walk slowly and quietly, and they stopped from time to time. She saw part of the yard, the space in front of the dwelling structures, and the main tower entrance. She expected some strangers to be standing on guard there, if not one of the brothers, but she saw absolutely nobody as if the castle was deserted. At one point, she peered through a crack in the wall, staring at the kitchen door. The door was half-open, but once again – not a soul could be seen. She stood there for a moment and listened. Not a sound. She checked the perimeter, and as she went up the hill to the opposite side of the castle, the dog suddenly stopped without a signal and growled quietly.

"Shh ..." said Sophie, almost lying on Droog's neck and putting her hand on his broad nose, "Easy, boy, very slowly ..."

The dog went silent and made a few more steps forwards. Sophie encouraged him to take one step at a time until they approached the corner of the concrete fencing on the western side, right next to the tower. There were some thick green shrubs, but they were not tall enough to provide reliable cover.

Sophie pressed gently on Droog's neck, and he lay down, lowered his head, and then crawled forwards on his stomach. Now, if Sophie could stoop over him, the green branches would also cover her. They moved forwards, and this time Sophie saw a whole group of people. They were strangers to her, standing on the cliff's edge, facing the still-dark western sky. Their heads were lowered, and it was clear that they were standing in front of the small black hill of a fresh grave.

Two big men in military uniforms were leaning on spades taken from the castle shed. Another one in the same uniform was leaning on a crutch. His left thigh, right arm and head shone in the morning sun with white bandages. The shorter man with glasses and a shaved head was supporting two crying women and spoke quietly.

One of the women cried so much that she could hardly stand. Sophie did not know her, but she felt something tickling her nose from inside, and her vision blurred.

A few minutes later, two other men appeared from behind the tower. They carried one of those stone slabs that were in abundance in the courtyard. Sophie did not see their faces through tears, but they were not dressed in Cruiser robes. They carefully lowered the stone on the grave, and one of the big men activated his hand weapon. The bright ray must have written a name on the slab, and one of the women, black and slender, covered the grave in the autumn wildflowers she had held in her hands. The other woman fell to her knees, and Sophie could hear her sobs. The wind blew from the sea; what Sophie's eyes failed to see, Droog's nose didn't. First, he whined, and then his tail started to wag. He produced a high yelp and rose above the shrubs before Sophie managed to calm him.

Everyone, apart from the woman on her knees, turned around and covered their eyes from the rising sunlight, trying to see the red-headed girl mounted on the huge dog.

"Droog! Sophie!" she heard Arthur's voice say, and her mount galloped towards its master, still squealing happily and wagging his tail. Sophie did not fall off his back, only because of the leather straps securing her on the saddle. Dogs may be the size of large ponies now, but they still run like dogs.

Chapter 24. 3411. Out in Space – Massimo

Massimo stood still by the campfire, looking Vist in the eyes. He did not appear to be afraid or even surprised by the fact he had been discovered. His arms were relaxed along his sides; his deep purple skin had no micro-scales, and his smooth cheeks reflected the flames like a glaze. He was not wearing his knitted tunic anymore. His trousers and shirt were made of a soft black rubbery material that was not a product of village craft. He was not barefoot this time but wore shoes with proper soles for climbing, running and walking long distances. He looked unarmed, and Général lowered his fist and signalled Steven to do the same.

"Who is this guy?"

"This is Massimo. I mentioned him before. He is an adviser to the High Martyr in the village," said Captain Darkwood. "Vist, how did you know he was up in the tree?"

"I heard him."

"But how did you know it was him?"

"I did not. I assumed it would have been him if anyone had followed us from the village and stayed invisible. I am glad I was right. Let me introduce our guide. Am I right again?"

Massimo nodded and smiled, showing his perfect teeth.

"I was hoping to speak to you before you left the village, but Your Grace was so convincing at impersonating another believer, so I decided to watch you first. Just to make sure." He smiled like a man who definitely does not belong in the village, with the High Martyr or the Lord himself. This time, his smile reflected his mood rather than his offering a service. "I am not just the High Martyr's adviser, but also a city spy. I have lived in the Salty Village for almost a year, keeping an eye on Shafran's activity and intentions. When I received a message from Raja, I wanted to meet you first and prevent you from going to Shafran. Still, my orders were clear: to let you find the village, observe your behaviour, learn about you as much as possible and protect you if necessary."

"From what?" asked the captain, returning to his seat. Général also lowered himself on the mat, but Steven walked around the purple man in black and stopped behind his back.

Massimo completely ignored Steven and answered, "From those things you have managed without my help. Watching you, I decided you were not a threat to the city and would be welcomed there. You can call off your scouts. You are quite safe in these parts."

"And *you* can sit down here and tell us who you are and what is going on," Tom said, inviting Massimo to the mat by the fire. The young man accepted the invitation and sat next to May.

May looked at Massimo wide-eyed.

"Massimo! You did not leave the city by exile? I wanted to ask but couldn't."

"No, May."

"I thought it was so not like you."

"I know."

She looked somehow pleased and explained to the others, "We used to go to the same school. Massimo, you probably don't remember me there. I was four grades younger and read your articles on artificial selection in local grasses. I was so surprised when you arrived in the village and I was afraid to talk to you. Now I understand why you never ..."

She stopped, blushed and pretended she was checking on her daughter, who woke up and whimpered a little.

A few minutes later, after regrouping, Mik and Tolyan searched Massimo for suspicious items but found nothing apart from a small communicator in his earring. Then he had to answer a few more questions. The young man submitted himself to these precautions willingly and calmly.

"So, was there an ambush in the eastern hills?" asked the captain.

"Yes, but not by Shafran's guards. He is not stupid and knows his guards' worth, but he knows very little about you. The tribe of the svoloch was spotted a few miles east of the sea. They sometimes come down from the nearest mountains during their breeding season to feed on the eggs of the local amphibians. Kendra suggested they would kill or force you to return to Shafran if you went east. He doesn't want you to reach the city, and he wouldn't mind weakening you and forcing you to seek his protection."

"Kendra ... that hag? What's her problem?" asked Steven, "She is horrible!"

"Kendra is too clever for her own good. She is a hundred years older than my generation; therefore, she is ancient history to me. In her time, Kendra was unable to become the High Martyr because she was a woman. Believers treat women as inferiors, but she and Shafran are the only people in the village who were kicked out of the main colony. She was a wife to one of his predecessors here. Before that, I am not sure, but I think that in the city, she was a corrupt politician or cheated during her election. Nevertheless, she is dangerous and hard to deceive." Massimo turned to face Vist. "I am not sure how, but you managed to fool her. Maybe she is not as sharp as she used to be?"

"Why doesn't Shafran want us to reach the city?" Rod asked.

"Because he can see a certain value in keeping you for himself. He dreams of taking over the city or at least sabotaging it. But he has no means to do that apart from a few dirty tricks in his pocket. He hoped to use you one way or another. At first, Kendra suggested using an armed mob to imprison you in the pit until you cooperate. I said that you might not be alone and another few of you might destroy the village using the technology we know nothing about. And I was right too," Massimo said, grinning again.

"Yes, you were not too far off," said Mik, but he did not return the smile.

"What can you tell us about the White City," Vist asked.

"May already told you enough, and you figured us out pretty accurately," said Massimo. "I can add that Shafran's description of the city was not entirely wrong either. He just served it to you as an ugly thing, using plenty of negative terms. You will have to see it for yourself."

"I am sure we can make up our own minds."

There was a loud snore. Steven prodded Tolyan with his foot. The big trooper rolled on his back with an open mouth but did not stop rumbling. Everyone suddenly felt very tired.

"In that case, we need to get there as soon as possible. But to do so promptly and safely, we need to sleep first!" said the captain. "The routine for keeping watch still stands in the usual order. Somebody has to wake Tolyan, as he will be the first on guard. Everyone else – bedtime! May, you and the baby should take the storage tent. Steven, take our packs out of there and cover them up in case of more rain. Massimo, are you staying with us or returning to the village?"

"I am going back to the city. With you."

Chapter 25. 3416. Back on Earth – Novices

"Sophie!" Arthur said with surprise, then helped her get down. "What are you doing here?"

Nat was beside Arthur, but neither of the boys looked like they were in trouble.

"Looking for you! Who are these people? Where is everybody? Why aren't you wearing your robes? What happened last night? I was sick with fright!"

"Wait, Sophie, come with me. Let them finish. This is not the right time or place."

He took Sophie by the hand, nodded at Nat, and whistled to Droog to follow them. All three of them and the dog went back to the shrubs and stopped there.

"Not the right time? Why didn't you come last night? And you!" Sophie turned to Nat angrily and said, "You promised to bring him back! What's going on? Where are the brothers? Where is Sister Volna?"

"I would have kept my promise if you had just waited a little longer," Nat said, "but they needed help, and we offered."

"*They* needed help? I can't believe it!"

"Sophie, these are the astronauts! They just returned from a young, colonised planet where people live and work for themselves. We can go there too, all of us!"

"What? Arthur?" Sophie spoke slower, "What are you saying? Do you mean our prayers have been answered?"

"Forget about that. There is no Lord to save us, but these people will. They were caught by the brothers and dragged up here to be turned or killed. Now look at them. They were beaten and tortured, and one of them died. And that blond guy bandaged all over – he killed Brother Otto. Can you imagine? Two strong and healthy people had not been able to get him in the past. See the Black one? Even Brother Patrick failed to get to him. Do you remember anyone who Brother Patrick preached to who did not turn or die?"

"So this is why you took your robes off? Are you mad? Arthur, have you forgotten what Father Ontha did to me when you went swimming and left your robe in the tent?"

"Father Ontha will never hurt you ever again, sweetie! He will not be able to wipe his own arse, never mind spank novices. The twins will not make you clean their feet anymore, and Mark will not rape anyone ever again. You don't have to do their laundry, cook for them, and kneel on the gravel with bare knees during the service three times a day. Sophie, we are free, we can leave this place! We can leave Earth!"

"I don't understand you, Arthur! Did you take your Bliss this morning? Your pupils are not dilated; you can't see our Lord's way!"

Nat, who had not interrupted his friends until now, put his hands on their shoulders and said, "Guys, there is no point in arguing. We will take them to the camp, and they will explain it all to the rest of us. Then those who want to stay can stay ... And those who want to leave won't be stopped. The captain gave us his word. I trust him."

"Why? Can he talk like Brother Patrick?"

"No, actually. Brother Patrick talks a lot, but you can't really follow him. These guys say very little, but it is just ... clear. The captain makes you think; the Word-Bearer tells you not to."

"Tell me, Sophie, did you really believe that the fathers would save us? That we won't all die here when Earth burns?" Arthur asked.

"Mum used to say it would not happen for another hundred years."

"But it will be very bad here much sooner."

"Our souls ..."

"What about our bodies? Sophie?" Arthur took her hand and placed it on his chest. "What about our future? You said you want a family. I would love to have children with you one day. What about their future?"

"But if the Lord wanted to?"

"What do you want, Sophie?" asked Arthur and Nat almost simultaneously, laughing heartily.

This made Sophie's face relax, and she smiled.

"I will listen to them," she said, "then I will see how I feel."

"... and think," said Nat, "That is what counts. You feel different every day."

An hour later, Nat's deep voice called all the novices out of their tents. It was late morning, and usually, everyone would have been busy working after receiving an order or two. This time no brothers came with orders. There was no bell calling them to the yard for morning service. And it looked like there would be no breakfast, just like there had been no dinner the night before. After praying and chatting, all the novices returned to their tents, where they worried and waited. Only Jade the Stitcher was still sitting at the entrance to her workshop – a wooden shack with a plastic roof. When she saw the group of people approaching the camp from the direction of the gates, she disappeared inside but left the door ajar to hear what was happening.

A few voices from the tents said happily, "It's Nat! Nat is back!"

But when all twenty people, aged between thirteen and thirty years old, came out, they stopped in confusion and stared at six strangers dressed in uniforms of different ranks and units.

Sister Volna, who had spent the whole night in the kitchen cellar with the chef's body, was brought out too. Now she was standing next to Tolyan, with his iron fingers around her forearm in a vice-like grip.

Tom Darkwood looked at the young faces, one after the other. All the novices were in their robes, marked with Cruiser insignia stencilled with spray paint – a cross inside an oval that looked like a fish standing on its tail. Arthur explained earlier that it was actually a space rocket. All the girls wore a scarf on their heads; all the boys had hoods on their short robes. He could also see tracksuit bottoms, pyjamas, jeans, long skirts, baggy trousers, boots, trainers and sandals. This group would probably look pretty motley if it wasn't for those miserable robes.

Nat and Arthur were walking among the novices, telling them in excited voices what they had already told Sophie. Sophie did not say much. She held Arthur's hand as if she was afraid to let him go again.

The oldest of the novices, a man called Virgil, was the first to address the strangers. "You came to preach, so go ahead. Is it true? Will you take us to another planet in your ship?"

"No," Tom answered. "We can take you to the Resistance. There you will be able to build your own ship."

The disapproving and rather disappointed murmur rippled through the group of young Cruisers.

"I knew it. It's all rubbish. How are we supposed to build a ship?" asked a boy in a baseball cap, "We can hunt, fish, cook, stitch, and clean ... we don't build ships."

"You can do all of that to earn your chance to evacuate. But this time, you will work for yourselves."

"Sounds almost exactly like what we were told here," said one of the novices from the back row.

"Not at all, because you can learn how to build ships just like you learned to do other things ... or you can pay for one to be built, or work hard and buy one."

"This is the test!" came the voice from the workshop. Jade stepped outside but did not go far from the door, "They are testing your faith! Don't listen to them!"

"Do you expect Jade to come and build the ship too?" Virgil said, and a few people chuckled.

"No, I expect Jade to make her own choices when she is there. She is an old woman. The first ship might not be built in her lifetime, but she – or her own children if she has any – can help you to build your ship by doing what she is best at. She can have her own tailor shop and make a decent living among friends."

"What are you going to do with Sister Volna?" Virgil asked.

"Sister Volna is free to do what she wants," Tom answered and nodded at Tolyan.

Tolyan opened his hand, and Sister Volna looked at him in disbelief for a moment. Then he walked to Virgil and stood shoulder to shoulder with him.

"Did you kill all of our fathers?" Russell asked.

"No. Father Deessa jumped out of the window of his own volition. It was not high but he broke his neck. We were not there to stop him," Mik answered, "Father Ontha is still alive, I think."

"What about our Word-Bearer?"

"He lives. But I am not done with him yet," Tom said, "I have a few questions for that man."

"What other choices do you have?" Zina asked. "This Brotherhood is finished. Where will you go?"

"We are not going anywhere?" said Jade, stepping down to join the group of novices. "This is our home. We live here, and we pray here."

"There are other congregations," Virgil said. "We may still be saved on the Moon. The Mooners never refuse to take back their lost sheep," he said and looked at Sister Volna, and she returned that look with gratitude.

"We don't have to stay in tents now, right?" Vira said, "We can move into the castle. There is plenty of food in storage, unless you plan to rob us?"

"We are not taking anything but some water, dry fish and a couple of loaves of bread," Zina said.

"What do you want us for then? Just leave!" Jade said.

"I believe this elderly lady wishes you well ... but what about tomorrow? You are all young, you still have a chance to start again and learn!" Marta said.

Tom stepped forwards. "It is up to you to believe us or not, but at least hear me out. People on Earth have only a few decades of liveable conditions. A few more years will be possible in underground settlements and the nearest colonies for a handful of those who, for whatever reason, chose to stay behind and die with their planet. Their existence will be simple, not very comfortable, and death will be unavoidable. But for now, the rest of you have more than one option. You could join the gang of Thieves, who don't believe in the evacuation. They are marauders who don't want to work for their living here and exist for short-term goals, stealing from anyone ... including their own. That life is a dead end."

Tom allowed that to sink in and carried on, "You can remain Cruisers and allow yourselves to be slaves to those who lie to you and use you. Whatever they do, your future is not their concern. You might lose precious time and get stuck here hopelessly. The Moon Plan will fail, and I think you know that, but Father Ontha's idea would not work either. I admit, stealing my small ship just for himself, torturing and killing my pilots to get to the colony, all that was more realistic than drifting off on the Moon. Unfortunately for him, it was a little more than just stealing supplies and fuel. The consequences of these crimes are more severe."

"Then what are we supposed to do?" asked a boy with dreadlocks called Roy, "The Rebels will shoot us on sight!"

"We are Rebels and did we do that?" Mik said. "You are still alive, and we are talking to you. I killed only those who threatened us. Ask your friends here."

Arthur and Nat nodded.

Tom continued, "The Resistance's new evacuation plan is called Object. Hundreds of scientists have been searching for a way to relocate the people of Earth to the colony in the Vitricus System for the last twenty years. We are lucky to have a loader, and now we have the technology to deal with the evacuation's time, distance and the biological issues. Not everybody will be able to just go. Still, those who care for the survival of humanity as a species, those who want to help their children evacuate, and those who simply want to live their remaining lives here to create something great are welcome. Object will create lots of good jobs to provide a decent and honourable life in the final years on Earth, worthy of a civilisation of our race!"

"So, all this means we can't go to the colony now? Or even soon?" Virgil asked.

"No. No one can."

"But you have that ship! Why can't you just take us there?"

"Do you want us to take just you there?" Marta said in anger as her face reddened, "Okay, how about this? I see about thirty people here, including us. I can squeeze twelve passengers into the ship. Tell me, young man ..."

"Virgil."

"Virgil! Who am I to take and whom do I leave behind? Mm? Shall I take half and come back for the rest in five years? And if you get there now, what are you going to do? Life in the colony is not a free ride. In fact, it is much harder. The colony is still developing. You will find yourself in an unfamiliar and strange place, where everyone is more qualified than you in whatever your trade is. What are you good at?"

Virgil said nothing.

"But if you go there in thirty or fifty years in your own ship, you will get there faster than now, you will be better prepared and the colony will be better prepared to receive you."

Tom took Marta's hand to calm her down and said, "We will be in the castle until noon. Then we leave, and those who want to leave with us should come to the tower. You have a lot to think about and a lot to do. Your dead comrades are on the grass by the gate. Bury them, burn them or make Angel Flesh out of them. It is your choice."

Tom turned around and walked back to the castle. His team followed him.

Nat, Arthur and Sophie started to call out some names, "Yazabella! Come on. You can still go to school. They have schools in Resistance settlements."

"Rick, don't be daft. Come with us!"

"Vira, I hope you will come."

"Eric, Milana, what will you do if Thieves attack again?"

But soon, they stopped, grabbed their modest possessions from their tents, and rushed to catch up with Tom.

Droog ran ahead of them, barking and showing a complete lack of care for what was going on. The dog was just happy that Sophie and Arthur were together again.

Chapter 26. 3411. Out in Space – Quarantine

They watched Massimo's small and agile figure hop from rock to rock across a stream and then sprint beside it towards the white tower of the city gates.

"Just run this by me again, please. Why didn't he take us straight to the gate?" asked Tolyan to no one in particular.

"He did. Here it is. Any villager would gladly give up their share of weekly rations to be allowed here right now," answered Mik.

"Can we trust him? What if this is really an ambush or some other trick of Shafran's?" said Steven.

"In Vist's opinion, this boy has been super-honest with us. And I trust Vist's gut," said Rob.

"I don't trust my own gut. Why should I—" started Steven.

"No one trusts your gut, Steve," said Zina. "Général, why don't you sit down here on this rock? I don't like your breathing."

"I am fine, girl ... just glad we have stopped. This hot wind is not easy to breathe in ... but I must say ... I, too, don't think the boy means us any harm. Why would he allow this young mother and her child to come with us? He could have sent her back. I am thinking more of ... What are they? Are they still humans? He is purple ... she is scaly ... That's not right."

May used the break to let her little girl out of the sling. She walked her daughter on the warm sand. Steven noticed that Nadezhda appeared to be quite comfortable with the wind and heat. The girl squealed and drooled with delight, pulled up, and tried to run in the air with her tiny legs. Her almost white skin, with a hint of violet, shimmered a little in the red light as if she was gently dusted with glitter.

"She saw his cover being blown and could tell the others," said Tolyan quietly.

"Guys," said the captain, "it is not like we have much choice. He might just be a real city agent who has orders and instructions. We are outnumbered here anyway. Not by village peasants but by colony forces, perhaps. What is the point of getting suspicious now? Let him do his job. Vist, what does Chang say? How long until the next storm? How are they in the Wasp?"

"Four hours and seventeen minutes. They are fine." Vist looked at the screen projector and noticed the low power indicator flashing. "Rod, you said you have spare batteries charged. Can I have them? Rod?"

Rod did not move.

"Rod?"

"There is a cat," said Rod without turning his head. He was staring towards a small growth of shrubs and grasses between two cliffs.

"What?" Tolyan and Zina said simultaneously.

"Did you say *cat*?" asked the captain.

They all turned and looked. Two yellow eyes were examining the travellers from about fifteen metres away. Indeed, between bluish-green branches and grass blades, almost invisible in its stillness, was a cat.

"Hey, kitty," called Zina with that voice people use to talk to their animals. "Hello, pretty thing. Come out and say hi!"

"Is it real? How is it possible?" said Tolyan.

"Careful, Zina. It is an alien cat, and it's huge!" said Mik.

"It is another city spy," added Steven, "what do you say, Vist?"

"They must have bred cats and dogs, too, like some other farm animals. This one looks comfortably at home here. It might be hunting those small fat creatures living in the soft soil."

The cat looked very different from the few remaining cats on Earth. Those were smaller, incapable of finding their own food, and with blunt nails instead of claws. This beast was a large tabby with a shiny coat, magnificent whiskers, and an unmistakable build of a hunter. Its gaze was indifferent, but when Zina made a few steps towards it, the cat turned around and disappeared into the grass silently. Its twitching tail was long, with black rings.

"I say this is good news," said Rod. "If these citizens have pets, they are not doing too badly in the long term."

"Massimo is waving to us," said the captain. "This is it, guys. Let's go."

Steven jumped onto a middle stone to watch out for the whole group. Everyone, in turn, started to cross the shallow stream like Massimo had done. They jumped on the stepping stones in a long line. The small army of troopers went first. Mik carried the little girl in his arms, ignoring her loud protests. Zina and Rod helped May, followed by Vist. Tom Darkwood was the last to cross the muddy water. In the middle of the stream, Steven noticed Tom looking at Vist in a strange way. Was Tom attracted to Vist?

The city wall looked like it was indeed made of the same salt spheres, an unpleasant association with the village. Rod seemed to accept that he had lost a bet to Tolyan and Steven. Still, upon closer inspection, it turned out that the concrete wall was only lined on the outside with convex salty fragments, which made it look like giant polystyrene foam. It was at least twenty metres high and, as discovered later, the whitest thing in the city.

The strong city gates were just big enough for a truck to pass through. They were not white but made of metal and looked a lot like a hatch for a cargo bay in a spaceship.

Rod frowned. As they walked through, he said quietly, "I think we have found *Noah* … or at least some of it."

There was no time for conversation. Massimo explained that the first thing the visitors should expect is quarantine for all of them, including May, her baby and himself. So as soon as the gates had automatically closed behind them, he led the whole party across a yard with a few trucks and vans parked there. The vehicles looked ordinary, but they could carry heavy loads and up to ten people. They could take out a small expedition and bring goods from the local farms. Apart from the familiar smell of carbon fuel, the mouldy aroma of pink wax clearly dominated here.

On the opposite side of the yard was another wall with a smaller automatic door.

"I contacted your aunts, May," Massimo said, opening the door for everyone by dialling the code on a touchscreen on the wall, "They will ask to appoint a decision board about your issue. For now, we need to sort ourselves out. Even if you and your baby are not staying, we all need to reduce the risk for the citizens. Showers are there for us to use. The equipment must be turned off and placed in a niche for dry sterilisation. It will destroy microorganisms and remove excess radiation. The city is protected by a dome of an invisible field, as it is safer for unaltered plants and animals and for you – our new friends."

"How long is this quarantine?" Steven asked.

"Follow the instructions inside, and it should not take more than one hour to clean yourself and one hour after that."

"See you in a couple of hours," said Steven, walking into the building's small vestibule.

The cleansing facility consisted of ten individual shower rooms. Steven saw Vist disappear into one of the rooms just like the others.

"One thing loaders cannot do is to purify themselves," said Steven quietly.

He closed the door and looked around. His changing room was clean, cool and brightly lit, with a comfortable sofa by a small table with refreshments. The wall screen ran a pre-recorded message giving instructions on what to do and where to find a towel, toiletries, medicine and clean underclothing if needed. Instructions included a demand to take two portions of a laxative suspension that worked within twenty minutes. These twenty minutes were rather pleasant, as Steven's feet and hands were dipped into bowls of scented water where tiny worms removed all the dirt from under his nails and dead cells from his skin. This manicure worked like those done on Earth by certain fish. After his guts had been completely flushed twice, he took a dose of antibiotics with a glass of cold tea that tasted a little like ginger beer.

A few minutes later, Steven stripped and stepped into the shower cabin, which was programmed to clean his body of microorganisms, dust and grease using three kinds of ray, including ultraviolet rays and airvibra rays. These dry rays were followed by hot water, soaps, gels, body lotions, moisturising oils and creams ... pretty much like how they would have done it on all the large ships equipped for long journeys in space and between stations. The towels were like those in the best hotels of the Platinum Age. Except for these laxatives, Steven would welcome this quarantine daily. He took the final portion, apparently created especially for them. It was a culture of gut bacteria that should have restored his internal bio-environment by adding a few new species to help him digest local food and keep his weight under control. He sat on the sofa and examined the table. He found a pot of real coffee, blueberry muffins and what he took for a cold prawn salad there, but those prawns looked more like large insect larvae. Steven did not mind this ... it was delicious.

He dozed off despite the coffee and realised that he had been in the room for a little longer than two hours. He lifted himself from the sofa; the green light above the second door was inviting him into the common room.

He approached the door and heard a noise behind it. It was the raised voice of Tolyan, but he could not work out the words. Trouble! He thought then burst into the common room.

Chapter 27. 3416. Back to Earth – Casper

"Casp!"

The miller's assistant jumped up from the chair and blinked at his stepfather, who asked, "Where is Vist?"

The still-bright orange sun winked for a second through a slit in the thick clouds and almost blinded Casp through the window glass. He shaded his eyes with his hand and looked around the room.

"He was here just a ... What time is it?"

"Almost ten in the morning. I had to work an extra hour to compensate for the night adventures. I brought coffee for you two, but he is nowhere to be seen."

"I fell asleep. It was still dark at three, I am sorry!"

Casp felt unsettled by Vist's disappearance. The mysterious night guest, almost killed by the anxious youth, had disappeared at dawn into the autumn storm in the valley. There was no evidence of him having removed anything valuable from the mill tower or its storage apart from one poly-bottle of water. The miller said that Vist had popped in to check on his sleeping patient and had thanked Mrs Herman for the good news of the receding fever before leaving. The computer had been powered down and had no files added, removed or copied. It looked like Vist had indeed done nothing but some MESH browsing and had used an electronic post exchange, probably from his own account on one of the crew-salons or polit-forums.

The miller suggested that this was not a surprise because MESH was the only thing the new government had not yet seized control over. If Rebels have to communicate long distances, this would be the safest way. Vist would likely cross the river and head towards the Dead Forest to meet up with the Resistance. All was well. Casp could sense that Mrs Herman did not expect to be involved in politics so soon – she had avoided accepting Rebel refugees in their house until this day. Now she seemed worried that the Cruisers would suspect more strongly that the miller hid Rebels occasionally, and there would be plenty of trouble. The little girl, Hachi, woke up wet from sweat and hungry, and her mother rushed to the kitchens. Casp overheard Mr

Herman mumble behind his wife's back that he had already hidden a couple of Rebels in the past well enough for even Mrs Herman not to be able to find them.

Casp said that the wind was strong and Vist could not have gone far in weather like this. He pulled his goggles over his eyes, jumped on his quad bike, rushed along the road to the bridge, and interrogated the old caretaker about the time of Vist's crossing. The caretaker insisted that no single man had crossed the bridge in the last twelve hours. There had been a group of men and women in an electrical cart just a few minutes ago, and there was a woman on foot earlier in the morning – a shy, pretty and very polite one. Doesn't he know what women sound like? Ha ha, he does indeed! The robe? Yes, but every sensible person and faithful child of our Lord wears a robe in weather like this. No, he did not see a handbag. It wasn't his business to fill his eyes with sand checking people's luggage unless it was a vehicle compartment or a large truck on wheels.

There was no point looking for footprints, as sweeping ground waves of sand erased them as soon as they were left. Casp peered over the river through his goggles but failed to see the other end of the bridge. He asked himself why he even cared; the man called Vist had not done anything wrong, apart from scaring the hell out of him on his arrival at the Daisy Mill. But it was nothing compared to shooting Vist with a shotgun in return, right in the heart. That man had done exactly what he had promised – helped Casp's sister and left the mill untroubled – but Casp felt something else through a certain amount of guilt. He discovered that in this moment, he wanted to be by Vist's side no matter where Vist was. He admitted to himself that the last night spent in the room watching this mysterious person was the best time he had had in ages. They had hardly talked, and Vist had been very busy pushing through complicated images, adding something to the paragraphs in different languages, frowning and sometimes laughing at something that Casp did not find funny.

He vaguely remembered Vist's story about the Oak. It turned out that the rumours were true that in just two days on foot, in the middle of the Dead Forest, there was the largest and oldest of the giant trees. If it wasn't for all the dust and sand in the wind in his region, Casp would probably be able to see it from the top of the mill. The Great Oak, oddly enough, was still alive. On the upper branches of its crown, the leaves were green in summer, and acorns ripened.

Many years ago, when it stood tall as ever, one of the last data-loaders built an entire commercial health resort called the Tree House. The trunk and branches were wrapped in staircases and elevators. On the thickest branches and in the hollows, residential premises, guest rooms, indoor gardens, medical quarters, gyms, a restaurant and even a swimming pool (rains cannot fill it anymore) were built. Under the roots, there were office spaces and transport facilities. A vacation there used to cost serious money in the Platinum Age. Nowadays, the Head Board of the Resistance "lived" there. The Tree House was hidden in the dust clouds. Satellites protected it against any attack from the ground or from orbit. The lifts and stairs have been removed from the trunk, and you can only get up there on the tetrahoders – that climbing machine designed and built by the legendary Baker family.

At some point, Casp became sleepy and continued seeing Vist at the desk through the inverted images of the holo-screens. He dreamed of Vist having some inhuman powers and speed. In his dream, he saw Vist looking straight at him for a moment and then ... Vist removed the nail of his own thumb. From the thumb, he pulled out a wire, thin like a thread. He inserted the end of it into the input port on the panel. Vist closed his eyes, and those screens shone gold instead of the usual white and blue. Casp could not remember any more of the dream. And now, even this memory was such a disproportionate and fluctuating sensation that he shook his head and turned back to Daisy Mill. He decided he had read too many sci-fi books about loaders in the master's library.

Soon he said to himself out loud, "If only that was not a dream! It would have been so damned cool!"

Chapter 28. 3411. Out in Space – White City

Steven stopped. There was no threat in the quarantine facility's common room. But there was an argument unfolding. Massimo sat on a bench with his top off, facing Tolyan, who was in his underpants with a towel over his neck on a parallel bench. They were having a rather emotional debate, at least for Tolyan. Everybody, including May and her baby, seemed to enjoy watching them. Vist was fully dressed. Steven spotted Zina and felt even better. Oh, boy, she looked stunning with her hair down!

"Don't get me wrong," Tolyan boomed, "I appreciate your kind offer, but the cold water in our thermo-flasks is no worse than the water in your ... fancy container. What's it called?"

"A thermoreg," Massimo said, scratching his purple and quite hairy chest. He looked almost like a child next to Tolyan.

"Yeah, that. We are not stupid, you know. Rod, tell him. We also know how to exploit exothermic and endothermic reactions."

"I am sure you do. Why do you think we know of it? We were not the first to discover those things." Massimo was obviously better at self-control, but he was clearly not used to having this type of conversation. "I just assumed that since you have been on the road for a couple of days, surely you could have run out of ..."

"Oh! Are you now suggesting that we are not capable of restoring our supplies? We are not those villagers of yours ..."

"But this is not why ..."

"Of course not!" Tolyan sat back and folded his huge arms on his mighty chest, "You think you are so much further ahead with your technology, don't you? Do you think I was impressed with those fancy showers and your arse-washing bogs? We have things like this too and even better. We did not hibernate for three hundred years ... for your information. For example, we have prolonged the average life span to a hundred and sixty."

"Yes. That was before you sent colonists here. We live longer here, thanks to you. We also stay young and fertile much longer than before. My father looks almost the same age as me."

"So? We did that too. Men have no problems with their prostate or with blood pressure, and they stay healthy longer! Young women can have one of their ovaries removed and preserved for thirty years and have it back with all the hormones and eggs—"

"We don't do that!"

"Aha!" Tolyan looked triumphant.

"Instead, we can clone the whole reproductive system and replace the old one. Men's too, you know. Just like any other organ."

"Grrr!" said Tolyan and threw the towel on the floor.

Captain Darkwood intervened. "Tolyan, leave him alone. It is not very polite to challenge your hosts in this manner. Don't forget, over the last three hundred years, we have had wars, the entire population of Earth working out their differences. You know, mass production takes time and resources and involves politics. But these people have had to face – Vist, what did these people have to face?"

Vist's metallic voice answered readily, like an information desk. "This handful of people had to face an alien world with a handful of technological inheritances and the objective of surviving in an environment full of surprises."

"There! Take away the time they spent in stasis and then in station conditions, although you can add that this planet offered some new ideas and materials. No wonder they progressed faster. They had nothing else to do."

"Well ..." Tolyan would not give up easily. "Not such a handful anymore. Thousands of them now."

"Oh, sweetheart! Just make your mind up and admit that they have done pretty well," Rod said, "I already have many questions about the things I have seen."

"About the bog, I assume?" Steven asked.

"No, Yes – about that too, but I am more curious about your ensemble, Massimo. What is it made of? I thought it was rubber, but may I feel it?"

"Sure," said Massimo and handed Rod the shirt he was holding. "It is made of ucha-silk, made from the sap of the ucha-tree."

"Hmm. It is thick and stretchy. Soft like a fabric, breathy and at the same time, Vist, check this out! You might want to use it to upgrade your bio-suit. This is not just a shirt – it's a device, a bit like your robe. I would like to learn how it works. Now Massimo, tell me this – why are you purple?"

The screen on the wall turned itself on, and the violet face of a woman said that their tests were confirmed to be negative. May and her child needed to stay a little longer to see a paediatrician, and Massimo had to see a nurse about some of his old scars, but the guests from Earth were safe enough to enter the city.

Tom and his crew got dressed, took their belongings, and entered another corridor, leaving May and Massimo behind. The passage brought them into the square, where a few people were waiting for them. Two were dressed in a uniform and may have been city guards.

The man, who did not look much like a community leader, stepped forwards. He spoke with an unusually deep and powerful voice that did not match his small height and face, which was completely covered in hair. All you could see was his dark bottom lip.

"I was hoping so much that this event would take place in my lifetime, but I never even dreamed that it would be my honour to say these words, 'Welcome, people from Earth!' For many reasons, I am glad you finally came. I am the Grand of the city. I have no other name until the next election."

His thick brown hair and bushy beard were trimmed evenly around his neck and just above his shoulders so that he resembled a porcini mushroom. He wore sunglasses, very light, comfortable trousers and a shirt of properly woven fabrics. His clothes and the clothes of the people with him were decorated with some colourful patterns. Luminescent and metallic dye chemically enhanced the colours and made the fabric reflect the light. In the dark world of Noverca, this was the brightest sight seen by travellers so far. Each colonist had a small flat light device on their chests, worn as a necklace. This time Captain Darkwood took his rightful place as a mission leader and introduced himself and his companions.

"I am glad to greet you in the name of everyone we left behind. The objective of our visit was pre-planned and has not changed since your predecessors landed here. May I assume you are aware of it and still accept its necessity? It has been a long time since the last communication between our worlds."

"Everything we have done here and managed to achieve we did for one main reason. To build a home for humanity – for us and for those still to come. You are the first. But all I see is a delegation – as I expected. Our sensors detected one small ship, but we could not say if there were more out of range. May I ask how many of you are here, and when should we expect the rest?"

"I am afraid this is it for now. I have my pilots waiting for my orders with the ship, but it is a small ship indeed. You may say we are a delegation from Earth rather than a specific party of new colonists. We are not here to stay."

"Then I anticipate a lengthy conversation. If you can afford to travel on round trips this time, then we definitely have things to discuss. Today is a day of true historical significance. Let me take you to the town centre," said Grand and pointed to the vehicle that was most definitely built using models from Earth, at least to some extent.

Rod said that the last time he was on an electro-train was when he was a child visiting an old entertainment park in Nevada. This elegant and almost luxurious train, with transparent wagons, was not made for children's entertainment.

The Earth delegation was taken across the city with an opportunity to see truly reassuring sights. It was a normal civilised establishment like common academic districts built around the Earth in the twenty-second century. Streets were formed in rows of two and three-storey dwellings, none of which looked alike. The gardens, squares, roads, rail networks, stores, markets and teashops could easily belong to any Platinum Age town, but to forget where you were would have been impossible. The colours here were alien, and the massive, strange building rising above the city was definitely not a bell tower or city hall.

"First, we will make you comfortable. You are welcome to stay in any hotel of your choice. The city budget will pay for accommodation, although I suspect the owners will be happy to offer you the best rooms for free. To have such special guests is a priceless advertisement and very good for business. The same goes for restaurants. Only on this matter, I hope you will allow me to make a few recommendations—"

"What is that?" Tolyan interrupted, pointing at the tall building.

"This is our temple of O'Teka," answered Grand, "That device on top of it connects all of us to the temple via these amulets," he said, touching the flat device on his chest. "And it controls the city walls, maintaining the protective electromagnetic field. You might not feel it yet, but this place is screened from space radiation and from the rays of Vitr."

"Vitr?" Rod asked.

"I think they abbreviated Vitricus to call it their sun here," Mik said.

"I would like to go to the temple first," said Vist, making his or her wish clear, and it was clear that he or she would go there first.

Chapter 29. 3416. Back on Earth – Preacher

"So what did they do with them in the end?"

Zina sat next to Tom, folded her arms, and put her forehead down on them.

"I don't think they have the stomach for protein processing," she said, "and I feel so relieved about that. Digging or building a fire for ten corpses appeared to be too much trouble for people they all hated."

"Ten? So?"

"Yes, Ontha didn't make it. He was old; he died about two hours ago. I tried to make him comfortable and offered him food and drink, but he asked for Bliss and refused to tell me how to contact the nearest neighbours and get some help. Maybe they really don't have access to MESH here."

"They must have – if they didn't hack the satellite cannons, how else could they have shot us down?" Tom said, sighing. "So what did they do with the bodies?"

"They dragged them to the wet mud, further towards the sea and left them there. The bodies got sucked into the sludge within minutes. Dangerous business. I don't know how they did not get stuck there too."

"And Patrick?"

"Tolyan and I took him off the cross, dressed him up and left him on one of the beds upstairs. He should be able to walk again by now."

"Any novices turned up?"

"So far, just four. At first, it was just one girl with a small sack and a grey goose in the birdcage. She said she would go anywhere with us if nobody ate her bird. So now we have Roy, Yazabella, Eric and Milana. I wrote down all the novices' names. Most of them are healthy, but if we take them to the Oak, Selest must examine them, especially the girls. They were frequently abused."

Tom gritted his teeth, clenched both fists, and slowly put them on the table.

Zina carried on, "Mik has found almost all of our things, including our weapons. One zapper was dismantled, and some of my painkillers were missing. Marta's portable com-station was blown up on the way here. Steven's blade was found on that Virgil guy. Not sure why *he* would have it."

"I will ask him myself. How is Steven?"

"Steven is Steven. He still thinks he is indestructible, but at least he heals faster than you and I would. Tolyan will be as good as new by the time we leave. Mik's wound is fresh and will need a few days, but he is pretty mobile."

"And Marta?"

Zina paused then said, "I don't know. She does not say much."

"Is she still sitting with Chang?"

"Yes, she is by the grave. But she does not cry anymore. She just sings something sad in Ukrainian."

For a few minutes, they sat at the dining table of the tower's second level in silence.

Zina lifted her head. "Tom?"

"Mm?"

"Do you miss him?"

"Who? Chang? Yes, of course."

"No, I mean Vist," replied Zina, "Don't you wish he was here with us? Everything is simpler when he is around."

Tom visibly relaxed and took a deep breath. "You still think Vist is a man?"

"I ... don't know. I actually don't care. I know I miss him ... or her."

"Nobody bets on it anymore, but I think Vist is a woman," Tom said.

"Sometimes I think that too. You like her, don't you?"

"In what way?"

"That way ..."

"Is it even possible?"

"Can I speak freely, Captain?"

"Zina, you already do."

"Everyone likes Vist, even if they don't admit it. Or at least respects her, as our troopers do. I know Rod never was completely positive. But Tom, if you like someone *that way*, would you even care whether this someone is male or female? Does sex always have to decide for us who we are to love? Only immature people's love starts with physical attraction."

"Hey, were we talking about love?" asked Tom and looked at Zina.

"Maybe you misunderstood me, but yes. Let's talk about love. Do you love Vist?"

Tom Darkwood moved his eyes from Zina's face towards the narrow vertical line of the grey sky in the window.

"There was a time when I knew exactly who my beloved was, and I still could not answer this question. Perhaps I don't know what love is or who I am myself."

"What? You suspect you might be like Rod?"

"No, I don't know what I want. Do I care about Vist? Sure! I feel something like love when I convince myself she is a woman. But when I suspect she is a man, everything in me refuses to believe it, and I almost hate her for the torment her mystery causes me. Maybe I am immature."

"Then I say you don't love her. You are anything but a coward, Captain. If you loved her, you would not be afraid to love her, no matter what she is. Say you love her as a woman, and she turned out to be a man ... What are you going to do? Stop loving him? You don't love a man or woman ... you love Vist!"

"Zina!" Tom almost shouted.

He got up and walked to the window that Father Deessa had jumped from. It was about six metres above the ground. This window was the largest in the tower, but how a fat man had squeezed through the frame remained a mystery. His heavy dark-blue robe lay on the floor by the window.

"Is the Word-Bearer ready to talk?"

Zina also got up.

"Yes, Captain. Here is the key." She dropped the key on the table.

Tom stormed past her, grabbing the key on his way.

"Tom!"

"What?" Tom stopped at the doorway.

"Love him! If he is a woman, that will be a bonus."

Tom gritted his teeth again and stomped up the stairs. He couldn't get the key into the keyhole for a long time, and he opened the door with almost a kick.

The small window did not let in much sunlight, and the room was lit mainly with a few large candles. The Word-Bearer sat in the chair by the fireplace with no fire. He was chewing on a creamy fish pie and had a mug of tea in his hand; he held it as if it were a glass of wine. The Word-Bearer's movements were slow and deliberate. His thin fingers reminded Tom of the old portraits of ancient aristocrats. Brother Patrick was in his sky-blue robe, but his neck was wrapped in a silky white scarf, tied in a large bowknot on his chest. Who does he think he is? Tom thought. A cardinal or a bishop of some kind?

"Finally!" Patrick said without looking at him. Instead, he carefully examined the last piece of the pie before moving it into his mouth. "The Black woman said that some 'space captain' would talk to me. Are you him?" he added with his mouth full. Sour cream from the pie whitened his lips, returning Tom to his unpleasant memory of Shafran eating tocks.

Tom was too wound up to waste time on ceremony.

"Where is the connection in the castle?" he asked, "How do you send messages? MESH, phone, radio?"

Patrick swallowed, wiped his lips, shook some crumbs off his white tie and slowly got up. He walked towards the window, still not looking at the captain.

"You've searched the castle, haven't you? I assume if you had found something, you would not be asking me. The others did not tell you anything useful either, am I right?" He turned around and faced Tom for the first time. "What makes you think we have such ungodly items in this holy place? Yes! Holy place!"

Tom did not say anything; he studied the strange man in front of him. Patrick appeared calm, but Tom noticed a sparkle of perspiration on his forehead. He realised that this calmness was achieved with great effort. Patrick was nothing like what Mik had described ... a very different person! How many faces did he have?

The Word-Bearer smiled and spoke again, "Captain, do you know what these ruins are?

These walls," he said, making a circular motion with his left arm above his head, while still holding the mug in his right hand and swirling it lazily, "used to be the walls of a cathedral, built for a very special purpose – to get closer to our Lord. The earthquakes lifted it up on the hill. It was rebuilt five times. The sea came closer to its steps and receded again. The towns around it are long gone – claimed by the forest. The forest is now dead, but these walls are still here. For thousands of years, people have come here to communicate with our Lord. Even when this became a museum, nobody dared speak louder than a whisper when walking in. Did they use a radio or telephone? No. Our Lord does not need these things to receive our messages, or send his. Only your true heart can reach him through your prayers."

Look at it now, Tom wanted to say, but he remembered Vist's advice, "Do not try to reason with the unreasonable," and said nothing. Patrick waited for a second and carried on.

"So, as you can see, I can't help you. If you came here for information, I could tell you many useful things, but nothing about technology."

"I was asking about your means of communication with people, but you hear what you want to hear. Okay. Don't you want to ask about your fellow Cruisers? Do you care what happened to them?"

Patrick shrugged.

"I am sure what happened was exactly what the Lord intended."

"Don't you want to know?"

"Oh, go on then, tell me," said Patrick capriciously. He sipped his tea and grimaced.

"Father Deessa committed suicide, or maybe it was an accident. We are not sure. Father Ontha was responsible for the death of my pilot. Ontha tried to escape after he had me in the torture chambers, but he collided with the man you had met earlier and died from a serious spinal injury. All your brothers died during an attempt to detain, torture and poison my people and me for information. Your holy place was built on human blood and bones, and now you insist on carrying on the good traditions. Give me one reason I shouldn't drag you into the dungeon and beat your smugness out of you with the club they used on me?"

Tom spoke these words as if he was thinking aloud, calmly and quietly, but Patrick's smile slowly slipped off his face and was exchanged with an expression of pale concern.

Tom continued, "The women and children are given a choice to stay here or to come with us if they want to. But even if one of the young ones decides to stay, I can't allow you to twist their minds any longer."

"Are you going to kill me too?" said Patrick.

"That will depend on how useful or harmful you really are."

Patrick sipped the cold tea from his mug again. "Okay. You sound like an educated man. I am not sure about that dark demon of yours, though, who so heartlessly left me upstairs alone. Your kind likes reasoning. Ok, let's reason. Just summarise for me once more – what problems do you have with religious faith?"

Tom sighed. He suddenly felt tired. "It's a wicked manipulation tool and a force that has slowed down the development of the human race and its individuals for thousands of years."

"That was too generic."

"You said – summarise."

"And yet your summary is so vague. I believe if I try to do the same for my conviction, I can do a better job and be more concrete. Ready? There is a god! That's it. See? Simple and concrete! You people talk too much. You are demagogues. I know what you will ask. Why do I believe there is a god? How do I know he exists? Again, my answer is simple and pure – because I do. I don't need *to know*. I need *to believe*. You can believe only in what you cannot know. That is my understanding and therefore – my knowledge."

Tom felt a headache creeping in, and he summoned memories of Vist's voice in his head again. He blinked and tried to reach out for that voice like a drowning person reaching for an outstretched hand. Do not try to make sense of it. It is like trying to build a jigsaw puzzle from the pieces of ten different sets.

Patrick was still talking, and his voice was getting stronger with every word, but the mockery in his eyes gradually turned into deep sympathy and kindness. "The recorded human history over millennia shows the consistent presence of religion. Pagans believed in many gods of natural forces. Simple savages believed in the spirits of their ancestors; Muslims, Christians, Hindus and ... whatever ... created thousands of versions of our Lord, including the faith of atheists. Choose according to your taste. What does this mean? It means that there is a *need* for it! You can deny it as much as you like, but you need to believe in something. Without faith, you have no foundation, no morality, no order, no comfort and no reason for living. This world is nothing but an illusion created in our minds by Satan. It may feel real to you, but one strong knock on the head and it is gone. The real world is the one you *need* to find your way into while you are still alive. This is why you were born: your soul has just one lifetime to find the Lord, and you will be safe. Don't resist, my brother. The Lord is calling you. He is still waiting for you; he still loves you. He is forgiving, and even you, Captain, can still find peace and love." Patrick now stood in front of the captain and looked right into his eyes with the warmth and tenderness of a nurse in a psychiatric hospital.

Tom had no idea of how Vist was able to listen to this sort of thing. How could she play along as she had done with Shafran? Tom realised that he couldn't do that. He would likely end up strangling this man in the blue robe if he did not shut up.

"Captain! Come on, you have nothing to object to such clarity with. Why don't you just believe? You have so much to gain and nothing to lose."

"Except for my mind and my full responsibility for my actions. Please stop talking. I don't like white noise. Tell me about your evacuation plan, or you can return to your cross. I spoke with Brother Mark before one of his victims interrupted us. Mark did not know much, unfortunately. He said that the evacuation was in the hands of the Lord. You better not try the same line with me, Brother Patrick."

"I do not understand. What evacuation plans?"

"You have a rocket in your insignia. Ontha wanted to know where my ship was. He also wanted my pilot and my loader. I want to know what for?"

For a moment, Tom felt like a completely different man was standing in front of him, but it was the same Word-Bearer, although his posture and facial expression were suddenly more like that of a politician. His sympathetic eyes became cold and his lips tightened.

He spoke with short and sharp words, "Simple. We need a ship to the colony you returned from. We don't believe in the drifting Moon project. We want to go to our Promised Land!"

"How did you know about us?"

A soft and lazy voice said, "There is a true way to know things, my brother. The Lord spoke to us. Ouch!" Patrick grabbed his own nose, which bled immediately. The white scarf was now covered in red splatters. "What did you do that for, son of a ...? You broke it!"

"None of that shit!" Tom said, "Tell me the truth!"

"Okay! Okay! Jesus! Oh, fuck! That hurts!" Patrick's deep and almost singing voice changed dramatically into a squeaky whine.

"Where would you prefer to go from here? Up to the loft or down to the dungeon? Heaven or hell? Since you do not want to stay on Earth?" Tom asked.

Patrick laid down on the bed, then held his nose and tilted it upwards.

He spoke like an ordinary man with a blocked nose. "We intercepted your communications with the Rebels."

"So you do have a radio in here?"

"Not in here, gosh! I will bleed to death! It's in the van! Portable. Virgil used to work as a communications technician for the new government. I recruited him and persuaded him to steal the com-van. He is the one who hijacked the military satellite and instructed it to shoot your pods down as soon as you all left the ship. Missed mostly, stupid fucker! The last pod left a few seconds late and scrambled his timing. He was not experienced enough to compensate but at least he got two of you."

Tom was already running downstairs to the yard. He found his troopers there, called out to Steven to secure the prisoner in the tower, and then told Tolyan to get Virgil. He turned to Mik.

"Are there any structures in the castle that can conceal a vehicle?"

"No, sir."

"But if you had a van here, how would you hide it?"

"In the woods or in a cave ... if there is one."

When they arrived at the camp, Tolyan stood among the few remaining novices and swore like he only did when drunk.

"Where is Virgil?" Tom asked.

"He and Volna are gone! The bastard was hiding an e-truck or something in there." Tolyan pointed towards the woods. "He covered it in branches, and these guys," he said, pointing at the novices, "apparently did not think to tell us."

"You expect too much of them!" Mik said to his friend. "Where would they go?"

The captain sighed. "I don't know. To other settlements, Thieves, other Cruisers, Mooners. Maybe Virgil was hoping to find the *Wasp* by himself and then think about how to fly it. He will not be able to trade any more of the intercepted information because we will change the frequency and codes from now on. Funny, he left for the unknown in his van when he could have flown away in a spaceship of the same size in just a few years' time. Communications technicians are paid well in the Resistance. Much more than the new government used to pay him, and definitely more than he was getting here."

Chapter 30. 3411. Out in Space – The Colony

The town was not big, with just a few thousand people. You could easily get to know it in a day or two just by wandering the streets. The colony was not just a city. It also included a few farms, some of which were quite remote. In the city, most people moved around on foot and used slightly faster e-trains. Outside of the city walls, they travelled by tracked vehicles and wheeled trucks. The economy was also simple and, according to Vist, resembled the economy of the early American states, with one or two differences: a lack of taxes and churches, but with the benefits of advanced technology. It was a New Year's tradition to contribute voluntarily to improving the city.

The only city temple was nothing more than an electronic repository of information. The principle resembled MESH on Earth, but with hardware backups and hard copies of crystal records. Inside the temple, there was not much room for people because the information was accessed remotely. You could read it or add your work anytime and anywhere, using personal amulets – a small box with a voice-control panel.

The amulets were worn around the neck and powered by solar radiation, and they could open a holo-screen of any size. Since the sun was always there, it was always available for charging. The amulet was secured to each person through biometrics. All the systems in the colony settlements were fully end-to-end homomorphically encrypted, as were all connections.

Data fraud was almost completely eradicated. Communications across a fully virtualised network infrastructure were instantaneous, lag-free and completely wireless. Permanent settlements were connected in a network. Each tower projected a wireless net over hundreds of miles. Personal amulets were connected to it, providing communications and distributing computing power. Persistent connections to centralised storage allowed all data to be recorded and stored perpetually. Colonists used them to talk to each other, study, work, access bank accounts, make payments for goods and services – and for writing, of course. The colonists recorded everything – their thoughts, their achievements, their discoveries – and they called it an offering to O'Teka. Two cycles after entering the city, every guest from

Earth was presented with an amulet and learned how to use it. Unfortunately, taking them home as a souvenir was out of the question. All they would be allowed to take away was information since they brought nothing but knowledge. And this is why they needed Vist.

The colony was a new and separate culture in which trade principles were essential. It sounded so simple at the start. The colony would benefit from accepting more people – the bigger the community, the more members could contribute to its development. People from Earth needed a new home, which is why they sent the *Lyra* ships in the first place. The colony's purpose was to build that new home, but the travellers could not help but feel as if they had come to a completely alien planet and were asking for refuge.

"This is why I need to talk to the colony's leaders as much as I need to talk to your scientists. After all, it is not just a matter of technical and biological issues, but a matter of politics too," Vist said when Grand made another stop by a college field camp outside the western city gate. Here, all the *Wasp* astronauts regrouped for the final trip to the farms.

It was almost four cycles since all ten guests had come to the city and examined every corner of it, including Paradise – the garden. May, who Massimo vouched for, was allowed back to the city after three cycles of rehabilitation. This meant she could show the astronauts round Paradise herself, much to everybody's delight. Grand took them outside the city walls to show them the farms and research stations.

"My dear friend! You will have no problem here. I am sure by the time your people arrive, we will find a way to integrate them into society. Right now, you need to focus on biological differences, and there will be no shortage of help from our scientists. To survive in this world, you must become a scientist to a certain degree anyway, regardless of your chosen purpose, other skills and professional occupations. You saw what happens to those who do not accept such a necessity. But our colony flourished because our majority understood and embraced science." Grand looked around and beckoned one of the students to come closer. "Vist, meet John. He is one of the average students of this school, but he is very resourceful and has already succeeded in more than one discipline. After all, why should we be anything less than our founders?"

The short young man who approached Grand stopped and waited for a question. He looked at Vist with a strange expression, almost as if his expectations were fully met, yet he was still fascinated by what he saw.

"What are you working on, young man?" asked Grand.

"Bioengineering is my main goal, sir. I want to invent a new way of combining microorganisms with electrical equipment. I study the work of Kim Schroder on biogel-based refrigerators. I will try and modify her bacteria species to improve solar panels. I also study wind sculpturing and write essays on the principles of society formations."

"And what of your ambitions if you fail all three subjects?"

Vist's question did not surprise the student. "If I fail on all three, I will write a novel about you, sir ... ma'am."

"You can go, John," Grand said and turned to the rest of the guests, "Do you all see why your colleague Vist is so concerned? You have to compete with colonists to feel at home here, but I am sure you can prepare the people of Earth for both environments within a couple of generations. Vist, you need to talk to Samantha Nguyen. I think you are right, and your evacuees need to be thoroughly prepared biologically and mentally. They have to be able to integrate into our climate and our society. From what you told me, to bring just anyone will be just as dangerous for us as it would be if we opened the gate to the villagers. We may not survive the new fractionation."

Chapter 31. 3416. Back on Earth – Tom's Message

MESH message

TDarkwood_17.05@@Parsecmail.mesh.

Voice record of Captain Tom Darkwood, in command of *WSP-41* (05.09.3416–13.45 EN-time) Earth. Bow-Bridge station.

Encrypted for the personal attention of Rezeda and any Chieftain of the Oak with the authorisation of Object and Vist.

Hello Vasily, Fleur, Josh! Whoever gets this first, thank you for your greeting message. It is nice to know you are all in good health. I am sorry for the long silence, but Cruisers detained us, as you probably figured out. Not Mooners, no. These ones call themselves the Moses Movement. We managed to break free, but we lost Chang, and our troopers are not in their best shape. Marta told me the last words she sent you before destroying her station were about Rod, Général and Vist being missing from the landing party. I hope you found them. I saw the message from Vist on my MESH port, but it was too brief: "I am alive, see you on the Oak." The good news is that we have located your second beacon and know where to go. The first operational MESH access was here, on the bridge, so as you can see, we are very close.

Our detention was in the ruins of St David's cathedral. There we found a handful of brothers and liquidated them with their leaders. All the details will be in my official report. We also found almost two dozen youngsters, brainwashed and "blissed out." One refused to come with us and escaped with their only sister there. He needs to be blocked from MESH urgently and found ASAP. With possession of official technology, he has control over one of the satellite cannons and can potentially mess something else up. All the names will also be in my first report, but this man is Virgil Gull. You will find him in the com-staff personnel list, and he has stolen a communication van from one of their safe-return teams. You may find a young woman with him who goes by the name Volna. Check her out, too; I suspect she is not a simple sister.

I intend to take the rest of the former novices to the nearest watch post, so please check the map and send someone there on tetrahoder to help the three of them return to their families. They are all locals. The rest have decided to come with us or have nowhere else to go. I have not been on Earth for almost five years and am relying on you to know what to do with them. I hope you have more cabin camps now in Object.

Whatever you decide to do with the ruins, you have to know there is little value in them. The ruins are not completely deserted, as an old woman and one Bliss addict are still there. I had no way of dealing with them, and my priorities lay elsewhere. I assume they won't be able to defend themselves if Thieves pay them a visit. I leave it to your authority to decide their fate.

I also searched MESH for the location of Chang's family. I have written to his mother, but his cousin is with you on the Oak, so I will be very grateful if one of you will formally notify him. I have attached the coordinates of the grave here if he needs them.

Please pass the message on to Selest from Marta that she needs to see her as soon as possible. Our pilot is pregnant. Since she is also a widow, she will need lots of support.

What else? Oh yes. Don't worry about the quarantine; we have completed all the necessary stages on our way back while on Wasp, in line with the protocol. The samples of the important materials should be with Vist. They are the only hazard, but Vist will head straight to the labs, so tell them to prepare the seals if you have not done that already.

I may not have any more access to MESH on my way to the Oak. I miss Earth food, so please tell Nick the Catalonian that I will have anything but worm stew. I hope to see you soon.

Voice command Four-one-three, send.

Chapter 32. 3411. Out in Space – *Ark*

"I want to know what happened. Why did you split up? What made religion reappear among people who had left it behind generations ago? I have some ideas, but I would prefer to hear your account." Vist's metallic voice displayed a trace of impatience.

Tolyan made a gigantic step forwards and said, "Yes, please. I also want to know. Those bubble villagers do not look very advanced. They are reversing. Are they an experiment? The girl we met said that you exile people."

Grand looked him in the eye and then stared at his hands for almost a minute. Everybody waited. Finally, he opened the door of his strange vehicle and said, "Get in. I want to show you something. It is not far – about twenty minutes away and the road is good. You will know most of the details by the time we get there."

The road was good indeed. It looked like a typical country road you would see in most of the hot regions on Earth, where clay and rare rains cemented all frequently used routes into recognisable dusty tracks. Tom sat on the bench next to the driver and could now feel Vist's back, as she – or he – sat right behind him. Not being aware of this contact was hard, and his neck muscles tightened immediately. Tolyan sat back-to-back with Grand, and Général faced him on the opposite seat. Rod sat next to Général, and the rest took their seats in the same order. They had already visited most of the settlements arranged like this. The engine sounded surprisingly quiet, but the tracks on both sides made a constant rustling noise – too loud to have a conversation, but with Grand's voice booming even louder. He did not have to worry about traffic, as he was the only driver on the road.

"In a nutshell, the first few generations never even thought about faith or worship. The trouble started long after every member of the original colony founders had gone. The day arrived when survival was particularly hard. A series of natural disasters and bad weather almost destroyed the first four farms. It took two years to restore them to full prosperity. I should tell you about two men who changed the world for the colonists, and you can see for yourself whether it was for better or worse. One, and his name has intentionally been forgotten, happened to be a troublemaker. He is usually referred to as the Selfless. He was probably very smart, but being rational is not the same. He was the first person who was not enthusiastic about working, risking his life, or thinking hard for the sake of the colony. Some people said that this was because he did not have a family. Others thought he didn't value life and didn't care about dying. The records noted that people heard him saying things like 'I'd rather die' and 'What's the point?' It is true – he did not do well as a kid. He was jealous of a girl who did not like him, tried to hurt other kids during training, always wanted more than those who worked harder than him, and he was the first person in our history to lie about something."

"Sounds like the first colonists failed to pass the necessary understandings on to some of their descendants," Vist said. It seemed as if Vist had not raised his or her voice over the noise. However, the voice still sounded as clear as if someone had just turned the volume up. "There was an IVP programme for your founders by KOSI relocation – an educational course to balance colony prioritisation and individual-value prioritisation. Still, why was he a surprise to the others? His behaviour lacked that balance but wasn't unnatural. Surely your phycologists recognised that?"

"Psychology was not in high demand back then, as you can imagine. Surely it was an error, but the colony at that time was still like an under-populated ant-hill! One person technically could destroy the whole colony, just like one crew member could sabotage a spaceship, leading to the death of all. Today we value human life more than anything, but in those days, I am afraid the circumstances claimed several lives as a price for the colony's survival. While everyone was expected to realise that what they were building was bigger than their individual lives, it was the only thing those lives depended on, and that one day, things would be different if they succeeded. What happened to the Selfless may not be new for Earth, but here – nobody had any experience of dealing with someone who had completely failed to understand his and the colony's interdependence."

Grand turned his truck from the field into the woods and then said, "The colonists didn't practice exiling people back then and were completely unprepared to deal with such unexpected occurrences. Also, there was nowhere to exile them to. Even scouts could not last outside the city walls for more than three days. When people were tired of his whining, the Selfless was invited to choose the job he wanted but with one condition: he would do his best. This was after he had almost burned down his place of work. He was first assigned to the electrician's team. On the day of the accident, he was locked up in his quarters for ten cycles on minimum rations and became a burden to the colony. He said he wanted to work with literature. So his new assignment was to replace the old woman in the Information Block – the first brick in the temple of O'Teka. The keeper was a firstborn here, a feeble but proud woman. She volunteered to give her job up and went to the kitchens. This was a bonus for everyone as her crisp pie is one of the colonists' favourite recipes, even now. But she died soon after, at the age of just ninety-nine. In the meantime, the Selfless mainly delegated his duties to his junior co-workers and spent his time reading. I don't know what material he chose, but people then noticed him talking about strange things and becoming very close to the second man I mentioned. This man was called Tor Goodman, and his friendship with the Selfless turned him into a monster. A few years later, he called himself Godman and was responsible for a real disaster. The colony, too, was partially responsible for it by not acting soon enough. But everyone was busy; there were neither the means nor the people to deal with him, and nobody expected that a simple burden could become such a disaster. Godman started the first secret group, targeting anyone who would listen. For those who felt lonely, he became a friend. For those who lost their parents, he would become a father. If someone became frustrated or sad, he would make them feel even worse at first, and then offer a solution that no one had thought of. Some young people were convinced by him that they had been treated unfairly, exploited and turned into slaves. He had charmed some young girls so much that it was enough for them to give up on their dreams and even their purpose. Some stopped working entirely and demanded easy jobs, more food and comforts based on being disadvantaged in one way or another."

"Sounds like he left his mark!" Général said under his breath.

Grand continued loudly, "One story has become a sort of legend. There was a young girl born with a disability due to local radiation. She only had two fingers on her right hand and one on her left. That was before artificial limb technology was improved and we started using genetic testing. Her parents brought up the girl to be a fine and determined colony member. All she could do with her three fingers was to assist the botanist in the greenhouse laboratory. She operated magnifying equipment for four hours a day and kept the dome-glass clean for the rest of her working hours. It was an easier life than that of the others, but everyone appreciated her effort. One young smart-arse spotted her, decided he had had some health issues too and demanded his hours of wall-insulation maintenance be shortened. The doctor failed to find anything wrong with him and suggested observation. Of course, the lad was found to be a fake. An attempt to discipline him ended up him seeking Godman's sympathy and understanding. This boy grew up and became the first preacher of what we were forced to recognise as a Way of Ancestors."

"What year was that?" Vist asked.

"Sixth generation period, year 186. The colony was just over a thousand people at the time."

"Thank you. Please carry on."

"I am glad you find it interesting. So, where was I? Aha! Similarly, the colony lost thirty-two young members to Godman in the first four years of his teachings, including six mature-but not-very-smart men. The Selfless, the young preacher and Godman spread dark ideas like a disease. The Way of Ancestors started to weaken the colony's foundation. The fewer people remained committed to human survival, the harder it was for the colony to progress, and the easier it was for a small sect to fool new members with the idea of something else taking care of them. They spoke of an entity leading our ancestors on Earth for thousands of years – one that would look after you if you believed in it and trusted it. To persuade people to give up on this idea was not easy since the alternative was much harder and demanded bravery, hard work, stamina, strong will and the ability to reason. Naturally, all this led to a complete reformation of the managing system. Rules evolved into laws as the population grew. The task of creating positions to enforce the law became rather urgent. A few quarters were built to detain those who became destructive or dangerous. Several more educational issues had to be addressed, and more attention had to be paid to people who might refuse to follow the principle of survival. The colonists managed to slow the decay but did not prevent a final societal split. The Way of Ancestors group was growing in numbers and strength. It took just eighteen years for a small group of troublemakers to become an army of god worshippers. They armed themselves secretly, searched for and read historical books, organised gatherings and chieftain elections. One day they started a revolution."

"What did they want?" Tolyan shouted from the back to overcome the noise.

"Independence, I guess," answered Tom loudly.

Grand laughed, "That would have been easy. The believers had already stolen enough equipment, tools and resources to build their own base and could potentially start it on one of the farms. This is what the colony was prepared to give up, as long as they left us alone and stopped preaching to everyone. But to start a new base was too much work for a bunch of moaners who wanted an easy ride and were really not skilful or resourceful enough. They were like spoiled kids who wanted to do what they liked but still expected food and protection from their parents. Unfortunately, these freedom seekers weren't kids anymore. They took hostages and demanded the surrender of the original dwelling base to them. The main colony was forced to leave and start from scratch."

"Why didn't they fight?" Tolyan asked.

"The fight would have cost too many useful lives, although they outnumbered the believers four to one. They could die fighting or leave the station, but if the committed colonists left without tools, equipment, materials, medical supplies, etc, then they would have died anyway. There was nothing to fight for one way or another, so the colonists suggested to the believers that the two groups split up, and the believers agreed to fifty-fifty. By agreeing to leave, the colonists managed to take everything they needed to start again. It was not a fair deal, though, as there were fewer of them."

"What about your library?" Vist asked.

"The colonists kept almost all of it. The believers were interested mainly in video entertainment and a handful of old texts about various religions, myths and magic tales. But the colony lost the *Ark* to the Way of Ancestors."

"They were allowed to take the whole spaceship away from the colony?" Steven looked furious.

"Yes, but the colonists still had *Noah*. It was a floating settlement and was used to rebuild the colony. It took weeks to transfer everything to the furthest farm. This is where our White City was built, and so was the temple of O'Teka."

"That explains why we couldn't find *Noah*," said Rod.

"Since then, we have built four small submarines that are very efficient and multifunctional. You did not detect them because you were looking for a large metal structure and specific radio signals. Unfortunately, there is limited time when they are on those frequencies. Some local marine life is very sensitive to radio waves and the waves can alter its behaviour. So, Yam, Ham, Shem and

Japheth open communication only at scheduled times and in cases of emergency."

"Is that why the new shift-postmen haven't been built? You had to prioritise."

"Yes, Vist. These events slowed the colonisation down in many ways."

"Of course," said Mik and spat some dust overboard. "Instead of using all the resources to build and grow, you had to deal with those selfish bastards."

"Hey! We are here."

The track stopped in front of something that resembled an enchanted forest from one of the past fairy tales. Or it could have been the ruins of an ancient city in the jungle. Instead of stonewalls and towers, the travellers looked at the remains of what used to be *Ark*, the spaceship. First, they transferred into the surface station, then to a colony town, then a mass of shacks, then into ruins of the latter, and these ruins had now almost disappeared under dark-blue bramble-like plants and lianas.

"What happened here?" Général asked.

"History backwards happened here," answered Grand and turned to Mik. "Selfish ... you say? They did not gain anything, as you can see. First, they denounced and destroyed the priceless ZPE-converter left for them as an ungodly attribute, then they tried to run *Ark* their own way, but without enough people and only with a few who knew what to do. Of course, these people were not the ones who made decisions around here. Their leaders slowly changed this part of the colony into a monastery or a slave camp. People initially became followers to avoid hard work and thinking for themselves. Living here alone, pretty soon they all had a shortage of ... well ... everything. They consumed all the food, but couldn't make, grow or find enough for everyone's needs. Naturally, they broke into castes. The higher castes had more than the lower ones. The equipment started to malfunction as they could not service or maintain it properly. There were no trained engineers, medics or builders. The leaders had to persuade and threaten their people to work for food and safety. They preached altruism, promises of the enjoyable afterlife, punishment and blessings – all things that had worked on Earth. They tried to raid and rob our farms, but we fought them off, ready this time. They did not ask for a new converter but tried to steal one. They tried sending infiltrators into new settlements, but the colonists were prepared for that with resources and training. We are still perfecting ways to protect ourselves, but they keep finding new tricks like a mutating virus does."

"When did they leave this place?" Vist asked.

"No more than twenty years after taking it over. By that time, they had stripped it of everything they could use, so there was no point in claiming it back. Our scouts visited this place to recycle materials, but only if it was easier than synthesising new ones. The sect lost many people to accidents, disease, undernourishment, fights and the planet itself. It was still a much harsher environment back then. Now Gera is an Eden compared with those years. In fact, they would have become a subject of extinction if the atmosphere had finally not improved so dramatically. The climate is also better now, thanks to our terraformers. Walking on this planet became not just possible but also enjoyable. When no more than a hundred believers were left, they migrated towards the sea, where it was safer and easier to find food and building materials. Now they have become a completely different culture over the last few generations. They do not have their own demographic growth; their population varies greatly in size and is replenished solely by the exiled. Unfortunately, they are not a safe neighbourhood and constantly present a threat to us. We had to use spies like Massimo to be a few steps ahead and prevent their attacking our water supply. Once, after discovering a blue root, they had this great idea of poisoning our water and then taking over the city. Now our filters are placed underground and are well secured. They tried to send their own spy, who was discovered within a day. Oh, my friends ... you name it, they have tried it."

"Don't they suspect and discover your spies?" asked Mik.

"They do, but it is hard for them to dismiss every new arrival, as they need capable people to exploit. Although it is hard for our spies to be perfectly convincing, they outsmart them almost every time. It's a shame to use Massimo's great talents in the Salty Village instead of the White

City, but what else can we do? That old crow, Kendra, puts newcomers through nasty tests."

On the way back, everyone was silent. Nobody wanted to talk about the fate of *Ark-8*.

Finally, Steven said to Vist quietly, "*Noah* had three sons."

"There was a fourth, apparently, but he drowned in a flood," Vist replied.

"To name a submarine after a drowned man – any superstitious person would have a problem with that."

"Don't be daft, Steve," said Zina, trying to shake the dust off her black hair, "Superstitious citizens? No way!"

"I think it is a good name," said Tolyan, "They all are. A bit mocking. Hey, Vist. What would you call the first spaceship that the colony will build one day?"

"I don't know ... maybe ..."

"*Icarus*," Steven said.

"*Enterprise*," Zina said.

"*Gagarin*," Tolyan said.

"*Tardis*," Rod said.

"*Mik*," said Mik.

"Stop it," said Tom.

"*How?*" Vist said.

"Just shut your gobs and ..."

"No ... I mean, *How?* as the name of the ship. This is the very question that people always ask and try to find the answer to. The ship enables them to move forwards and find out *how* things work, along with *why* and *what for*. Asking good questions was always a positive force for humanity. It's the reason we exist ... as human beings. What happened here is an indicator that other things that weren't great on Earth could happen here too. Who knows, maybe one day, people here will fully adapt and become too comfortable. The struggle for survival will recede eventually, and the colony will count its people in millions. Then perhaps other earthly troubles will start. Religious wars, racism between purple and hairy citizens, wars over territory, discrimination, fascism and totalitarian regimes? What disaster might we start if we bring people from Earth here? I want to know how to prevent all those things from happening."

Once again, the group fell quiet.

On arrival back at the city, Général said under his breath, "I would call my spaceship *Way Out*."

Only Vist heard him.

Chapter 33. 3416. Back on Earth – Jade

"Hurry up, Jade, you old bitch! It has been hours."

"Brother Patrick, I brought some food and locked the door downstairs. You told me to—"

"I also told you to hurry up with a shot. I need 3.5 milligrams. NOW!"

"Okay, okay. I am moving as fast as I can. I am not as young as Sister Volna, you know. I am afraid I might not be able to serve you as well as she could."

Jade the Stitcher helped Patrick, wrapped in the mazarine robe of Father Deessa, to lift his legs on the bed, and covered him with a satin pink cover. He sank into Sister Volna's pillows and thought they must have been stuffed with dove feathers instead of hay. He extended his arm to Jade. She rolled his sleeve up and squeezed his bony upper arm with her large hand.

"Well, I don't know," Patrick said, closing his eyes as the needle entered his blood vessel, "another shot and you will do just fine."

"How do you feel now, my Word-Bearer, any better?"

"Fine. It will take a minute to work. Thank you, my dear Sister Jade. You don't mind if I call you that, do you? Since I am now the only one who can. And you can call me father. You can have my old blue robe. I always thought the darker blue would become me."

The wrinkly cheeks of the old woman became almost the same colour as the blanket.

"Oh, Br ... Father Patrick. Thank you. Thank you. Lord, be praised! You made me so happy!"

"Where is Volna, anyway?" he asked and squinted, responding to some stomach discomfort.

"I told you, she escaped the Rebels with Virgil, in his van! That is why she did not pack her things. Our Lord saved them both as he saved us! The Rebels did not find the vehicle once they had gone."

"Shut up, woman! Stupid old cow. I could have done with that van. If Volna went with Virgil, ha! He is a dead man! Now leave me. I need some rest. Today was so stressful."

"But father! I thought you asked for Bliss because ..." Jade got up and pointed at the old alarm clock on the bedside table.

"It's almost time for the evening service. We missed one last night, and there was no chance to pray during the day ... You have to do your duty to our Lord."

"Fuck it ..."

"What?" The old woman gasped, not believing her own ears.

She stood there in deep confusion and disbelief for almost a minute. Her face became pale, and her lips whispered some sort of apology to her god. At that time, the new Father Patrick started to snore. She came closer to the bed and tried again.

"Father Patrick, you are the Word-Bearer! Wake up, it's time to serve our Lord."

Patrick opened one eye and looked at her.

"You again. I told you, I am tired and stressed. My nose hurts! I just had a late dinner and need to gather my strength. We will do the prayers tomorrow."

"But this is even better ... an inconvenience for you to suffer. You always do the best service when you are hurt!"

"Not tonight."

"But why?"

"Stop questioning me!" Father Patrick turned away from Jade and curled on his side to face the wall.

Jade was close to tears.

"This is a sin, father. What have they done to you?" She tried again, slowly pulled the pink cover off Patrick and saw that the bottom edge of his shirt had rolled up and uncovered his bony back, covered with old marks from the whip.

"Maybe I am not hurt enough. Now go!"

"Shall I bring a whip?"

"And I will flog you with it if you don't leave me alone!"

Jade sobbed once and wiped her eyes with her fist. She sat helplessly on the floor by the bed and desperately called for the last time.

"Our faith, father. The Lord will punish us, will punish me if I don't do something to make you pray!"

"Idiot," mumbled Father Patrick, half asleep, as the Bliss started to sedate him. "You were the only one with the faith here, he he ... and you are not even a Cruiser."

Jade shook her head, covered her face with both hands, and sat in the quiet room for a while. Then she sat up and looked at the half-empty syringe on the bedside table with determination. Patrick did not hear her when she started to speak quietly and calmly.

"The Rebels have broken you, haven't they? But you don't have to worry about anything anymore. Anything at all, father. You will thank me tomorrow, and we will pray five services one after another to compensate. We will redeem ourselves. Have you seen what those sinners did to Father Ontha? This was the Lord's way of giving me an idea."

She got up, took the syringe, and lifted Patrick's shirt on his back a little higher. His ribs rose and fell as he exhaled and inhaled, and his vertebrae stuck out like the knuckles of a clenched fist.

Jade laughed a little, happily, with a new soothing note in her voice, "The Lord is truly great. He foresaw all of this. Praise the Lord. Don't you worry, my angel, I am a stitcher. I know my way with needles and ..." She pushed her left middle finger under the elastic of his underpants and found the coccyx. The man was so thin, it wasn't difficult at all. Then she gently moved her finger up his spine, counting to four. She pushed the needle in between the fourth and third vertebra and finished the sentence, "... not only needles."

Patrick was already heavily drugged, but his body jerked once or twice. He made a single moaning noise but snored again as soon as Jade pulled the needle out. Jade got up, covered Patrick, and tucked him in.

"It might be permanent if the Lord would wish for it. But you will still be using your arms and feeling pain above your waist ... enough to suffer for all our sins. Your brother, Jesus, did not even dream about such glorious suffering. Father ... Even Prometheus would envy you. You will be able to see your feet but not feel the toes removed. I will clean you, feed you and bandage your wounds. I will even carry you to the cross ... you are as light as a child. I will look after you and make sure we do all the services as we should. Our Lord will be pleased."

She got up, folded her hands on her stomach, and looked again at the sleeping Patrick with overwhelming emotion and a loving smile. Then she blew out the candles, quietly left the room, and retired to the lower bedroom.

Thieves did not come for another four weeks, and the Resistance arrived only after six. Father Patrick, or what was left of him, was still alive when they did.

Chapter 34. 3411. Out in Space – Samantha

The colony's head of science, Samantha Nguyen, and Vist came out to the top of the city wall through the small door in the tower. They walked slowly along a stretched balustrade towards the northern part of the city, casting long shadows on the floor in front of them.

"This wall reminds me of one of the Seven Ancient Wonders on Earth," Vist said.

"The Great Wall on the Chinese continent?" Samantha asked.

"China was a vast country, but the continent was much larger."

"It is hard for me to imagine vast lands. I saw the Earth maps, but only with some effort could I accept how small our Gera really is. It seems big enough when you live here all your life, not only for a person but for the entire population of the human race of Noverca."

"Did you travel? As a population?" asked Vist.

"Not by your standards," Samantha said, smiling, "even by the standards of Christopher

Columbus, we only went for a little walk around our backyard. The future colony can potentially occupy a territory hundreds of times bigger than the existing estate with all its farms and research stations. Further south, it is too hot to grow anything, but the deep fishing there is very good, and even further down, as long as you avoid the Galtstream current – it boils anything. Along the islands stretching east and west, the climate is relatively mild, but there aren't so many large fields. The islands are marshy and rocky and need lots of work. The North is also very unattractive, as you can imagine. It is dark and freezing, but if we want to dig up some natural resources there, we will have to find a way, eventually."

"So, what is your plan?"

"Grand and the whole leadership suggest the way forwards is further artificial evolution. According to O'Teka, the colony started to flourish only after serious alterations were made to colonists themselves."

"I can see why. You have done a great job in genetic adaptation here. You now have a rich life stock, and you have covered Gera with impressive gardens and forests," Vist said. "Even the people are not the same as the ones that landed here so long ago. I looked into the last reports that were never sent to Earth. A few things are not mentioned. For example – what caused the purple pigment in the skin?"

"An insignificant side effect. We altered some melanin to be like the phioletine in a shell of a local slug we call rock snails – very nutritious molluscs, by the way. You probably missed them at Laguna as they look like black pebbles in tiny slime pools."

Samantha put her hands together as if holding an egg, then wrinkled her nose and laughed like a child. She was a tall slender woman with a hawk nose and shiny copper hair. Her beautiful eyes were the colour of grey pearls, and her skin would have been almost white if not for purple freckles on her face and arms.

She carried on, "The first colonists were not aware of them for many months, but their discovery was a true gift. As a result, our skin reflects some of the radiation. A useful trait, but now we vary from lilac tints to deep purple and even crimson, depending on the amount of our natural pigments. We are so used to it that we may have just considered it not worth mentioning."

Vist stopped to look at Samantha with new interest. "So skin colours are not an issue, but I have seen other unusual characteristics in the city. Tell me, did you promote hypertrichosis deliberately?"

"Yes. They are much stronger, although shorter. Grand is one of few who don't shave," Samantha said with a shrug. "Most people do, just like some of your men shave their beards off or remove follicles. If you want to see it, visit our hairdressers. Some styles preferred by women are truly stunning."

"Are you creating a new race to colonise the north?"

"That is not how it started, but now you mention it … Indeed, we have already started breaking up into different races. Nordians are better adapted for survival in darker and colder parts of Gera, and Uzhans are more comfortable in the hot regions. Both would be able to successfully coexist and trade here, in the Terenian zone. If you look closer, you will also notice that they have very different pupils, like nocturnal animals, and a special way of distributing body fat. Do you find us too ambitious?"

Vist shrugged. "Not at all, not even if you started growing gills and colonising the seabed."

Samantha laughed again. Her laughter was easy and honest, "It is too early to think about that, but who knows. One step at a time. At first, we had to survive where we were. First genetic alterations were focused on radiation tolerance and the need to deal with the excessive salt in practically everything. The genes of the European scurvy grass were invaluable for many plants now adapted here. We had to rebuild the biochemistry of all our species. It worked for animals and plants, and now it works for us. For example, ionic blood cells extract radioactive particles from the tissue. One of our kidneys is now fully responsible for the filtration of these particles from our blood into R-urine. We can dissolve twice as much salt in our blood and excrete it through our tear glands. We have a second lymph system—"

"... and a higher count of erythrocytes at sea level than citizens of La Rinconada," said Vist with a smile.

"Not anymore. That was only necessary before our chemo-physicists sorted out the oxygen level in the atmosphere. Now Gera's living conditions are not very different from equatorial zones on Earth, although the average range of radiation levels is still not good for you. You won't be affected much here for another few days, but if you stay for a few months, you and your friends will have to wear your protective gear and submit for regular purification treatments. But if you decide to stay for good, we will have to clone some of your organs with genetic alterations and perform surgical replacements. I guess it will take a couple of years and at least nine operations ... for you. Fourteen for your friends. You are different from them, aren't you?"

There was no sign of doubt in Samantha's voice, so Vist did not deny it.

"Yes. I have already adapted to living inside space stations and on Mars. But how fascinating! You have achieved more in three hundred years than Earth managed in the last millennium."

"We had to ... in extreme conditions. We are not as efficient as natural evolution but are more accurate and significantly faster. We used genetic surgery to adapt plants and animals much sooner than natural processes would have done. Without our interference, they had zero chance of survival here. There was a day when the first colonist was born through genetic selection. And then there was a genetically engineered baby, just as happened on Earth a long time ago, only we also had the first baby with animal genes and finally – with alien genes. And yes, without Earth's experience and achievements, we would not have lasted for a year. I guess we have to be very grateful that even in the Dark Ages, there were people who advanced science despite all the obstacles. Look how far back it goes."

"You mean the times when one of the very first successful and useful genetic transplants took place in the twentieth century?"

"Exactly! The human gene responsible for insulin production was inserted into the DNA of bacteria. A few decades later, a vast culture of genetically altered bacteria provided various patients with necessary hormones and saved many lives. A hundred years later, humanity not only had unlimited access to any functional proteins they needed, but they could grow any type of tissue to treat people with deficiencies and patients recovering from illnesses and injuries. In another hundred years, any internal organ could be grown from the adult stem cell of the patient, under the right conditions. You could create a genetically compatible medicine in a month and a new vaccine within a few cycles."

Samantha continued talking and produced an instrument that looked like a small windmill spinner from her shoulder bag. She lifted it above her head to measure the wind strength. After taking the readings, she put them away and continued, "Our ancestors left a world where head transplants were already possible, all genetic disorders and predispositions were removed from the human genome, and new mutations were carefully monitored. Not only have human incubators become yesterday's news, but artificial wombs for the whole seven months of foetus development were available for any couple of any sex. Chromosomes in a donor ovum could be replaced with the selected sets of two men, extracted during the meiotic division of their cells to give them a biological son or daughter of their choice. I was always fascinated by how far your genetic engineering went! Tell me, please, what else has been done recently? What is *your* body capable of? After all, a few more centuries have surely pushed it even further. Have we become a completely different species, or are we just varieties of the same one?"

They approached the corner of the wall to the west. Vist stopped and looked back over the balustrade. The river reflected the Vitr's light and appeared full of burning blood.

"If you know the history so well, you probably know about all the dark ages that from time to time slow progress down," Vist said, sighing, "nevertheless, I am not just a product of genetic architecture but also of bio-electronic engineering. Your colleagues Shar and Doctor Hawk would probably be interested in comparing our ways of integrating metal with living tissue. I am more resistant to certain conditions than my friends, which is true. I also have enhanced abilities and sensors. I have electronic implants that help me in many ways, including accessing and processing information more efficiently than an average human brain. My spinal cord is wired, and a few of my bones have been replaced with devices that serve specific purposes, but I can't tell you too much as ... it's kind of personal for me. Maybe one day, if I return here to stay or if I know for sure that I will not. In any case, I promise to make an offering to O'Teka and leave you with information that you may find helpful enough. Right now, the most pressing matter is the natural expansion of your population and the expansion with the new arrivals from Earth. The number of colonists on Noverca may increase in the next fifty or seventy years. I can make it possible to bring thousands of people here. A new genetic pool, as Grand called it. I am prepared to exchange some of our current knowledge for ways we can prepare our new generation for this environment and for your type of society."

Samantha thought for a moment and said, "You know ... it makes perfect sense. I am sure Grand and his team will help you with the latter. To prepare your adults for this relocation biologically, I would say we have very few ideas, and you can take them all back to Earth. We can do more for unborn children, but they will also need some system alterations on their arrival here. The children born here can become comfortable much more easily. It will be good for both our populations if we can still interbreed. I know, it is not much I can offer now, but ..."

Vist shrugged, "Every little help ..."

Samantha suddenly took Vist's hand and squeezed it with almost childish excitement.

"Vist, I think we can help each other. I need your knowledge and computerised head for a task I have worked on over the last few years. You and your comrades can help me to succeed. We are missing a gene that can help us spread much further on Noverca in no time. You know about the creature that lives in the Northern Mountains."

"The svoloch?"

"Yes. It periodically comes to our woods to feed and breed, but most of the time, it survives in very hostile conditions. The temperature in its natural habitat drops to minus fifty degrees centigrade, yet they live there without fire or clothing as far as I know. Maybe they have fur we can also grow or metabolisms we can borrow. Maybe they have completely new homeostasis mechanisms. Maybe they simply hibernate there, but we don't have seasonal changes. How and why would they do that?"

"You want to find out how they can live in the dark and cold hell and see if you can do the same?"

"No, I do not want us to live in hell. I just don't want us to die there if we need to visit those lands and bring light and heat with us so that it can become comfortable artificially."

"What if they live in the deep caves heated by geothermal warmth?"

"Fine, that means we can go there too ... But we need to know all of that to master those lands! A remote underground town could be built in suitable caves."

"Something like our colony on Mars? Possibly. The warm zone of Gera might become overpopulated one day!"

Samantha let go of Vist's fingers and threw up both of her hands.

"Maybe. I don't know. That would be the job of environmentalists. My job will be to ensure they can do theirs when arriving in those lands."

"But what can *we* do to help?"

"One thing we never had to do on this planet is to hunt. Nobody knows how to do that.

O'Teka describes some hunting skills, but nobody on Earth had to hunt the ghostly creature we have here. We need that svoloch alive to study it. But so far, nobody has ever seen it. Those soldiers of yours are skilful trackers. They might be able to track it down and bring it to the city labs. You and I can combine our knowledge, and we will find out why it is so robust. Vist, we have to know this not only for our own sake but also to find a way to make your people feel as good here as if Noverca is their real mother."

"Okay, I am sure the guys would love the idea, and I shall talk to Captain Darkwood. But apart from its habitat, what makes you think the svoloch can be that useful?"

Samantha took a deep breath.

"Oh, Teka! I have so many questions for this creature. Please don't think of me as crazy, but I don't believe it belongs to this planet any more than we do. You see? On Earth, all living things share the molecular structure of DNA, at least enough to suggest kinship between members of different kingdoms, to some degree, and their common origins. The same applies on Noverca if you look at native living organisms.

We have introduced Earth life here with its genetic code and managed to adapt some of it to this environment, as you already know. We took genetic engineering as one of the quickest ways forwards; we introduced Earth genes to local life and vice versa. That was a very difficult task. The best results are produced by passing the gene from one Earth species to another because of their genetic relation. On Gera, we have organic life structured by the same principles. It is also carbon-based, and its DNA chemistry is remarkably similar. Even the double helix was unavoidable, just like two independent architects would not be able to ignore the property of the same material they used to design a specific structure. Of course, significant differences allow us to distinguish the local life too. One is easily spotted as a number of membranes in the nucleus, and another is a totally different energy organelle. The local plants had very similar chloroplasts, but the rest of multicellular life didn't have our mitochondria until we forced it."

Samantha thought she heard a faint click in Vist's head.

"Just a minute," said Vist, stopping and closing both eyes, "I remember now what Professor Bianchi called fusionchondrias as a joke in his theory of Noverca's first bacteria before he actually identified them as part of any cell. They are like tiny nuclear reactors producing energy for organisms. You even have a device that can find local life by detecting this reaction in nests and trails. Do all local plants and animals have them?"

Vist opened one eye and then another as if rearranging something in the mind's filing cabinet. Samantha nodded.

"Yes. Every plant, every dirteater, every bug, every blobster and protozoa, even photosynthesising algae, although very few are capable of respiring too."

"Are you telling me that the svoloch does not have it? What does it have instead?"

"According to the detectors we used on their campsites, it does not and ... I don't know. It is the largest animal on Gera. Almost our size, I bet, so it relies on oxygen. We have just one sample of svoloch tissue, although it is very inconclusive and probably a little contaminated.

It also suggests that this creature doesn't share its DNA with local life. It is an alien resident of Noverca, just like we are. The svoloch is not only a potential threat but also a very difficult subject. It appears to be extremely rare, and its behaviour makes it hard to track down. The believers are convinced that this animal is a doomed spirit that takes the solid shape of flesh and blood as punishment. There is hardly any description of it in our records, and the only evidence proving their existence, migration, estimated numbers and habits comes from the svoloch's interaction with the environment. For instance, we know that they are omnivores and cannibals that feed on all that is edible without any waste, including their own dead. We did not find a single body, unsure of what they do with the bones. Most of the leftover scraps were too old. We found plenty of dry skin flakes and faeces, but the heat and radiation make it almost impossible to conduct reliable DNA tests. We never found anything fresh enough until one very recent event. Right now, all I know is that they travel in couples or in very small groups of up to eight. We know this because when they camp to sleep, they dig little beds in the dirt, which allows us to count them. They leave some fur behind, but we cannot be sure that it is theirs, as it varies too much, and we did not find any follicles. It buries excrement and food remains, as some other animals do, but it has a humanoid or primate shape. It can also control its body temperature and therefore has very interesting homeostasis."

"If no one has ever seen a svoloch, how do you know it has a humanoid shape?"

"We have thermo-video footage of the sleeping svoloch. It was pure luck. One of our geological drones spotted the pattern against the cool soil of the bedding hole by the Ribbon's east bank. The drone was flying just a few miles away from a group of scouts following the slow pack in the conviction that this particular svoloch might have been wounded or sick. They rushed there but found that the pack was gone and the one they spotted must have been in labour during the recording. It most definitely gave birth, but whatever fluid, blood or tissue was produced in the process, it was meticulously mixed with dust and pushed into the river. Why do they hide the evidence of their existence so hard? I have no idea ... What if they are aware of us? All the scouts managed to bring back was a drop of dark fluid smeared on the grass at the edge of the camp. There were just a few broken-down cells, but I need more to confirm my theory and learn enough."

"Samantha, I will try to help, but I have to ask this: if the creature is hostile and might also become a competitive species in your new territory, how likely is it that we will cause its extinction?"

"Whatever it is, we will try to coexist with it. We want their genes, not their extermination. If we need their home, we will have to find a way to protect ourselves from them and them from us. I speak for all the principles of the colony when I say that only a threat to the human race's survival will force us to destroy another species, race or congregation. Do you disapprove? Vist?"

Vist did not reply immediately. The line of clouds appeared above the mountains and poured down the icy slopes like heavy smoke. The wind strengthened. It was time to return inside. Vist's voice mixed with the wind and flew away, but Samantha heard the word nice and clear, "No."

Chapter 35. 3416. Back on Earth – Général

"Général, don't get up, please!"

"Vist, you are alive! I am so glad to see you, lass!"

Vist gave Général a feminine smile and pushed the plastic stool closer to Général's wheelchair. It was warm in the green room that morning. Here you could forget about the weather outside. It had only holographic windows, projecting a sunny day in the ancient rainforest. The water fountain was quiet, and few canary birds sang in the aviary between real tropical plants in the large pots.

"Vist! My lass! When did you arrive? Rod told me that your pod also went off course!" The old man was still talking into his oxygen mask, but his eyes sparkled with genuine delight. "Sorry about this, minor lung damage ... So, were you lost?"

"Yes, but not too far from here. I walked for three days, was authorised yesterday morning to come up the Oak and got pretty busy in the laboratory. Joshua Garcia was on duty and had nine people already assigned to assist me. Once all reports were done and samples catalogued, I was free to go and check on you, commander. Where is Rod?"

Général squeezed Vist's hand with gratitude, "Rod and Tolyan are having a little reunion breakfast. They got rid of me by leaving me here. Lovely place! You see, the rest of the team only caught up with us last night. Steven is still in the hospital branch, at least until tomorrow. It looks like my lads had a little adventure with the Moses Movement without me. But what about you, lass? Did you manage to do your part?"

"You could say so."

"What do you mean? Is Object safe?"

"Yes, although it might become a little harder than I had hoped for."

"Why?"

"On the way here, I was shot. In the chest."

"My word! But you are alright?" Général said.

"I don't bruise easily," Vist said, then winked and touched the robe's fold of ucha-silk.

Général shook his head a little in realisation.

"Oh no, your cross straps! What did you have in those pockets?"

"Tissue samples from the colony. Most of them are okay, including the ones on my back straps. But all the svoloch capsules were shattered. I lost every single cell."

"What would it mean to the mission?"

"Our progeny will still go, but it will be harder for them to adapt. There will be more losses among adult travellers."

"I must say, I am sorry to hear that."

"Don't worry, Général. Svoloch's genetic properties were the cherry on top. We didn't know about them before and still had plenty to plot."

Général sighed and turned his wheelchair towards the fountain, "I am afraid my usefulness to the Object has expired. Tom took me on this mission only because he felt sorry for his father's old friend. I am sure my lads also had something to do with it, but I was nothing but a burden all the way."

"I did not feel burdened by you."

"Of course, you didn't. Nothing seems to get to you, bloody tin man!" Général laughed at his joke and then frowned. "Do you know why I survived the crash? According to Selest, there was venom in my blood, which protected me from the awakening shock. Nothing she has ever encountered before. Any thoughts?"

Vist's cheeks blushed a little.

"I have no idea."

"I think you do. Someone slipped a couple of goon-flies into my pod. No way could they be found now, but I wonder who could have thought of such a precaution. Rod is sure that it was you. Everyone else hates those bastards. I say you have scored a few points with good old Rod. Nothing to say? No? Okay, but whoever it was, I am grateful. They have saved my miserable, useless life."

"Not so useless. Don't forget, Général, the many great ideas we would not have if it was not for you."

"Nice of you to say that, lass, but Mik was the real leader there. And what now? What can I do now for Object?"

"Your troopers still need you. They look up to you; they measure themselves by your honour. You are what keeps them strong."

"Eh ... They probably think one thought or two ... Listen, lass! I might have about thirty years left in me if all goes well. But by the time of the evacuations, they will be the same age I am now. This means they won't go, they will stay ... Why would they try so hard? Why are they loyal to Object? They keep going, but not because of me."

"Every one of us has more than one reason, Général. They care for the survival of us as a species because they think this is the right thing to do. Also, they are human! Their instincts and their conscious desires are to pass on their genes to a new generation. They will have children, and this way, they will continue, like all the people before them. I think those are good reasons."

"What are yours?"

"I share their reasons, but I am also a loader and extremely self-centred. This is not just a job or care for the sake of others. It's personal."

Général was puzzled.

"You mean *you* are going to get something out of it?"

"I carry on the mission my family has started. I happen to love it. Like those first colonists who were born for their purpose, so was I. Altruism does not suit me. There is great value for me in seeing Object succeed. Everything I do, I do for Object. It is my real art, and I enjoy seeing good results. Imagine what my masterpiece will be like!"

Général thought about it for a moment, then he seemed to remember something, "I don't have children, Vist."

Vist didn't reply.

Général carried on, "I want my genes to be passed on though. I, too, want those chromosomes of my ancestors to be part of the colony! I don't know why I didn't think about it! So selfless of me ... I had a chance once, you know," Général said, smiling into his oxygen mask, "Her name was ... Nina. No, Janina. All I remember now is that she wore ruby earrings and red underwear. Oh! It is too late for me now."

"Général, you and your lads donated your cells to Samantha's lab, which will be activated on Noverca before the first people arrive. You will be cloned there and have children this way. Would it make you happier, knowing that they will be there?"

"Oh, I don't know. I have to ponder it."

"You have thirty years you just promised me. Is that enough time to think?"

"It will have to be, lass. Hey, what about you? Will you have kids? You are young enough to become a mother and ..." Général looked embarrassed, "I have to ask this. Between you and me. Are you a lass or a lad? I promise I won't tell anyone."

"I believe you, but I can't answer that."

"Are you like Rod or like Tolyan?"

"Neither. By the way, they will try and have children too. But you want to know about me. I am just another person with a few additions." Vist's voice was merry and not serious enough to talk about the question that had been bothering everyone for a long time. "Before you ask, I do not have any extra chromosomes. I am not an asexual synthetic or cyborg being. I had no reproductive alterations. I am enhanced and full of useful implants, but only for cognitive and creative abilities. I probably will have children when the time is right. I just have to conceal my identity for a little longer."

"Conceal from whom?"

"My real name or gender will not make any difference to anyone in the Resistance or the Moses Movement. I have personal reasons."

Général took his mask off and coughed as he said, "I did not ... understand much from what you just said ... ahem ..." He had to put the mask back on. "Lass ... I don't want to feel like a total jessop calling you a lass if you are not."

The door opened, and Tolyan and Rod walked in.

"Vist!" they said at the same time.

"Dude! How long have you been here?" Tolyan gave Vist a bear hug and almost lifted the loader off the floor.

"I never thought I would be glad to see you!" Rod said and pushed a small paper bag into Vist's hand. "Here, you can have my sandies!"

Chapter 36. 3411. Out in Space – Reunion

The entire Object team gathered again for a family meeting on board the *Wasp*. After Tom Darkwood received official authorisation from Grand on the very first day, Tom ordered Chang and Marta to bring the ship to a spare farm field just one kilometre from the city. It was so great to reunite and to exchange experiences! The Broadsky couple did not waste time, and they collected a massive amount of data on the planet's biology, geography and geochemistry. No matter how comfortable the offered accommodation in the city was, everyone decided to stay on the ship for the rest of the trip. The *Wasp*'s small sleeping cubicles felt like home.

After Vist introduced everyone to the new plan and everybody expressed their views on the matter, a few decisions had to be made. Tom expected the younger troopers to be excited about the idea but felt rather surprised to see his old friend's eyes sparkle like snow in the sunlight.

"But Alan – Général – I will be even more worried than Zina is about you going back into action. Our troopers don't need much training. They did their fitness routine on the ship, in the city and even in the woods. But you are more than twice their age and, forgive me, not as light on your feet anymore."

"Nonsense, Tom. Yes, I am old, fat and ugly, but I am strong enough to lead my little army during the attack. We don't know the numbers of our enemies and need every man on the field. Plus, I just would not let them go anywhere without me."

"But this is not a military operation. Massimo will take us to the lake in his truck; there is just room for two more. Rod will go because his scanner is better than Samantha's. Grand said he could spare a couple of guards."

"We don't need his guards!" Steven said, "We would rather have our pilots, you, Vist, Général and Zina, with us. It's true that colonists are better adapted to this planet, but they are still not as physically capable as we are."

"I agree, Captain," Zina said, "I looked at their health charts. They are very agile and fast, but they are, how shall I put it, they bruise easily. With a simple cut, they bleed a lot. Massimo is a very good example. That rubbery armour suit he wore is his second skin, to protect his body from accidental scratches and more serious wounds."

"Also, Général isn't fat at all," said Tolyan. "How long will it take for Rod and Vist to make a trap? A couple of days? By the time we set off, he will be back in shape with these alien enzymes' help, don't you worry!"

"But that thing is too dangerous!" said the captain, "Vist, do you still have a record of the first encounter? What do they say the svoloch did to them?"

Vist squinted slightly and read the recently uploaded posts in their head:

We did not know about our neighbour until the first expedition to the mountains. The first explorers did not return. Their radio message only said they felt like they were being watched. The rescue group found what was left of them – a couple of bones ... but not a single item they had on them that day. What sort of predator takes equipment? Maybe it likes to decorate itself or its nest, as some Earth birds and crustaceans do?

"This record does not have a precise date," Vist said.

"I assume that was before the colony started to split?" Mik asked.

"Before even the first farms were built," replied Vist and carried on, "This is just a quote from a report by Andrey Donko, head of soil research, on the fifth day of the harvesting month in the year 162, 'I fired a blind shot but most likely missed. There was no blood, and the soft ground looked like someone had started digging a grave with a teaspoon. That is where I found Issa. His liver, heart and most of his limb flesh had been removed. The svoloch must have teeth as sharp as blades. I thought they had escaped the camp because I forced them away, but now I had to run. I heard them coming back and legged it. They did not chase me; they probably did not fancy a pursuit on a full stomach. I went there the next day to bring Issa back, but apart from two shallow holes in the ground, I found nothing. They took everything away, including the torch I dropped in haste.'"

After a moment of silence, Tolyan said, "Sounds like a challenge. We *do* have weapons."

"We need it alive and intact if possible," said Vist, "There are more reports describing various events and suggestions of their preferences in food and mating rituals. Apparently, they kill and consume infertile females, weak males and deformed newborns. I do not see how that can be concluded based on such limited data, but no one insists their ideas are right. Most of it is just speculation or even a series of myths. One very certain thing is that the creatures come from the mountains about once a year for a few weeks, probably to give birth. Why they do that – remains unknown. During those times, the colonists try to monitor their numbers at least, but even that is not easy. The size of groups is changing, and the resting camp locations are too. How to get closer to them? Well, they have not allowed anyone yet. They avoided previously attempted traps and cameras, so they must be excellent at mimicry. Telescopes and other remote observations also failed. We have to outsmart them, but we must hurry. Their time in the woods is almost over. All packs have started migrating back north, including the one wandering by the local lake, and they won't return for almost a year."

"So our chances are very slim. We need time to prepare, to build a trap," Rod said.

"The one Samantha has targeted in the woods by the Plato Lake is different because it is alone, and his movement radius has been quite consistent. He might be old and single, therefore – our best chance. Massimo knows where to look for him. What kind of trap do you propose?"

Rod scratched the tip of his nose and answered, "The fastest and simplest way is a net. If we cannot see the svoloch, we might be able to lure him in. We stretch the net on the ground, and once the creature walks over it – we pull it up and ensnare the svoloch like wildfowl. Is there anything we can offer him as bait?"

"Samantha said the svoloch has a weakness for local caviar. We enjoyed seeing it during the village feast, the large and smelly eggs of some aquatic life form. Otherwise, the bait will be ... us," said Vist. "When it is caught, we will have to sedate it. Doctor Hawk has some drugs here based on a high concentration of goon-fly venom. We can use those."

Rod nodded.

"Okay, let's say we placed some eggs in an ambush spot. How can we know which way the svoloch is going to approach it? Where shall we stretch the net?"

"When our ancestors wanted to lure something, they used the same methods for hundreds of years, during hunting and wars. You look for a spot with only one good way of getting to it," said Mik, "In the case of our secretive friend, it can be the only path where he can stay hidden as he approaches. If he lives by the lake, we set our trap between its home and the bait. And as close as possible to the lakeside. Shame we don't have day and night here, but we must visit the lake and find the right spot first."

"Okay then," said Tom, getting up, "you and I will ask Massimo to take both of us to the lake to do some land mapping right now. We will try to avoid the animal and be quick. Since a farm is nearby, our hosts should help you find something to make a net out of. Talk to them, Rod. The more people participate in the weaving, the sooner the net will be ready. So everyone – get on with it. No doubt Vist will know how to weave and teach you all in no time. When we are ready, Général will lead a hunting party of myself, Mik, Tolyan, Steven, Rod and Zina. It is always good to have first aid on standby in a dangerous operation."

"But I am not a doctor!" Zina said, "I am a surgical assistant."

"The local doctors are good, but they have not seen non-altered humans in their lifetime. You are more qualified to treat one of us," said Vist.

Zina blushed.

"And you are more qualified than me!"

"Vist will be busy with Samantha, getting ready to receive our game," said the captain.

"I protest you going, Captain," said Chang. During the meeting, none of the pilots said a single word. This time, Marta appeared to be very timid, and Chang was unusually quiet. "Let me go instead. You are our captain and the leader of Object. You can't afford the risk."

"Neither can I afford to risk any of my pilots? I know about your heart problem, and we need you to fly us back."

"I also don't think you should go. Plus, Massimo's vehicle can only take five more people. Six, if one of them is Rod," said Vist. Everybody else agreed that this time the captain should reconsider his priorities.

Tom gave up and concluded the meeting. As people were leaving the room, Vist followed Marta and stopped her on the way to her room.

"Mrs Broadsky, what's wrong?"

"I don't know what you mean," said Marta, lowering her voice.

Vist also spoke quietly, "Marta? It's me. I know something happened while you were parked in the *Wasp* by the sea. What was it?"

"Please don't ask." Marta looked worried.

Chang, who was almost in the room, suddenly reappeared in the doorway.

"I knew it," he said, "Nothing can be hidden from your scanners, Vist."

He took Marta by the hand and gently pulled her to go behind him.

"Chang ..."

"No, Vist! Not this time. I beg of you, leave it. Nothing is wrong. We had a bit of a problem back there. Nothing to report. It's personal." He looked as if he suddenly had an idea and said, "We argued. Yes. Every couple has problems from time to time. We will be fine."

"But are you both safe?"

"Yes," said Marta, "yes, we are. Please do not alarm anyone for no reason. We have too much to do in so little time to worry about our little quarrel. We will join you briefly to help you with the net."

Chapter 37. 3416. Back on Earth – Marta

"Marta, why are you up so early? Never mind that! You won't believe it! Vist is here! Yes! Has been here for days! Oh! Marta! I was so worried about him, I thought I would die."

Zina found the pilot in the passage, by the window between the showers and the training block. Marta stood there absolutely still, looking through the dirty glass at the dancing branches of the oak. The wind was strong again, but the thick glass was soundproof. Zina could even hear a single water drop falling from Marta's wet hair to the metal floor.

"Marta, what is it? Are you alright? Have you been sick again? Do you want to talk?"

"I want an abortion."

"Woah! Hang on! You told me that you are glad ... so this way you will always be with Chang. Why? Have you changed your mind?"

"Today Selest figured out when I am due ... the dates do not add up. It is not Chang's."

Zina felt as if the silent wind somehow blew everything out of her head, including the ability to think. She couldn't say anything for a whole minute, but Marta did not say anything either. All Zina could manage was to step closer to her friend and put her arms around her.

Finally, Zina whispered, "But how? Who? You would never ... Was it one of our guys? Even Steven is better than that. When?"

"During the first two days on Noverca. Oh, I was so sure I conceived before that, on the ship!"

"But that makes even less sense. You were alone with Chang after we left for Laguna."

"Not alone enough. I persuaded Chang not to report the incident, but we were attacked on that semi-island. I was raped by one of the colonists from the woods."

"But we were told that the villagers did not go to those parts. You were supposed to be safe on the *Wasp*. The whole village would not be able to break into that ship."

"I don't know. I have not been to the village."

"Then it was the other colonists? Scouts from the White City? After what we have seen, I can't imagine that. Not so civilised after all?"

"Nothing was civilised about those men. Chang was so afraid for me, but I did not tell him everything. I just avoided being intimate with him ever since. And now he is gone and I regret it all so much!" Marta started to sob but remained still.

"Tell me everything. Actually, no! Come with me to see Vist. Tell him. He will know what to do, he will figure it out."

"Figure out what? I don't even care! It does not matter whether it was a villager or a citizen. I just want it to be cut out of me. Wouldn't you?" Marta turned and met Zina's eyes.

"I suppose I would. It's not only a horrible way to get pregnant, but ... your health could be at serious risk. Your quarantine tests showed no infection, but those purple people might not be compatible with us. We know little about all their mutations and how those mutations might affect foetus development. Yet another reason to see Vist!" Zina let go of Marta and walked around her, still talking, "Their embryos are designed to adapt and to mutate as they grow, to assure their sustainability to all those alterations. Your foetus can start taking from you what it should not. Please come with me to Vist. I will tell him anyway. I must. I am sorry, but I am really worried about you."

"It's too hard, Zina. You do it. Just tell him, or her, if you have to. Selest told me to think about it because babies are so rare now on Earth, but there is nothing to think about. If she doesn't help, you have to do it for me. Please, Zina."

"Your life could be at risk whether you go through with it or not."

"I have very little reason to live anyway, but if you manage to terminate this pregnancy, I can still be useful to Object. On the other hand, if I die, I will welcome death as a relief. If no one helps me, I will do it myself. I have an Adieu pill my great-great-grandfather received from the pharmacist a day too late." Marta sniffed with bitterness. "Funny, I kept it in case of imprisonment by the Cruisers. But when I was caught, I didn't even remember it."

"Don't say this sort of thing! I am so sorry! Let me walk you to your room. Can I get you any food?"

"I don't want to feed it. Maybe later. But this has to be done today, Zin. TODAY!"

Zina took Marta by the arm and led her along the corridor. A couple of minutes later, they entered the room for female astronauts. Zina noted that Vist did not stay there. But as far as she knew, he did not stay with the men either. Were there rooms in Rebel settlements reserved for loaders?

*

Marta waited for almost an hour. She could not even sit down until Zina had left the room. Maybe it was a mistake to tell her. Now she would tell Vist, and this shameful fact would be stored forever in Vist's loaded head, which was male, according to Chang.

Chang! She missed him so much, but every time she tried to look at his image, she would cry and cry as if she was full of nothing but tears. Why did it hurt so much? Was it because he was dead or because he died in agony, tortured in front of her eyes? Was it the pain of being alone with his body in that dark room for what felt like an eternity? Was it because their happiness was so deep but so brief? Maybe he was not only a husband but a part of her essential core on a new, deep, sub-particle level, and now ... she would never be complete without him. In the end, his heart failure freed him from the pain and horror, but would they still be together now if he survived the torture? No. She was unconvinced that she would ever forget that terrible night in the Cruiser's castle when looking at Chang's reconstructed face as a constant reminder. But if he was a true part of her, shouldn't she ... no matter what? Marta frowned, lifted her face towards the grey ceiling and closed her eyes. If, instead of him, they would cut *her* arm off or destroy *her* face, would she be able to live happily ever after with a prosthetic limb or scars? Wouldn't that be the same kind of reminder? Do you need reminders so you never forget such an experience? With his injuries, Chang might have become a very different person – and not only on the outside. Marta shook her head. Wouldn't it be nice to feel brave and to say that she would love him no matter how different he would be? But in reality, no one can be certain. You have to be there and feel what it is like afterwards. Would she be the same person, then?

How strange, but for the first time Marta felt something like a relief. Nobody ever stays the same, anyway? People stay together only if they change together. The door opened.

Zina walked in, shaking with agitation. "I am sorry, Marta, but I could not stop him."

Vist followed her quietly and calmly and sat in front of Marta on the folding stool. His eyes looked with the usual warmth, but they appeared to be very tired this time. Vist said, "Hello, Marta. I am very glad to see you. I have been told what happened to you all on arrival in Gera and then on the return home, and it seems like you had the worst experience anyone can imagine. My condolences."

"Thank you, Vist. Good to see you too. To me, it seems like you have arrived with no trouble whatsoever. We had problems because the Cruisers wanted to know where you were."

"Marta!" Zina sat next to her. "They wanted to know many other things. But imagine what would have happened if they had caught

Vist with us? What would have happened to Object?"

"It's quite alright, Zina." Vist's voice managed to sound compassionate even through all that metal. "Our loyalty has to be with what is dearest. This is the real reason why you refused to help the Cruisers, Marta. But if you had agreed to do what they said in an attempt to save Chang, no one would have the right to blame you."

"When they cut him, I cared neither for Object nor for you, Vist," said Marta and looked straight into Vist's olive-green eyes. "If I knew where you were, would I have told them? Be sure of it, but I could do nothing. First, I was fainting, and then ... his stroke." Marta started to cry again.

"This is why *nobody* knew of my location." Vist touched the small fresh scar on his forehead. "When I sensed that our signal had been intercepted, I had four seconds to decide whether to save my friends or humanity. I still don't know what the right answer would be. But I chose to land elsewhere because I carry with me something that does not belong just to you or me. Had I chosen differently, then everything my friends and I tried to achieve would have failed;

everything they had given up for it would have been in vain. You would never forgive me in any case. And Chang would not, I assume."

"Don't you dare decide for him ..." said Marta before stopping and thinking for a moment. "Vist, you are probably right! I am sorry, but I had to lash out at someone."

"Understandably."

For a while, nobody spoke.

"Go on," said Marta, "you did not come here to talk about these things alone."

"Are you ready to talk to me about what happened in New Portland?" Vist said.

"No more than when you asked me before ... on that farm."

"Zina said that—"

Marta interrupted Vist and said, "I will tell you all about it. Just do not record it, please."

"I won't."

Marta got up and walked around the room. She was anxious at first but soon became as calm as was possible in this situation.

"The first few hours after you left were wonderful. We talked, we enjoyed working together as a family, and we were looking forward to having some romantic time when all the tasks were completed. There were only a few minutes left before break time. We were outside, not far from the ship, collecting soil samples. Our sampling-auger was broken, and we took out shovels. That was fun too, but hard work. Then it was time for regular contact with the captain on TR-1 communications as we agreed. Chang wanted me to join him, but I said that the wind would contaminate the vertical sediment section we cut out in the ground. I didn't want to start such a chore all over again, and I only had a few more extractions to make. He left hesitantly, and after a few minutes, a strange feeling crept in as if I was not alone. I was so frightened, I could not even describe it. Of course, I left the section and ran towards the *Wasp*'s hatch. I had to pass ... this thick growth of dark shrubs. They looked like ferns but were black and much larger. Someone rushed at me from under those leaves, grabbed me with both hands and threw me on the ground with my face down, really hard. I lost consciousness."

Marta stopped pacing the room and sat down again.

"I woke up from the pain ... I felt him inside me, but I was also bleeding from the wounds he left – I assumed – when slicing my trousers."

Vist stopped her. "Forgive me ... but what were you wearing?"

Marta blushed. "It was so hot ... We were dying in that uniform and went outside in our yoga kimonos."

"Please, carry on. I want to understand why the locals would do such a thing. The village mystics were somewhat careful about crossing certain lines."

"Maybe it was a village maniac," said Zina, "that is why he was so far from the bay."

Marta frowned at her and said, "Then they had more than one out there ... You know, he did not get off me by himself. Somebody pulled him off – at least one more colonist. I thought it was Chang at first. I was freed and heard fighting behind me. The sound was a pure roaring, and I heard words uttered in a language I failed to recognise. Minii, minii! And then – ajaa."

"In Mongolian," said Vist, "*minii* means *mine*. And *ajaa* is *run* in Finnish. All the colonists enriched their lexicon with words from various languages."

"Well, they did run off. At least one of the bastards did, the other one chasing after him. By the time I got up, there was no sign of them. I saw footprints in the sand, but they disappeared in the wind almost immediately too. I did not wait for them to come back. I rushed to the ship and went straight into the wet room. I cleaned myself up from the dirt and semen, bandaged my thigh, changed my clothing, and found Chang in the communications room with his helmet on. I told him only that the colonists attacked me, so we armed ourselves and agreed that we would not ever separate or walk that far from the ship. But I was so ... unsettled. I can't describe to you how I felt. I made Chang promise not to tell the others about the attack. He couldn't understand why and disagreed with me at first. He was right; this was not the behaviour of the wormhole ship's pilot. We have obligations and direct orders to report everything that happens. I couldn't explain why I wanted to hide the whole thing from you. I somehow felt that I must. So I complained about stress and nausea and promised Chang to report the whole thing myself when I felt better and to avoid further trauma. But you ... you could tell." Marta lifted her eyes at Vist and took a deep breath.

"I wish I did not have to ask, but can I see the cut you received that day?"

Marta did not care anymore about Vist's gender or for her own sense of decency in that moment. She had just practically, once again, relived the two most horrid episodes of her life and felt almost numb. She got up, turned around, and lifted the folds of her dressing gown. There were six-week-old scars on the back of her right thigh. Vist's fingers did not touch her but measured the size of the marked area.

"You are right, Zina," said the metallic voice. "We have to take her to the surgical branch as soon as possible. Marta, when was the last time you ate?"

"I had some sandies yesterday but could not keep them in."

"Good. Have a glass of water now, but do not drink or eat anymore. I will be back to fetch you in a few hours. Zina, go to Selest and ask her to prepare everything for a surgical, not chemical termination. This has to be done under sedation. Marta, trust me, it is better this way."

Chapter 38. 3411. Out in Space – the Net

Zina felt uncomfortable. Here was Vist, right in front of her, on the opposite side of the circle. His robe sleeves were rolled back above the elbow. His hands were beautiful, with long fingers and clean nails, moving so fast as if he had been weaving nets all his life. Zina dropped her head and looked discreetly at Vist's face. He was focused on his work, his brows furrowed, his lips pressed tight in concentration. One lock of chestnut hair fell on his face. Vist blew it off and then pushed it back behind his ear with one quick movement of the left hand. Such a simple gesture, but Zina's heart fell into a bottomless chasm with it. She turned her eyes away from Vist, took a deep breath, and let the air out slowly and silently. That short glance at Vist was like flying. She had to wonder ... How would it feel if those long fingers touched her face, or if those strong arms closed around her. What do those asymmetrical lips taste like? Zina felt red heat spreading from her face to her neck and ears. She hoped that her blushing could be explained by the hot air if anyone noticed.

Vist had to be a man, probably her age, plus or minus five years. His robe hid his body under those folds, but judging by the shape of his arms, he was stocky and quite muscular. Although his wrists were so narrow! Zina shifted on her stool as if adjusting the edge of her net and looked at Vist sideways. He had a beautiful profile. It used to look so ordinary when she thought Vist was a woman. Now this remarkable person, unlike anyone she ever knew, made her feel at home in this strange world. He was a good person, resourceful and easy to talk to. He knew so much. He could do practically anything, or at least he had mastered anything he had tried so far. Being next to him felt ... safe. Zina's mouth was dry, and she coughed.

"Here," said Samantha next to her and passed Zina the last bottle of water, "I shall go and bring some more, and maybe something to eat. It is quite warm here indeed."

All the crew members had walked into this shed a few hours earlier, which the farmer had called a storage house. It turned out to be a wooden structure like a barn on a typical American farm or something like a small private aeroplane shed at the same time. The interior looked more like a museum of human tool evolution. Fishing rods, spades and shovels, scythes, carts, wooden hay forks, axes and saws were neatly placed with parts for electrical pumps next to a small solar tractor. Rod could not stop saying how strange it felt seeing a simple motor harvester hundreds of years out of date; a harvester that had been a prototype for his own huge and effective crop collector, capable of cleaning sixteen hectares of fields in one hour.

"Such an advanced civilisation does not know how to make a net trap? Why not?" Tolyan said quietly.

"They never needed it," Rod answered. "There is no fishing by the shores. Submarines are using acoustic traps. The sea dwellers can be picked up from the mud during the low tide. There are no wild rabbits or birds. The football goalposts are force shield arches."

"It is always good to keep the knowledge of the olds," Steven said, "it might come in useful again. The ZPE-converters on Earth were misused, and so people returned to solar panels and windmills in no time."

A grey coiled rope hung on the wall. It looked old, as such ropes were used on farms only in the early years.

"This is a lot of rope," said Vist's metallic voice.

"Enough?" asked Zina.

"Should be enough for the net we need. To make a trap, we should manage with about three or four square metres."

"Yes!" Steven said, "Just like in those jungle adventure stories. Spread it, cover it with leaves on the path, and pull it as the bastard walks over it. The creature will be dangling in the air before he knows it."

"We will build a trigger. Manual timing will be too risky with only one shot."

"Do you know how to make a trigger? Or a net?" Tolyan turned to Vist.

"I haven't made one this big, but the principle is the same. I will not manage it alone, though. Not in one cycle. I will show you what to do."

Everybody watched how the thin but strong rope became a double knot in Vist's hands and was then undone and stretched again. It took careful measurement and practice, but soon everyone sat in a semicircle and weaved like ancient fishermen. Even Samantha got carried away, biting her purple lips to white with effort.

Then she got up, stretched, threw the end of the rope around her stool, and left the shed.

Zina drank the water, and her eyes met Rod's gaze. Oh no, he had been watching her all this time.

"What you bleeding looking at?" Zina said, imitating his way of talking.

"I am looking at you, Zin, and wondering how hard it might have been to be the only woman in this landing party."

"Not a big deal. Why should it be hard? Are you suggesting I am weaker or less capable than you are?" Her voice sounded angry.

"Not at all. Physically and mentally, you can compete with most men I know. But psychologically, don't you feel alone? Marta is always busy on the ship and spends most of her time with her husband."

"Thank you for your concern, Rod, but I am fine. I can talk about anything with anyone. Even about my period if I have to. You are lucky I don't have to."

"Guys, guys! Please change the subject," said Tolyan. "If light conversation can make this chore a little less daunting, let's talk about something beautiful."

"Are you calling me ugly?" Zina asked, sounding even angrier.

"No way!" Tolyan answered.

"Careful, Tolyan, you may not leave this shed alive," said Steven. "Don't listen to him, Zin. We all think you are beautiful. Isn't that right, Vist?"

"Absolutely," said Vist, winking at Zina.

She emptied the bottle in one gulp and wished she had something stronger in it.

"Vist, tell us about Mars," Tolyan said, trying to save his skin.

"Yes," said Rod, "We know that you lived and worked there, but what did you do in the cave town for fun?"

"I am not sure I know what you mean. There was fun in everything I did."

"What about times when you did not work in the archives?"

"And when you did not study or train?" Steven said.

"Or practise new skills?" Rod added.

"Mars's population is not big. Most of the people were busy with various duties. But we also socialised, made friends, met for dinners and barbecues, went on dates and visited the theatre and cinema together. We also enjoyed games, sporting events and concerts."

"But you – what did *you* do?" Steven asked.

"All of it."

"I did not know you had restaurants and theatres there," said Tolyan, "Hang on. All of it? Dates too?"

Suddenly everybody was wide-awake and alert. Zina felt like her stomach was turning into a block of ice. Now she was thinking toxic thoughts about some unknown Martian woman who had been waiting for Vist on Mars in the underground colony. How incredible she would have to be to catch his eye. What chance did Zina have? She tried to imagine her rival but didn't even know where to start. But that woman would have to be beautiful, smart and talented. Just like him. Is she a loader too? Zina sighed. Vist wouldn't spend his precious time with someone just out of boredom. After all, he is never bored. She has to be very special to drag him away from his work.

In the meantime, Vist replied to all questions at once, "Of course, I won't tell you about my date. I am surprised you asked. We don't have restaurants there. We cook for each other and have friends for dinner. There is a cinema hall to watch flickers and a decent sports facility. The theatre, yes. That was a special thing indeed. It was too impractical to facilitate professional theatre in the first-ever colony. The need and interest in it – call it a trend – is a relatively new thing. We performed there ourselves. We participated in concerts and produced plays. There was an old man who worked in the cargo department. A few years before he died, he used to come up with brilliant ideas for an annual play to celebrate New Year. He selected actors among us to play the characters and invited us to try the art of acting. I watched many of his performances. He was very good and inspired others to carry on the tradition."

"Did you act for him too?"

For some reason, everyone expected a negative answer, but Vist said *yes*. It took a minute for another question to come.

"What part did you play?"

Zina could see that every person in the room was thinking the same thing: this is it! But Vist spoiled it once again.

"I have only done it twice. Once I played Master Cornelius in *Morning Colours.* And once I was Marlona in a twenty-fourth-century musical comedy called *Times and Dynasty.*"

Zina noticed the disappointment on everyone's faces. It was quite explicable.

To break that awkwardness, she asked, "Can you still remember the words? I always liked Cornelius's monologue in the second part."

"Yes, Vist. Give us a quote. Great idea, Zin," said Rod.

"I am not sure. Okay, we all can use a break, I guess."

"Oh my! I would like to see that!" Steven said, "Mik and the captain are going to miss out."

Everybody stopped working and stared at Vist in expectation once again. Vist hesitated for a minute, then put his hand under the scarf on his neck, pressed two fingers to his throat, adjusted his larynx, and hummed. Satisfied with the result, he placed both hands on his knees and looked in front of him. Zina did not expect such a change. His eyes suddenly looked empty, and his face aged at least ten years. There were ages of suffering in this face, the pain of unbearable loss, and heavy thoughts. He was not looking at anything in the shed. Those eyes saw something through the walls ... through space and time. Vist's chin appeared to be made of stone, his jaws became square, and the small muscles in his cheek moved in obvious anxiety. Then came the voice in the complete silence of the shed. The metallic distortion was gone.

It was the voice of a man, "Again. Sleep won't come. The night was over, but my problem would not leave. It never will. The question that I ask has no coherent answer. Why must I make this choice? Why can't things be right and wrong, at the same time? Why can A not be B, and why does the transformation take ages? My wants and needs ..." Vist closed his eyes. "It would have been so easy if they were the same. But I am torn." He opened his eyes, but they were full of angry fire this time. He looked down to the left as if trying to extinguish that flame. His voice was full of bitterness. "The others – it seems so effortless for them to preach honesty and lie, to cheat and then demand justice if someone cheats them out of ... what? What do they value? Their love?" Vist closed his eyes again and shook his head, "They are full of hate! Their lives? They kill themselves but slowly. Oh, men! Your kind survived in contradiction with itself for thousands of years. But just imagine ..." Vist lifted his head, then looked ahead once again, with all his face as bright as the Orion Nebula. "What will I be the day I made my choice? What will you be if you ... What am I saying? There is no use. The transformation will take ages. The universe's age is very hard to guess." With these last words, Vist's voice was dying, and the light dimmed until his face became a mask of a dead man – hopeless and lifeless.

For a moment, Zina was speechless and then started to applaud. She could not help herself. That was truly the best version of the character she ever saw, even in Bolshoi. The rest joined her clapping, maybe not so enthusiastically, and Steven whistled, while Tolyan insisted on hearing more. Rod asked for a different character. Zina discovered that she did not want to see Marlona. Vist was so wonderful as Master Cornelius. She feared the magic would be gone if he played a female part. The shed was full of noise loud enough for the people outside to hear. The door opened, and Captain Darkwood walked in with Samantha. They carried water and packed lunch bags for everyone. Grand, Mik and two young apprentices from the farm kitchen followed them. Massimo came in with a bucket of frog eggs, but Samantha told him to leave it outside. Tolyan explained what had just happened, and everyone wanted to see some of the play. Samantha said that she loved theatre. They have two in White City but had never heard of the *Morning Colours* as it was too new. But they were familiar with *Times and Dynasty* and wanted to see an extract. Grand and the Captain found that they would like that too.

Zina was going to protest, but she could not find a good reason.

The work was forgotten as everyone took their share of cheese, pickled nar-bulbs with dry fruits, dry rock snails, and barbequed larvae on a skewer with honey mead in a mug. They sat on the clean wooden floor, and Tolyan demanded that Vist show the colonists how to act properly before eating. Vist chewed his lips in deep thought and then stood up.

This time he did not touch his throat, but his audience observed another transformation. Zina refused to believe her eyes. Vist's shoulders lowered, his back straightened, and his chin lifted slightly. The wrinkles of the old man disappeared, as his facial muscles relaxed. His skin started to look softer and lighter. It was a very feminine face indeed. Zina knew this was just an act, but it appeared that even Vist's eyelashes became longer and thicker. This illusion was supported by a suddenly capricious expression on his face and a girlish pout. Reddened lips formed a white-toothed grin, and green eyes sparkled with confidence.

Vist crossed his arms on his chest, stamped his foot, and suddenly started to sing, "I refuse to wait for another minute. He drives me mad every day and night. My heart is his if he chooses to win it, but this time he just has to do it right."

The song went on for a verse and chorus. Vist was not going to do the whole aria, but the final part only. He finished with a bow and blew a kiss towards his roaring audience. The room was filled with applause, cheering and laughter. The comical part of the naughty widow from the play was meant to be screechy and annoying. Any man could have sung this song in a mocking manner. Still, Zina could not help but gain the impression that she just saw a woman singing in the wooden shed without the acoustic effect of the more appropriate hall. Not every man could pull such a deep soprano in the final line. Zina started to feel a horrible doubt creeping into her mind, and the vague image of the mysterious woman on Mars turned into the figure of the not so mysterious man. That man was Vist. It was the same Vist she had seen as a man just a few minutes ago. Zina forced a smile and clapped with everyone else, but the icy fear in her stomach started to melt into corrosive slush. She looked at her friends. Nobody cared about Vist's true nature. They are curious, nothing more. But for her, this could mean a broken heart. Look at their happy faces! And here, Zina spotted the captain. Tom also clapped his hands and laughed. But that laughter had a very different note of happiness in it. She recognised it with the almost physical pain of envy. He was full of the same delight she had experienced after seeing Vist as Cornelius. "Oh no you don't!" Zina imagined saying to Tom, feeling how her heart was becoming light and joyful for a new and unexpected reason, "She is mine!"

Chapter 39. 3416. Back on Earth – Object

The conference room was not in the Tree House at the Oak but under the giant tree. A few huge arching roots created the entrances into the Mole Tunnels, where the Resistance kept its arsenal, food storage and garage for the tetrahoders and electrotrucks. All the participants were already leaving, talking about nothing else but what they had just heard. It wasn't a large group, considering the importance of the event: only forty-three representatives from various Rebel factions of the continent most dedicated to the Object and KOSI evacuation. After having been verified by security, the rest took part via the MESH link, and their holo-screens were already gone too. Everyone had left. The chairman of the Resistance, Vasily Lindberg, sat back by his terminal. He nodded along to his thoughts in silence for almost a minute. Finally, completely alone, he turned on the MESH recorder's playback. He fast-forwarded to the end of the reports and played the meeting's next part.

It started with his own voice. "I believe I can speak for all of us here when I thank you,

Captain Darkwood, for your detailed report, and your team for their dedication, effort, bravery and investment in the Object mission. Does anyone in this room have any questions? If you do, please enter them in the live stream. Our secretary, Mr O'Connor, will allocate them accordingly. I want to take advantage of my position to ask the first one. Captain Darkwood, I understand that data collected by your pilots and your engineer during the last shift has already been processed theoretically and tested by model programs. Tell me, what have you achieved since you introduced it to specialists on Earth and Mars?"

"Thank you, chairman, but this type of question would be best answered by a specific member of my team who was directly involved in the process. Vist, please."

The metallic voice from the speaker was loud and clear, although the microphone was much further away from this strange person.

"Thank you, captain ... chairman. If you don't mind, I will summarise for now and address the more detailed propositions directly to the planning group. Tonight I need to be as brief as possible. So! Some of our calculations worked. It took the whole team from Mars and Earth, but a single wormhole is now achievable. Getting to Noverca will take just one shift instead of several. If you all work hard and stick to the Object plan, you will manage to design, build and test it in your lifetime. That is, if the sects don't interfere much. If Earth lets you down too soon, you will still have a few decades on Mars to launch from ... provided you take back the PSS transports from the Cruisers to relocate Object to Mars's underground stations. The last to leave will be the operators on the Jupiter KOSI station, of course."

"But it will be a very narrow wormhole, I was told. What ship can we build to go through it? Even class WSP's energy ripples will be too big and may crash the vessel."

"You don't need big ships. You need a modified, simple escape pod capable of launching and landing. It allows the pod to shift by itself, opening the wormhole from the KOSI ZPE launch station. However, it is a one-way ticket. This type of wormhole cannot be maintained to offer any chance of return. Even the shift-postmen would not be able to find the stream. But you would be able to send out a swarm of small, podlike vessels, each with two or three adult persons in stasis and with modest luggage. My assistants called them pod-fliers."

"But there will be millions of people to evacuate. How will we manage? Even with the state budget, we can't afford the mass production of such pods."

"Unfortunately, mass production isn't an option anymore for two reasons. First, there won't be that many people left. I met with our MGP representative, Selest Dvali, who showed me the graphs of the population forecast. It looks like she was correct to point out that there is no rational incentive for people to reproduce anymore if their children don't have a long life or happy future. Anyway, they will be advised to stop entirely in the next thirty years. On the other hand, the death rate is growing due to the lifestyle under the new government. The current course of events suggests that the entire population will be completely restricted to protective stations here and on Mars in fifty years. Synthetic food only – all animals and plants will be gone and no more than ... well ... It is hard to tell. When you published realistic expectations of evacuation four days ago, almost everybody who responded to the MESH forum expressed a desire for their bloodline to continue somewhere and somehow. New generations of genetically enhanced colonists might be able to afford to fly their own pod-fliers to Noverca mainly on autopilot. But the rest of humanity will have to travel in the form of micro-life material: as cell nuclei in eggs and sperm banks, as undeveloped clones, embryos or zygotes inside incubators or in frozen, dormant states, which will be much cheaper. Nevertheless, you will need someone capable of operating the process. The whole planet must become a new Resort of Hope and pursue this common goal. You are lucky if you will have between twenty and twenty-five thousand people in the whole solar system to actually travel by shift and deliver what remains of humanity to the Vitricus System. How many will be able to buy or build a pod? Well, that is up to them, as long as they don't use force to obtain one. That is the second reason."

"Yes, I had heard that there would be fewer of us, but I did not realise how few ... Mr O'Connor?"

"Here is a question that came through from our South American Representative. Please, go ahead."

"Zalia Shwetska. What do you mean? What you just said sounded like not everyone will be able to evacuate. Wouldn't Object try to save everybody who will be left on Earth? Isn't that what the KOSI relocation originally planned?"

"The KOSI founders planned the colonisation of all before the Moon Cruisers took over the government. We are not living in a Platinum Age anymore. I agreed to work on Object with a few terms and conditions a few years ago. One of the conditions was not to bite off more than you could chew, to avoid choking. The Cruisers have a plan that won't work but that could create obstacles for Object, and this is their choice. Nevertheless, you can make the economy work for human survival until the end. If the Cruisers become renegade, and they come to buy or earn their part in Object – sure, why not? But the number of people who can be evacuated to Noverca will depend on how much they can earn. Of course, the best way would be to evacuate as many people as possible. That can be achieved by supporting a healthy economy and fair trade of goods and services. Allow people to make their own funds. In the past, people worked to get a pension plan, a better house or a car. Now they will work to buy a pod for themselves and their special someone or something. That was my second condition. As the Object mission recognised before we went to Noverca, trying to save all at the cost of a capable few may result in the death of Object itself. The mission will fail because such charity will slow things down too much. The end of the world will not wait. A noble attempt to save the maximum number of people might lead to a minimal number being saved, if anyone at all. Pod production will need substantial funds. People who cannot contribute anything can send some genetic material cheaply, and this material will be treated the same way as the rest. Still, they would not be able to go themselves or send members of their families. Those people who worked hard and saved enough to go or to send their unborn children can be sure that they will be the first to be activated and walk among the colonists. Mr O'Connor?"

"Next question, please."

"Ryth Cotra, Mediterranean WildLife. Madam, will Object at least pay for other living things to continue on Noverca? After all, the first colonies had more of those to take, and they did not take up much space. Thank you."

"Of course, it will be reasonable and useful for the colony to receive surviving animal and plant genomes, but not at the cost of human life. Non-human micro-life material should go together with human micro-life material if there is room for donations. Thank you, who is next, Mr O'Connor?"

"Alexander DuPont, Active Opposition Group. Sir, Mooners control budget funds across the world. So what of it now if Object becomes a commercial enterprise? Can Cruisers just come and buy themselves an armada of capsules? I'd rather not fly anywhere, but I won't let them either – because of what they did. They are responsible for the fact that we are evacuating almost at the last moment."

"I agree that this won't be fair. I believe that your head economist, Darius Rossi, is in this room. I will ask him to tell us about his idea. Please?"

"Thank you, Vist. The idea is not mine but one of our young consultants. Nevertheless, I like it very much and would share my reasons with Mr DuPont. Although it has not yet been thoroughly worked out and should be ready for a full presentation next week, I can briefly convey its essence. Factors such as time, financial means and the number of workers and specialists will not allow us to evacuate everyone. Selling capsules for stolen funds does not appeal as a moral option to anyone. At the same time, we can increase the number of evacuees if they take an active part in Object. A new currency or, if you want, credits that guarantee pod ownership can only be earned in the project itself. There is nothing else left to do on Earth. The so-called New White City can be established on every continent. It will resemble the Resort of Hope in Canada, where the first colonists were raised and trained. This time we will grow and educate our young ones and ourselves and build pod-fliers for all members. Like any other urban structure, it needs housing, food, clothing and other basic amenities. It will need hunters for materials and resources. It will also need protection. Anyone can enter Object with nothing in their pockets but determination and start from scratch to earn credits for their own evacuation. The longer you live and work there, the more you earn on your method of relocation. When this structure is worked out, and here, a lot of things need to be calculated and tested, then all the residents of the city who were born since the project started will have every right to be evacuated. We should be able to guarantee this much to them. Yes, there will be fewer of them. Unfortunately, the number of children has to be limited. But they are the ones who will complete our project and become the new humanity of Earth that can join the colony, prepared both socially and biologically. An example of the structure, the White City of Gera, brought from the colony by Captain Darkwood, will help us choose the most favourable Object policy. But as I said, we need to work on the details."

"Thank you. Benjamin Novak. Independent E-Bank. Mr Vist! What will happen to our dormant evacuees when their cells arrive at the colony?"

"All will be activated or in vitro fertilisation will be used to produce carriers of the donor's material. Those carriers will become colonists themselves and contribute to the diversity of the genetic pool of the planet. No one can tell how long it will take for colonists to activate them all, not even the colonists themselves, but they will have much longer than fifty years to prepare and build the facility, as they had already started. So, many changes will take place. Everything we do still might be wasted if history repeats itself there. The question is, will we take this chance, or will we just perish in passivity?"

"Next question comes from a bio-group in Central Asia. Please."

"Thank you, Mr O'Connor. Tamar Weber. I would like to know about the new species of humanoids that you have mentioned in your report. Is it true that the colonists found a life form on Noverca that is very close to humans? Would you mind telling us more about that creature? Captain Darkwood said it was captured for the first time while you were there and is a monstrosity."

"We will have to agree on the definition of a monster first, but the truth is: there is a creature whose genetic material might be crucial for the fast adaptation of our descendants. The svoloch is an incredible survivor. Its genes could allow the colony to expand further north and south."

"What exactly can they do?"

"My personal involvement was shortened by our need to leave the planet. Nevertheless, I have learned that those creatures have a unique metabolism. They are capable of fast regeneration, partially reflect radiation, and when necessary, they can convert it into different types of energy: kinetic, thermal, etc. As a result, they do not rely on respiration as much. Which explains their tolerance to low oxygen in the air. They can heal incredibly fast, especially when resting. Their fur is not only a good insulator but also one of their essential sensory organs. Imagine being mostly covered in something like cat whiskers. I could tell you more, but I would rather refer you to my essay on MESH under the restriction code of Object."

"Thank you, Mr O'Connor. Lidia Omondi, New York, Free Media for Resistance. Mr Vist, if I understood correctly, you are planning to introduce many of their genes to a human genome. Is there a risk that we will not be human anymore after such a procedure? I mean – our descendants. At the end of the day, we are trying to preserve humanity, not transform it into something else. I understand purple skin, new types of retina cells and a second lymphatic system, but if we go too far, would we not become monsters ourselves?"

"We are here because we change all the time, just like all living things. Evolution is an inevitable and necessary factor of our continuation. Both our cultures, on Earth and on Noverca, took control over evolution, just like we took control over selection centuries before we even knew what it was. We can promote evolution and survival as long as our gene bank exists and we keep perfecting our technology. For now, the conditions on Noverca are still pretty harsh, outside of our comfort zone. But that can change, and I am sure we can too. Even if we look different and will not be called humans anymore, our "bloodline" would make it possible. Finally: since we are capable of reasoning, what makes us human might not be our physiology but our virtues and values. Next question, please, Mr O'Connor."

"Rudolf Wu, Sixth Greenland Research Centre. Mr Vist, you have played a great part in Object so far. I was told you are a loader. The last one! Is it true? What is your real name, and what will you do from now on? Thank you."

"I belong to the second generation of those appointed and loaded by the KOSI relocation laboratory. The lab was indeed destroyed. The rest of my kind is long gone, exterminated by Cruisers. My name is Vist. My work for Object ends as soon as I pass my all findings on to your scientific society and get my payment. After that, I intend to investigate a certain relevant matter as much as possible here and on Mars, then ... I will go back to Noverca to complete my work."

The chairman heard his own voice again. "I don't think we can authorise that. We don't have any more of ... your kind. I am sure we can use you here."

"Sir, I wish I did not have to remind you that because the loading project was terminated, I have had to survive by my own means. I am neither an employee nor the property of the Resistance. I agreed to do what I did to help humans to continue to be. I did it for my own reasons and ... for a price. What I am about to sell you is worthy enough to grant me my own ship."

"I see. I can't argue with that. After all, that was agreed, and that agreement is still stored on MESH. What ship do you want?"

"I will take the *Wasp* and see if I can hire a suitable crew."

"Okay. Mr O'Connor has more questions listed here for you. Will you answer them in recording?"

"I will indeed."

"I have one more before we close the conference. I thought your samples of svoloch cells were destroyed on your journey here."

"Yes, sir, that is what I thought. But it turned out that I have access to enough of what we need. I cannot tell you more than that."

The chairman stopped the playback and lifted his head.

"Well? I hope you heard that" the chairman said to the empty room.

"Every word," answered the communicator's speaker.

"Do you still think opposing a loader is a good idea?"

The voice sniffed and said, "We wouldn't be the first ones."

"And what good came from it? I don't know, father. But your plan is very risky."

"Have faith, Vasily. This person is an abomination and ..."

"Father! This abomination is our only chance!" the chairman almost shouted. He took a deep breath and lowered his voice, "Why can't you take over Father Deessa's plan, and then we will both be on our way to the colony in no time? The Broadsky widow is not the only pilot who can fly class WSP."

"Because we need to do something larger than ourselves. We have a noble cause, and the whole point is to save as many children of the Lord as possible. Including us. Production of new pods *is* our only chance indeed. But if the new government takes over Object by denouncing the Mooners and offering budget funds instead of the new currency, we need to propose a prioritisation scheme. Old chaps like you and I should go to the first automatic pod-fliers."

"But that still might take years. I don't want to wait. I am sixty-two already ... by the time it is built, the best half of my life will be in the past."

The chairman pressed his cold hand on his burning forehead.

The voice answered, "So why don't you take the *Wasp* for yourself? You don't know where it is, do you? You need my help to find it for the price of new pod blueprints."

"That bastard reprogrammed its course before jumping off. It did not go to preset coordinates."

"How do you know that?"

"You heard him. He asked for WSP, the last one of her kind too. We knew he would do that. But he ... she did not ask for its location, being well aware that we are the only ones who should know it."

"What is he ... she going to do with it?"

"She will modify it to her standards and go to Noverca. The selfish bitch will be the first to evacuate! She ... he wants to return in ten to fifteen years, but I doubt this will be good for our plan."

"Why? If this loader of yours is right and our plan will slow down the evacuation, we will need him or her to fix it and speed it up again."

"Father, I am not dealing with a hero here but with a businessman. If he or she returns and learns that we didn't fulfil this part of the agreement, she will just turn around and leave for good."

"Then you will have to make sure she doesn't, and you finally take control. The loader outsmarted you and Deessa, and you had to learn a lesson from that mess."

"Deessa killed himself, and I need another agent. Or did he...? Did you? Or Lord! How?"

"Never mind that, Vasily! Volna is a good girl. She follows every order, unlike your captain. If it wasn't for Darkwood's insubordination, we would have taken both Vist and the *Wasp* five years ago. The loader would have gone to the colony with Ontha and his men, and Ontha knew how to make even loaders do what they are told."

The chairman suddenly smiled.

"Now we have Baker back. We can build another *Wasp*."

"And how will you explain *that* to the Resistance Reps, whose priority now is Object and nothing else?"

"You could kidnap him! If you can't have Vist now, you can take Baker and make him—"

"Don't be stupid, Vasily!" The speaker's device almost shook with anger as the voice rose to a shout, "One man is not enough to actually build a pod or a ship. You will need a factory, a whole team and materials and time. To do it secretly is even harder and will take longer. Why do you think we gave up on the Moon Plan ages ago? It has been nothing but a diversion for almost ten years now! You are better off waiting for the first set of pod-fliers. The only way to go sooner is to persuade Vist to take you with her. Man or woman, you know for sure that Vist can be bought."

"Bought maybe, but not bribed. Father, don't you think I wouldn't. But I remember too well what happened to Maiser, and after everything he did for that ungrateful bastard.

Damn you! I am surprised that you are willing to wait for so long. You are older than me."

"I want to do the right thing and save humanity!"

The chairman made mocking faces at the speaker, knowing that no one could see him, and then asked, "But why? Seb, I've known you for years. You don't give a shit about humanity any more than Ontha did?"

"*Father* Ontha, my friend. *Father* Seb. Don't forget the formalities. They are what really matters. Those who will follow us to Noverca ... even if it's only a handful, they will always remember *who* at least tried to save them all. *We* will be remembered, not some heartless superhuman who did everything for a price and did not care if some poor stranded souls were left behind to die. He also said that fewer people would evacuate than we thought. Good! We can make sure there are even fewer than that."

"You want to become the new martyr on Noverca!"

"Why not? Looks like this title has a certain weight there."

"In some peasant village ... not in an elite society. This is far from good, Sebastian. Things can change for the worse in so many years. They might completely forget about martyrs, the Lord and the faith by the time we arrive."

"True, but that village is proof that what could be forgotten can be remembered again. Things can change in our favour just as likely. Think about it, Vasily! The children of the Lord are waiting for us in a different system. They will take over the colony, just like we took over the Platinum Age. This process is inevitable! We will get there and say the right things, and then ..."

"But don't forget about the biological factors. Without genetic modifications, we will depend on their technology and their scientists. We are not salt-villagers, Father. We don't have purple skin and reflective micro-scales. How will we survive?"

"Power! Vasily, this is why we need to be in power. If you don't care about power, you better freeze some of your sperm cells while you still can."

"Fine, have it your way! But what are we to do with Vist for now?"

"Let Vist have the *Wasp*. Let Vist even have his or her old crew. They were away for too long and won't be so easily corrupted or tricked. Plus, we don't need too many witnesses."

"But if they go back to Noverca first, they may influence what happens there. You will be the first to hate this!"

"Don't worry about that. It will take a while for Vist to prepare; anything could happen to her in the meantime. She might get sick or have an accident. Thieves may attack her. If that happens, the crew will stay too. Shame there is no one left from the old unloaders. Anyway, the *Wasp* can be ours. It is always good to have a plan B."

Chapter 40. 3411. Out in Space – Svoloch

"We underestimated it. We thought we were so skilful and trained to deal with hostile people and animals, and then we were beaten by a hostile but completely unknown creature. We should have studied it first. Citizen's data is too limited."

"Calm down, Zina ... this is what we are trying to do here, aren't we?" Tolyan spat on the ground and added, "To study it, we need to catch it first, or at least see it."

"At what cost?" said Zina with a trembling voice, "Who screamed?"

"Rod," answered Tolyan, kicking the mycelium of some luminous mushrooms, which then burst into blue fairy dust in the darkness of the shade. "Trust me, I know his voice very well, I hope he is alright."

"Vist would have known for sure."

"Your precious Vist is not here. Stay down. I will go and see for myself. Why did you even come with us?"

"That was not a scream of horror but pain. You need me here. You are not hunting wild boars, you know."

"I am sure five of us are capable of overcoming one alien monkey."

"Six of us have more chances. I am going with you."

"Wait, someone is coming. Sounds like Général."

The thick black shrubs moved like a bear trying to make its way through.

"Are you sure?" said Zina, but she immediately had to rush forwards to catch the old man stumbling and almost falling into her arms. Tolyan helped her to sit Général down on the brown moss.

As soon as his commander caught his breath, the huge trooper asked him, "Any new orders, sir? What happened there?"

Général did not reply. He rolled his eyes, his face full of strange expressions, and just pointed towards the direction he had come from.

"Take it easy, Général. That's it. Where is the rest of your squad?" asked Zina.

"I never believed in god." the old man finally answered, "but I am ready to believe in Satan. I never saw anything move so fast: the ugly bastard almost got me. He would have if not for Steven. I am here to fetch you guys. We will have to carry both of them."

"Both of whom?" Zina asked.

"Steven is in pretty bad shape, and that demon is sedated, thanks to Rod."

According to Général the creature remained almost invisible until it entered the trap. Its dark skin and shaggy mane camouflaged the svoloch perfectly in the shadows of the black plants. The trick worked, and the svoloch became entangled in the net like a butterfly. The creature was stronger than anyone expected and almost broke free, but Mik, Steven and Général fell on the creature like a bunch of wrestlers and tried to hold it down. Despite its allegedly acute vision, the svoloch did not seem to have noticed Mik immediately. He shook Général off his back like a coat and went straight for Steven's blond head. The strong trooper could not even dodge with all his brilliant reactions and skill. He received a series of paw blows – strong and as fast as lightning.

"It would have been the end of our brave Steven, but Mik pulled the svoloch's head back with all his might and forced his mouth open. Rod did not bother with syringes and emptied the whole flask of dope into the frothy gob but was bitten, as you probably heard. Tolyan, make sure you do not start joking about the svoloch mistaking Mik for one of his own kind," Général said to his young friend.

"Is Rod okay?" Tolyan asked as they walked back.

"Your sweetheart hurt his finger. He will get over it."

"You should have let me go and take your place," said Tolyan. He sounded like a child who had missed all the fun.

"I was not convinced I could protect Zina if she was found by that thing. But after seeing it in action, I would say none of us could handle the beast alone. That's right, my boy. Here we are. Make haste, Tolyan. Mik is building stretchers, and we need to help him."

In the opening, Rod stood by the hairy body on the ground. Tolyan nodded at him and went about following his orders. Zina was already kneeling by Steven, whose head and upper body were covered in blood. He was conscious but made no sound, squeezing his teeth hard and waiting for painkillers to fill his blood vessels. Zina was too busy washing and bandaging his wounds to pay attention to the creature lying just a few inches away. She bowed over the beast when she was sure Steven was taken care of.

"Careful, Zin," Rod said behind her, "I would not risk any twitching."

Zina turned around and saw pale Rod standing with his hands pressed to his stomach. His front was also stained with blood, and Zina felt terribly guilty for almost forgetting about him.

"Gosh! Rod, I am so sorry. What did it do to you?"

"Minor injury, according to Mik," answered Rod and lifted his right hand. His middle finger was gone, "That bastard has eaten a piece of me, along with the soporific, I hope it works. I would be pretty upset if all of it was for nothing."

Zina took his hand and examined it.

"Clean cut, like it was taken off with secateurs. Here, I have used almost all disinfectants on Steven, but this should be enough. Where is that bandage? Here we go – nice and tight. Now keep it upright so that you don't start bleeding again. Are you sure it is not lying around here somewhere? I have an ice case, they can sew it back on in the city."

"No, I am pretty sure this bastard is digesting it already," answered Rod and sat next to Steven, "Are *you* going to be ok, mate?"

"I will live. Might not be as handsome anymore though. But if I have to get injured to get Zina's attention, then ..."

"Actually, you don't have any deep cuts ... just too many of them. Général is right, and you should not walk back. You have lost plenty of blood."

Zina turned to the svoloch, which was already bound and loaded on the stretcher. She took the large paw and lifted it. It was not a paw – it was a hand with five fingers. There were no claws but nails – large, black and badly chipped but not sharp or long enough to cut seriously through the flesh.

Zina stood back to see the rest of the strange creature. The skin was dark grey, rough and leathery. Scruffy black hair covered its head, chest, groin and most of its back, but on the neck and shoulders, it appeared to be long, straight and glossy as if oiled and brushed. It looked almost like a lion's mane but much longer. Zina walked around to face the creature and said, "This is impossible! Is this some kind of joke?"

The sedated svoloch breathed with a heavy snore in its sleep. It had the face of a man, ugly and rough. That was not a werewolf snout, or even that of an ape; it was unmistakably a human's face.

"Surprised?" asked Steven, shifting himself onto the stretcher Mik had brought to his side, "That's the reason I hesitated. Don't you think he looks a bit like Abraham Lincoln?"

"Don't be silly, Steve. I say he looks more like ... actually, I know what you mean," said Tolyan, "He is not so big and heavy though. As Rod cannot use his hand for a while, Général and Zina must carry him. You are huge compared to this wild bastard."

"Thank you, darling. Did you hear that, Zin?" Steven laughed shortly and immediately flinched.

"We need to move," said Mik, working in silence, "We don't know how long the sedative will last. I will not relax until we cage the creature. And no, Tolyan, I am not talking about Steven."

Zina picked up the rubbery handles of the military stretchers and was truly surprised by the svoloch's weight. The creature was no heavier than the average human adolescent. She walked behind Général towards the track and studied the creature in front of her. Its feet, head and hands were large, but the rest of the body appeared slim, sinewy and dense. Its physique made her think of a cheetah or greyhound. The svoloch was probably a very fast runner or excellent climber, or both. Since it was known as the largest predator on Gera, this agility was not for running away. And yet he didn't have any of the usual features of a killer. No fangs or claws. Okay, those teeth could bite through small bones effortlessly, but there was nothing to hunt in his habitat. He must feed on smaller animals and plants. Maybe the svoloch could crack the shell of rock snails, the skin of tocks or cream roots. Nobody knew yet, but perhaps he occasionally went fishing in the sea and picked the young blobsters there. And what if this was an intelligent humanoid who cooked his own food? Even if Samantha was right and the svoloch was a cannibal and an omnivore, so what? There are cannibals among people on Earth even now.

It took them about an hour to get back to Massimo in his truck and another forty minutes to get to the city gates. Mik's concerns were wasted. The huge dose of the sedative kept the creature asleep for a few hours. Vist and Samantha managed to measure Abraham – as his catchers named the creature – and examined it thoroughly on the surgical table. DNA samples were taken, and at this stage, the results failed to shock anyone but instead created more new questions and added to the mystery of this native species ... that maybe was not native after all.

Chapter 41. 3416. Back on Earth – Selest

Doctor Selest Dvali was a ninety-two-year-old professional surgeon from Gudauta, and she had been the head of the Med-Group of the Resistance on the continent for the last twenty years, remembering very little of her life before that.

Her family was destroyed and scattered around the world by the Mooners. She never married, and as far as she was concerned, her only family were her staff and patients. She mainly managed health care for the Resistance. She was personally involved in the treatment of such important individuals as astronauts who returned from Noverca, and now she was specifically tasked with leading the research work on genetic evolution for evacuation. Selest was devoted to the cause, and she was among those few people convinced she was not going anywhere.

"But why not?" Marta asked, still lying on the bed, tired and pale, "Surely, with your contribution to Object, you can afford several pods."

"Mmm," said Selest and stared at the monitor above Marta's head, "I don't like the colour of your face, but your heart rate is fine. Move your toes for me ... Good, the drug is wearing off. Any pain? No? Are you sure? Okay, to be honest, I would rather give my credits to those kids who will be born among the Thieves and Cruisers despite all warnings and advice. I will be too old to go."

"But you will have at least twenty years of perfect retirement on Gera if you go. I am sure you will like it there. Just because it is different."

"You don't believe yourself when you are saying this, Marta," said Selest, laughing. "If it will make you feel better, I will donate my cells to the gene bank. You have done well. One of the nurses or Doctor Fry will check your blood pressure in about two hours, and then you might be free to go. Did you eat?"

"Oh yes, I forgot what it is like to be hungry and not feel sick after breakfast. Zina brought so much, I thought I would not manage, but look." Marta pointed at the empty poly-containers on the tray. "The best collection of snacks from Nick and two milkshakes."

"Don't go mad. If you get up, take care and be slow. The anaesthetic needs more time to wear off. Take two of these if the pain returns. I have to go now."

"Okay, thank you, Selest. How is everybody? How is Général?"

"You can ask them yourself in a minute. You have a whole line of visitors outside, but I will allow only two at once. The room is too small for more."

Selest opened the door of the recovery room and said, "Zina, Alan, you can come in now. Don't make her too weary!"

She waited in the doorway for a minute, watching all those greetings and questions about her wellbeing. Then she closed the door and stopped by the waiting hall. She nodded to Rod and Wes, who were waiting in the company of three huge men in uniform. She did not know them well, but she had treated their injuries on the day of their arrival. In the next hour, she checked on a few more patients who were victims of the most recent incident involving Cruisers. Then she listened to the report of Doctor Cazacu on the physical and psychological state of the newly arrived former novices, and went to the laboratory. She found Vist surrounded by holographic screens.

"Well?" Selest asked.

"Yes," answered Vist, still looking at the screen, "I reckon this is even better than if we had the original material. Although ideally, I would prefer us to have both."

"You are getting greedy. You did not count on either at the start. Tell me, Vist, that creature, was it intelligent? Could you communicate with it?"

"The specimens we have encountered could communicate. We already knew that they lived in tribes with certain traditions and rituals, much more complex than our wolf packs, prides of lions, or even ape groups are all known for. Their vocabulary is poor, but they could express their immediate needs."

"Did you learn their language?"

"No, they already knew words from Earth languages when our *Ark* and *Noah* arrived."

Selest stood back in shock.

"How is it possible?"

"Because they are humans. Well, they used to be." Selest gasped, but Vist continued, "Thankfully, now I know what not to do so that we do not repeat their mistakes."

"With all respect, this sounds very doubtful. Such a transformation, by your own account, would take thousands of years unless it is an artificial mutation. And this is on a planet that was even less comfortable not so long ago. The very first Lyra set of ships was sent recently by comparison! How did they get there, and why did they become these back-to-nature things?"

"Believe me, Selest, I have no answer to this mystery. Yet! But the fact is, they are the only other native life on Noverca with human genes; they still have human facial, physical and vocal features. The internal organ structure resembles ours, as the scanning allowed me to see since I had no body to do an autopsy on. There has to be an answer, and I am determined to find it."

Doctor Selest stepped closer to Vist, put her hand on Vist's back, and said thoughtfully, "The fact you have some of its DNA now and here ... is pure luck."

"Luck for me, maybe, but misfortune for Marta. You still think she is better off not knowing?"

"What do you think?"

Vist turned away from the screen and looked at the old woman, "I care for Marta enough not to distress her any more than she already has been."

Selest sighed with relief, "I wouldn't want to be the one to tell her. The poor girl has been through a lot. To find out that she was raped and impregnated by a mutant ... that could be the last straw. Zina told me that Marta almost took her own life once already ... in the castle."

"Yes, and you might have saved her life here. Does anybody else know?"

"As far as Doctor Fry and the nurses are concerned, this was just an abortion, unavoidable after the prolonged radiation exposure. You and I are the only ones who know."

"Have you done to her leg what I have asked?"

"The teeth marks? Yes. They are gone. The scar now looks like it was a blade wound."

"Thank you. Now, look here!" Vist pointed at the screen. "You will find everything I extracted from the amniotic tissue in this file – the poor thing has already mutated, but *this* second file only has some svoloch's DNA, still unchanged as far as I could compare. Here is the real gold: some of the chromosomes in these pairs did cross over. Have a good look at my notes. This is it, I think. What have you done with the foetus?"

Selest shrugged. "Just took samples for you, and that is all it was good for. Although it grew faster than ordinary human embryos; it was only ten weeks old and already the size of a broad bean."

"Then you have it all. You know what to do. Here are all my notes on the svoloch and other species. Ask Vanessa and Deo to look at the blobster material since they are specialists in marine life. They will find its salt excretion mechanism more than interesting."

Vist turned the terminal off and detached the neuron wires from it. "Now you have all you need. Good luck."

"Are you sure you don't want to participate? How can you stand not being involved?"

"Selest, I am involved. I just have to start a new stage. I can't do both because even loaders can't be in two places at once."

"When are you going?"

"As soon as Marta is fit enough to fly. To Mars first."

"Did she agree to go back?" Selest sounded surprised.

"She said she will help me with the *Wasp* and then decide on her next move. She said Chang donated his genes for cloning in the White City, just like the others. She said she wanted to use these genes to set things right. By the time we return to Noverca, there might be fully grown, purple and shimmering clones of Chang walking about. I cannot say I am comfortable with her idea, but how can anyone tell her how to feel and where to look for closure? I hope she just finds a way to move on."

"Did you leave yours?"

"What?"

"Genes."

Vist laughed. Metallic laughter that sounded a little like a broken piano. "My clone won't be of much use to anyone without my implants."

"Where are you going now?"

"To the archives. I am not hopeful, but I just might find some clues there. Tolyan hinted about a Siberian attempt to send a probe to the Vitricus System in 3061. I want to have a look in case they sent more than just a probe. The Dunhuang Secret Terraforming Project is also worth looking at. I will check the Mars archives. Some materials are less damaged there than those in Greenwich Library."

"Okay, but don't forget to drop in to say goodbye before you take off. Even if you return to complete the evacuation, you know I will not see you again."

"I will do that. Thanks, Selest."

Vist hugged Selest and picked up the backpack.

"When you don't frown too much, you look just like your father," Selest said, "but you have your mother's features too. Tell me, for goodness sake! I delivered both of you after all! Are you my gogo or doli?"

"Goodbye, Selest."

Vist walked out of the room, and the old woman stood still for a few moments, fighting back the tears. Then she went to the lab vaults, passed the incubator facility, dialled her personal security code on the door and entered the section of artificial wombs. Once upon a time, all of them were in high demand and busy year after year. This part of the med-branch had no personnel duty and was completely deserted. Only one unit was lit with the gentle blinking lights of operational indicators. It was clicking and hissing from time to time, ever so quiet. The small observation window looked like the bright pink eye of a giant fish. Selest peered through the glass, which was also a magnifying lens. She looked at a small nubbin of tissue the size of a broad bean suspended in the thick liquid among a few artificial vessels.

Selest sighed and said quietly, "I will name you ... Piliali."

Chapter 42. 3411. Out in Space – John

"Can I? I am sorry if I ... You are leaving soon. Can I talk to you, if you don't mind? I feel I must. I'll never have another chance."

"We met at school, right? Please come in ... John? I thought so."

A short young man of no more than sixteen years, in a stripy top and scruffy trousers made of some rough bluish cloth, walked into the room and stood there, looking at Vist with an expression of excitement. He did not look shy. He just didn't know how to start. Not many people knew how to talk to Vist. Both studied each other for a moment without knowing how similar they were in the given space and time. The boy appeared to be fear-free too. He looked straight into Vist's eyes; his shoulders were relaxed and square. This young man's calm smile and confident posture reminded Vist of a young alpaca with a proud neck and fearless eyes. Vist spoke first.

"Do you have questions for me?"

"Millions. But I have very little time, so I will ask a couple at least."

One of Vist's eyebrows shot up.

"Really? Okay. Let's not waste any time, then. Come with me to the window. I am enjoying your sun for the last time. It looks spectacular with a few clouds around it."

"For the last time? But surely you will be back. I know I will not live to see it, but, sir ... Can I call you sir?"

"You can if that makes it easier."

"You will try to come back, won't you?"

"I promise I will try."

"Excellent! I would like my sons and daughters to meet you. I am planning to have a big family when the time comes."

"So why are you here?"

"You see, I am interested in the development of societies on Earth and here. I spent hours and hours for the last four years praying to O'Teka. I found many answers, but not to all my questions. Is it true that you have a temple of O'Teka in your head?"

"You may call it that, yes."

"Then you might have bibles that our temple does not have, right?"

"The ones written in the last four hundred years on Earth, I would say."

"Then you might have those answers."

Vist sat on the low windowsill that also served as a long soft bench. This way, he could see both things – the bright redness of the sun and the shiny face of the boy who sat next to him. This face was paler than Massimo's – the reflecting scales shimmered on his nose only, and his eyebrows were thick and bushy. Vist noticed the incredibly narrowed irises and figured the boy was a Nordian, with shaved and styled hypertrichos. A great mass of curly brown hair was twisted into a bundle and wrapped in a net, the newest fashion among young colonists. Over the past few days, White City schools had been filled with nets, shaved heads, robes, spectacles, beards, long braids, yellow curls and pairs of swirls like cow horns.

"What do you want to know?"

"Some of your thoughts on religion. The first colonists did not bring it here with them. Even the Chronicles of Human History doesn't teach it; it merely describes religion as part of our ancestors' culture. How come it has reappeared here, so far away from our roots?"

"Are you talking about the villagers' faith or your religion?"

"We don't believe in their entity. We believe in ... in fact, no. We don't believe. I would say we *know*, sir. The belief here in the city is a concept of trust, not faith."

The boy's eyes were full of defiance, which is typical for that age of discovery. Vist smiled with a hint of mockery so hard to resist, and said, "But you have a church, bibles, you are god worshippers yourselves, or you are going to tell me that your god is true and their gods are false?"

"We worship knowledge. Worshipping does not have to be applied only to gods, sir."

"True, John. You can – and should – worship anything dear to you. Your job, your home and the people you love and respect. You can call books any word you like, 'praying' instead of 'reading' when learning from them. You can reuse other religious terms to mislead those tempted by faith, but you cannot change the need for faith in certain types of people."

"Do you mean there are *types* of people who will always find faith and infect others? Is it a virus or a gene Professor Nguyen can isolate and remove from our genome?"

Vist's face had become serious again.

"No. One of your greatest writers, I mean, preachers said in his bible, *The Evolution of Minds*, that 'Every society, even the most rational, will produce believers—'"

"But he did not say why!" said John. "He talks about religious leaders who trick the others into believing. That they are hardly ever true believers themselves."

"Yes. Why do they need to trick the others?"

"To manipulate them?"

"Into doing what?"

"Into serving their gods, sir."

"Are you sure? Think of High Martyr as an example."

John frowned for a moment. His huge eyebrows joined into one hairy wave, and then his eyes brightened again, "To serve them thinking they serve the gods. But why do they need to be served? They can have anything they want anyway."

"Do you know what they want? This is why I mentioned those certain types of people. We don't always want the same things. Sometimes this difference goes further than taste in music or food. You and your friends here in the city want to achieve the same wonderful things. You want to find the purpose that will make you and everyone else happy. But you also have the High Martyr in the Salty Village, who shares all the characteristics of his predecessors here and on Earth. I know you have never met any of them, and I hope you never will. But look at what they all cling to: comfort without effort, feelings of self-worth through their power. They attempt to turn their vile passions into morally justified virtues – an inability to create anything useful, the desire to destroy what they can't control, lust for imaginary greatness and hate for real greatness, even self-deception to escape depression. Can you think of more?"

"I do not care for those leaders. To me, they are nothing but harmful mutations of society that deserve nothing but expulsion from it. But those who follow them, what do they gain? Faith replaces accountability; it compensates for the lack of facts, discourages independent thinking, and creates a fear of the unknown and, at the same time, the avoidance of knowing. Sir, why would anyone want that? This is what I fail to understand, and I can't find any sound explanation."

"Same here."

"But... Sir!"

"You can't get inside their heads to understand them completely. You have to be one of them for some time to grasp their values and moral standards. Imagine a frog trying to understand why a fish prefers to be permanently submerged, although it may remember what it felt like to be a tadpole. All we can do is speculate. I guess they see decision-making as a burden and are afraid to fully grow up. Your new heroes – Mikael King, Anatoly Grin and Steven McLeod – are convinced that true believers are hiding from the pleasure of self-challenge. Our captain is sure they prefer to live in an imaginary world full of fairy tales. All may be right. The believers are also not the same; if you ask them, they will tell you something very beautiful and convincing. I doubt they ever reasoned with this question because such a process would contradict the essence of faith itself. And yet, some managed to snap out of it and return to reason. The majority tried to change reality on a whim, without admitting their real fears."

"Fear of what?"

"Fear of death perhaps? Or fear of life? Maybe fear of failure, judgement or responsibility? In this case, a godly entity is very convenient and comforting. For thousands of years, the people of Earth created thousands of different gods. Some people said this was only one god that presented itself differently to various nations. Some people pointed out the differences in the holy words of different gods causing wars and the death of millions, and some interpreted the opposing guidelines as the same message despite numerous contradictions. It is hard to tell who was manipulating the others and who was a true fanatic of their faith. Both types have proven to be devastating enough to learn from and not repeat. And yet here we are. A sect of Moon Cruisers on Earth is trying to doom humanity, and here on Gera – a similar tumour is growing inevitably."

"Will they become our doom too? Will they overtake us eventually?"

The boy's voice had a hint of worry in it for the first time. His fingers went to his chest and touched his amulet.

"They will certainly try. The more comfortable this planet will become for humanity, the greater the risk of what I call the 'too comfortable,' which will become what you might have to face."

"How is that a risk?"

"You might start feeling less of a need for that purpose of yours, which every colonist has to find. I see that is what drives you more than any other motivation, and I really would like to know how you guys do that. We can learn from you. So I hope you are more rational than we were and will bear that in mind – consciously deciding not to give in or channelling it in ways we could not even imagine. After all, this universe is wonderful for providing us with endless challenges. As long as you don't repeat the fate of the svoloch." Vist pulled both feet onto the bench and rested his arms on his knees. "Seems like only yesterday I thought that nothing worse than the need of god and corruption could happen to the race of men."

"Surely the whole population cannot lose their sanity."

"This one had. Maybe not sanity but reason. The svoloch started here as humans. That is clear. It is necessary to learn what happened to them, how and when they came to this planet and how they evolved into ... the svoloch. It will have to become a purpose for some of you to find out. I would like to know why we did not know about them until now. I have nothing in my database about earlier colonisation attempts on *Lyra*. I need to go back to Earth and search for the answers. Whether it is a destroyed or missing record, my library is incomplete without that information."

"I wish I could help," said John, rising from the bench. He glanced at his amulet. "It was good talking to you. Now I have commitments to attend to in a few minutes, sir. My wish is that you did not have to go at all, but I understand this is bigger than I imagined."

"I'll tell you what ..." Vist got up, walked to his backpack, and pulled out a small book no bigger than his palm. It was an old type of notebook, made of paper and leather, written in ink and with a faded picture of four playing cards on the front cover, "I want to give this to you."

"Oh, I know what it is, sir. It's an ancient bible!"

"No, it is most certainly not. This is my personal collection of short poems and quotes. I started it with my sibling when we were your age. Each has a little philosophical message from the wisest ones on Earth. They are good to ponder or meditate on. Something I occasionally enjoy accessing by just reading. I have decided that before I give up my amulet, I will use it to go to your church and donate to O'Teka certain things stored in *my* temple." Vist touched the left side of his head and carried on, "Some of the data files, called Object and Vist, will have restricted access. Only the reader of this book with a certain mind can decode it if the key is found on its pages. I predict that if you don't manage to decode it, then one of your children will. That would mean your colony is ready for that specific file and will use it well."

"That's so crafty!" said John with delight, then he got up and opened the book. "I must not get obsessed with this puzzle!"

"You won't. You are not wired that way."

John had obviously never handled old books before.

He flicked through the pages with his finger and read out a few lines randomly, "The language is old indeed! So many commas. *'When I want to understand what is happening today,'* Wow, there are hundreds of quotes! *'A world of dew.'* Sir, you could hide tonnes of keys in this little book. *'I have clients in order to build,'* This is so unfair! What is that? I don't know what dice is. *'The mind is out of tune with the heart.'* Okay. Sure, I accept the challenge. Thank you."

The young man carefully pushed the book into his breast pocket. "Sir, you wanted to know how we look for our purpose. You are sort of lucky; you never had to look for yours. It was forced onto you with all that knowledge in your head. Good thing you accepted it. Do you sometimes wonder what you would have done with yourself if things were different?"

"There were times when I didn't wonder about that."

"Then please take it as a message to your young ones on Earth. I want to share with them my understanding of purpose. They must try to find theirs if they want to survive in this world. It might not be a perfect way of life since we still have few people who failed, but O'Teka suggests it is the best one so far. Here we start as soon as we can learn, but it is never too late unless your delay is deliberate self-harm by procrastination. Knowing what you truly value and what you are good at is not enough. You have to gain that value completely by yourself, without relying on others. If you can't do that, then you are already on the wrong course and have to make a turn to pursue different talents and passions. It will only work if you make yourself happy in the process. Only then will you be able to care for your colony for hundreds of years because, I assume, your happiness includes the wellbeing of your grandchildren too."

It was as if John was looking for that audience he was addressing there. Vist stopped blinking. John's pupils dilated from excitement despite the sun shining into them. John stepped close to Vist and his eyes were almost level with Vist's green eyes.

John carried on, "And what tools should you use? I suggest using versatile study, hard work, reason, consistency, accountability, integrity and judgement. If you don't dismiss those, you will soon see how much your colony depends on your personal happiness and how your individual state depends on the happiness of the colony. Interdependence is almost ecological."

"Do they teach you all of this in school?"

"No. We would not take it seriously if they did. You have seen our schools. They give us an environment and conflicting materials to figure it all out. Figuratively speaking, they put you on a ship called *Look After Yourself* and push you into space to find *your* colony. You have to learn how to sail and where to as you go."

"And if you crash the ship or get lost?"

"You will be rescued and set off once again, though you don't know that on your first journey. However, on the second trip, you know it won't happen again. If you don't succeed, you will become a miserable burden for the colony.

So failures are very rare. Humans are pretty ambitious and capable creatures, don't you think?"

"Creative and proud too." Vist nodded. Any member of the Object team would have paid a lot to see Vist's face right now. "What about competition? How do you interact with your fellow colonists if you look after your interests?"

"My parents taught me very early to value what is truly good for my growth as a person. I can't help but love those who are better than me. If they judge me by their standards, I feel honoured. Competition is a great motivating force. For example, I will strive to surpass my parents and be a bad father if my children don't surpass me. It is in your interest at the end of the day. Thinking about it, and about everything you said, I reckon it is not only about looking after your own interests. It is also about being aware of how other people do that. People usually judge others by how they treat their fellow humans, but hardly ever by what people do to themselves and by what means. Tell me how you treat yourself, and I will tell you how I shall relate to you. In that way, we decide on how we can coexist. Would you remember this, sir?"

"I have recorded it. Thank you," said Vist, then he blinked.

Chapter 43. 3417. Back on Earth – Who is Vist?

MESH message

TDarkwood_17.05@@Parsecmail.mesh.

Voice only record of Tom Darkwood, unemployed. (18.04.3417–20.20 EN-time) Earth.

Encrypted for the personal attention of Rod and Tolyan Baker.

Guys, I wanted to say that I wish you were here, but that would be a pretty gnarly thing to do.

I don't want to spoil your honeymoon, but I have to. I have bad news, and our regrouping has been postponed until further notice. Since Vist came back from Mars to visit Tibet, there has been another attempt to assassinate her, but this time she had only Nat, Zina and Steven with her. I received a message describing a fight via MESH from their host. Two members of his staff are dead, but so is the assassin. And you would not believe who it was! Sister Volna with a zapper under her silk gloves! Yes! Deessa's murderer, who we thought was long gone. She made it look as if she had accidentally bumped into them, but Vist could sense a fake from afar and immediately sent Nat out of the room. Steven zapped Volna when she opened fire. He ended up wounded as usual, but Zina is in a coma this time, barely alive. Both are in the same Nagqu hospital, but Vist left in a hurry almost on the same day with Nat alone. Apparently, the last thing she did was whisper something into Zina's ear, tell Steven to look after her, and disappear. Mik is still waiting for her on Mars. All he cares about is his commander's worthy retirement. I will go there too as soon as I make sure our guys are ok and ... I make my mind up.

She has found something. I am sure of it. It is not like Vist to just ... Oh, whom am I kidding? It is a lot like Vist, but even she would not leave her friends in such a condition. I am afraid she will go to Noverca with Marta and Nat and leave the rest of us behind. But that is hard to imagine. Okay, it is not hard, but something in my gut tells me that she would not ... Oh! Guts, right? My whims! My wishful thinking! What a torment! Hang on, I need a drink!

Okay! In my head, I understand her reasons! She doesn't want to endanger our lives any longer. She is better off alone. I, too, don't trust anyone anymore. Who could have known that so much would have changed here in just five years? Instead of making a wormhole and building the pods, the Resistance has to investigate and capture the corrupted members. Where would it lead? I don't know. I am torn! Shall I stay and fight for Object, or shall I follow my heart and help Vist in her search? Heart! She would have laughed at this sentiment and reminded me that my heart pumps blood and does nothing else. My reason is fighting with my feelings. I am failing to integrate them both. If I focus on Vist's search for the truth, I have to ask myself, what is there for me? Why is she doing this? To what end? Why does she need to know so much where the svoloch came from? Is it personal? Is she just curious? After all, she cares little about what people will do with the information she got for them, risking her and our lives. I know that much. Until now, she was helping the Rebels, as long as they cooperated and did everything her way. She is a loader, not a leader. Why should they follow her? So, as soon as they became inconsistent and breached the agreement, she lost interest in them and the rest of humanity on Earth, is that right? Lost interest in Object, in the evacuation, in the whole human race. And for myself ... Guys, I am telling this to you because you understand love more than anyone I know. Zina understood too. I mean, she does. And Steven, If I only knew. I need another drink!

Good one! So, Rod, Tolyan ... tell me, am I mad to follow Vist for love, not knowing who Vist really is? This should not matter. It doesn't matter to you, you lucky bastards. Sometimes I think I am in love with an imaginary Vist, but the real one is ... pretty real too. This is not some romantic, crazy and quick svoloch-hunting trip. If we go with Vist, okay ... if I go with Vist – that would be a lifetime commitment. Vist might not come back to Earth after what Vasily did. You will say that most Rebels are still willing to follow her plan, but if she loses her trust in humanity? And what can I say here for myself? What do I want? Do I want to find the svoloch? No! I don't care about the svoloch, but I would say – yes, if I do it with Vist and she is a woman, and she loves me too. But if Vist is a man, my friend, my brother-adventurer ... will I not bother myself with what everybody else would do, as long as we both feel like a happy team of space striders? Marta is doing that very thing, right now! But they are just friends, business partners, and she is desperate to feel better. Young Nathaniel is Marta's apprentice. He has found his destiny and his purpose. Am I desperate too? Zina never cared and followed Vist, loving her or him without asking Vist to love her back. How can she do that? She always told me she would give her life for Vist. Steven follows Zina, knowing well that she is mad about Vist. Why can't I do the same? Because I want something in return. That is why! I will not be happy not knowing that at the end of the day, I will hold Vist in my arms. How selfish of me! Or selfless? I don't know if I am ready to invest my life in the unknown, being aware that the process of pursuing this mystery could be quite good fun anyway, although very fruitless. I don't know if I am prepared to accept that my investment will never be paid for with anything else. Is there enough value in it for me? What are my values? She might be a woman that will never love me back anyway, then what? Can I love a person for both of us no matter what? Is there more wine?

How ironic. Every member of my crew is where they belong but me. And I was your captain, for goodness' sake! A leader of the Object trip! Maybe I belong with Vist, but in her shadow, I have lost all my confidence. I wish I knew where she is now and what she is up to. So many questions! I don't know the answers. I must believe

– I thought I would never say that – I must believe that she will wait for us. For me, that is my faith, my religion. Believing in the unknown – believing that Vist is a "she" and she can love me back, believing that we will travel together uncovering the mystery, with our friends by our sides. That is the faith I can live with and give my life for. Am I strong enough, and am I in love enough? Is this me talking? Hah! I am so pissed!

Right! Guys ... Hic! Enjoy your trip, and I cannot express enough how much I hope we meet again on Gera or anywhere else on Noverca! I don't care! I am so going to regret this letter tomorrow ...

Voice command four-two-two, send.

To be continued ...

Book 2 Construct and Vist, an Official Trailer:

Steven's voice interrupted them through the music, "Hey Mik, today's special includes fresh tocks ... I am also ordering sandie soup and rabbit roast for the girls. What do you want? The usual?"

"Sure," answered Mik and turned back to Nikolaya with a certain interest.

"Tock platter to share for a starter, one sandie shchi, one rabbit with pea mash, one goat de volante with lemon and one flame beef burger with potato and extra chilli for mains. No seaweed on the peas, please. Oh yes, and two bottles of Mik and Ann Jello from the year 1005 or 1006. We will decide on the desserts later," said Steven into his amulet.

Tilda leaned over the table and said loudly enough, "Nikolaya was trained in one of your scout academies. Show him your brows, Nikkie!"

Black eyes flashed a green reflection at Mik once again. Nikolaya turned her slow smile directly at him and frowned. Her extra muscles under the skin of her forehead contracted, and her eyebrows, which looked like ordinary broad and smooth arcs a moment ago, unfolded. Every hair had become erect and happened to be almost five centimetres long. Now they looked just like the bushy whiskers of the *Felidae*.

Tilda squealed with exaltation and clapped her hands. "I love it when she does that! I wish I had the same implants, but I am not entitled to them as I have chosen a very different purpose. I am so glad they let her keep them."

"I have seen this before, you know," said Mik, "Vibrissae come with eyes for most of the Nordian scouts. But if you didn't graduate above pride-grade, you will not receive maintenance treatment, and the superfluous neurons around your eyes will atrophy. Your antennae will become useless in a year or two," said Mik.

"I have a plan to take care of that … and some help," answered Nikolaya, returning her eyebrows into a flat position and smoothing them with her thumbs.

"Then my second question would be – what help? I am still waiting for the answer to the first one."

Nikolaya stopped smiling and frowned again, but this time her face didn't bristle. "Your friend is no fun at all," she said to Steven, who was watching all of this with interest.

"Oh, but he is … just play along and answer his questions. Avoiding direct requests is the first sign of dishonesty. Very unusual for the colony. I would even say it is frowned upon here too."

ABOUT THE AUTHOR

Author Anka B. Troitsky was born in the USSR in 1968, grew up in Kazakhstan and left for the UK in 1993, not believing that Russia would become a European country during her lifetime.
Philosopher, biology teacher, translator of books, police cases, Courts hearings, and NHS... writes about everything she has understood and learned in her favourite science fiction genre.